A NOVEL

POSTER GIRLS

MEREDITH RITCHIE

ISBN: 978-1-954614-58-1 (hard cover)
      978-1-954614-59-8 (soft cover)

Edited by: Betsy Thorpe
Chapter heading illustrations drawn by Randi Koistinen
Author cover photo taken by Ali Hogston
Author cover photo background is "Coronam Magnam" painting
  by Kristen van Diggelen Sloan
Cover art created by Eva Crawford

Authors Note: The "courage" quote on page 306 was inspired by Mary Anne Rodmacher.

Published by Warren Publishing
Charlotte, NC
www.warrenpublishing.net
Printed in the United States

For Tom Fidelle

Prologue

SUMMER IN CHARLOTTE, 1944

After mastering this trip more than a hundred times, and on darker nights than this, his feet knew all the safe spots to land along the path. His body angled, squeezing behind the back fence to avoid the nail that loved to ruin his shirts. He was alone, heading for the rear service door of the main cafeteria. Any lingering diners had moved on to complete their night shifts. He could have closed his eyes and let his stomach lead the way.

Walking down the aisle that separated garbage piled into stacks of blue and tan canvas bags, he inhaled, expecting the smell of leftover biscuits stashed in the usual spot by the back door. Instead, he took in acrid, peculiar air, and stopped. To his right, he caught the first flicker. The summer heat in Charlotte hung around long after the sun went down, but his brain registered an extra warmth coming from the right. He stopped mid-aisle, sure the darkness was playing tricks on his eyes. Another flicker, this time growing into a tiny flame.

Fire.

His thinking slowed. Despite his training to respond quickly, it felt like the gears in his head were dripping with tar. Starting as a dishwasher in this building, he'd since worked his way up to third-shift assembly. Each new training program brought the same sober lecture on the dangers of fire at the plant. Gunpowder wafted past every inch of the two-thousand-acre campus. A fire in one building might explode and domino through the other two hundred fifty, killing thousands. He seemed to be the sole witness to this fire.

Think. He willed his mind to clear and his fire-training protocol to kick in. Instead, he remembered the many jokes he and the boys had whispered behind their hands when the gray head of their instructor turned away. It felt better—more manly—to laugh about this place blowing sky high, taking all these dames with it, curlers and lipsticks littered for miles. *Serves all of 'em right,* they'd sniggered, *trying to take a man's job anyway.* The city was smart to fuss about the dangerous, rapidly built plant facility just outside its limits. Hiring all these women and coloreds only made the danger worse.

The flames grew. He ticked off his options. If he left now, he might reach safety in a neighboring field before the whole place blew straight up to Peter's pearly gates. No one would be the wiser that he'd been there, should any of them survive. Then again, all these late-night extra biscuits might slow him down. How far could he really get?

If he stayed, he should follow the fire protocol. He pictured his safety instructor, a former drill sergeant, pacing the room and saying, "Big fires start small and follow the wind. Time is your best friend, so don't waste it."

The man now licked a finger before holding it high in the air. The wind was still. That was good.

Thoughts coming faster now, he remembered the need to stop a fire *well before* it reached the volatile free-burning stage. The first person to discover any fire—*Lordy, why did that have to be me?*—must try to smother it, cool it, or take away the fuel. The warmth coming from his right radiated across the aisleway and heated the blue bags to flashpoint.

Flames grew on both sides. He yanked a fire extinguisher off the outside wall and walked back up the aisle, aiming at the biggest flame. As soon as it left the hose, the intense heat converted the powerful stream of liquid into useless steam.

Why isn't anybody coming from the kitchen to help?

"Help! Fire! Somebody, come help!" he screamed over the back fence, but heard no replies from any fellow third-shift workers. The main cafeteria presented the greatest fire risk, so it'd been built two hundred feet away from any other building. Too far to hear his cries.

There had to be *somebody* inside, even at this hour. And where were the blasted Navy patrols? They usually came every half-hour.

As he raced inside to call for help, he heard a pop, followed by the cracking and hissing sounds of an advancing fire. He hit the floor as the building contents ignited with explosive force. His ears rang loudly, but he was thankful to still have ears. And the higher flames would certainly draw attention and more help. Fast crawling from the flames, he prayed for more time to escape before the whole building went up. Hearing a deep cough, it took him a moment to realize it wasn't coming from him.

"Help! Please!" his ears caught, coming from someone trapped in the kitchen. He squinted through the thickening smoke. A large mound, crouched in a corner, came into focus.

"Please, help us!" He recognized the Negro woman he called the biscuit lady. *Damn, why'd it have to be her?* She matched him pound-for-pound, if not more, and that was saying something. This would not be the carry and rescue scene from the movies.

She appeared to be searching for something. Chalking her up as too dumb to save herself, he tried to block her cries as he rose to his feet. This place already had too many women and coloreds for his taste, but then he noticed a clear path between them. No time to think it over.

Head down, he reached her fast, then tried pulling her up. Her arms were locked into her sides, clutching something to her massive bosom. The blind terror on her face made him question his decision. Another explosion was imminent.

"You're gonna to have to walk on your own," he yelled.

She shouted back. "I can walk, but they cain't."

He looked around for more bodies. "Where are the others?"

"They's two more, but I cain't find 'em." She held out her arms.

The objects came into focus. Two kittens, knocked out from the smoke. She wasn't talking about two more people. He scanned the floor and made out two small balls of fur near a desk. He cursed loudly before grabbing them by the necks and leading all six of them out the front door.

The night air filled their lungs. Violent coughs forced him to his knees as screams and shouted orders landed all around them.

Firemen, looking down like a wreath above his head, were the last thing he remembered.

Chapter 1

Two men in uniform stood on her front stoop, their starched postures fighting against the weight of heavy news. "Are you Mrs. Charles Slone?"

She could not answer, only hug the doorframe, no match for her greatest fear playing out before her eyes.

A droning priest appeared, bringing with him an endless line of strangers mumbling in apologetic tones. Wanting to run, instead she stood riveted to the flag-draped coffin, descending too fast. A clump of dirt followed down the hole, echoing against the shiny wood, loud enough to break the spell.

Maggie woke.

Shivering, she got up to yank the drapes open, then the blackout curtains behind them. Finally, the warmth hit her shoulders, and she rested her head on the pane. "It was a dream," she whispered, until it sank in, and she began to thaw. She looked at the sun, knowing it had just finished shining on her husband somewhere in the Pacific.

Behind her, the writing desk held her latest, half-written letter to Charlie. It also held a tall stack of his letters to her, chronologically sorted and wrapped in red twine. She would finish that letter before sunset, filling it with happy news about their family, and leaving out her bad dreams.

Charlie's wardrobe drew her like a magnet. Pulling on both doors at once, she waited for the scent of her husband's favorite Lifebouy soap to ride out with the flow of escaping air. Disappointment hit her instead. Too much time had passed. It smelled like any other part of the house now.

Her hand brushed over his abandoned shirts and suits, stopping on a tweed jacket he'd worn the night before he shipped out.

The soft music, the smell of his cooking, and her second glass of wine had worked their magic that night. "This seems like an elaborate ruse to get me to forget what tomorrow will bring," she'd said.

"Don't let tomorrow ruin tonight," he murmured into her hair as they danced, before framing her face in the candlelight—his best move to garner her complete attention. "I have created this so-called ruse to help us remember." He kissed her—tortuously, slowly—then pulled back. She watched the light dance inside his gorgeous gray-blue eyes, before he added, "Lest we forget."

In the middle of unpacked boxes, stacked high in every corner of their newest home, they had danced slowly enough to stop the song from ever ending. How could that have been a year ago now? She lifted his same jacket from the hanger, felt its weight, and pushed her arms through the sleeves. Moving back to the window, she hugged herself, feeling the scratchy fabric beneath her palms, like she'd done when he was her dance partner.

Morning giggles reached her ears now from her daughters' bedroom, the cure for any sadness. She smiled, wishing she could bottle that sound. Returning the jacket, she closed the doors on her sorrow. By the time she poked her head through the girls' bedroom door, she was almost back to normal.

"It's almost time for church, ladies. The bathtub is filling now." Maggie shooed them out of their room, along with their groans.

A Chippendale brass pull in each hand, Maggie tugged on the heavy drawer in search of the right outfit. For each girl, she laid out a copy of the same white dress with a coral sash that tied in back. She carefully placed a hat, rimmed in the same coral ribbon, on each bed, then added gloves and socks trimmed with lace. At the foot of each bed, she displayed an identical pair of shiny, black patent leather shoes. Opening their jewelry box, she drew out two necklaces, straightening the first communion crosses that dangled from each.

Her mother-in-law, Grace, would expect to see her latest purchase on display this morning. Determined to get it right this Sunday, she counted out all the layers and pieces required for church in Charlotte. Church in Boston had been less formal.

She stopped in the hallway, catching her daughters' high-pitched dialogue coming from the bathtub. They spoke in the character of their dolls, navigating through the mysteries of the adult world. Maggie sighed, wishing they could stay little forever, or at least until Charlie returned.

Maggie could tell one doll spoke as the child and the other as the mama—quite a bossy mama it seemed. She grimaced. Did she really sound like that?

Stepping into the bathroom, she saw Daisy's hair half-covered in suds and Demi's maybe two-thirds washed. Immersed in their pretend world, it took them a few minutes to notice Maggie's hands-on-hips presence. Before they did, she took in their perfect skin and button noses, holding on to this ordinary moment, then descended to her knees. This last little part of the bath is what they needed help with. She poured more shampoo into her hands and let her fingers lather a good sudsing for each sweet head. Their eight-year-old conversation kept on going, despite Maggie moving their heads this way and that.

The mammoth tub with its clawed feet hardly fit inside the bathroom, but it was the reason Maggie finally agreed to live in a house they could barely afford. Charlie had played her like a fiddle, knowing it favored the English tub from their honeymoon, where she had languished for hours. Her in-laws had shocked them with tickets on a transatlantic ship to Europe, a huge surprise delivered right after her own parents revealed their gift of a hope chest that had been in her family for years. Such was the contrast between their families—presumptuous and extravagant, versus personal and precious.

Maggie grabbed the rinsing cup, letting streams of water pull the curls out of each brunette mane, reaching halfway down their backs, before springing back into place. Each sister took turns giggling at the other's sopping wet head. Maggie wondered briefly if that honeymoon tub even existed now, or had that part of London been bombed? She pulled herself up and checked the old wall clock. They were running late. Again.

An hour later, they swam through a sea of well-dressed men and women at the fellowship hall at St. Patrick's Cathedral. Young and old faces, mostly unfamiliar to Maggie, greeted each other warmly. She spotted Grace. It was hard not to.

Grace Virginia Slone and her court gathered around a table with a huge sign, "War Gardens for Victory." Grace had baskets of fresh vegetables on display from her own garden. She passed out samples of bright yellow squash, deep green zucchini, and pamphlets explaining how other parishioners could grow the same. Maggie could recite the spiel by heart. "Grow vitamins at your door! Sow the seeds of victory so our farmers can keep our troops fed!"

As Grace finished, Maggie tapped her shoulder. Grace spun around and Maggie braced for what she and Charlie used to joke as: The Grace Virginia Inquisition. With one sharp, lightning-fast glance, Grace assessed the Sunday morning state of her family members. It started at the shoes and rose until the last hair stood judged. Maggie hoped they passed inspection.

There was no sign of George, Charlie's father, at the table. He was wise to steer clear. Nearly a century before, George's family had founded St. Peter's Cathedral downtown. Now Grace and George were prominently involved with getting St. Patrick's, Charlotte's second parish, going in Dilworth. The twins attended parochial school here during the week, so after properly greeting their grandmother, Daisy and Demi hurried down the hall to meet their friends. Maggie felt something close to jealousy watching them run off. They made friends so easily.

Grace watched them scoot away, likely finishing her inspection of their ruffled backsides, then faced Maggie. "Our girls look absolutely precious this morning, don't they?" Not waiting for an answer, concern shadowed her expression. "You look nice too, dear, but a little tired. Are you getting enough rest?"

Maggie ignored the backhanded compliment. "I do have a lot on my mind. Last night I couldn't stop thinking about the Shell Plant."

Grace lowered her chin and voice. "Oh for Heaven's sake, Maggie, please don't mention that awful facility. No one here agrees with their little experiment to recruit women away from their children."

"It's not an experiment. It's a paycheck. It's a j—"

"There now, if it isn't Eliza McGovern as I live and breathe? Don't you look pretty as a picture!" Grace gushed and stepped in to kiss the air around the elderly woman who had just arrived at the table. Maggie dropped the subject. Clearly, the plant was taboo. She gently shook Mrs. McGovern's bony hand and played her part of doting daughter-in-law.

Maggie would never forget the day she overheard Grace talking to a friend and trying to explain Maggie's unique background. Grace had prayed hard for Charlie to find a suitable bride. She kept her prayers to three simple things: Irish. Catholic. Southern. Grace got two out of three in Maggie and supposed she should be grateful. Charlie had attended many a cotillion dance full of candidates that fit the bill perfectly, but her son had an awfully stubborn side. He broke Grace's heart by moving with the Army to Boston and meeting his future bride there. Maggie, on the other hand, had never expected to meet a good Catholic boy from the South. She assumed only Baptist churches were allowed down here.

"If you'll excuse me," Maggie politely interrupted Grace and her friend. "I'm going to find the girls and save our seats. Meet you and George in the normal pew, if it's not taken."

"Well, I can't imagine who would do such a thing," Grace sent a knowing glance and wink in her friend's direction. "*We* sit there every Sunday."

"I can't imagine," Maggie said, as she walked away from the table and started looking for the girls. Feeling self-conscious, she excused her way through a large, happy reunion of women. Despite the prominent family she had married into, Maggie was still very much an outsider. Women here were polite but more aloof than the friends she'd left behind in Boston. After living here almost a year, she had yet to make one real friend from church. Only Kora from the library.

Maggie found the girls and their usual pew, where they waited for the service to start. As she watched the girls take turns drawing *Xs* and circles on the back of the program in their game of noughts and crosses, she tried to rub away tingles she felt at the base of her neck—the kind that come from stares that change into polite smiles, once discovered. What if these stares belonged to friends of old what's-her-name, the blond from Charlie's high school photos? Charlie often thanked Maggie for saving him from her.

Grace and George started coming up the aisle. With so many hands to shake along the way, it took them a full five minutes. Her in-laws always played to an audience. Finally, they slid into the pew, the girls sandwiched between them. Grace beamed at her granddaughters.

The service began. Daisy and Demi sat, stood, and kneeled on cue, knowing the rhythms after years of practice. Church was important to Maggie, but not for the same reasons as Grace. Every Sunday, the familiar service brought Maggie's parents back to life. She felt their presence in the pew. It brought a strange mix of loneliness and peace. Her mother and father couldn't pass on these traditions to their granddaughters, but she could bring the girls to church in their honor.

Father Fitzgerald began the homily. Light passing through the stained-glass windows tinged his white hair in violets and blues. He measured out careful words, instructing his flock to embrace God's will, but also acknowledging as part of our human nature the struggle for acceptance. The struggle for why.

With a voice that rose and fell hypnotically, the priest continued, "Sarah doubted, Elizabeth laughed, and Rachel lamented. God tested their wavering faith and rewarded them with the miracle of Isaac, John the Baptist, and Joseph."

Maggie glanced at the surrounding pews. If faith was measured in number of children, these were some high holy folks. Some families filled a whole row with ten squirming children in scratchy collars and uncomfortable shoes.

Grace's perfect posture reflected her serious attention to Father Fitzgerald. His words must be hard to hear, knowing how much Grace had wanted a big family. It had to sting for the priest to link God's will to a faithful woman's womb.

When the sermon ended, a young mother and her parents were invited up front for the baptism of her sleeping baby boy in a long, white, lace gown. Grace caught Maggie's eyes, then looked back at the family on display. Maggie realized this was the family Grace had spoken of last week at supper. Her shoulders sagged along with her heart, remembering the funeral for this child's father was just last month. The war ensured he would never meet his only child. The young woman and her parents appeared to still be in a state of shock. The congregation held its breath for fear of adding more pain to this tragedy.

The priest kept to the script for this normally joyous occasion. "What name do you give this child?"

"We name him Charles Peter," the young mother said softly. The same names Grace had chosen for her only son. Maggie and Grace's eyes filled with tears, but avoided each other. *There but for the grace of God, go I*, Maggie thought. Daisy and Demi watched her closely for signs that they too should be sad. Her carefully shackled sadness rattled its chains. *Pull it together*! she warned herself.

A sergeant in the Army when she met him, she and Charlie had both agreed to pursue civilian life in Boston. He had found insurance sales challenging enough to hold his interest, though the pay was less steady and brought some lean years. Ones she insisted his parents never knew about.

The war changed everything.

Anger settled into her body, pushing out her sadness. Her crossed leg began to swing as she remembered their fight in Boston, the night he re-enlisted.

"I have a plan, Maggie," he'd said. "It will all work out. Trust me." Charlie's face was suddenly painted with doubt, and he tentatively asked, "You do trust me, don't you?"

"Of course, but how can loyalty to men you don't even know yet be stronger than your loyalty to us?"

When he stood, his chair scraped against the ancient hardwood floors and his palms punched the table. His sudden movement must have produced a louder effect than intended, because he softened his posture instantly, reflecting defeat, only not quite. Not Charlie. "I'm sorry to put you through this."

She stood too, quieter so not to disturb the girls, but just as dramatically. "You fulfilled your duty to your country already, Charlie Slone. We need you more."

He moved to her side of their small kitchen table, gently holding Maggie's elbows in his hands. She kept her arms tightly crossed. "I know you'll need support, that's why we're moving home."

"*Your* home," she corrected.

"My family's home," he said, before wrapping his arms around her tight, melting her, like only Charlie could. He whispered just behind her head. "You are my family. You are my Irish Rose, one that's stronger than she knows."

Now, sitting in the pew, Maggie waited to feel anger's familiar shadow—guilt. It washed over her, right on cue. Sacrifice was celebrated everywhere she turned. In magazines. In movies. In posters. And especially in conversation with others who had given up much more than Maggie. She couldn't win, and that upset her the most.

They stood for communion. Walking down the aisle behind the girls to receive the sacraments, she worried about having to greet the widowed new mother after the service. Every word tested in her head sounded thin and hollow. What comfort could she give without starting to cry over her own potential loss? The service ended and members greeted one another customarily in the narthex, on the way to gather for coffee and doughnuts.

The girls ran toward the smell of fried dough. Maggie's worries were wasted. The young woman and her parents had departed as soon as the service ended. Awkward words of congratulations and sympathy, while not easy to give, are even harder to receive.

By the time Maggie reached the food table, the girls were covered in crumbs. "Leave some for the rest of the church, please," she whispered, handing them a napkin to share. "Here comes your Gigi."

Grace came up behind the girls, extending both perfectly manicured hands. "Young ladies, there are some people Gigi would like you to meet." It seemed important for Grace to parade the girls in front of her friends, but Maggie was rarely included.

Each girl grabbed a hand and the three of them walked away, leaving Maggie to fend for herself. Her stomach started doing flips. Why was this so hard? Would it ever stop feeling like the first day at a new school?

She looked around for anything to make her sudden isolation less conspicuous. To her right stood a group of mothers about her age that she was sure Grace had introduced her to at some point. Sneaking glances, she recognized at least two from the girls' school, but the names escaped her. For the past year, making friends had taken a back seat while she moved her home, said goodbye to Charlie, and settled the girls into school. She picked invisible lint from the front of her dress, until that felt like a spotlight on her solitude.

"Mind if I join you ladies?" she asked. "I'm Maggie Slone, in case we haven't met yet."

"Why Maggie, we know exactly who you are. Your sweet mother-in-law can't stop talking about you!" said one, extending her white gloved hand and introducing herself. Her very Southern double name Maggie couldn't quite get, but she didn't want to ask again. Trying on a bright smile, Maggie put aside her suspicions about what Grace was telling others about her. The rest of the group nodded their hellos, politely expanding their circle to make room.

Their conversation continued. "I told Retha once again she is no longer allowed to take the children to Morgan Park, but my children put up such a fuss! Can you imagine?"

"Mine too," the other agreed. "It's such a puzzle."

"My children say it's more fun than the other parks."

"Who decided to build such a wonderful park in Cherry? I've never been there. Do we know if they have better facilities than other parks?"

"What ever happened to separate, but equal?" This comment drew several laughs among the group. Maggie suddenly understood what was different about Morgan Park. It was one of the few accessible to dark-skinned Charlotteans.

"Mine love the games the other children play there. I finally gave up and let Mabel take them."

One of the mothers looked over at Maggie and asked, "Which park does your maid take your children to?"

"We don't have a maid," answered Maggie, her voice trailing off. "We haven't tried any of the parks yet. My girls play mostly in our backyard."

"I'm sorry, where do they play? I wasn't clear on your last word."

"They play behind our house mostly," Maggie finished quickly. She kicked herself. She tried to avoid words like yard or park—not to mention *car*—when talking among a group of belles like this. Her Boston accent always yielded the same confused response.

"How sweet," one remarked, the words dripping from her pretty pink lips. The pause that followed bore the weight of difference between Maggie and the other mothers. Charlie's butter-soft drawl had garnered the opposite reaction up North. It was one of the first things that drew Maggie to Charlie, and often made her friends swoon.

"Maggie, what part of North Carolina were you born in? Your accent is so distinctive. Is it Tidewater?"

"A little further up the east coast. Boston."

They offered polite nods. "I hear it's lovely," one of them said, like she'd never care to verify the claim.

One of the more familiar faces softened, before adding, "Such a big city. Do you miss it?"

Maggie's reply caught. *Every day*, she thought. She cleared her throat, briefly twisting away from the circle of polite faces to reset her emotions.

"You must think of our Charlotte as a mere cow town." The woman Maggie was sure she had met before at the girls' school filled the awkward silence.

"Not at all," said Maggie, not wanting to offend. "Boston is big, but we keep to our own churches and neighborhoods, just like here."

She willed Grace and the girls to return, rescuing her from this conversation. Glancing over the circle to check, she almost cried out in relief.

"If you'll excuse me, I see my family." Leaving the circle, she offered a hurried smile and a wave. "See you next Sunday."

Chapter 2

JUNE, 1943
KORA

Maggie Slone would be late to her own funeral, but Kora could do nothing about that today, only sit tight and wait. Alone inside Maggie's car, parked at the library, Kora looked out the window, confirming her suspicions: that was the same gray sky she had seen the first day she arrived in Charlotte—three years ago—on a bus from Montgomery.

Worried about meeting her new husband's family, sleep had refused to come on that bus, for her at least. Rain tapped a slow tune on the roof, drowning out the noises sleeping souls never knew they made. James had given up his window seat so she could see the countryside, but nighttime converted the window to a mirror.

The reflection caught her handsome new husband asleep on her shoulder. She patted his head and James mumbled something sweet. Mister and Missus Bell. Plenty of "Bell" jokes had surfaced at their recent wedding celebration—silver bells, wedding bells, even Southern belles.

Raindrops hit the roof of Maggie's car. On the passenger window, Kora now watched the window beads form, join together, change shape, and begrudgingly follow the laws of gravity, streaking toward the dirty window casing.

James had been right about the move to Charlotte. It didn't take long for her to find a job at her favorite place in the world: the library. Books fed her soul for as long as she could remember. Every night she revered them, if only to dust their spines and make the floors beneath them shine.

Cleaning was the only job Kora was allowed to perform at the Carnegie Library, where she had first met Maggie a year ago. That first night, Kora had arrived a few minutes early. The doors hadn't yet locked before the long Labor Day weekend. The librarian must have left early, knowing Kora would lock up. On her way to do just that, she noticed a white woman with an armful of books trying to back out the front door.

She's going to drop all those heavy books, thought Kora, right before it happened. The heavy books clapped loudly as they hit the floor, scattering around her feet. Kora observed the woman stare at the fallen books for a full moment, then curse loudly. Kora froze mid-step, unsure what to do.

Eyes wide, the woman's hand flew to cover her mouth once she discovered her audience. "I'm sorry, I shouldn't have said that word. Or try to carry all these books in one trip. I forgot my bag in the car and I was afraid to get locked out if I went to get it."

"I can help you get out the door, ma'am." Kora bent down for the books. "My heavens, you've checked out enough books for the US Army. You a teacher?"

"No, I've got two girls at home who love to read as much as I do." Bending down to help, she added, "I lose all sense of time around books. They're a good distraction."

"Yes ma'am, I understand," Kora replied.

"My husband's serving overseas and books help pass the time a whole lot better than crying." Two stacks formed on the counter as she continued. "I was worried I wouldn't have enough to get me and the girls through the long weekend. My name's Maggie. What's yours?"

Kora had to really pay attention to the words this Maggie spoke. She talked a lot, like she was nervous, with an accent Kora had never heard. "I'm Kora. Kora Bell. My husband is off fighting somewhere too."

They both nodded awkwardly, without a clue what protocol might belong to this situation. "It's nice to meet you, Kora Bell."

"Yes, ma'am." She noticed Maggie wince at the required formality. Another uncomfortable silence stretched out, while Kora picked up the last book from the floor and read its surprising title. "You checked out *Native Son?*"

"My sister told me to read it. Have you?" Maggie asked.

"Yes. I'm just surprised ...." Her words trailed off. White people made her suspicious. You never knew if their intentions—however good on the surface they appeared—were rooted in self-interest.

"What do you do here at the library?" Maggie rested her hand on the counter, glancing up at the chandelier hanging from the grand ceiling. "I used to dream of living in a library when I was little."

"I clean this place at night," Kora said, before a memory made her laugh, loud enough that she had to share it with Maggie, so as not to appear rude. "Back in Alabama, I went to school with a girl whose whole family lived inside a library. She was real smart and that place sparkled like a church!"

Maggie laughed. "You're not from Charlotte either?"

Kora shook her head. "Born and raised near Montgomery. I moved here with my husband. He has family here. Where are you from?"

"Up North. Boston," she said, then paused. "You remind me of a girl I grew up with. Her mom worked with mine."

Kora nodded, suspecting exactly what that meant.

"What's your favorite book, Kora?"

"The Bible. And anything by Jane Austen."

"Oh, I love her too."

Thinking this might be her longest conversation ever with a white woman, Kora kept it going. "What's your favorite book?"

"Well," Maggie hesitated, turning toward their reflection in the darkened window. She turned back with a smile and tilted her head. "I have twins named Daisy and Demi. Does that give you a clue?"

Kora solved the puzzle right away and nodded. "I must've read *Little Women* a hundred times!" Both of them laughed, then Kora asked, "So you have a boy and a girl?"

"Actually, my Demi is a girl. Identical twin girls, so I guess that's a little different than the book. Who's your favorite March sister?" Maggie asked.

"That's easy: Jo. Yours?"

"I think I relate most to Meg, but really there's a part of each sister I love for different reasons."

Kora took another look at this fellow bibliophile. "I'm sure they have a book group you could join here. That was a great way for me to make new friends. I started one at the Brevard Street Library last year." Kora hesitated a second. "That's my library. I volunteer and clean there too."

"Oh," Maggie dropped her gaze to the floor. "I guess I can't join your group then. Or could I?" Maggie's eyes stayed low, but her voice raised higher than normal at the end of her question, betraying a vulnerability. "If I'm being honest, this is the easiest conversation I've had outside of my family since moving here."

Kora looked away too. She certainly didn't expect to feel sorry for a white woman tonight. Or ever, for that matter. An image of them walking through the door of the Brevard Street Library together flashed through her mind. She saw the stunned faces of her book group as everyone treaded through the awkwardness. No, that definitely wasn't possible.

Kora's voice sounded strange as she heard herself say, "Maybe just the two of us could talk about a book together?" She would never forget the happy smile that spread across Maggie's face.

A year later, sitting in the same library parking lot, Kora watched that face approach the car, half-hidden behind an umbrella and a wobbling stack of books. Each month, Maggie would check out the latest book for them to share and discuss. She took a long time selecting the titles, but she was good at it. Now she opened the car door with only a pinky finger.

"I got some good ones today!" she said, heaving the stack over the front seat. They landed softly. Kora read one of the titles upside down as Maggie fiddled with closing her umbrella.

"*A Tree ... Grows in ... Brooklyn!*" Kora exclaimed, thinking it sounded familiar.

"I couldn't resist that one." Maggie smiled wide. "It's the Brooklyn up North, not yours here, but everybody's talking about that book."

Kora would've had to wait at least six months for that copy to find its way to the corner of Brevard and Second Street. When they first realized that different libraries carried different books, Maggie and Kora devised a plan to broaden both their minds by sharing and talking about the same book from different perspectives.

"I'm late to pick up the girls from Grace," Maggie said, as her key found the ignition.

"But I need to be dropped off at Brevard for my next shift. Before six." Kora barely kept the annoyance out of her voice.

"I'll get you there on time. I just can't be late. Tonight is bridge club and I need to stay on Grace's good side." Maggie twisted toward the rear window, slowly backing the car out of its spot. "I'm making your casserole this Sunday. I know it will help when I break my news."

"You're telling your in-laws about your job this Sunday, huh?"

"Yes. Boy I'm nervous! I've got to convince them. I've already signed up to take the test."

"Test? What kind of test?"

"Some kind of competency test."

Kora wondered if everyone got the same test. "Does anyone fail it?"

"I don't know, but I'll keep an eye out for anyone who runs out crying. That is, if I can convince Grace to watch the girls."

"You'll do fine, just fine. Our husbands need you."

"I'll admit doing *something* feels better than all this waiting for him to come home."

"It must feel real good," Kora said softly, watching the parade of grand Myers Park homes outside her window. They rolled up a long driveway as Daisy and Demi bounded out the front door, followed by Grace Virginia Slone. Most everyone knew Grace's full name since she often referred to herself as such. Grace's face tightened as she recognized Maggie's passenger, then Kora caught her scanning the sidewalks for any neighbors paying attention.

"Mama!" the twins squealed. Maggie got out and was nearly knocked down by the force of their hugs.

"Hello," she said, laughing. "I guess you missed me?"

"Yes, but we had fun with Gigi," Daisy reported. "She taught us how to walk with books on our heads!"

"That's swell," Maggie said, looking at Grace. "Training for their debutante balls so soon?"

"It is *never* too early." Grace said as she reached the car.

Kora avoided direct eye contact, but smiled politely and watched Grace's thin lips form a fake smile.

"How are you, Kora dear?"

"Doing fine, Mrs. Slone, mighty fine," she said, nodding. "Can't complain." Kora kept her smile carefully in place as the girls jumped into the back seat of the car and discovered the library treasures.

Maggie slid back into the driver's seat, rolled the window down, and thanked Grace for watching the girls.

"Anytime, dear. We will see you for dinner this Sunday. Just bring yourselves and any new letters from my son." Grace waved as Maggie backed down the driveway.

Maggie stopped the car, then tipped her head out the window. "Have fun at bridge club tonight!"

Kora noted Grace's puzzled look and chuckled softly. "Now you know there's not a bit of fun happening at that bridge club."

Cranking the window back up, Maggie laughed too. "That's true. Grace carefully picks bridge partners to challenge but never exceed her card skills. *Or* her attractiveness."

"They take that game so seriously," Kora said.

"Another reason I do not fit in here," Maggie said. "I would rather play *anything* but bridge!"

Maggie pulled the car up to the front door of the Brevard Street library right on time. Kora jumped out, shutting the door behind her. She leaned into the open window for goodbyes.

"Good luck on Sunday," Kora said. "You're gonna need it, delivering that kind of news to Grace." She tipped her head toward the back seat. Both girls had noses buried inside their new story pages. "Do they know yet?"

"I told them yesterday." Maggie twisted around. "Daisy, what do you think of my new adventure?"

Daisy lowered her book and flexed the muscles in her skinny arm. "Mama's going to get big arms like the posters. *She* can do it!"

They all laughed as Maggie mirrored her daughter's sign of strength. "Oh! Almost forgot." Maggie pulled her sleeve back down, lifted two books, and extended them toward the open window. "Here you go. I can't wait to read these after you finish."

Kora stuffed them deep inside her satchel. She waved goodbye and hurried inside, anxious to return to her favorite place in the world.

Chapter 3

JUNE, 1943
MAGGIE

"**D**aisy and Demi, let's *go*, please!" Maggie shouted up the empty stairs a second time. "We don't want to be late for Gigi and Papa."

"Coming!" The girls ran down and Maggie raised her casserole dish higher to allow them to scoot underneath. She joined them on the front stoop and did a quick inventory of their outfits and shoes as they fought about who won the race.

"No fighting on Sunday," Maggie warned, before leading the way down the sidewalk.

They kept their feet to the cooler, grassy edges, grateful for the shade cast by the willow oak canopy. The cozy houses they passed, tucked into smaller lots on their street, changed as they turned onto Queens Road West with its grand houses and sprawling yards.

Maggie tried to listen to the girls' chatter, taming the reflex to compare these homes to hers. As her mother used to say, she had less than some but more than most.

"What's in there?" Daisy tried peeking over the dish's lid.

"While you two were playing all afternoon, I was busy cooking."

"Uh oh," the girls said, scrunching their noses.

"What? I can cook. You're not starving."

"That's not your ham surprise, is it?" Daisy said, holding her tummy.

"You make great sandwiches," Demi said brightly, like this was a consolation.

Maggie feigned shock but wasn't really upset. Everyone knew she struggled with cooking. Her recipes never turned out like she planned. Not like Charlie's, who often cooked in their family. Her mother-in-law loved to point this out about Maggie, like she had three heads. It was why Maggie asked Kora for cooking lessons—to prove to Grace that she could learn new things, hoping this would show that she could also handle her new job.

"You'll be glad to know Miss Kora is teaching me how to be a better cook."

"Daddy could teach you too," Demi said softly. "Soon as he comes home."

Maggie bent to match her daughter's height. Demi gently tucked an unruly brown curl behind Maggie's ear. Maggie inhaled the moment. Demi, with her tender touch, was her nurturing child, but Maggie needed to be the strong one now. "Daddy loves cooking for his girls. I bet that's the first thing he does when he comes home." She braced for the word that often came next. *When?* An impossible question to answer. The only thing worse was when they stopped asking it, like they did now.

Draping her free arm around Demi's small shoulders, Maggie went on. "How about we write him another letter tonight after dinner? In his last one, Daddy couldn't stop raving about what a grown-up writer you're becoming. He loves your letters."

"He loves my letters too!" Daisy said with furrowed brows, inserting herself into the conversation.

"He certainly does!" Maggie set the casserole dish on the grass and held out both arms for a hug. Their arms entwined. Maggie gave thanks for these small moments—they meant everything this past year.

"I can see Gigi and Papa's house from here, why don't you have a rematch and race there?" The hug ended abruptly as they pushed off her body at the same time, launching themselves toward another finish line.

Maggie watched them sprint away. Lifting the casserole from the ground, she walked and rehearsed her words one last time. She would break the news to Grace and George today and she had to get this right.

The senior Slone's house held its own among these grand estates. Tall white columns flanked a wide, brick porch, and twin entry doors welcomed the many guests her in-laws entertained.

Grace's front bay window displayed a flag for all to see. Its thick, red border around a white square held a perfectly centered blue star, telling the world a member of this family was fighting in the war. A similar flag hung in Maggie's front window—also with a blue star, not gold. Gold stars were never coming home. Gold star flags represented her deep fear of being a widow and raising the girls alone. She made another deal with God—she'd lost count how many deals this made—keep her star blue and she would do everything in her power to bring him home, starting with this new job. Assuming she could convince her in-laws to help.

Maggie crossed the threshold, allowing herself to be politely welcomed and hugged. She could hear the girls in the living room already making a fuss over Percy, Grace's white toy poodle.

"What *is* that you are carrying?" Grace asked, pulling away from their hug.

"I told you I was going to help this time and bring a dish for dinner."

"Yes, but I didn't think you'd actually bring one."

"Well, I did … so here you go!" Maggie placed the casserole into Grace's hands.

"Is that grass?" Grace asked, checking the glass bottom.

"Sorry, we stopped along the way." Maggie wiped off the warm grass as best she could.

Grace let her finish cleaning, then frowned at her now grassy palms. "How lovely. I'll have Lucy add this to the table while you wash your hands." Turning toward the sitting room, Grace called out, "George, Daisy, Demi, y'all make your way into the dining room now, you hear?"

Maggie cleaned up, then followed Grace into the kitchen, passing the girls pulling the poodle by the collar toward the dining room.

"Percy is not allowed at our dinner table." Grace pointed to the door. "Outside, please."

"Awwww!" the girls harmonized, but released the curly cloud of a dog out back.

"Maggie, please select a trivet so Lucy can add your delightful contribution to our table."

After a year of Sunday dinners in Charlie's childhood home, Maggie knew exactly which drawer held Grace's collection of elegant trivets to protect her many antique surfaces. With a filigreed knob in each hand, Maggie pulled the drawer open.

"Are the trivets already out?" she asked to the air behind her, loud enough for Grace to hear. "The drawer's empty."

Grace's voice came through the wall. "Check George's study. Mr. Jeffrey was repairing one with a broken foot and letting it dry."

Maggie entered the study, layered in tanned leather and dark woods. If a manly smell could be bottled, this would come close. Atop one of the end tables, she spotted the trivet. She couldn't help stopping in front of Charlie's portrait on the wall. The towheaded boy of five proved that his inextinguishable dimples were present from the start. She noticed several features of her girls, including their dark blue eyes and small chin clefs. They favored him.

The trivet lay in front of a framed picture of Charlie in his football uniform, his team fanned out behind their captain. Looking every bit proud, sure, and serious, he appeared destined for the leadership roles he would later claim in the military. This version of Charlie, while attractive, was not why she fell in love.

The first time she had seen the picture, on her first visit to this house, she had remarked on his firm gaze and chiseled resolve.

"I suppose. I practiced that face often enough." He gave her a demonstration, then changed his face to a silly grin. "It was all acting. I knew so much less than what was expected of me, but I hid those doubts."

She couldn't help asking, "What kind of doubts?"

"Like there was a ticking clock over my head, and it was a matter of time before I made a mistake and someone figured me out."

"You wouldn't be the first person to get something wrong."

"It's okay to be wrong if it only affects me. Only I couldn't stand someone else paying the price."

"Like one of your men?"

"I couldn't bear that," Charlie answered, then seemed to want to lighten the mood. "Eventually you learn more and doubt less, but it takes time."

She smiled at her humble and kind soon-to-be fiancé. He left the Army soon after they married, finding security in complex insurance calculations instead. He embraced his power to mitigate loss, rather than agonize over it.

Maggie picked up the repaired trivet, but kept her eyes on the young captain Charlie, trying to mimic his outward courage, if just for today and the conversation she faced with his parents.

Leaning into the swinging door that partitioned the kitchen and dining rooms, she breathed in more comfort—this time from the smells rising off the formal table. She held the door for Lucy, whose face was strictly business, on her way to land each perfectly timed dish on the table before leaving for the day.

Nobody she knew in Boston had a cook, so Maggie often stumbled through her interactions with the Slone's household help. Lucy's skin was the color of a beautiful live oak, and her posture just as erect. Wondering if Lucy had her own family yet to cook for this Sunday, Maggie gave her a wide berth.

Lucy brushed past with her famous glazed ham, then lowered it next to her buttery mashed potatoes, and green beans bathed in bacon drippings. The aromas blended perfectly. As intoxicating as the wine George now poured for the adults.

Lucy's cooking was a bright spot in the decision to move south. Maggie found out Lucy and Kora were neighbors, and often competed for the prize of best cook in Brooklyn. It didn't take much to convince Kora to teach Maggie to make a casserole that would rival Lucy's Sunday menu at the Slone's house.

"Everything looks wonderful, Lucy. Maggie brought a trivet for her new dish." Grace winked. "See you in the morning, Lucy."

George teased several giggles out of his granddaughters. He looked just like Charlie. Not for the first time, Maggie wondered if Charlie's hairline would age as well as his father's perfect touch-of-gray temples. She prayed for the chance to find out.

The family of five stood behind their regular chairs. All heads turned to Grace, who nodded for everyone to take their seats. Grace and George claimed opposite ends of the table. The girls sat on one side and Maggie the other, placing her chair in the middle to minimize the gap Charlie left in the family.

Grace looked sweetly at her granddaughters. "Now, who said the blessing last Sunday?"

The girls instantly pointed to one another and said, "She did!"

Grace smiled knowingly. "Well, isn't it lucky that I remember who gave thanks last week? It was Daisy. Demi, please lead the table in prayer."

All bowed their heads as Demi recited, "God bless the food we are about to receive. Give bread to those who hunger, and hunger for mercy and justice to us who have bread. Amen."

"Amen!" George said, his wide eyes clearly anticipating the spread before him.

Grace beamed at Demi. "That was lovely, darling. Everyone, please eat."

All five began the ritual of lifting the closest serving dish, adding a portion to their plates before passing to the right.

Maggie tried to forget how nervous she was.

As hostess, Grace led the conversation. She asked the girls about their week and their friends. In the middle of the girls' reports, Grace took her first bite of Maggie's macaroni and cheese. "Why

Maggie Slone, this is *good*! However did you manage it? You've been holding out on us!"

Relieved and a little bit proud, Maggie said, "I'm so glad you like it. I had some extra cheese stamps." She paused half a second, remembering how Kora had to get creative around the shortage of her usual cheese ingredients. "Kora taught me how to make it."

"Kora? The one who cleans the library?"

Maggie nodded.

Grace looked exasperated. "Sweet Maggie, why would you not just pay her to cook for you? We could pay her, right George?"

"Of course," George said, hearing his name after clearly not paying strict attention. "Who do I pay?" He cocked his head, then sliced himself another bite of ham.

Grace ignored him, turning back to Maggie. "I dare say you have denied her the opportunity to earn an income. There are certain expectations here." As if it were widely understood but not politely discussed, she whispered her next sentence. "There are societal protocols."

"Kora doesn't want my money. She's my friend and friends learn from each other."

"Haven't you made friends from all the bridge clubs I've gotten you invited to?"

Maggie kept her eyes level with Grace's, though she longed to roll them toward the chandelier. "I already feel like an outsider. My abysmal card playing skills only amplify that fact."

Grace's eyes did reach the chandelier, clearly in exasperation.

Her husband, perhaps anticipating further conflict, raised his glass. "I would like to make a toast!"

Daisy and Demi hurried to clutch their grape juice glasses, arms stretched high in the air. They loved toasting like the grown-ups. Grace and Maggie slowly raised their glasses too, as a silent truce.

George's buttercream drawl boomed over the table. "To friends and family that make life bettah!"

Five glasses clanked and voices rose. "Cheers!"

Maggie set her glass down. "That was a lovely toast, George, thank you." Charlie had explained to her long ago that Grace was the imposing force at home, so the rest of the family had claimed whatever territory she did not. For George, that meant the banking world was his. Over the years, each respectfully adhered to subtle signals whenever a line was about to be crossed.

Maggie tried to listen to the conversation while judging the best time to make the bold announcement she'd practiced all day. She was running out of time, but it couldn't feel forced. She willed her voice to stay strong. Keep the focus on Grace and everything Grace would gain.

"I've taken a job at US Rubber Company," she said in her best casual, run-of-the-mill dinner conversation voice. "You know, the Shell Plant."

Grace's fork slipped from her hand, but she caught it before it made a sound. "What's that, dear?" she asked slowly.

"I've taken a job at the US Rubber Company Naval Ammunitions Plant," she repeated, even slower, then let it sink in. What an awkward mouthful of words, even to her ears. No wonder everyone shortened the name to "Shell Plant."

Grace's long lashes batted, and her lips stayed parted. "I'm not sure what to say." She threw her napkin over her plate, like her appetite had vanished.

"You could say congratulations?" Maggie took a sip of wine for courage. "My first day is next week. I know you don't agree with my decision, but I would be grateful if the girls could come here before and after school. They will have daycare soon, but I'd much rather they stay with family." She paused for effect. "Plus, you might enjoy the extra time with them. And I *know* they would benefit from your influence."

Grace looked across the table at her husband, who nodded his agreement to her silent question. Raising her own glass to lips, she let it hover in the air between her and Maggie. "This can't be about money, dear. You know we'll cover anything you need. Anything."

Grace held Maggie's eyes over the rim as she finally took a sip, then set the stemware down with purpose.

"Money is one of the reasons." Maggie looked down at her plate of fine bone china. "Charlie has always had expensive taste."

Grace shot back, "It's not a crime to like nice things, dear."

"That's true. He also wanted to buy a house close to you, but it has stretched us too far and the war has gone on longer than he planned."

"Do they know?" Grace tilted her head toward the girls.

"Yes, we discussed it last week." Maggie noticed her squirming children. "Girls, I think I hear Percy whining at the door for you. Go keep him company outside for a bit, please?"

The girls pushed back their chairs and stood.

"Please carry your empty plates to the kitchen. Lucy will get them tomorrow," Grace said.

Once they were out of earshot, Grace threw her hands toward the coffered ceiling. "There *has* to be another way."

"His pay allowance isn't covering all our bills." Maggie kept her voice level. "Charlie's plan is not playing out like he thought. No one's is." She looked to her father-in-law. "It's sweet of you to offer money, but what the girls and I really need is your time and support."

George leaned over to pat Maggie's hand, but he understood not to speak first on such family matters. This was not his territory.

Grace continued, "That plant is dangerous, Maggie, with enough explosives to affect half of Charlotte. George said as much to the Chamber, but got outnumbered." Grace looked at the door the girls had just exited through. "Their father is in grave danger. Now their mother too?"

"I understand how you feel," she said to Grace before turning to George on the slim chance it would help. "You wouldn't believe the safety protocols they follow there. They are military precise. This was not a fast decision. I truly weighed every risk and benefit."

Maggie turned back to Grace, took a deep breath, and threw down her ace card. "You spending more time with the girls will be a gift for all of us." She'd practiced this last sentence carefully, knowing Grace was always eager to impart more of a Southern influence on her only grandchildren. Grace stayed quiet, hopefully considering the possibilities, as Maggie continued, "It's important to end this war as soon as possible. Charlie has already missed so much of the girls' lives. I know it's dangerous. Trust me, I've never had something I've been so scared to do—and scared not to do—all at the same time. I'm also tired of waiting for our lives to go back to normal." Conscious of talking too much with her hands, Maggie let them fall in her lap. "I need to do *something*."

"You are raising two perfect children. Isn't that enough? You could grow a victory garden like me. Heavens, I've practically begged you to come to my Junior League volunteer meetings. Maybe then you'd finally make a few friends here."

George cleared his throat, with obvious timing. Grace had crossed a line.

Maggie fought the urge to leave the room. She wouldn't let Grace bait her so easily. This was Maggie's decision to make and theirs to support, not the other way around. "Those are things *you* are good at, Grace. Not me. Besides, haven't you seen these posters and billboards popping up? Uncle Sam needs women like me."

Maggie could almost see the wheels spinning inside the matriarch's pretty head. Finally, Grace broke her silence with clear, measured sentences. "I want my son home safely as much as anyone, but you and I both know Charlie wouldn't want you to go to work. They say we all have to make sacrifices, but mothers belong at home with their children."

"Charlie isn't here. He can neither confirm nor deny your theory. He moved us to here so we would have your support. Today, I'm asking you for a bit more of that support." Maggie continued, softening her tone. "The girls'll hardly know I'm gone. I'll work first shift while they're still in school. I just need a little extra help before and after the bells ring."

The two mothers locked eyes. Maggie pulled away first, quietly lifting the wine bottle and topping off each glass. She caught Grace dabbing a slender finger to each side of her face. She was pulling her "I've got something in my eye" trick. The one Maggie and Charlie had laughed about many times. Her gesture provided the illusion of both pain and strength, as she bravely masked the hurt she'd so obviously endured.

Maggie took it as a good sign. Grace would see this as an opportunity to help her son's family and at the same time rear the "North" out of the twins.

Grace managed a weak smile. "Well then," she said.

Maggie kept stone still, despite wanting to cheer. Though it would never be spoken, Maggie had won.

"Another toast, please." George's baritone cut sharply through the silence, his arm raised in anticipation. Grace and Maggie slowly raised their glasses. "To family, sacrifice, and bringing our boys home in victory!"

Maggie was impressed, if not a little humbled. She gave her father-in-law a broad smile. With just a few words, George had brought the solution into focus: a common goal for the women at the table.

"To victory!" they echoed as three glasses came together.

Chapter 4

JULY, 1943
MAGGIE

The gray bus slowed, and its huge tires crunched through the gravel. When it finally stopped on the circle drive, passengers stood and poured into the center aisle. Maggie waited so she would be last. Her mind replayed this morning's sad goodbye with the girls. The guilt was physical. She had hugged them too long.

Daisy and Demi had seemed just fine, but her heart broke watching their animated waves as she pulled away. Now tattooed into her memory, the image replayed several times. This wasn't natural. Charlie should be the one headed off to work with all three of his girls smiling and waving him off.

Looking out the bus window, she studied the massive web of plant buildings before her. *So many*—how would she ever learn her way around? She must've paused too long before descending the stairs.

"Everything all right, miss?" the driver asked behind her.

Startled, Maggie nodded and said over her shoulder, "Sorry, everything's fine, thank you." She took a deep breath and the first step down.

A sign pointed new hires toward the administration building. Folding tables were set up around the room's perimeter, and one displayed a handwritten sign that read "NEW PERSONNEL." The woman sitting behind it looked a lot like Maggie's mother had before she died. This woman was older, with pretty features, but those were dwarfed by huge, rhinestone, cat-eye glasses.

"What's ya full name, honey?" The woman's New York accent made Maggie feel more at ease, less self-conscious about her own.

Maggie spelled out Marós Fraser Slone, quickly adding, "but everyone calls me Maggie."

Cat Eyes scanned her list before adding a check mark. She paused before looking up. "Marós is a beautiful Irish name. Means Rosemary, doesn't it?"

"Yes, it does. My father chose it, but my mother insisted I go by a more American-sounding name," she explained.

Cat Eyes blinked through an understanding nod. "Maggie it is then!" She crossed off Marós and wrote above it, then pointed to an empty row of metal chairs against the wall.

Maggie sat and placed her pocketbook on her lap. Not wanting to stare, she pulled out her billfold instead. Flipping through the black and white photographs inside, her mind filled in the colors with happy memories. Boston, before the war, where it had been easy and effortless to mold herself into a life with Charlie.

The first photograph showed a young Maggie and Charlie when they were first dating. A friend had snapped it at an outdoor party. Charlie looked handsome and relaxed, even in his starched military uniform. One of them must have said something funny, because they were both laughing, holding each other for balance. If only she could remember what was so entertaining.

Maggie moved on to the next pictures, mostly of the girls. One showed the twins as babies, sharing a buggy. The next-door neighbor's daughter was also in the picture. The young girl, on tiptoes and peering over the handlebar, wanted to "push her babies" down the sidewalk. Maggie had forced a smile for the camera, with her foot jammed under one of the rubber wheels to keep the twins from rolling away. She shook her head remembering the twins as babies—long days and short years.

She turned to the last picture. Charlie had invited all their Boston friends over for an early surprise party for her birthday. She missed those friends. She ran a light finger over each blissful, unknowing face, frozen on December 6, hours before their spirits sank alongside the ships in Pearl Harbor. Her own naïve expression in the photograph was illuminated by the glow of thirty-three candles. She kept this picture to remind herself how life can pivot on a dime.

Maggie put the pictures away and subtly checked out the office surroundings. Among the sounds of clacking typewriters and ringing phones, she noticed so many women, busy in smart skirts and heels. Some, yielding pens and paper, followed behind important-looking military men. Others nodded or shook their heads through questions asked from the other sides of tables and desks.

It had been almost ten years since she'd worked in an office. What might she have in common with these young women?

The men were mostly in uniform. Maggie had a clear view of one office window. A serious face was framed between two huge stacks of files, one on each desk corner. Occasionally a woman entered his office, adding new folders to the pile, while removing others from the opposite end.

More women—also new, she assumed—found seats next to Maggie. Some seemed to know each other. The low hum of chatter added to the rhythm of the bustling, noisy room.

When all the seats were filled, the woman in the distracting cat-eye glasses instructed everyone to stand and follow her. Maggie found herself dead last as the long line of women snaked down the hall. They entered a small room with seven or eight rows of tables and benches, which brought back memories of college classrooms.

Maggie picked a seat next to a younger girl with a mass of dark wavy hair and her face turned down. The instructor began calling names and handing out folders.

"Betty ... Svendsen?" She scanned the room before finding Betty's extended hand.

"Wilhelmina Neal?" the professor inquired, glancing around.

The girl next to Maggie shot up, almost shouting. "It's Billie. My name's Billie." She grabbed the folder and sat down just as quickly, keeping her head low after a quick glance in Maggie's direction.

Maggie tried to smile and make eye contact with her, but Billie seemed intent on the document in front of her. *Well, this is off to a swell start.*

The instructor began her lecture, pacing back and forth in front of the room. "The US Rubber Company, Munitions Division, welcomes you. Our three shifts cover every hour of the day, employing close to ten thousand people from Mecklenburg and the surrounding counties. Over two hundred and fifty buildings that make up this facility were built during the last half of 1942. Our mission is to bring a speedy end to the war, without ending our own lives in the process.

"If you only remember one sentence that comes from my mouth today, make it this one: Safety is our number one goal. In layman's terms, we are surrounded by materials that explode if they get too close together. Your adherence and enforcement of our safety rules will keep us all alive.

"In your folders is a map of the campus—over 2,200 acres. This'll show you exactly where to find our plant hospital, fire station, change houses, and any one of our seven cafeterias."

Here the instructor looked up from her notes. "Our hair and dress code are described on page eleven of the employee handbook. I hope you ladies like the color blue." She didn't bother hiding the sarcasm from her voice.

Maggie listened and took notes on the backsides of the papers in the folder. "We assemble rounds of 40 mm anti-aircraft artillery shells," the woman continued. "Also called 'little shells with the big wallop,' we assemble over 100,000 a day. That seems like a big number, but one single ship can go through half-a-million shells in a sixty-minute battle."

Maggie felt the bench shake as a nervous Billie pumped her leg up and down. Craning her neck to see further down their row, she caught other women wearing annoyed expressions, as if Maggie were the culprit.

Maggie reached into her pocketbook and placed two pieces of pink bubble gum in front of her. Loud enough to attract Billie's attention, she unwrapped one piece of the rationed treat and popped it in her mouth. She slid the other piece in front of Billie, causing her to look up.

Maggie held Billie's gaze and gently placed a hand on the jumpy leg, signaling that it would be all right. Billie stopped the shaking, and their silent dialogue ended in shy smiles. Maggie had found a friend.

❄ ❄ ❄

Two weeks later, bells jingling in her hand, Maggie wound through her latest shortcut between buildings. Her last job had been in a legal office before she had the twins, where she knew the precise location of every last paper clip. Here in this massive place, she couldn't find a thing and asked a thousand questions all day long.

Today's training assignment felt simple on the surface: push large carts between buildings. Only these carts were filled with explosives and had a nickname, "Angel Buggies." If pushed too close together, she might get her own set of wings. Maggie felt awful enough leaving the girls for nine hours a day, but the thought of leaving them without a mother entirely ....

Seizing the last empty bench in the crowded change house, she tied the first set of bells around her ankle. To any passers-by, the bells offered a loud and clear warning: steer clear of this buggy's deadly contents.

Maggie was assigned to shadow Ruby and Deborah. Jingling all the way, the three of them left the change house toward Area 9. Greeted by a wall of July afternoon heat, Maggie shaded her eyes until they adjusted to the sun.

Ruby and Deborah walked ahead, looking to Maggie like the characters "Mutt and Jeff" from the funny papers. She guessed Deborah wasn't yet twenty. Ruby might be a few years older and was a good six inches taller, eight if you counted her thick auburn hair pinned high on her head. They were already deep in conversation.

"That's your problem, Deb. You gotta learn to think on your feet better."

"I wanted say something mysterious. I try this, honest, but my words sounded silly, so I stopped."

Maggie's heart melted for this beautiful young girl with the thick Polish accent, just trying to fit in.

Ruby seemed more impatient. "But we practiced this over and over, Deb."

"I know it! Those big blue eyes make me forget. Oh, what the use? My parents would never let me date a goy."

"What's a goy?"

"I tell you later," Deborah answered as they reached their destination. A man pointed Maggie and Ruby to a large buggy with sides almost taller than Maggie. On tiptoes, Maggie peeked over the side, wondering how much of her rationed sugar might have been used to make all that gunpowder.

With Ruby on one end, Maggie gripped the opposite rail of their cart. Deborah pushed a much smaller carriage in a different direction, promising to wait for them at Area 10.

So far at the Shell Plant, Maggie had learned to assemble fuses, insert primers, and load tracers into empty shell casings. These new details swam inside her head. Soon, she would receive her permanent line assignment, hopefully the same one as her new friend, Billie.

Maggie and Ruby kept quiet, letting the sound of their bells part the sea of people along the path. A group of passing naval officers whistled long and low in Ruby's direction. With striking red hair the color of a deep gemstone, a very tall Ruby stuck out in a crowd. Her head never turned, but Maggie caught a knowing grin.

Maggie tried to make conversation. "Did you say your parents work here too?"

"No, ma'am, they work at the Army supply house north of here. At the old Ford plant."

Maggie winced at the reverence to her age. "Ruby, you don't need to call me 'ma'am.'"

"Oh, yes ma'am. I mean Maggie, sorry," she said, using the inside of her elbow to wipe sweat from her hairline. "Blasted heat ruins my makeup."

"Where'd you say you were from again?"

"Marshville," Ruby said, finishing the last syllable like she had a mouthful of something.

"Where is Marsh*vull*?" Maggie tried to mimic.

"East of here a ways. More headstones than upright people though. Charlotte's *much* more exciting."

Pushing their cart up to the Area 10 dock, they found Deborah waiting. Each one grabbed a new, smaller cart for herself. Walking ten feet apart with Ruby in the middle, they started down a new pathway. Maggie was impressed by how Deborah and Ruby picked up exactly where they had left off in their previous conversation.

"What's a goy, again?" Ruby asked.

"It's non-Jew," Deborah answered.

"Is it a non-Jew who's also a boy?"

"It's anybody who is non-Jew. See? *You* are girl, who's also goy," Deborah explained.

"Oh, I get it. There are girl goys and boy goys." Ruby giggled. Maggie did too.

"Yes, but you are missing point." Deborah sighed. "My parents are old-fashioned. Mama is always scheming to fix me up with NJB from AJW."

"Are you speaking in riddles?"

Maggie laughed out loud, enjoying their rapid banter. When was the last time spontaneous laughter had escaped from her? She used to be known for it, often at the most inappropriate times.

"Sorry. NJB is Nice Jewish Boy," Deborah said, flashing an embarrassed smile. "AJW is Association of Jewish Women. We live with my Great Aunt Sarah. She's big in AJW. They drag me to all boring meetings, trying to match me with sons of friends."

"They sound swell," Ruby said.

"That's my point." Deborah seemed frustrated. "I expect I will marry NJB someday, but not until I am good and ready!" She raised her voice to compete with a passing train. "Is this clear?"

Maggie looked at Ruby and shrugged. Their thick Northern and Southern accents harmonized. "Yes, ma'am!"

Ruby said, "Well, as soon as I marry my rich husband and live in a mansion, we will have you and your NJB over for a fancy dinner of champagne and caviar."

Deborah seemed to relax, then wrinkled her nose. "Why do rich Americans like fish eggs? We had lot of money in Poland, and never ate those."

"I can't say I've actually tried caviar yet, but I'm sure I'll grow to love it when I'm rich." Ruby glanced sideways at Deborah. "Do you still have lots of money?"

Deborah's pace slowed. "All left behind. Along with my friends and teachers. In middle of night." All eyes fell on Deborah as the three stopped pushing their buggies. "We are rich now, for very different reason." Deborah's voice trailed off.

They walked on. Only their bells sounded the rest of the way.

Chapter 5

AUGUST, 1943
KORA

Finding the streets empty, Kora crossed as the bus pulled away. Today was Alabama hot. Heavy with books and secret recipe ingredients, Kora shifted her canvas bag to the other shoulder on her walk to Maggie's house.

Kora had never lacked for friends, and here in Charlotte was no exception. She was blessed by her husband's sisters, her Brooklyn neighbors, and her Grace Church community. But none of them knew of her friendship with Maggie. She probably would have told James about Maggie if he were home. He was a good husband and kept all her secrets.

Reaching up to knock on Maggie's side door, she had to admit she looked forward to their monthly book discussions. Some were hard conversations and some easy, but all were honest and thoughtful.

Demi pulled the door open. "Kora's here!" she yelled behind her.

In the middle of pouring two glasses of milk, Daisy set the jug down and ran to hug Kora.

"What's in the bag?" she asked.

Kora pulled out two books she'd checked out for the twins.

After thanking Kora, Demi tucked one book under each arm while her sister grabbed the milk glasses. As the girls passed their mother on her way down the stairs, Kora heard Maggie caution her daughters, "I'm suspending the 'no food or drink upstairs' rule *for today only*. Please don't make me regret my decision."

"We're being careful Mama, see?"

Kora listened to the stairs' creak slowly with each small, careful step. She set the chicken, eggs, flour, and lard neatly on the counter and then removed an empty tin can and strainer from her bag. As Maggie approached, Kora explained, "We'll need this tin after, to drain the fat for the butcher. They turn it into glycerin to make explosives. You've cooked chicken before?"

"I've never made fried chicken. I've baked it before, but it comes out a little dry."

"Well, we'll fix that today. My chicken never turns out dry."

Maggie unrolled the top of a small brown bag and Kora enjoyed seeing her face change when the smell hit her nose. Kora caught the intoxicating scent too, instantly hungry.

"What kind of seasonings are in here?"

"The secret kind. My grandmother taught me to keep it that way, but always keep a bag ready for friends. This one's my gift to you. If you can get this right, that is!" Kora pointed to the ingredients on the counter. "She had some mighty high standards when it came to her fried chicken," she teased.

"I'm ready. Let's get started!"

"We start by you getting to know that chicken right there."

Slowly approaching the pebbly, yellow meat, Maggie's enthusiasm seemed to wane. Kora had plucked the meat clean to make it easier, knowing this was the part Maggie would need to push through in order to impress her mother-in-law. Grace's favorite meal was Southern fried chicken, and Kora's was the best around. Even Lucy, who worked for Grace, had asked for Kora's recipe, but she wouldn't budge.

Maggie held the knife and her breath before starting to section the meat into clammy chunks as instructed.

Kora stretched up on her tiptoes, pulling down two bowls from an overhead shelf. One was for the flour mix, the other for eggs. She glanced at Maggie, who was wrestling with the firm but squishy flesh. "I finished *A Tree Grows in Brooklyn*."

"What'd you think?" Maggie asked.

"I liked it. That Francie made me cry at the end." Kora pointed over her shoulder. "I brought the book today. Couldn't recall when it was due, and they wouldn't like me returning it none."

"I'll take it back. What were your favorite parts?"

Kora reached for the book and turned to the first page she had marked with a piece of torn paper, as was their custom. "Most of mine are around Francie. Here she talks about a very sophisticated numbers game she played in her head. She gives each number a personality. It's gonna sound like I'm making it up, but I created games just like hers to learn arithmetic. I thought I was the only one, but here some writer from New York I never knew did the very same thing. Did you ever do that?"

"I can't say I enjoyed math enough to make it a game."

"Well, here's one we can both relate to. In Chapter 48, she tries to remember every last detail of the day 'War' was the headline in all those newspapers she had to read. Francie made a time capsule out of an envelope with newspaper headlines, a poem, and a lock of her own hair. When I read it, I thought, *Now that is a sensitive child. An old soul.* If I ever have a daughter, I'd want her to be thoughtful like Francie."

"Do you and James want children? Someday, I mean."

Kora looked at her sideways. "I don't love that question, but you're not the first to ask it either. Wanting children doesn't seem like it's enough. If the good Lord blesses us with them, I will do my best to raise them in His glory." After a quick glance toward the heavens, Kora shook her head. "But I can't worry about that."

"I understand. Let's change the subject. My hands are so messy. Can you pull that piece of paper off the fridge for me? I wrote my page numbers down. Read me the first one?"

"Page 381. Francie thinks to herself, 'Seems like I'm the most dissatisfied person in the whole world. Oh, I wish I was young again when everything seemed so wonderful!'" Kora finished reading the passage and waited for Maggie to explain.

"I saw myself in Francie all through this book, but that moment of her young life really stuck with me. I think she was only fourteen, starting her first real job in the city when she said it. She realized she couldn't get her innocence back. I distinctly remember that feeling as a girl. You cross a line and can't go back. You long to be grown up because it seems so wonderful and liberating, then when you do, it's not like you hoped."

Kora stepped closer to inspect Maggie's chicken pieces. She asked for the knife, made a few extra cuts, then set them aside, pointing to the sink for hand washing. "I don't remember anything from my childhood being so wonderful. My parents were kind, hard-working folks, but my daddy had to move around a lot to find work."

"Did you move with him?"

"Not once. He left me and Mama with my grandparents a lot. It always made her sad. Before Daddy would leave, he'd sit me down to tell me again that it was my job to make Mama happy. Too much pressure laid on tiny shoulders." Kora saw sadness and agreement reflected in Maggie's eyes, but not pity. Good. She almost felt bad for judging Maggie on her reactions, but so far she was doing okay.

Kora demonstrated how the flour mixture came together, adding half-a-cup from the seasoning bag last. She stood back to let Maggie take over and picked up the book. "Remember when Francie and Neeley get their vaccines before starting school?" Kora began. "That Mama made them go alone because she couldn't bear to take them, couldn't stand to see them in pain. I'd have trouble with that too."

Maggie stirred the flour mix. "I think I marked that page too, but for a different reason. Didn't the kids make mud pies before that vaccine appointment?"

"Yes, I think that's right."

"Well, with no adult reminding them to wash up, their skin was still caked with dirt when they showed up to the clinic. That doctor and nurse embarrassed Francie and made her cry. They assumed Francie had a low IQ and wouldn't understand. Their awful words hurt Francie worse than any needle."

Kora stayed quiet, because the behavior of that doctor and nurse was the most ordinary part of the book for her. Francie and Neeley, because of their appearance, were judged as less. Maggie appeared to be waiting for her to speak, while Kora debated over how much to explain. Yes, they had things in common, but here, in this conversation, their perspectives diverged, separating like oil and water.

Kora had almost pointed out the obvious to Maggie last year when they talked about *Native Son*. The conversation had started down an uncharted path about what the author, Richard Wright, was trying to convey. After reading the confused look on Maggie's face, Kora dropped a crumb to remind herself to stay clear of that topic in the future. Maggie couldn't understand. It was best not to try.

But now their friendship spanned almost a year. Would bringing it up again this time be different? Before Kora could decide for sure, she heard herself say, "I understand Francie's pain. I feel it every day."

Maggie was quiet, then set the mixing spoon down. "You're right. I'm embarrassed I didn't see that before."

Kora turned up the heat on the skillet and demonstrated how to test the grease using small drops of water. Once they skittered to the side, Kora dipped the first piece of chicken into the eggs, dredged it through the flour mix, and gently placed it in the hot pan, which sizzled and popped like applause. Maggie mimicked each step, proving to be a good student.

When the pan was full and covered, Kora turned the heat down on the stove and on the conversation. "There ain't no point you apologizing for the way things are." She opened the book again, flipping to her last marked page. "I also liked the part where the bartender calls on the family to share funny stories about Francie's daddy after he died. Francie didn't like this man one bit on account of all the liquor he served her daddy, but that visit puts him in a new light." Placing a finger on the page, Kora read the words out loud. "'He was a short stocky man with thick hands, a short red neck and thinning hair. Who'd ever guess, looking at the outside of him, that he was so different inside.'"

"Francie changed her mind after she got to know the bartender." Maggie nodded. "She has a lot to teach us."

"That she does," Kora agreed, turning each piece of chicken for the last time. The magic of the secret spices filled the room. She turned off the stove, sensing it was time. "Call the girls to eat. This'll be a good batch."

Chapter 6

AUGUST, 1943
MAGGIE

Billie stifled a yawn while Maggie drove a corner in the sleepy Woodlawn neighborhood a little faster than she meant to. The rubber wheels squealed in protest.

"Take it easy! Where you gonna find new tires if you wear out these?" Billie asked, before lifting out a small paper booklet from her purse. She separated three squares, using the perforated lines. "That reminds me. I'm putting my gas stamps in your bag here."

Stopping in front of a modest brick ranch, the rear door of the Ford flew open. Ruby and Deborah slid across the wide back seat. "I didn't know you were training for the Indy 500. We could hear your squealing tires a block away," Ruby said.

Deborah came to Maggie's defense. "It's not easy being driver, Ruby. You want to go back to the bus?"

"Nevah!" Ruby said dramatically.

Figuring now was as good a time as any, Maggie picked a magazine off the floor.

"Watcha got there?" Billie asked.

Maggie unfolded the front page. "Oh, just the latest Saturday *Post*." She held it high and turned on the overhead light so they could see in the early morning darkness. "Ladies, we're famous. By association, at least. Look who made the front cover!"

"You don't say," Billie said.

Ruby gave a low whistle. "Well, I'll be."

The girl on the cover was dressed head to toe in an all-too-familiar shade of blue with machine tools and a metal lunch box resting on her sturdy lap. A rather large ham sandwich suspended very near her mouth, proved her labors had caused quite an appetite.

Her brassy hair was hastily pulled back, springing out beneath the straps of her safety gear. A saintly halo gleamed in contrast to her dirty face, and bright red socks stuffed into her deep brown penny loafers offered the outfit's only color contrast.

"Look, it says 'Rosie' right there on her lunch box," Deborah said. "Just like song!"

"Sure is a government gal, isn't she?" Billie leaned in closer. "I don't even recognize some of those buttons on her shirt. Wonder what they mean?"

"How can you talk about buttons? What about her *enormous* arms and legs?" Ruby cried. "That's some kind of artistic statement, right? I won't get those man hands from all this military work, will I? Or muscles like that?"

"Relax," Billie said. "Your scrawny arms and legs could never look like that. We just have to worry about getting an arm or leg blown off."

"On that note ..." Maggie dropped the paper to the floor. "I thought you'd get a kick out of it, but we'd better get moving." She twisted the radio knob before pulling down the gear shift. As if on cue, the "Rosie the Riveter" song came through the speakers.

"I love this part," Ruby said. "Turn it up, will ya?"

All four heads bounced to the perky beat, singing whatever lyrics they knew. Maggie sang her favorite part louder than the others.

Rosie's got a boyfriend, Charlie
Charlie, he's a Marine
Rosie is protecting Charlie
Working overtime on the
riveting machine.
When they gave her a production "E,"
She was as proud as a girl could be.
There's something true about
Red, white, and blue about
Rosie ... the Riveter!

Deborah stopped short of rolling her "r"s for the chorus, letting the other three drag it out like a rivet gun. "I cannot do rolling like that, but I *can* harmonize like we practiced." Deborah pointed to each as they sang their part.

Their planned pitches layered, filling the car with a sound no single voice could ever achieve. "Rosie, Rosie, Rosie, Rosie ... working the assembly line!"

The road changed from paved to dirt and the city became fields. Maggie surveyed the still-dark sky, thinking they'd make it in time, when the steering column began to shimmy. The wheel pulled hard to the right as she wrestled it left. The car erupted with confusion, questions, and screams until Maggie stopped between the edges of road and field. She didn't need to get out to know she'd blown a rear tire.

Charlie had searched long and hard to find four new tires before he left, swearing he didn't need to teach her how to change one, because he was confident in his return before they had a chance to wear out.

So much for his plan.

She turned toward the others, wondering who in this car full of skirts knew how to change a flat tire. Their wide-eyed faces mirrored the same question back to her. She faced forward again, noticing a set of headlights in the distance.

"Billie, get out of the car," Maggie said, as she released her own door handle. No time to consider options, she stepped near the edge of the dirt road, waving arms back and forth. Billie appeared next to her doing the same.

The old pickup slowed. It was too dark to tell if it was painted brown or just rusted, but the engine purred. Maggie took that as a good sign. The driver cranked down his window, revealing two men who looked like they had just discovered an open lion cage at the zoo. Round eyes gleamed against ageless mahogany skin.

"Our tire just blew." Maggie pointed to the trunk. "Could you help us? I have a spare in back."

They turned to each other. Floppy straw hats masked their expressions and Maggie didn't catch their low-spoken words. The driver then poked his head through the window looking up and down the otherwise empty road, before finally addressing Billie and Maggie. "Stay right there."

"Where would we go?" Billie asked, getting Maggie's elbow in her side.

The truck made a quick three-point turn and pulled in close behind, headlights illuminating the deflated tire. Billie and Maggie approached the driver's window again, but stopped in front of one of his palms. "That be close enough. We gone walk you through this."

"Won't you get out to help us?" Billie asked.

"No'm, we cain't do it. You understand it's not safe fo' us."

The truth washed over Maggie. Their intentions could be misinterpreted by another passing car. The driver leaned his head out the window and issued exact instructions, talking louder than his still running engine. The passenger kept his eyes on the road, head bobbing left and right. They seemed ready to bolt at the first sign of headlights.

Illuminated in the truck's beams, Maggie and Billie did as they were told. Their skirts doubled as towels wiping away dust, sweat, and grime from their hands. Billie was wrenching the last bolt into place as Maggie lowered the other tools back in the trunk. A shadow moved across the lid. She turned just in time to see the truck spin out, returning to the road without a chance for a proper "thank you."

A new car full of men slowed down as it approached. Maggie didn't like the feeling this car gave her, and was glad the other two girls had stayed inside. "Billie, get back in the car."

"I don't take orders from you," she said, crossing her arms.

The big car stopped. Heads poked through rolled-down windows. The car had come from the direction of Charlotte, and Maggie thought she recognized these boys from the plant. They were young, too young to enlist, but old enough to make some extra money for the summer. Not that they needed much extra money, she assessed, given the size of their automobile.

"You ladies require assistance?" The snickers floated out with the scent of new leather.

"Thanks, but you're too late, gents. Just finishing up here." Billie lowered the trunk lid and clapped dust from her hands.

"Who was that helping you? Sure left in a hurry."

Maggie put hands to hips. "You know? We never did catch a name on their police badge." She turned toward the fading taillights of the truck. "We all better stay under the Victory Speed Limit today, huh?"

The boys looked at each other in alarm, their mischievous grins wiped clean. She'd guessed right. The hint of authority put enough caution in their minds. They'd keep a safe distance between their car and the Good Samaritans' pick-up.

"Thanks for stopping, but we'll be fine from here," Billie said with her friendliest wave.

Back on the road, they recounted the strange adventure. Thanks to those men, Maggie could add "changing a tire" to her growing list of new skills. She would deal with finding a replacement tomorrow.

The road changed from dirt to gravel as they approached the entrance gate. Old Glory waved atop the enormous flagpole, and a much smaller Navy flag few beneath. As the morning light broke on the horizon, Maggie stopped at the guard house, and cranked down the window so the guard could view all four Employee Passes.

"You know, you ladies don't need to show me those," he said with both elbows on the window frame. He winked at the magazine cover of Rosie, thrown up on the dash. "You gals are famous now," he teased. How ironic, Maggie and Billie were now just as dirty as the girl on the cover. He let them through.

They curved through the gravel roads of the "Fightin' 40" campus and parked behind the closest change house. They rushed in to change.

Back in blue coveralls, they went their separate ways. "Meet you at lunch today, Billie?"

"Sure thing," Billie said, before disappearing around the corner.

❋ ❋ ❋

The main cafeteria was a popular place, likely due to the baskets filled with dime store cigarette lighters at every door. Smokers borrowed and returned the lighters that were forbidden everywhere else.

Maggie could do without all the smoke hanging in the air. She came for the lower ceilings and more intimate setting. *Like a roadside diner,* she told herself, because the line buildings could feel so massive. Whether to strike a match or conversation, the building offered the only oasis of normalcy, despite the danger outside.

Unpacking her lunch, Maggie set her milk carton next to her mustard and bologna sandwich, wishing it were ham and Swiss. She had been lucky to nab the last open booth in the loud, crowded room. Billie slid across the opposite bench. Her light olive skin went almost pale.

"You look like you've seen a ghost," Maggie said.

"I might just have," Billie whispered, nearly hunching over the table. She released a few brown curls from behind her ear, hiding her face before glancing back over her shoulder. "You see that older man in line?"

Maggie followed her gaze. His dark hair was cut almost military short into a flat top. A healthy tan made him look younger, in contrast to his graying temples. "I see him, what's he to you?"

"His name is Harry Stillman. Works with my daddy in Gastonia. He's known me since I was little."

"Are you afraid of him?"

"No. It's just awkward is all. His daughter Katy and I used to be thick as thieves, before we stopped being friends. Haven't seen him in years. He looks the same … only sadder."

"What happened?"

"That's a complicated answer. My first question is why he's here and not at the mill."

Maggie stared over Billie's shoulder, signaling that he was headed their way. Billie spun around as he tapped her on the shoulder. "Mr. Stillman!" she said with surprise on her face, then stood up to accept a long hug.

"No more of that 'Mr. Stillman.' You're grown. Call me Harry like everybody else."

Remembering her manners, Billie launched into introductions. "Harry, this is Maggie Slone. Maggie, meet Harry Stillman."

Harry extended his hand and Maggie shook it.

"Will you join us?" Billie asked.

"I'd like to. Thank you." Harry found a space for his tray next to Maggie's. "It's fine to see you, Billie. Been too long."

"You too, Harry." The three of them busied themselves with food.

"How's your daddy?" he asked.

"He's good. Daddy didn't tell me you'd quit the mill."

"It all happened fast," Harry said before a swallow. "This place needed men who understood production, and I knew I needed to get outta Gaston County. It wasn't good for me to stay there no more."

"I heard about Mabel. I'm so sorry."

"It's been mighty hard, so I thank you." He sipped his coffee before continuing. "She died of a broken heart, after Katy. Made it easy for me to leave when this job came calling. Not one damn thing left for me in Gastonia."

He turned his attention to Maggie. "Now, when did you two come to work here? Didn't always agree, but now I think it's the right thing to recruit you ladies."

"We started the same day last month. Maggie moved here last year. She has twin girls. They're eight."

"You married?"

"Yes, my husband is …" she stopped, surprised by her own failing voice and stinging eyes, this time not from the hovering smoke.

Billie leaned forward, adding loudly enough for Harry's ears, "She thinks her husband is fighting over in the Pacific somewhere."

Maggie took in a long breath, before her cheeks blew out as she exhaled. "I'm sorry, this really should be an easier story to tell by now." Her voice finally leveled out. "His letters can't say where he is exactly … it just feels so strange not to have any idea."

Harry's arm found its way around Maggie's shoulders. A stranger no more, she leaned into him and relaxed a moment.

"Keeps them all safer that way," he said taking his arm back. "Lot's left better unsaid these days."

They resumed eating, but the gaps of quiet felt more comfortable. Maggie picked at her canned peaches, disappointed that they, too, tasted a bit smoky. Harry pushed around his meatloaf and potatoes, then nudged his tray forward to make room for his coffee cup.

"You boarding here in Steele Creek, Harry?" Billie broke the silence before popping her last bite of sandwich into her mouth.

He tapped a pack of Chesterfield cigarettes on the table, catching the tallest jumper between his lips. Maggie was surprised he'd waited this long to take them out. It seemed like every smoker here was dying to light up as soon as they walked in, like it was the first normal thing they'd done all day.

Harry seemed to consider Billie's question as he spun the borrowed lighter around his right thumb, catching it firmly in his palm every time.

Billie watched, mesmerized, before admitting, "Katy and I spent one whole summer practicing your boomerang lighter trick there, but never got it. Smoking never took root with us either."

Maggie heard the flint crack as he lit the tip, pulling the fire through with a deep inhale. He shot a smoky line straight up to the low ceiling, well above their heads. Maggie watched it swirl around them, wondering when he would answer Billie's question. It seemed Harry was the kind of man rarely in a hurry.

"I've been renting a room from a widda in Charlotte. Her husband's been gone some time and her boy's off fightin'. She's plenty tore up about it. Right after I started here, another supervisor sent me to check in on her one night and I just stayed." He inhaled, making the end a beacon, glowing brightly. "Does your husband know you work here, Billie?"

"Yessir, or he will soon at least. Mail takes longer than you think." Billie's cupped hand ran across the cool, laminated tabletop. A few crumbs fell into her napkin.

"Where you living here?" he asked.

"I rent a house in Charlotte. It's small, but enough. Maggie lives in *Myers Park*." Billie finished the last two words in a fancy accent. Maggie wished she hadn't. "I became friends with her anyway," Billie added with a wink, like it was all her idea.

"You always were a real good friend, Billie," he said, in a sad way.

His sentence chased away all traces of Billie's playful smile. "I've tried to be," she answered, before changing the subject again. "Maggie's giving me rides to work in her big ol' automobile."

Cheeks flushing, Maggie had to explain. "My husband grew up in Charlotte. He moved us here to be closer to his family."

"Where's your family from?" Harry asked, leaning in to be heard over the noise.

"They were from Boston. My parents died in a fire, but my sister is still up there. My father worked at Gillette for thirty years. Maybe plant work runs in my family."

"Sounds like you've had your share of loss too," Harry said softly, then he pulled out his watch and rose from his seat. "Ladies, it was a pleasure."

"It was nice to meet you," Maggie said.

"I'll be looking out for you two from now on. Let me know if you ever need anything. Billie, you tell your daddy 'hello' for me. He's a good man and I hope he understands why I've been so poor in keeping up with him."

"I'll be sure to the next time I see him. Goodbye, Mr. Still ... I mean, Harry."

Both women watched him cross the room and stop at the exit door. He could have been any smoker, going for the deepest possible hit before returning to a world filled with dynamite.

Holding it steady with a two-fingered pinch, he shortened the butt with a long last drag, then mashed it in sand. The lighter was returned to its basket, ready to brighten the next worker's day.

Maggie stayed quiet before asking, "Want to talk about it?"

"Nope." Billie stood up to go. "I wouldn't know where to start. Besides it's time to go back to work."

"Wait!" Maggie rose from the table. "At least tell me more about who Katy is."

"Was. Katy was. She died two years ago. She was pregnant too. That man lost his only child and only grandchild on the same day," Billie said plainly, then turned and walked away.

❋ ❋ ❋

A week later, her chin in hand, Maggie watched her latest trainer through heavy lids. The girls had a summer cold and had begged to sleep in her bed last night. It was hard to appreciate how four skinny arms and legs could cover that much space on the bed, crowding her into a small corner. Their stuffy-nosed snores ensured she hardly slept a wink.

To avoid nodding off, she focused on his words. When he used an acronym she hadn't yet mastered, Maggie raised a hand. "What does QC stand for?"

"Quality Control."

She wrote it down, then raised her hand again. "And what does that mean?"

He straightened his uniform collar, causing her to wonder if he invented the term. "It means we got inspection points at every part of our process. Before, during, and after. As a matter of fact, the success of our QC has forced the brass in DC to find Charlotte on the roadmap."

"Thank you," Maggie said. His bragging made her sleepy again.

"DC likes us so much, they're talking about filling our third production line. Not sure where we'll get the hands for that. This plant needs more workers." He whispered on the back of his hand, "You watch, they'll be letting in Negroes next."

At his last sentence, Maggie's ears perked up. Her mind raced through its possibility, as the trainer's words replayed through her head ... *the plant needs more workers.* Maggie thought only of Kora.

Chapter 7

AUGUST, 1943
KORA

Growing up, Kora hadn't appreciated her nickname. Her cousin used to tease her with it, until it caught on.

"I'm gonna start calling you Candora," she had said one day.

"Why?" Kora asked. They were finishing up a new puzzle together. At twelve, her cousin was a couple years older and worlds wiser, always teaching Kora lessons on how to act. Kora was better at puzzles though, and she could tell that stuck like a burr in her cousin's side.

They had been talking about Kora helping their teacher after school. Miss Washington asked Kora a thousand questions about the other children's behavior. Kora bragged about answering them all honestly.

"Is it 'cause I can do anything?" Kora asked.

"Nope. You're too dang honest. You can't see how some situations call for less candor. That woman was pumping you for information. Now all them kids are gonna get in trouble 'cause a you."

Kora bristled, lining up her defense. "You know I can't help it."

"Uh huh. She knows it too. Everybody knows it ... Candora!" Her cousin finished her sentence, then launched into an all-out run. She made it out the door first, with Kora right on her heels, ready to throttle her.

To Kora, honesty was a good thing. Didn't the Bible say so?

Over time, Kora would learn when to be honest and when to keep quiet, even when asked a direct question. Her mother caught her talking back to a white woman once. Kora would never forget looking up to meet those wild, blue eyes as the woman accused Kora of taking more bananas than she'd paid for. Kora knew she had done no such thing, and their argument caused a scene.

Mama was by her side a second later, wedging herself between her daughter and her accuser, now loud and angry.

"You're right, missus. I thank you for bringing this to our attention. Will this be enough to cover the difference?" Mama placed three shiny new coins on top of the counter. The woman swiped all the money up and turned in a huff. Mama was unusually quiet as they walked back home, but Kora fumed.

"Why did you lie to that woman? I paid the right amount for that fruit. I know how to multiply. You know I do."

"I know you understand numbers," Mama said, her voice stoic and strange.

"You're always saying I'm good at math. And the Bible says not to lie."

At that, Mama stopped and turned her shoulders so she faced her daughter. Kora expected that famous finger might start wagging any minute, shaming her about something she should have learned by now.

"The Bible says a lot of things, Kora. It's been used to justify all sorts of evil. I hope you never understand how much." Her mother softened. "Now, you can be good at math, but not better than that lady. You're big enough now to know the rules."

After that, Candora learned to curb her honesty, but her nickname stuck. She was happy to leave it behind in Alabama.

✳ ✳ ✳

Maggie took the turn a little too fast as she drove Kora to her shift at the main library. Kora's mind had wandered as Maggie talked a mile a minute about something, but now Kora recognized her repeated sentence.

"Kora, did you hear me?"

"Sorry. Didn't catch it."

"You looked a thousand miles away. I asked what you'd heard from James lately." They traded husband stories. Kora appreciated the ride after their latest book discussion, but Maggie complained about being late for something-or-other as she pulled through the circle drive to let Kora out.

Kora stood and squinted through the evening sun. She looked up, assessing the Carnegie Library's two-story roofline. The gutters needed cleaning after all this rain. She made a note to tell her boss as much before she left for the evening. She turned back to catch what Maggie was asking and leaned into the open window. Maggie's arm was extended across the seat.

"Can I ask a favor? These were due yesterday, but I ran out of time. My fines are adding up."

Kora read the book titles in her outstretched hand. Titles she wasn't allowed to check out. She quickly calculated if she'd have enough time to sneak them back without getting caught. Before she knew what was happening, Maggie declared her a lifesaver and drove off.

Kora tucked the books safely in her waistband. If she'd known, she would have worn her fuller skirt. She could hide a whole circus tent in there. This one would have to do, she told herself as she went inside to start her shift.

Emerging from the cleaning closet with her supplies, she passed a line of women waiting in front of the checkout counter. Kora kept her head down, praying the books would stay put behind the waistband. She approached the book return table, like she was there to clean it, but seeing how empty it was, she stopped. Her plan was to slip the books among the normally tall stacks waiting to be checked in as the last task performed by the desk clerk. She had witnessed the overflowing mess of a book return table a hundred times after the library closed. Why did this night have to be different? she wondered. Kora got her answer, seeing the fancy dress and perfect makeup worn by this young desk clerk, clearly anxious for a big date.

If she could have checked them in herself after everyone left, Kora would have, but that was impossible. *Here goes nothing*, she thought, before leaning across the table to "clean" the far corner of the table. Bent over, she quickly added her books to a small stack, hoping no one would be the wiser.

Relieved to be done with Maggie's errand, she got busy cleaning the rest of the room. The room emptied out, then the checkout girl stopped and stared at the return table like it had grown wings. Kora's heart beat faster as she went deeper into the stacks with her feather duster. It didn't take long for her boss to come looking for her.

"Kora, may I have a word?"

Not liking the sound of that question one bit, Kora followed her into a small, wood-paneled office. They passed the young lady from the checkout counter on her way out the back door. Kora's face grew hot as she felt the woman's stare.

Her boss shut the door, sat down at her desk, and launched into a full interrogation regarding the books.

"While there is *no* greater champion of literature than I, it is my suspicion that you too revere the written word, Kora. You clean these books and this building like it's your own home. Only it is not *your* home, Kora, and you must revere our rules as well. This is not your library. Do you understand me?"

Kora nodded, not in agreement or even understanding, but knowing it was expected. She continued to take her medicine, but was surprised by the personal attack. She had been a good employee, and this was her first offense.

"You should know the law is quite clear on this matter. There is no room for misinterpretation. Certain books are only available at this library. The fact that you were caught tonight returning two books that you never checked out, can only mean that you stole them."

Panic rose in her throat. Should she bring up Maggie's name? Would that drag Grace into this? No, this was between her and her boss. Kora chose to say her truth.

"I didn't steal those books," Kora said, hoping her own words might carry some weight, while also doubting they would ever be enough.

"The irony is rich, because these titles would have made their way to the Brevard library shelves in six months' time."

Kora gave a small sigh. Her boss wasn't listening. She wanted to stand up and shout it: *I did not steal those books!* But she stayed silent, praying for it to be enough to keep her job. She thought of the small amount of money she and James had saved to buy a house when he returned. She needed this job to make that dream come true.

"I'll make you a deal, Kora."

Kora was instantly suspicious. Deals never seemed to benefit her in the end.

"While you can no longer work here, I have written an endorsement of your skills. Feel free to share this with your next employer." She rose, extending the letter to Kora, completing the firing process.

Kora numbly accepted the contents of the second pale, outstretched hand of the evening.

"I trust you will respect our rules more after this experience. This will conclude your employment at all our city libraries. It's a shame to end this way. You did good work here and at Brevard."

Kora heard herself ask who would finish cleaning tonight. The woman seemed to consider the question, ruling herself out.

"You may finish up. I'll stay and lock up behind you."

Feeling her tears well up, Kora stuffed them down, as she'd learned to do. Anger and sadness stored away for another time. She finished dusting the books, bidding them a proper goodbye.

She came to Betty Smith's *A Tree Grows in Brooklyn,* the very book she'd broken the rules to return earlier. This kept her eyes dry. Like little Francie, she would never let them see the impact their *rules* could carry.

Chapter 8

SEPTEMBER, 1943
MAGGIE

A low hum started from a distance. Maggie looked down, waiting for the belt to deliver its slow rows of empty shell casings. She picked one up, felt the weight in her hands, the first of thousands she would lift and assemble. Training was over, it was the first day on her permanent line.

Running earlier to find her new building and, just in time—her new seat—left no room for introductions. Already missing Billie, Deborah, and Ruby, not one familiar face surrounded her. All four of them had been assigned to different buildings.

On Maggie's new line, each worker settled into assigned tasks. The rhythm took root in her head. Line work was not much different than laundry or dishes. Repetitive tasks allowed her to think, but her train of thought was broken when two Navy men walked up behind her, inspecting her work while carrying on their own conversation.

"When's he getting here?"

"Already arrived this morning. Crumley's been reassigned to Georgia."

"What's the new guy's rank?"

"This one's a commander. More senior than Crumley. Younger too. Some hot-shot."

"Gettin' a hot-shot means we're doing good here," the first one said as they moved away. Trying to decipher their cryptic clues, Maggie's new coworkers filled in the blanks.

The woman beside her began talking. "I don't like to gossip, but ya know who they're talking about, right?" Not waiting on an answer, she tucked her chin and continued. "We've got a new IO. He arrived this morning when I was in the admin building."

"Do tell," another encouraged.

"Well. He's tall, dark, and very handsome. *Very Navy.*"

"Go on."

"I woulda noticed him just for that, ya know, but he also walked funny. Had a bit of a limp."

A limp? This got Maggie's attention.

"When he left the room, they said how that limp kept him out of combat."

Maggie couldn't help herself. "Did you catch his name?"

"I never heard a first name, but his last name was kinda plain. Like Commander Smith or Jones or something. Maybe it was Martin. Can't say I recall exactly, but I'm sure they'll post it soon."

Maggie shut out the rest of the gossip. *Be reasonable, Mags, what are the odds?* Very slim—practically minuscule. Martin was one of the most common names in America. She jumped as a passing train whistle blew loudly. *Pull it together.*

"You all right, dear?" the woman next to her asked, concern written all over her face.

"Yes, thank you. You'd think I'd be used to that sound by now," Maggie said, a little embarrassed. She spent the rest of the morning doing her job while listening to more idle chatter. At lunch, she scanned the cafeteria for a familiar face. Her friends must have been on other break schedules. She chose a table filled with women who seemed nice enough to pass the time.

She kept an eye on the door. Each time a man in uniform appeared, her breath caught. *This is crazy*, she thought, before excusing herself from the table and tipping her tray into the rubbish on her way out. The bulletin board stopped her. She scanned every face posted there but only found the old IO smiling back. *Lt. Commander E.C. Crumley, Naval Inspector of Ordinance* was written below the photograph.

Back on the line, the afternoon passed quickly. Toward the end of her shift, she jumped again, this time from a tap on her shoulder. The young naval officer apologized for startling her. She waved it off.

"Mrs. Slone? I've come to escort you to the admin building. An issue with your paperwork needs resolution," the officer said crisply.

"Oh. Yes, of course. Should I get my things?"

"No need. It shouldn't take long. Please follow me." Once outside, he opened the Jeep door for her, hesitating like an awkward first date.

The bumpy ride ended at the stately admin building, its bright white, two-story exterior reflecting the sun's rays. Her driver pulled up and pointed to a long line of women. Assuming they were waiting to take care of similar matters, she added herself to the back of the line and glanced at her empty wrist to keep track of time, before remembering the no jewelry rule again. The wall clock said half past two. Her carpool of friends would be waiting on her within the hour. She willed the line to move faster.

"Name, please?"

"Maggie Slone. I was told there was an issue with my paperwork."

The clerk scanned her list, then looked up as if inspecting Maggie's face, making her uncomfortable. "Come this way." She led Maggie up a set of iron stairs. The second-floor doorway opened into a stark white hallway, long enough to toy with her depth perception. She followed her guide past identical office doors spaced ten feet apart. Some were open, revealing the same desk and chair combination inside.

Finally, her guide stopped in front of one. She pointed inside to a long bench against the wall, across from an empty desk, telling Maggie to wait there.

The all-white room had two doors. One Maggie had just entered through. The other, also closed, was located behind the desk. Maggie heard voices behind it, but before she could understand a single muffled word, the door opened to reveal a smart-looking woman with thick, silver-streaked hair.

She took a half-step back after catching sight of Maggie on the bench. Turning her head back through the crack in the door, she said, "Looks like your fourteen-thirty is here." No response came, but Maggie heard footsteps behind the door.

Flashing a pleasant smile, the woman placed her pad and pencil on the desk, grabbed her pocketbook from a drawer, and left. Maggie watched her go, then twisted toward the mystery door, wondering what in the world this was all about.

The door swung wide. He filled a good portion of the frame with his height and presence. His hair and face showed more fullness of age, but the years had left his eyes alone. The same eyes she had told jokes and secrets to as a child. Her first crush, her first love, and first loss.

His dress blues and shiny buttons made him look older, wiser than she remembered. As they kept to their opposite sides of the room, Commander Leland Martin seemed to assess her appearance too. Her mind couldn't catch up to the reality. They hadn't been in the same room for fifteen years.

He finally spoke. "This was the best way I could come up with. You know? To dull the shock." Hearing his voice was like opening the lid of a long-forgotten memory chest. She had loved that voice once. Her eyes closed in response to the familiar sound, then she heard him cross the floor in four uneven steps to join her on the bench. He probably thought she might black out.

He was closer now. Her mind searched for reasons. "Why are you here?"

"I accepted a new position."

"At this plant?"

"Yes. My new job assignment."

"But how did you know *I* worked here?"

He flinched, quickly, then spoke softly. "Is any part of you glad to see me?"

Beyond the anxiety and shock, his presence brought an odd nostalgic relief. Seeing him felt like home, she admitted to herself, but wasn't ready to share that with him.

He seemed to be waiting for her to continue. *Too bad*, she thought, as her suspicions grew. *How did this happen? What did he expect after all this time?* She once knew everything about him, including how much he valued control. She doubted this random job assignment.

"I still don't understand. How did you know I worked here?"

"I was checking the roster and found your name. Not too many Marós Fraser Slones in the world. You may be the only one outside of Ireland."

She guessed that might be true, but that roster was thousands of names long.

"You haven't answered my question," he continued. "Is any part of you happy to see me?"

"Of course—a part of me is."

He seemed to relax.

"It's been a long time," she added.

"Yes. It has."

An awkward silence stretched the time. Unsure what to do next, Maggie's hand awkwardly sliced the air between them.

Surprised by the gesture, he took her hand. It didn't help when he added his other one too, completely enveloping hers. The warmth of his hands spread through her body, but the sight of their matching empty ring fingers rushed her hands back to her sides, where they belonged. Her wedding ring was home with the rest of her jewelry. *Was his there too?*

"It's good to see you again, Mags."

That crossed a line. She quickly stood, and crossed her arms. "I'm not your Mags anymore." Her anger, worn on her sleeve, was clear as the naval service bars on his. "I haven't been Mags for a very long time. Maybe since the last time I saw you fifteen years ago."

"I did see you once," he admitted, rising to his feet. "Nine years ago."

She let his sentence seep in. "The funeral. You *were* there," she said. Her mind fit this new piece into the puzzle. "I thought I saw you, but talked myself out of it. Your parents said you couldn't make it."

"I would never miss your parents' service, but staying after was more than I could handle, seeing you so sad ..." Leland looked at the wall. "And so pregnant."

His last remark brought a smirk to her face. "Twins will do that to a body." She remembered that sad day, then said, almost to herself, "It was horrible being pregnant for one of the worst heartbreaks of my life. The fire that killed them took a piece of me too." Maggie looked up at Leland again. "I half expected my girls to be born sad."

"Your parents meant a lot to me, but I didn't want to make a scene. Your sister caught me in the parking lot after. I made her promise not to tell you."

"She wouldn't have. You're not exactly her favorite person."

"How is Helen?" he asked.

"Helen is well. Obsessed with making tenure at Wellesley."

"She never married either?"

Either? Did that mean he wasn't married? She was afraid to ask. "No, not married, but that's never seemed to bother her. She loves spoiling her nieces though." The mention of her girls hung in the air. She waited for Leland to ask about them.

"How do you like working here?" he asked instead.

"I like it. It feels good to be part of something larger than me and my problems." She narrowed her eyes. "I'm still confused how your new assignment came about."

He lifted his shoulders. "Just lucky, I guess."

More questions churned inside her head, but so did the familiar feeling of being late. She checked the clock on the wall. After three.

Billie, Ruby, and Deborah would be boiling in this heat, waiting by her locked car.

She took a deep breath and chose to be direct. "Seeing you today has been ..." *What were the right words? Shocking?* Yes. *Confusing?* Yes. *Comforting?* She surprised herself with a yes to that too. Leland's face, his voice, even his accent, all of it reminded her of Boston—of the life she was good at, before all this change wiped it away.

He was waiting for her to complete her sentence. She started over, "Seeing you today has been surprising."

He nodded, looking a bit dejected.

How could she turn this to her advantage? Another breath and the answer presented itself. She continued, "But there is something you can do for me—"

His head snapped up. "Name it," he shot back before she could finish.

Chapter 9

SEPTEMBER, 1943
MAGGIE

Despite the welcome break in the heat, nobody on the line brought up the weather. Superstitions ran high, as if humidity itself were waiting to hear its name as an invitation to return. Maggie was grateful for more than the cooler air circulating through overhead fans. Billie, Deborah, and Ruby were now working beside her.

Her friends were at first confused by their sudden transfer, then excited. "How lucky are we?" they asked, hugging one another. Maggie had never mentioned her conversation with Leland, and hadn't seen him since the day he'd agreed to move them to her line. She'd been surprised when it happened so fast. The four friends shared a lunch break and carpooled most days.

Maggie had first asked Leland about a job for Kora. Anything to relieve the guilt she felt. The risk of Kora being fired had never occurred to Maggie as she casually passed her library books through the car window. Kora had used a neighbor's telephone to tell Maggie the news. Maggie was angry at the librarian, but Kora refused any intervention from Maggie or her family.

"Let it be," Kora said, ending the discussion. "I'll find another job."

That day in his office, Leland had also offered a third shift cafeteria assignment for Kora. Maggie was sure it paid more than the library. She would drive to Brooklyn and track Kora down. She planned to go after work today, before she picked up the girls from Grace. Maggie hoped a cafeteria job would be just the start for Kora, leading to something bigger soon. She pictured Kora's face here, among her other friends. It could happen.

Now lifting her next shell head, Maggie inserted a thin disk into the bottom of the tracer shaft. It was vital to find the right spot for a perfect fit. If slightly off, it could explode before reaching a target or fail testing down at Wateree Pond. Always top of mind was the plant's pursuit of the highest naval safety award, the coveted "E."

What they did was dangerous, so they tried to cover it with everyday gossip and girl talk. Maggie heard a woman say, "I saw another recruitment poster hung at Kress's. They're really gunning for more women here."

"'Gunning' is a poor choice of words, but yeah, I saw a new billboard go up on South Boulevard too. Uncle Sam's turning up the pressure."

"I heard the Navy wants more production lines here. Where do they think all these people are gonna come from? Tennessee?"

"They've got their own war facility in Tennessee. Something top secret."

"How can you show up to place every day and not know what you make?" asked Deborah.

"Beats me," Ruby said.

"Maybe it's a 'loose lips sink ships' thing," Billie offered.

"Could be," Ruby guessed. "That's said plenty round here."

Maggie kept quiet, letting her mind drift back to her own secret: Leland. Seeing him had broken the dam on so many memories. Best friends growing up, everyone back in Boston had thought she and Leland would be married someday, including her. She shook her head slightly, to clear it.

Ruby's loud laughter brought a welcome distraction. She was talking about that picture show again. The movie star had legs for miles and the gall to show off her perfect nylons when the rest of the country couldn't buy them. Maggie missed nylons too. She was down to her last two pairs.

"Of all the things to ration," Ruby said. "I just don't understand. Why's it necessary for my legs to suffer too?"

"You could always shave with Kewtie," Deborah said.

"Cutie?" Maggie asked, trying to sort through Deborah's accent.

"You know?" Deborah pretended to run an imaginary razor handle up the back of her leg.

"Oh, right, that cute little razor. You won't catch me using one of those," Maggie insisted. "Not after seeing my girlfriend's awful scars. I'll just live with pale, hairy legs, thank you very much."

"One of my magazines showed how to paint your legs. It looked exactly like nylons," Ruby said.

"Paint your legs?"

"Yeah, why not? You paint your nails, don't you?"

Maggie showed off her own chipped nails. "Not doing much of that lately either."

"Call it silly, but I plan to try it."

"Suit yourself," Maggie replied, thinking it over. "And let me know how it goes."

One of the supervisors handed Maggie a set of papers. "I need you to deliver this report to the admin building."

"Sure thing," she answered, telling the girls she'd meet them at the car.

Report in hand, she made her way between the maze of buildings. Once inside the admin building, she pushed out thoughts of Leland with his office only one floor above. Her steel-toed footsteps echoed over the black and white hallway tiles. Focused on her task, she almost didn't recognize Harry as he approached.

Billie had revealed a few more details about Harry's daughter, Katy. When Katy had started dating the richest boy in town—also the meanest—Billie lost her best friend. Not invited to the wedding,

Billie assumed she wasn't good enough for Katy's new husband and fancy life, but now she knew better. Billie had played right into that rat's plan to isolate Katy from everyone who loved her.

Harry slowed in front of Maggie. They exchanged awkward greetings, struggling for what to say next.

"I meant to tell you, my mother-in-law knows people at our church who have extra rooms if you ever need one."

"That's kind of you, Maggie. The widow and I are finding our way around each other. I'd kinda hate to leave her alone right now."

Maggie felt a rush of affection for this man with sad but kind eyes. Secretly knowing the details behind his loss made her uncomfortable, like seeing him in his bathrobe. She studied the black and white tiles.

"I thank you, Maggie. I really do. I don't mean to offend you."

"Not at all, Harry." Maggie smiled and met his eyes again.

"Especially since I'm your new foreman. Just got assigned to tracers." He gestured toward an open door down the hall, where he might've received news of this new assignment.

"How wonderful. I'll see you more often then." She lifted her report as evidence of her task. "I'm sorry to cut our conversation short," she began.

"You go on now," he said, with a nod and a friendly smile, changing his whole face.

Walking away, she decided what drew her to Harry. He seemed comfortable in his own skin, like Daddy and, now that she thought of it, like Charlie.

Chapter 10

SEPTEMBER, 1943
KORA

Kora's side ached. Her cheeks did too, thanks to the wicked sense of humor of her sisters-in-law. This was what Kora had missed out on, being an only child. These three sisters knew how to press every last button to get each other riled up. They had been serving each other huge slices of humble pie their whole lives. On the small front porch, Kora prepared the audience for their routine. The late afternoon sun had shifted, and Kora was sitting smack dab in the literal hot seat. She tried swatting the air with a paper fan as if the warm, fake breeze made much difference. Still, it felt good to laugh.

The sound of the engine stole their attention, eyes searching for the noise until a fancy automobile, foreign to these streets, came into view. Several jokes rolled off their tongues. *Couldn't get much more lost than that. Did all white people have such a poor sense of direction?* Kora was about to add in her own dig, when she realized she knew that automobile. And the owner.

She stood, more theatrically than intended, and the laughter died down. Stepping into the street, she could feel the sisters behind her, watching, but silent now. Maggie waved wildly through the windshield and Kora saw recognition and relief. Kora started to wave back, but self-consciously shielded her eyes from the sun's glare instead. Once Maggie stopped in front of the house, Kora approached her open window.

"I finally found you!" she sang out. This made Kora wonder how many streets Maggie had already tried.

"I couldn't wait another second to tell you the news!" Maggie paused. "Is this your house?"

"Mine's a few streets over. This here's my sister-in-law's." Kora gestured to the small white house behind her.

Maggie waved to them on the porch.

Kora addressed their confusion. "Sisters, this here is Miss Maggie. Miss Maggie, these is the sisters of my James." Nods and hellos properly exchanged, Kora watched the sisters head inside. She lightly braced both hands against the car door, in case Maggie was looking for an invitation to follow them. "What are you doing here, Maggie?"

Maggie's wide grin spread from cheek to cheek. She inhaled dramatically before blurting, "I got you a job at the Shell Plant!"

"A job? What job?"

"Third shift in the cafeteria. You can start as early as next week."

"Why did you do that?" Kora's mind tried to catch up to this unexpected twist.

"Because I want to fix what happened at the library—I wasn't thinking when I asked you to return those books for me. I made a mess of things."

Kora paused to sort this through. She trusted Maggie's intentions, but this still felt wrong. Working more nights meant hardly seeing her friends and neighbors. Her community had become even more important after getting fired. "Thank you, but I won't be taking that job."

"Why not? I bet you'd make more money than you were at the library."

"I have the support of family and my husband's military pay. Just like you. I'm not so desperate to take the first thing that comes along." Her words kept coming. "Besides, I don't want to work more nights, serving white folk. Would you?" Her mother's *rules* ringing through her head, Kora feared she might have stepped over the line with that last question, but couldn't help it.

Maggie wilted in the driver's seat, staring forward, as if finally surveying her surroundings. Kora followed her gaze. Hard-packed dirt lay between neat rows of front porches. Each porch skirted a wooden shotgun house elevated a few feet from the ground by a foundation of sloppy brick columns.

Most homes were painted white to best reflect the heat, but displayed proud, happy colors on trim and doors. In the distance, peering over the sleepy roof lines, rose the tops of several tall downtown buildings. Kora noticed several neighbors appear on their porches, heads turned toward Maggie's car.

"I'm sorry, Kora. I honestly thought I was helping."

"I know you did."

"I wanted to make it right."

"Ain't no part right about what happened at that library, but that's never stopped it from coming, long before you took notice."

Maggie got quiet again before asking, "What if I could get you a job working the line with me? During the day? It pays $25 per week."

Kora's eyes widened at the mention of that much money. She pictured the thin stack of flattened out dollar bills—her house fund—tucked safely under her mattress. That much money would help it grow faster, but she was still suspicious. "You can do that? How?"

"Leave that to me. I've seen Black men on the assembly lines, but you might be the first Black woman." Maggie tilted her head. "I can't see you troubled too much by that."

Kora nodded. "Yes, I'd be interested if it was that job."

Maggie's smile and enthusiasm returned. "I'll get on it right away. It would be loads of fun to see you every day." A new idea appeared to flash through her mind. "We could even carpool together!"

Kora pictured Maggie's gaudy automobile disturbing her neighborhood twice a day. "Let's not get ahead of ourselves," she said.

"Okay, it's a deal. You're still coming to my house next Saturday?"

"Plan to. If the buses are running."

"Good. I should know more then."

"See you Saturday." Kora stepped back from the car and watched it disappear around the corner, buying herself time to craft a story for her curious family and neighbors. She also considered all the things she could do with $25 a week, like connecting a party line to her house, so next time Maggie could telephone instead of driving up unannounced.

Doing some quick calculations in her head, Kora realized this money could bring her dream of owning a home a whole year sooner. She had avoided writing James about the library. Now she might be able to skip over that story altogether.

She pictured her husband's face as he read about her new job and wages. He would be tickled pink.

Chapter 11

SEPTEMBER, 1943
MAGGIE

Crossing the threshold, Maggie trailed behind his secretary, Mrs. Sexton. Maggie chose a seat, one with a massive desk between them.

"I've never seen such a large desk," she said, admiring the dark wood polish and carefully positioned items on top.

Leland looked down as if noticing it for the first time. "They mentioned some kind of historical significance." He looked up at the quite tall and ageless Mrs. Sexton as she walked away. "What's the story behind the desk again?"

Her answer came after pivoting in the doorway, elegant hair chignon on spectacular display. "It belonged to General Bragg in the Civil War." Smiling, Sexton added, "Apparently he liked everything around him to be big and intimidating." As her sentence hung in the air, the door clicked shut.

Maggie straightened, unsure how to act. She hated the awkwardness, so she jumped into the speech she'd rehearsed. "Thanks for seeing me, Leland. Your help getting my friends reassigned—truly—it means the world to me." She inserted her practiced pause to emphasize her gratitude. "The move to Charlotte has been difficult, as far as making friends. The first and best friend I made here is Kora, and she's out of work because of me."

Leland nodded. "I remember. The one you mentioned before. The Black woman?"

"Yes, Kora. I'm here to ask for a different job for her. On my line during first shift."

Leland didn't respond, but instead leaned into both elbows on top of the massive desk, which unnerved her. *Be patient and let him think*, she told herself, but couldn't help adding, "She's one of the smartest people I know."

His eyes focused on his folded hands. "I wish there were more I could do. Things are different here than up North. I can't just start hiring Negroes for any job." He looked back up. "Perhaps we could ease into this. What's wrong with third shift in the cafeteria?"

What's wrong? She suddenly imagined similar conversations—putting dark-skinned people in their place—happening over the same desk for the last hundred years. She took her time responding. Let him be unnerved, if that was possible. "So, your plan is to segregate the plant by time of day and department?"

"My long-term plan might involve integrating the plant, but that should happen slowly."

"Then explain why I'm seeing these recruitment posters everywhere, saying 'We're *all* in this together!' One just popped up at the A&P, of all places." Maggie did her best Uncle Sam impersonation, wagging her finger in the air. "Get your groceries and get a job, ladies!" She lowered the finger and asked, "How are you going to meet demand by ignoring such a large population of Charlotte?"

"I'm well aware of our need for more workers," he said, arms crossed. "But I also have to keep the peace here."

"Peace?" She had to look away at that one. "Peace," she repeated when her eyes landed on the wall behind him. She stood and walked closer to the familiar federal notice, placing a finger on Roosevelt's Executive Order. She read the words posted for all to see on Leland's office wall. "This order, to provide for the full and equitable participation of all workers in defense industries, without discrimination because of race, creed, color, or national origin—"

"Are you saying I'm violating a presidential order, Mags?"

She ignored his stubborn exploit of her childhood nickname, shrugged, and with her best neutral expression asked, "What do I know?" She sat back down.

The room grew silent. She matched his gaze with her most defiant expression. Leland looked away first, finding a spot on the ceiling. He exhaled loudly, then turned back. "I'll give it some thought."

Maggie's grin wouldn't stop. She knew she'd convinced him, but he couldn't admit it outright. Some things never changed.

"She'll have to pass the same exam as any other line worker. No handouts. And *if* I decide to put her on your line, I'm counting on you to make sure your production stays the same or increases. DC keeps track of those things, so it'll be easy to measure."

She squeezed her hands into triumphant fists by her sides where she thought he couldn't see. "Thank you, Leland." She nodded. "I understand."

"Our production rates are getting a lot of attention right now. The more eyes on our plant, the more pressure. I won't have that affected by your little social experiment."

"Yes. Understood." She couldn't wait to tell Kora.

"I have another meeting starting soon, but can we get together again?"

Maggie glanced at the wall clock too, then turned back to find his little boy face.

"What do you say?" he asked. "Two old friends catching up?"

Caught off guard, that question had never come up in the dialogue she'd rehearsed. "Can I give it some thought?" she asked, taking a page from his book.

"Of course." He chuckled. "Take all the time you need."

They stood and somehow got through another handshake. Rushing outside, she spotted the girls huddled under the only tree in the gravel lot, waiting for her.

"Why are you always running late?" Billie asked. "Where did you go?"

"We were getting worried!" Deborah added.

Ruby whined, "We were starting to melt!"

"I'm sorry!" Maggie fished for the keys. "Everybody jump in."

"You didn't answer the question," Billie pointed out. "Where were you?"

"I had a quick errand to run. Paperwork again."

The sky grew dark and the wind picked up. A late summer storm threatened. Maggie prayed it wasn't in response to her tale. She quickly crossed herself, in hope of forgiveness, before getting behind the wheel.

"I saw that!" Billie said, as she slid next to Maggie in the front seat. "Maybe later you'll tell me where you really were?"

"Soon," she replied with a smile. "It's all coming together."

Chapter 12

OCTOBER, 1943
KORA

Trailing the sidewalk, the line of mostly women snaked around the building. Kora had plenty of time to count all seventeen stories, as she waited downtown to take her aptitude test. Some of the women struck up conversations. Kora kept to herself.

Finally inching inside the door of the stately Johnston Building, Kora judged the too-tall ceilings and ornate moldings. A wide marble-floored hallway stretched between the entrance to a bank on the right and community room to the left. She waited her turn to occupy an empty spot at the long check-in table.

"Next!" a voice shouted. She approached the table. "Name?"

Kora recognized the woman behind the voice. She worked the picture show ticket counter sometimes, and would accept Kora's coin with thick white gloves, even in the hottest summer swelter.

"Mrs. James Bell, Kora Bell." She took a pencil and several forms from the woman, watching the picture lady record her name as Cora with a C, but didn't correct her.

Slipping into an empty chair, she began filling in the first form on her lap. The pencil lead wobbled inside its wooden frame, making it hard to write. She made do by twisting the pencil until she found the right angle to make a mark. Forms completed, she stood and straightened her own frame before walking to the next table. She handed her forms to a new woman, who flipped them over a few times, then looked up.

"It says here you completed high school. Is that right?"

"Yes." Kora nodded.

"Well, if that's the case, this test should be no problem for *you*."

Kora didn't like the way she emphasized the word "you."

The lady pointed left, "Head on into that room and wait for instructions."

Kora turned to leave, then stopped. She turned back and extended her hand. "I would like a new pencil, please. This one is broken."

The woman sighed, inspecting the end of the pencil before handing over a new one.

Minutes later, Kora was reading through the test, thankful Maggie had been right. The questions didn't look too hard. Many were math and the rest based on simple logic. She half expected a different set of harder questions for her, but was relieved to find otherwise.

Going over her answers and calculations a second time felt like being back in school. She was the first to finish then too. Glancing around, she noticed other heads down, still finishing. How would it look if she were the first to rise and hand in her test? Too uppity? She waited.

What if they interpreted her idleness as cheating? Growing weary of her own indecision, she approached the test proctor at the front of the room and handed in her test. Her pride swelled with each small check mark. Until that changed. Kora watched her add an "X" next to the last three questions.

"May I?" Kora asked with an extended hand and her friendliest smile.

"Be my guest." The woman handed it back.

Kora scanned the questions next to the three Xs. Two questions Kora had read too fast. Now she could see her mistake. But the last one?

"Isn't that a boat?" she whispered, pointing to the word "regatta" in her third missed question. She felt others starting to line up behind her.

"It's a boat *race*," answered the proctor. "And a fairly common English word, I might add." She pulled Kora's test back together and wrote the word "pass" at the top.

Kora narrowed her eyes but kept her smile. She fantasized the words she might use to educate this woman about the irony of the word—*race*—but stopped short. She wanted this job.

The woman offered a weak smile, trying to record Kora's score on her master list, but she was unable to match the name at the top of Kora's test among the Ks.

Pointing to her own name, misspelled among the Cs, Kora kept a straight face as the mistake was seen and corrected.

※ ※ ※

Long bus rides were great places to think. There would have been no thinking inside Maggie's carpool full of women, so Kora declined the offer and Maggie didn't push it. The bus rocked gently through a slow, right turn onto the gravel road. She enjoyed her front-seat view, because she could. Growing up, she wondered what all the fuss was about riding up front. One time, with a new driver in Montgomery, she took advantage of her light skin to find out. It was nothing special, still the same old bus.

Half of Kora's grandparents were slaves. The other half owned them. Lincoln's emancipation meant, for a little while, her parents could farm a small piece of land, but they knew which set of rules applied to their skin color. They kept to themselves on that farm, until the rules quietly changed again, and not in their favor.

Kora faced the window, feeling the air touch her face, and cleared her mind of things outside her power to change. Through pale green eyes—James called them the color of sea glass—she focused on the day ahead. This job was important. With such high hopes, she grew nervous the rug might be pulled out from under her again. Last night she had dreamed a severe-looking woman, declaring a mistake had been made, directed her to report to the cafeteria instead.

Maggie had described the line workers. Most were women, while nearly all the supervisors were Navy men, who talked like Yankees. Maggie warned Kora to avoid the few who didn't take well to the idea of working alongside Blacks, but she swore most were accepting. These were extraordinary times.

Kora found her way to the training room. She sped through the papers she was given to read. While she waited for the rest of the class to finish, she spotted a rolling, metal book cart against the wall, full of thick volumes with long-worded titles like *United States Naval Ammunitions Safety Production Performance Standards*. She wanted to walk over and open one of them, but worried about singling herself out further.

Kora watched the instructor, a Navy man, return to the front of the room to begin his lecture. He paced back and forth as he explained how Bofors worked. He wrote the funny word out in chalk and said it was Swiss. Lining the decks of naval battleships, Bofors guns were so big, they had a platform that rotated 360 degrees and needed a driver to steer their long barrels.

These guns could swivel on a dime to shoot down a plane high in the air or an enemy vessel too close to a ship full of American soldiers. Not just soldiers, but fathers, sons, brothers, and husbands. Her anxiety grew as she realized the gravity of what she was now a part of.

War meant kill or be killed. The mission here was to perfectly assemble these 40 mm shells so that Navy soldiers could safely load these Bofors and protect a ship under attack—to preserve life by taking it. A dangerous mission, both here and overseas.

Kora froze, suddenly longing for the safety of her old library job. She pictured James or another soldier suffering because of her mistake. But paying close attention to the instructor's words, her fear waned, and a new emotion settled in: pride. There would be no mistakes on her watch. This was the most important work she had ever done. Her whole purpose shifted in that moment and her uncertainty disappeared. She was the right person to do this job. She was ready.

Chapter 13

NOVEMBER, 1943
MAGGIE

Standing in judgment before the long mirror, Maggie couldn't remember the last time she had felt so bothered over what to wear. The first dress was too frumpy and the next revealed more than she was comfortable showing. She started to remove the third, then stopped, catching her frenzied reflection in the full-length mirror. What was she *doing*? Or rather who was she doing this for?

Maggie sighed, knowing she wasn't dressing for church or work this time. Those were easy. She was a married woman, and this felt like getting ready for a date. She pulled every pin from her hair, cursing the time she'd wasted putting it up, and thankful the girls had slept at Grace's last night. She would pick them up later, right after the park.

She ran down the stairs, yanking on her heels when she hit the bottom, but when she pulled the front door open, she felt the bite in the air. Blowing leaves ushered the cold across her lawn. She needed a coat. Closing the door again, she turned around to face the hall closet, knowing her only option was hanging inside.

Maggie had donated her winter coat from Boston, assuming she'd have little need for it down South. After using up her clothing stamps on her growing-like-weeds children, she had delayed buying a replacement.

She opened the closet, and there it was. The coat Grace had insisted she keep for brisk days that crept in, just like this one had. Maggie pulled it off the hanger, pushing her hands through well-lined sleeves. The coat eclipsed the very outfit she had wasted so much time debating.

On her way back out, she stopped at the hall mirror, wrestling between wanting to look good or bad for Leland. The coat looked ridiculous, but her hair looked good. *Too good*, she thought, drawing her fingers through several times, messing it up. Better. She left it that way.

This would be her third meeting with Leland in less than two months, and the first outside of work. It felt like she'd eaten butterflies for breakfast.

As she drove to Morgan Park, she ticked off safe topics they could discuss. One was Kora. Since joining the plant, her friend had earned her place on the line. Their production increased, pleasing the supervisors and foremen. Their gamble paid off and now paved the way for some of Kora's neighbors too. Maggie was grateful for all this, so she agreed to meet Leland at a park.

She pulled in beside the empty Jeep. He was early, of course. She scanned the park and caught him rising from one of the swings. She watched him cross the grounds to take a bench seat. There was a definite confidence in his stride, as each pant leg displayed a long crisp pleat. His limp was also there, though he'd gotten better at hiding it. There were a few others at the park, none of them paying a bit of attention to the tall man in uniform. Unique at the start of the war, military presence had since melted into the Charlotte landscape.

Maggie joined him on the bench and they exchanged shy greetings. The wind picked up and forced her arms into a tight fold. After hearing through the grapevine that there was no Mrs.

Martin and never had been, she almost canceled. *This is Leland, a friend from home*, she reminded herself.

She struggled for what to say next. "Lovely weather we're having, right?"

"What a difference a day makes. Yesterday was so warm, I was beginning to wonder if Charlotte had but one season. I hear the winters are short here."

"I've only been around for one winter, but yes, much shorter than we're used to."

She followed his eyes as they spanned the length of her crazy coat. "Go ahead, ask about the coat," she insisted.

"I wasn't sure if I should."

"Grace, my mother-in-law, had it made. She takes war salvage and scrap drives very seriously." Maggie stood up to give a better, full-length display. "She went through her whole attic to find old things to convert into something more useful." Maggie tried to feign a Southern accent. "That's where this lovely Carolina blue coat was born."

She slumped back onto the bench, leaving less space between them.

Leland touched one of her sleeves. "It feels like an old bedspread."

"It *is* an old bedspread."

He chuckled as she continued, running her own hand up and down one arm. "It's really a lovely chenille pattern. Grace had it sewn into a coat, then paraded through town. She basked in the attention it first drew, but once the idea caught on and others followed suit, she handed this one down to lucky me."

"Sounds like a noble commitment to war conservation," Leland said.

"Grace would be giddy hearing you say that. She takes supporting her son very seriously." The mention of Charlie felt blasphemous. She saw some kids playing. "This sort of reminds me of Quincy Park. Do you remember?"

"I do. Yeah." He nodded and looked over at the swing set. "I remember digging a path in the snow so we could swing in the winter. We used to get cabin fever so bad."

Tightening the soft blue belt on her coat, she said, "I don't miss Boston winters."

"Me neither," he agreed. "What do you miss most, though?"

Maggie thought a second. "The smell of fresh-baked bread at Quincy Market. And the bands that played there on Saturdays."

Leland shook his head and laughed, showing off one perfectly placed dimple. "Good music, yes. Good dancing, no."

Maggie laughed too, trying to ignore the dimple. "We were such bad dancers then, but we never cared. I'll add that to the things I miss: being too young to be embarrassed about what other people think."

He smiled and watched the ground. She tried to keep the conversation going. "Where have you lived besides Boston?"

"Everywhere," he answered. "I've seen forty-eight states."

"All forty-eight?" Maggie was impressed.

"That was my goal and I reached it."

"That must have felt rewarding."

"At first, yes, but once it was behind me, it felt a bit hollow." His voice trailed off. "Any big plans to celebrate our birthday this year? December eighth is right around the corner."

Maggie got quiet again. After sharing every birthday growing up, it was hard not to think of Leland each year, especially the December right after he had left. That birthday was especially hard without him around. Needing to get her mind off it all, Maggie had agreed—in a moment of weakness—to celebrate her birthday at a speakeasy with friends.

"I met Charlie on our birthday," she said, relieved to finally speak his name out loud.

"That so?"

"That's so," she said, wondering if he would ask more about her husband.

"Do your girls like sharing a birthday as much as we did?"

She got her answer—he didn't want to talk about Charlie. "I think they do. At least now. Who knows what they'll want as they get older?"

"It's hard to grasp what we want when we're young."

"True," she agreed. Were they still talking about the girls now?

He bumped her shoulder just like he used to. "So, what brought you here to Charlotte?"

"The war," she answered, her mood sobering. "We had wonderful friends in Boston, but Helen was the only family up there. She's so busy with her students and research. I think the idea of moving us two streets down from his folks made Charlie feel better about leaving." Maggie shrugged.

"I see."

What did that mean? Who was *he* to judge Charlie for leaving?

She kept those questions to herself. "I've tried making friends. It's been tough. My mother-in-law means well, but she's so Southern, and I'm … not."

"Is that why you asked me to make those assignment changes?"

"It was. Thanks to you, I have friends I see every day. They're outsiders too."

"Glad I could help." He looked like he was about to add more, but stopped.

"What?"

He paused another second. "I was surprised to see your name on the plant roster. Why'd you want to go to work and leave your girls?"

She tried to read his face before answering. He seemed sincere, but it was a very personal question. She decided to share the truth. "I didn't want to leave the girls, but we bought a home we really couldn't afford, and the war lasted longer than our savings." Maggie watched Leland, slowly nodding as he met her eyes, surprised at how easy it was to be honest with him after so many years. "I couldn't bear asking my in-laws for money, so I took Uncle Sam up on his offer instead." She chuckled. "There are a lot fewer strings attached to him."

"I see," Leland repeated.

His new phrase annoyed her. "You're certainly 'seeing' a lot today."

"I'm just making conversation."

"Well, I'm not so sure."

"Well, it's true." He shrugged as proof of his innocence, then appeared to remember something. "Say, your father-in-law doesn't work for a bank here, does he? George Slone?"

"Yes, that's him ... why do you ask?"

Leland chuckled. "What a small world. I just sent my RSVP for dinner at their house, along with some other big brass at US Rubber. Will you be there too?"

"Absolutely not," she said, louder than before. Grace and George entertained bank clients all the time. The United States Rubber Company would be no exception. Her stomach flipped as she thought of Grace and Leland at the same table. She needed to be careful. Grace's radar rivaled any military version.

She rose to leave, said a hasty goodbye, and made a beeline to the car.

Leland caught up just as her key found the lock. He turned her around. "Mags, I won't go if it makes you uncomfortable."

"All of this makes me uncomfortable!"

"I see ... I mean, I understand. You get what I mean." He was talking fast, then slowed. "We have a history and you'd rather not broadcast that fact. I'll send my regrets today."

She crossed her arms, considering the word *regret*. "It's probably too late."

"I'll say I'm sick. Simple as that. It's never too late." He ran a hand through his thick, dark hair. "Look, we're old friends. Nothing more. Drop all the Catholic guilt we grew up with. You've got your family. I've got my career. We both got what we wanted. I just want to be friends again. I've missed you."

His raw honesty took her by surprise. He looked scared, like this might be their last conversation.

Though his admission caught her off guard, she was most surprised with herself, as she slowly recognized the same—albeit confusing—feeling. It was nice to have him back in her life.

Chapter 14

DECEMBER, 1943
MAGGIE

"Thanks for this, George," Maggie said, pushing the car door shut and pulling her sweater tighter against the cold. She bent toward the open window. "I expect a perfect behavior report tomorrow, ladies."

"We'll be good. Papa's taking us to buy a gift for you," Daisy said, before Demi clamped a hand over her sister's mouth.

George turned to Daisy with one finger over his lips.

"That was supposed to be a secret for Christmas!" Demi said.

"Really?" Maggie asked, touched by their sweet plans. "Whatever you get me will be surprise enough. You three have fun." She waved them down the driveway, happy for the girls' shared experience with Papa George.

Back inside—alone in her house for once—Maggie straightened a few pillows and eyed the kitchen clock. Her mother's words whispered in her head: "Ladies don't drink before six unless they have a problem."

She turned back toward the neat row of wine, liquor, and soda bottles lining the counter like stiff little soldiers waiting for her party to start. What was wrong with starting a little early? She ceremoniously poured a glass, pushing the voice away.

A chorus of ice cubes hit the bottom of the glass, each with a new note, same as they did the night she met Charlie. She'd defied her mother's rules then too, sitting alone at a bar—a speakeasy, no less.

Maggie let her mind wander back to that first birthday without Leland. She had wanted to curl up with a good book, but her friends insisted on getting her out on the town and out of her funk. Their enthusiastic description of the fun bar safely tucked behind a drugstore soda counter piqued her interest. A birthday felt like a good reason to try something risky.

That night, Charlie claimed a seat just vacated by her friends on their way to occupy the small powder room. She braced for a line, like "You're a swell dish," but it never came.

"What'r'ya drinkin' there?"

"Vodka soda," she answered.

"A wise choice from a limited menu. It's hard to mess up a vodka soda." He flagged down the barkeep, placing the same order. She liked his adorable eye crinkles and smile full of straight teeth.

"This is my first time here." She took a sip to occupy her hands, wondering why she felt the need to share that fact with him.

"I bet everyone says that. You know, in case of a raid."

They glanced at the small, hidden door they'd entered through. The excitement of giving the right code word, now faded into regret. Maggie didn't want this man to think she was the type of girl who did this more than once.

She tried to think of something clever to ask, but her mind went blank. "You don't sound like you're from Boston," she said, enjoying his laugh that followed.

"You caught me. Yeah, the Army brought me north." He paused. "Did I hear someone say it's your birthday?"

Her eyes got big. He'd been watching her. She played it coy, her glass in the air. "Yes, Happy Birthday to me, I suppose."

He raised his glass too. "Happy Birthday to … ?"

"Maggie," she answered, impressed he got a name out of her so smoothly.

That night it was clear, Charlie had this easiness about him. It came from being liked by everyone he met. Her friends returned to mingle with his friends. Charlie never left her side. Everyone said they were a natural fit for each other. At least back then.

Now, waiting on her guests to show, she tried to remember the last time she had entertained. She walked through her wood-paneled living room and pulled back the lace curtains stretched over a front window, admiring her neighbors' door wreath across the street. War dampened the Christmas spirit, but couldn't snuff it out.

She wandered over to the radio, thoroughly enjoying her time without the girls to do whatever she wanted. Standing in front of the radio, she stopped to listen after each twist of the knob. Static rolled in and out between a boxing match and deep twangs picked from a lively banjo song, until the tuner landed on 1080 and Bing Crosby's deep, velvet baritone washed over the room.

Maggie straightened her crooked little tree. Underneath sat four packages, wrapped in newsprint. One each for Billie, Ruby, Kora, and Deborah. She imagined each face opening the new book she'd carefully selected.

She straightened Kora's book again, still hoping she'd show. Not that she could blame her if she didn't. Deborah and Ruby were nice enough to Kora, but Billie gave her the cold shoulder unless she needed something.

Billie seemed to resent Maggie's bond with Kora. Why did jealousies like that have to crop up inside friend circles? Maggie wanted everyone to get along. Finishing her drink, she debated pouring another when she heard a knock. A second later, Billie let herself in.

"Hiya, sorry I'm early," she apologized, arms heavy with a tray of food and bags of alcohol. Maggie rushed to help her unpack in the kitchen. Billie filled her in on her trip back to Gastonia, including her parents worrying over her living alone. "And drinking alone," she added, lifting the last bottle from her bag proudly. "But they didn't catch me scoring some of Mr. Brody's 'shine, fresh from the still!" She unscrewed the lid and offered it to Maggie's nose.

She took a whiff. "That smells kinda sweet, but also lethal."

"Yeah, Nick and I were known to split a bottle or two ... 'til he blamed the booze for my failure to get knocked up. Fat lot of good stopping did for us. Still no kids. He made me promise to only drink socially while he's gone." The doorbell rang again, just as Billie lifted the jar high in the air. "Here's to an appropriate social occasion to let loose!"

Maggie opened the door again to find Ruby and Deborah.

"Merry Christmas!" they sang, their excitement squeaking out like little girls, which they still were.

Maggie felt very mature, almost old, compared to them.

"I love your neighborhood," Deborah said, handing her tray to Maggie.

"It's absolutely charming," echoed Ruby's best sophisticated tone, then she put an elbow in Billie's side. "Beats living in the sticks, huh?"

Before closing the door, Maggie checked the empty sidewalks, hoping to see Kora walk up. No such luck.

Ruby found her way to the kitchen, adding food to the table and booze to the bottle display, while Deborah placed their packages under the tree. Billie measured out four glasses of deep brown moonshine and called for a toast. "To the best 'Rosies' a girl could ever hope to work with."

"To *Rosies*!"

Ruby took a sip. "It tastes like sweet tea. Could be dangerous!" They all nodded through a second sip. "Thank goodness for one thing, though," Ruby continued, "none of us have to live with the name 'Rosie.' My friend back home gets teased about it. A lot."

Billie raised her glass again. "To none of us being named Rosie!" More clinks and giggles.

Maggie was glad she had kept her given name a secret.

The party in full swing, they covered the kitchen table with bread stuffing balls, cheese whirls, and glory buns. Everyone exchanged compliments. Billie's cheese whirls tasted a bit chalky, but close enough to the real thing.

"What kind of meat this is?" asked Deborah, as if she'd read Maggie's mind. The salty taste was reminiscent of meat, but only after she forced her brain to ignore the texture.

"Spam hash. You like it?" Ruby asked.

"Uh huh!" Maggie swallowed another bite. "You know who else would like this?" She glanced sideways in Billie's direction, "Kora."

"Say, where is Kora? I thought she'd be here by now," Ruby said.

"She was hoping to come," Maggie said. "Maybe there was a problem with her bus?"

Billie poured herself another glass. Deborah and Ruby went on about Billie's bread pudding made with canned milk. They took their time migrating into the cozy living room to exchange gifts.

Maggie stopped to face them, extending the chain around her neck. "Like my birthday gift from Grace?"

They studied the thick, gold medallion Maggie held out for inspection. Maggie pushed the hinges of the locket open to reveal tiny ticking hands, and they all laughed.

"How many has she given you now?" Billie asked.

"Let's see, two watches and now a locket, but four if you count the antique hourglass she gave me last year."

Billie sank into the love seat. "Ah, nothing like the gift of time. Or a mother-in-law to emphasize your flaws!" She tipped her glass back, catching the last swallow. "Makes me glad mine's dead." Billie clamped her hand across her mouth and nose, leaving only her wide eyes exposed.

The girls stared back, not knowing what to say, before laughter busted through. Being the oldest and most responsible in the group, Maggie stopped her giggles and soberly asked, "Maybe you should slow down there, Billie?"

"You're right. I'm sorry," she said behind her fingers, looking to the ceiling for her dead mother-in-law's forgiveness. She pushed her glass across the table, out of reach.

Ruby saved the day. "Well, I am dying to get started on our gift exchange. Save mine for last, so let's start with Deb."

Deborah handed each a box containing a handmade scarf. They *oohed* and *aahed* over the bright colors, which were not blue. All agreed they were sick to death of uniform blue.

Billie made them open her gifts next. She had hand-braided each a necklace using special metallic string from her mother's mill scraps. Fastening the necklaces right away, they admired the craftsmanship, showing them off to one another.

Maggie handed out her gifts, setting Kora's aside. Everyone seemed to appreciate her thoughtful book selections. *The Fountainhead* for Billie, *The Little Prince* for Ruby, and the latest *Little House on the Prairie* book for Deborah. Each promised to start reading tomorrow so they could trade books later.

Then came Ruby's turn. She stood her full height, commanding center stage. She pushed the air down with her hands to signal quiet.

"Ladies, I have poured hours of thought and much of my paycheck into buying the absolute perfect gift for each one of you." She paraded the first box over to Deborah, laying it ceremoniously in her lap.

Deborah unwrapped a stunning journal with a satin, embroidered cover. "This is prettiest thing I've seen," she turned it over in her hands. There was a key taped to the back cover, which sprung the little lock. When opened, out fell a piece of paper congratulating Deborah on her one-year subscription to *The New Yorker* magazine.

"Read what I wrote inside, Deb."

Deborah found the inscription and read it aloud. "To my dear friend, Deborah. May this subscription unlock the key ... to finding your own NJB!"

Deborah and Maggie laughed and laughed at that one, leaving Billie to ask why. When they finally explained, she didn't find as much humor in the Nice Jewish Boy reference.

Billie was next. She painted a smile on her face, but seemed more than a little skeptical of what Ruby had in store. Billie removed the paper carefully. Once unbound, it took a second for everyone to recognize what she was holding.

"I love it." Billie flipped the box a few times and Maggie caught some upside-down words. It was a building model kit of the Empire State Building.

Billie raised her gaze to Ruby's. "You sure you're not a spy? When did I mention these? I don't remember talking about these kits."

"Of course we didn't. I think you enjoy being such a mystery." Ruby pointed back to herself. "I am quite comfortable with my ability to read people. Yet ... I gotta say I was the most nervous about getting this one right. But you are so good at putting things together. I took a gamble!"

Billie was still staring at the box. "Nick left some of these behind. I got bored and put one together, getting myself hooked." Billie looked up, embarrassed. "No one knows that but you guys. I keep them locked in a closet."

"I knew it!" Ruby said, taking a triumphant bow. "My natural gift giving talent reigns supreme."

Maggie waved off Ruby's ego, addressing Billie. "Why locked in a closet?"

"Because who would care?"

"You should put them on display."

"No one visits me, and besides they'd just assume Nick assembled them."

"*You* see them. Put them on display for you."

Billie listened, running her hand over the box cover again.

"Ah hem," Ruby interrupted, her perfect chin angled upward. "I've saved the best for last! Maggie, are you ready for my gift?"

Maggie nodded and took the package from Ruby's outstretched hands. "This is box number one," Ruby said.

Maggie lifted a metal contraption from the box. It looked like a horseshoe on a stick, with a long black pen running through the middle of the horseshoe. Not knowing what to say, Maggie couldn't hide her confusion.

"What is it, Rube?" Deborah finally blurted out.

"Not so fast!" Ruby warned. "Here's box number two."

Maggie tipped back her glass. She didn't react well to surprises. Everyone watching her closely made her cheeks flush with embarrassment. She tried to blame the wine and the cozy fire radiating from the corner, as she fought to quickly open the second box.

No one spoke as she unwrapped a can of paint. The lid revealed the color of the paint inside—somewhere between a light ivory and a peach skin color. Pairing this with the first gift, it finally clicked, and her embarrassment was replaced with wine-fueled giggles.

"Is this what I think it is?"

"You better believe it," Ruby said. "Uncle Sam's stateside answer to the wartime nylon shortage!"

Maggie jumped from her chair and rewarded Ruby with a big hug. "I love it, Ruby, thank you!"

Pulling back from their embrace, Ruby applauded herself.

"Ruby, you look like you swallowed the nylon canary," Billie said.

"Can I try it right now?" Maggie asked.

"Can we? Of course!" Ruby gushed as she pulled a stool to the middle of the room and directed her to stand on it. Maggie climbed up and rolled the waistband of her skirt, lifting the hem well above her knees.

Ruby made careful brush strokes down Maggie's bare leg. Maggie tried to be still, balancing herself and her wine glass through more giggles. She watched Ruby's serious face as her winter-white legs transformed to a perfect sun-kissed peach. After fanning her canvas dry, Ruby positioned the horseshoe-shaped pen along the back of Maggie's leg, adding the perfect black "seam" to the fake nylons. Then she handed the contraption to her model in exchange for Maggie's wine glass.

Maggie guided the stick up the back of her other leg, making one straight black line. Stepping down from the stool, she was afraid to get paint on her chair, so she hammed it up with a parade through the living room.

"Who's next?" asked Ruby.

Deborah jumped up. "I go!" She rested her foot on the stool and lifted the paint can. She pulled the brush down her calf in one long stroke. "It's cold. And wet!"

The four of them laughed so loudly, Maggie half expected to hear a neighbor's knock telling them to keep quiet.

Eventually the party began to wind down. Maggie and Billie waved goodbye to Ruby and Deborah from the front stoop.

Back inside, Billie lay on the couch with an arm draped over her eyes. "I just need to rest a bit. Stop the world from spinning."

"Take all the time you need." Maggie started gathering plates and glasses.

"It was a great party."

"It was, wasn't it? We should do it again soon. Maybe New Year's." Maggie enjoyed the vision. All of them counting down the last remaining seconds of 1943. "Maybe Kora will be able to come then too."

"I'm glad she didn't come tonight," Billie sat up slowly. "It would have been strange what with Ruby's gift and all."

"Strange? How?"

"Kora couldn't have taken part in the fun." Billie lay back down and said to the ceiling, "Not the right color paint."

Neither woman spoke. Maggie stood, balancing her stack of dishes, at a loss for what to say.

Billie finally blurted out, "I know what you're thinking. Stop it." She rose to collect her coat and gifts. "I know what it's like to be different, Maggie Slone. You do too. You shouldn't want to put Kora through that."

Maggie kept quiet, but turned toward the kitchen, leaving Billie to see herself out.

"I'll come by tomorrow for my dish," Billie said, over her shoulder. "Keep the booze."

The door closed for the final time that night. The rest of the mess could wait for morning. Before twisting off the last lamp switch, Maggie saw her painted legs in a new light. Was Billie right? Maggie had never intended to make anyone uncomfortable. Perhaps Kora knew that better than any of them and had stayed away.

Chapter 15
JANUARY, 1944
KORA

Kora stiffened her collar, capturing her breath inside the thin coat working overtime this winter. Crowded under the bus-stop shelter, her neighbors tested the strength of its weathered bench. They came with jokes about too much cold and not enough coat.

"Happy New Year, ever'body."

"I can smell your black-eyed peas from here, Miss Kora," one said. "Making me hungry!"

"Ever'thing makes *you* hungry," another teased. "But you right, those gon' taste good tonight."

"Miss Lucy in there makin' her greens too. We'll be startin' the new year off right."

Kora laughed with her neighbors. The outside chill was no match for how much they warmed her heart. The bus pulled slowly down Kora's street and they all grabbed whatever seat they could find. The air inside the bus warmed as more Brooklyn neighbors squeezed in at every stop, greeting the others with morning smiles as they made their way down the aisle. Kora loved her community.

Once at the plant, Kora hurried to her building. She placed her petite, sturdy frame on her stool without meeting any eyes. "Sorry I'm late."

Maggie looked confused. "But you're right on time."

"That's late in my book. My mama always said the best way to make a dream come true is to wake up early."

"My mother had a saying too: 'The problem with being early is nobody's there to appreciate it!'"

Kora couldn't help laughing. Maggie was funny. "I did wake up early today. Started cooking the black-eyed peas for my neighborhood tonight."

Maggie wrinkled her nose. "There's one Southern tradition I can't get on board with. I'm sure it's different if you grew up eating those things, but I'll be passing on the pea plate at Grace's tonight."

Kora and Maggie slid into the line's familiar rhythm. The shells were clipped together in sets of four. A tracer was added to only one of those four. When launched, the tracer's path illuminated the sky with a trail of light and smoke to reveal the accuracy of the gunner's aim.

Kora stole a quick glance at Billie on the other side of the belt. She hadn't seen her much since Christmas. That was probably a good thing, yet Maggie kept pushing Kora and Billie together. Wishing Maggie would stop trying might be the sole thing they held in common.

Harry entered on his daily rounds, but even the nicest white men brought her to high alert. Kora continued her quick work pace.

"Good morning, ladies!" Harry's deep baritone sang.

As he passed, several ladies said, "Morning, Harry!"

Kora tried on a casual smile.

Harry finished peeking over shoulders with high accolades for their quality. "Don't forget to let me know if you want to take on a shift at the testing grounds in April." He leaned one arm against the door frame, filling it entirely. "It's our turn to supervise that month. You'll get a front-row seat to how we keep our post-assembly quality high too."

He left, as he did every morning, booming out their catchy mantra. "Remember: *No spaces between the traces!*"

Ruby began the morning banter. "So, any resolutions, ladies?"

"Kora and I picked out twelve books for 1944," Maggie said.

"Yes, we did, one a month." Kora nodded.

"And she's going to teach me how to make her famous sweet potato pie, right?"

Kora hadn't yet agreed to that one. "I might could," she slowly said. "If you resolve to be on time this year."

"I always do," Maggie blushed. "Though that hasn't helped in years past."

Billie interrupted, "I already told you: resolutions are dumb, so don't ask me."

"What about you, Deb?"

"I'm going to write a daily letter to my teachers and friends back in Poland," she said. "Even if they've stopped writing back ..." Her tightened voice paused.

Kora and Maggie exchanged worried looks. No one talked much about the news from Poland. They weren't sure what Deborah knew. Kora's mind ran through hollow phrases, something helpful to say, coming up empty.

"My papa tells me stop. Not send more letters." When her English faltered even more through her rising emotions, Deborah cleared her throat and stood taller before declaring, "I *hate* Germans."

They all stayed quiet after that, until Kora couldn't help herself. "Hate will eat you from the inside out. Letting go of hate is a gift to *yourself*, not to them."

Eyes fixed on the empty shell in her hands, Deborah said, almost to herself, "Working here and write letters. It's all I can do now for them."

To avoid a slowdown of the belt, Kora quietly started working double time to make up for Deborah's slack. Maggie and Kora were stuck on the other side of the belt, too far to console Deborah. Maggie caught Billie's attention, then jerked her head in Deborah's direction. Billie finally picked up on the signal.

With a hand on Deborah's shoulder, Billie said, "It's the perfect resolution, Deb. You can still write a letter every day and save them to mail when everything's back to normal." Billie gently rubbed a hand once or twice over Deborah's small frame, then ended the contact with an awkward pat-pat-pat. This was hardly Billie's comfort zone.

Like it took all her strength, Deborah pulled up the corners of her mouth, then it was gone. There was nothing left to say, and Billie seemed to have reached her empathetic limits, so they got back to work. Kora waited for Ruby to offer a much-needed distraction, and she came in right on cue.

"So, I met my future husband yesterday." Ruby catapulted the bold statement into the middle of the conversation, pushing away unsettling thoughts.

"Did you now?" Billie asked, raising an eyebrow.

"Again?" Kora teased.

"Does he have a name?" Maggie added.

"I don't know his name—yet—but I really did talk to this one. A girl can't seem too eager for a name."

"Where'd you meet him?" Maggie asked.

"He was two seats down from me at Kress's counter. We both ordered the macaroni special and a grape soda. Said he goes there every Tuesday, so you know where I'll be next week!"

"What's he look like?"

"He's taller than me, which is harder to find than you'd think, with short, sandy brown hair. Looks great in uniform, and shows the cutest dimples when he smiles."

"I thought you were determined to land money and status, not cute dimples."

"This one's the full package. Get this—he paid for my meal and I didn't even find out until after he left. So classy!" Ruby fanned one hand in front of her eyes.

Maggie said, "I'm happy for you, Rube."

"Sounds like a real peach," Billie said.

"Thanks, but now I only have six days to decide what to wear next Tuesday."

When the lunch whistle blew, the belts stopped. Crossing the campus together, Maggie and Kora trailed the others. Winding through paths between buildings, they passed a sea of women doing the same. Lately, thanks to the new colored fuze and final assembly lines, Kora was happy to recognize more brown faces. Enough of Kora's neighbors worked here now to fill their own lunch table.

Almost to the cafeteria, Kora felt her stomach flip. She'd eaten with Maggie and the others a few times, but felt her neighbors watching. Navigating between those two worlds, some days she did better than others.

Pushing through the double doors, Kora and Maggie slid their trays down the rails and made their food selections. Kora paid first. As she waited on her change, she glanced over her shoulder to assess the room. Her friends from Brooklyn waved her over. Turning back, she saw Maggie's face change.

"I'll catch up to y'all on the way out." Kora set her tray back down, pretending to rebalance some items, but really she was buying time. She waited until Maggie crossed the floor to join Ruby and the others. Kora carried her tray the other direction, finding her own seat at the table.

Chapter 16

JANUARY, 1944
MAGGIE

L ocking the car, Maggie hurried to catch up to Grace and the girls. Their faces were illuminated with color from the Carolina Theatre marquis, displaying tonight's feature show, "The Song of Bernadette."

It was hard to miss Grace, whose massive fur coat brought a bear to mind. Other women wore furs too, taking advantage of the few days a year they were practical in the South, but Grace's drew the most attention with its size and length.

Annoyed by Grace's extravagance, Maggie softened when she caught Grace smooth Daisy's hair back in place, like a mother would. Grace did have her moments.

Tonight was the twins' first picture show, a rite of passage they'd begged for over the past year. If not for fear of them seeing wartime newsreels, she would have buckled long ago. Maggie didn't want to seed the girls' dreams with images of war.

The government used radio and picture shows to relay the war's progress. These days, Uncle Sam started every show, detailing battles won or lost on various fronts. Charlie had written about his unit being filmed at least once. Ever since then, Maggie wouldn't start breathing again until the newsreels ended, from dread or anticipation—she wasn't sure.

Grace gave the girls their orders. "Your mother and I will buy tickets out here. You two hold our place inside, at the popcorn line."

The ticket line included mostly women and the stray older couple. Charlotte had quite a few cinemas for a city its size, but The Carolina was *the place* where everyone went to see and be seen on a Saturday night. Never one to give up that opportunity, Grace left Maggie to keep their place in line while she greeted several friends.

Maggie pretended to be engrossed by various movie posters. Grace returned, quite flustered, and spoke under her breath.

"I just encountered the most unfortunate wig on Shelby Johnson. Poor soul's getting on in her years and it shows. A fact she may be the very last to realize."

As she started to twist her head in that direction, Grace grabbed her arm. "Don't *look*," she commanded, before turning to smile and wave casually at another friend. "But Maggie you must swear to tell me if I ever get to that point. That lopsided wig! In public, no less! Just lock me in the house."

Maggie tried not to laugh, unable to imagine Grace reaching such a state. The smell of popcorn grew stronger as they neared the flashy ticket booth.

Maggie changed the subject. "I'm glad we picked this movie. I hear Jennifer Jones is wonderful as Bernadette."

"I did hear she dies at the end. You're sure the girls can handle it?"

Maggie watched her exhaled breath hang in the air between them. "I could not put this night off any longer. They ask me every day—sometimes twice—when are we going to the Carolina Theatre to eat real movie popcorn?"

Grace's sigh dripped with resignation. "Looking on the bright side ... Saint Bernadette is one of my favorites, and I am honored to experience the girls' first movie. And being with you too, of course." The last part she added with three feather-light pats on Maggie's shoulder.

"So, you'll take them to the powder room before it starts. Like we planned? They don't need to see any part of that newsreel," Maggie said.

"Of course, dear. I remember the plan."

Some exiting patrons offered Maggie a gap to peek inside and check on her daughters. "The girls are almost to the counter."

"You run on in. I'll buy the tickets."

A few minutes later, Maggie and the girls stood close by, waiting for Grace at the coat-check table. The packed theater couldn't spare a seat for the bear-sized mink. Holding the overflowing popcorn bag between them, the girls picked at pieces. Maggie watched Grace eye the coat-check girl up and down before surrendering her prize.

Scouting the last four seats together, they excused themselves down a row of legs. Once seated, her daughters fought for control of the popcorn bag. Grace warned them to slow down—that bag needed to last the whole show.

Maggie asked the girls twice not to bounce so high in their seats, but it was like keeping coils from springing. It was their grandmother's warning look that convinced them to stop. Grace's "look" was legendary.

All the main level seats were occupied, and the balcony started filling up. Maggie looked to the wall murals high above their heads. With its layers of fancy moldings and filigreed chandeliers, the Carolina Theatre had always struck her as overdone. Too many loud, gaudy features competing for attention.

Grace stood to announce that a visit to the powder room was a necessity, and asked for the girls' company. Maggie offered to stay behind and save their seats, as per the plan. Taking the half-empty popcorn bag, she caught Grace smile wide and wave to someone farther back. Maggie saw her swell with pride and clutch her heart, mouthing the words "Thank you," and, "Yes they are precious," as she tightly threaded the twins back through the row of legs. The girls had always looked more Slone than Fraser. She'd endured many stories of Grace being mistaken *again* as the girls' mother.

They left just in time. Slouching into the crushed velvet seat as the lights dimmed, Maggie heard the clickety-clack of the film projector starting up behind her. The dust danced its way through a tunnel of camera light.

Mechanically lifting popcorn to her mouth, she didn't taste a thing. Marching troops, massive ships, and soaring planes dominated the screen, followed by dotted lines and arrows advancing on a global map. The narrator's voice seesawed between confidence in the Allied mission, and alarm for any Axis power and progress.

The uniforms and military haircuts made every man look like he could be hers. She scanned the black and white images as fast as she could for Charlie's familiar features, but came up empty.

Relieved when the movie started and her family returned to their seats, she looked across the girls' heads at Grace's expression, full of questions. Maggie shook her head no. No sign of Charlie in the newsreel. The girls reclaimed the popcorn as the beautiful face of Jennifer Jones filled the screen. Maggie let herself get lost in the story.

❋ ❋ ❋

Up way past their bedtime, the girls immediately fell asleep in the car. Grace offered to help as Maggie carried each one to bed. Afterward, Grace surprised her by accepting Maggie's obligatory nightcap offer. Doubling the ritual she usually performed for one, Maggie pulled two glasses from her crystal stemware cabinet. She watched the light play with the rich red color as it flowed from the bottle.

Like a good, superstitious Catholic, Grace raised her glass for a toast. "To childhood firsts and raising our girls right." She paused before adding, "And Happy New Year. We should do this more in 1944." Grace smiled, maybe at her own poetic last line.

Their glasses touched, and released a deep, melodic sound into the room. Maggie listened to it fade away. "Can I ask you something?"

"Of course, dear." Both women found a seat at the kitchen table.

"What does 'raising them right' mean to you?"

"Preparing them to be the best wives and mothers they can be. And the best citizens. Why?"

"What if they want more?"

"What if they don't?"

"My sister never married, and she has a wonderful life at Wellesley."

"They need to be prepared for all of their options, Maggie. They will have a *very comfortable* life here in Charlotte."

Maggie absorbed that last statement for its truth. Once pitched by Charlie as their brief Southern sabbatical, their time here would now occupy a large portion of their childhood memories. Moving back—leaving their school, church and new friends—might disrupt her daughters even more.

"Seems like it would've been easier if Charlie had married old what's-her-name from school, right?"

Grace picked at a flaking corner of the laminated table. "I don't know what would be different had that actually happened. I do know we are a family and we don't intentionally try to bait one another with questions like that, Maggie."

"I'm sorry, you're right."

"But since you asked," Grace began, and Maggie braced herself, "one thing has always been clear as crystal to me: you make my son happy. That's all a mother ever really wants, despite what might slip out now and again."

"I try," Maggie said, feeling a little more reassured.

"Anything important from the newsreel I missed?"

"No, just more of the same. No end in sight."

Grace took a long sip, as Maggie fished for something to say. Grace beat her to it. "How is everything down at the plant?"

Maggie chuckled. "I can't complain. Turns out I'm sort of good at it. I still miss the girls, but my friends—the ones I told you about—they've come to mean a great deal to me."

"That's nice, dear."

"How are you enjoying your extra time with the girls?" Maggie asked.

"Well, if I can borrow your words, it's come to mean a great deal to me also."

They laughed, but then fell into silence.

Before the awkwardness could stretch too far, Grace asked, "How are you *really* doing, dear?"

Maggie looked up, hesitant. It appeared Grace wanted a deeper answer, but she'd been tricked by this question from her before. "I have good and bad days," Maggie replied, twisting the stem between her thumb and middle finger. "I miss him. And I still can't believe it is 1944. They turn ten this year."

"Children do grow up, despite our needs or desire to freeze time." Pulling a loose thread from the window curtain, Grace twisted it around one finger, lips pressed tight, like she was physically holding back part two of her sentence. Having heard it a hundred times, Maggie's mind filled in the rest: Grace had had no choice but to smile through the pain of her only child and his family living so far away.

"Ten years old. How's it possible for time to move so fast and so slow all at once?" Maggie wondered aloud. The wine kicked in, and she thought, *What the heck, here goes.*

"Two years ago, Charlie left the house without saying where he was going. It was a normal day. Nothing unusual before he left, but then he was gone for hours. I began to worry, but right before I picked up the phone to start calling around, he walked in with the sunset." She took another swallow, noticing how little was left in the glass. "He brought in a new game for the girls and sent them to their room to play it, then he sat me down. The look on his face— so serious—scared me. He made me promise to let him get through his whole story before I asked any questions.

"He began to paint this picture for me. Where he'd been all day. How he'd weighed all the needs of those counting on him—his family and his country. He saw re-enlisting in the Army as the only way. He told me I was strong but would still need help, and you'd happily provide it if we were local. The girls were young enough, only seven then. He was convinced they'd hardly remember his time away. He'd be back before they turned ten. He got someone down at the enlistment office to agree that this war would be done in two years, two-and-a-half tops. America would arrive just in time to shut down the party and go home." Maggie paused to pour herself another glass.

Grace nursed her own drink, quiet for once. Maggie was afraid to guess her thoughts.

"He made me close my eyes while he painted his vision for me. He described the girls' tenth birthday party with friends and family all around. He swore he would be there to help blow out twenty candles all at once. He certainly had enough hot air, he joked."

Grace laughed softly, like she missed Charlie's sense of humor.

Maggie continued, "He seemed so sure of his grand plan, it was hard to argue, especially since he'd just come from signing on the dotted line. He'd set our family's course at the enlistment office that day, before even talking to me about it." Maggie stopped, having never been this honest with Grace.

"I'm angry with Charlie," Maggie said. *There*, Maggie thought, relieved to let it bubble up and call its name. "And at the same time, I'm terrified to never get a chance to tell him." Maggie's words faded and her insecurities kicked in. This was too much to share with Grace, unfair even. She was a mother first and mother-in-law second, but Maggie's own mother was gone, and she needed an ear to listen.

The matriarch took a full, agonizing moment to herself then said, "I love my son. Have always thought he hung the moon. But I think if I try and put myself in your shoes, I can understand why you're angry. You feel discounted."

Surprised by Grace's very direct statement—one she nailed like a hammer—Maggie waited for the other shoe to drop. She waited for Grace to insert a giant "but..." to the end of her sentence.

It never came.

Grace continued. "Even if he didn't tell you he planned to re-enlist because he knew how you'd react, he took away your chance to be supportive."

Maggie didn't dare say more.

"You know what I've always meant to ask you?" Grace asked.

"I couldn't begin to guess."

"I know you've told me why you picked those names for the girls, but remind me again."

Maggie gave a shy smile. "It seems trite now, but they're named after book characters. From a book my mother and I read many times. Why?"

"I do love those girls, but capturing your daughters' attention requires one to say their names quite often. Enough to make me wonder why you chose them, because Demi means half and a Daisy can be such a delicate flower."

"That's true," Maggie said slowly, not sure where Grace was going. "Should I have picked stronger names?"

"Not at all. Those girls are strong-willed despite their names, but it did get me thinking about how you got your name. I have a theory."

"Well please share it." Maggie was intrigued.

"Now, I only met your mother once at the wedding, but she was lovely. You claim Maggie as the nickname she chose to make you blend in as American, rather than Mary which is closer to Marós. I can't help but wonder if she picked it because it sounded like another flower, the strongest of them all: the magnolia."

This wasn't likely, but Maggie kept it to herself. Magnolia trees didn't grow above the Mason Dixon line, but a lifelong Southerner like Grace might assume their strength would be legendary throughout the country. "Are you saying I'm strong, Grace? Because most of the time I feel anything but."

Grace paused before answering, "Yes. And Charlie knew it too, but I'm sure I've shared my name theory before."

Slowly shaking her head Maggie said, "No ... no you never have ... but I'll take it just the same. As a compliment, right?"

Grace nodded.

Not sure if it was really Grace or just the wine talking, Maggie smiled, then marveled at all the firsts this night had to offer.

Chapter 17

MARCH, 1944
MAGGIE

Parked on the now-familiar bench outside Leland's office, Maggie's crossed leg kept awkward time with the steady typewriter beat. After sharing exactly one smile with Maggie, his secretary—Mrs. Sexton, she finally recalled—had pointed to the bench and resumed her work, leaving Maggie to wonder what she thought of these encounters. Did Leland call meetings with other line workers, besides her?

After Maggie walked in, Sexton closed Leland's office door behind her, leaving Maggie alone to hear his explanation.

Leland got right to the point. "Four Navy officials are coming from DC in two weeks. They say it's not an official inspection, but I wouldn't put it past them. It's important that we seize this opportunity."

"Sounds important," Maggie said, still wondering where she fit in.

"The skills of the staff I inherited are spotty at best. Further proof the best and brightest got battle assignments." His slight pause made Maggie think of the accident that limited Leland's own battle assignment potential. "I need someone I can trust to coordinate the preparations. I thought of you."

Maggie processed his words. He needed her. He trusted her. He thought about her. "So, let me understand. I would help prepare for a formal inspection?"

"Yes. Only it's not exactly formal, but we need to act like it is."

"In just two weeks?"

"Yes."

"How do I do that?"

"By communicating expectations to the lines."

Hearing the rhythm of military drills outside, Maggie watched the activity happening below the window as she let the idea sink in. Leland believed Maggie was the best person for the job.

She finally spoke. "What could this mean for the plant?"

"An E rating of excellence means more resources poured into this facility and more people hired from the community. People like Kora."

That got Maggie's attention.

"But these inspectors can be relentless. Trust me. Entertaining them the night before goes a long way to win them over. Wine and dine, if you get my meaning. Maybe you could help with that too?"

"But what about my assembly-line responsibilities? I can't take any more time away from the girls."

He gave a reassuring smile. "I understand. Your current duties will be suspended and resumed as soon as they leave. The girls and your friends will hardly have a chance to miss you."

Maggie paused, flattered he thought she could do this. She nodded. "Yes, I'll do it."

"Really?"

"Really. But I want the option to enlist my mother-in-law's help to entertain the guests … inspectors … whatever they are."

"Fine by me, but I would be there too. Don't forget you made me decline my first invitation to Grace and George's home."

"I did do that and with good reason. I'll work through your secretary to deal with Grace. Otherwise, my part would be too hard to explain. She's a proud banker's wife, known for entertaining important people in town. Grace and George could do this in their sleep. Just the same, I'd rather not share our history with them right now."

"I promise she won't learn about it from me." Leland rose. "First thing tomorrow morning, report back here. We'll talk messaging, then you will begin rounds to speak with each building supervisor. There are lots of them. Agreed?"

Maggie tried to picture herself talking to a supervisor with conviction. "Why would they listen to me?"

"Because I'll order them to."

"Well ... if that's all it takes," she said, rising. "It's settled then. I'll see you tomorrow."

❋ ❋ ❋

The next morning Maggie faced Leland, clutching the result of her late-night efforts. "I made a list." She smiled, extending a hand to show him.

He took a few seconds to glance at the list. When he handed it back, he took a few more to eye her outfit. "You look different. No coveralls today."

It was the dress. She'd wrestled with what to wear all morning, wishing she had asked yesterday. She finally settled on a yellow flower pattern, hoping it would please the supervisors she needed to convince. Now she second-guessed herself, worried for standing out too much. "I assumed since I wouldn't be working the line today ... ."

Inhaling, Leland said, "Smell different too."

She hesitated, aware how the dress cinched her waist. The perfume was left over from the last time she wore it, but he didn't know that.

Leland nodded toward her list. "It's a good start," he said, sitting down and pushing his own papers across the desk. "I had Mrs. Sexton type these up last night. It has exactly what to say at your first meeting with each supervisor, plus the check-up items for the week after. She included the name, rank, and building location of each one. Make sure every task is correct and complete."

She flipped through the papers. "There are so many buildings. Can I use a Jeep?"

"Hmmm, how's your driving these days?"

Her arched eyebrow offered him a clue. "Much better than you might remember."

"I'll take your word for it. See how much I trust you? This is all working out. I'll secure you a vehicle for the next two weeks. Think you can get to every building by Friday?"

"I'll try," she offered, then nodded. "I mean, *yes*, by Friday."

"There's a book around here somewhere, explaining each rank and title. You need to address each supervisor correctly."

"I am married to an Army sergeant. Not sure I need a manual."

Leland barely hid a smirk. "How should I put this? Army and Navy are *extremely* different. We'll grab the book on our way out."

"Where are *we* going? I thought I was doing this on my own."

"I'm coming with you. At least for the first couple of rounds in building five. I have a meeting down there anyway."

"That doesn't feel like trust."

"It's for them, not you. Enlisted men are not in the habit of obeying women. I'm more concerned with their response than your instruction."

"I guess I can't argue with that."

"Oh, *you* probably could," he teased, glancing up at the wall. "Let's go."

Minutes later, Leland's Jeep hummed over the gravel roads. He talked the whole ride over, feeling the need to hit every detail again. The more he said, the quieter she became. She checked her list for the name and rank of the supervisor in building five, Chief Petty Officer Miller. They exited the car at the same time, offering him no chance to open her car door.

She sped up as he walked faster toward the building's door. Arriving a second before, he grinned and held it open. She ducked under his arm, more than a bit annoyed by his special treatment.

Impatient to prove herself, she approached the first worker she encountered and asked, "Can you direct me to find Chief Petty Officer Miller?" While waiting, the two of them drew a decent amount of attention from the line workers. Her dress stuck out all right, but so did the commanding officer standing directly behind her.

Miller found them and pulled them into a corner. He properly acknowledged Leland with a salute. Leland returned the gesture, then introduced Maggie Fraser. He appeared confused by her stunned look back at him, then his face got red.

"Forgive me. Let me introduce Maggie *Slone* ... not Maggie Fraser." He finished with a cough to cover his slip-up on her maiden name.

Maggie didn't miss a beat. She did the talking from there, actually charming the pants off the fellow. He glanced at Leland a couple of times, expecting him to speak, but there wasn't a need. She managed every detail perfectly.

Handing over the inspection checklist, she told him when to expect her return. Before long, they were walking back to the Jeep.

"That was easier than I thought. Miller has a reputation for being a stubborn ass," he said.

"I suppose," she said curtly.

"But ... ? There's a definite *but* waiting at the end of that sentence."

"But ... I'm quite used to dealing with stubborn men," she finished.

"Now you're talking about me. I get it. You're mad."

"That's right," she nodded. "And I'll add another *but*. We don't know why it was so easy to handle Miller. Could have been you standing right next to me. If I'm going to do this, Leland, you can't be hovering around. You told me what to do. Twice. Now let me do it without a chaperone." She shielded her eyes from the glare of the sun. "Don't you have more important things to do?"

He tossed her the keys.

She caught them mid-air.

"Get to work," he said, and she rewarded him with a smile. "You can drop me off for my meeting, first."

Chapter 18

MARCH, 1944
KORA

etting down her bags—one filled with sweet potatoes and the
other with cooking utensils she couldn't do without—Kora
knocked twice at the side door. She checked the afternoon
sky, still threatening rain.

Mr. and Mrs. George Slone were hosting a dinner for some
naval inspectors, just arrived from Washington. Somehow Maggie
had talked Kora into helping Lucy cook and serve tonight's meal.
Understanding what this would mean for the plant and how much
extra money she would earn, Kora agreed, despite having to work
beside Lucy, who never missed an opportunity to show Kora her
place in the world.

Wearing her signature expression—somewhere between polite
and smelling something foul—Lucy pulled open the door. "You can
set those bags over there," she told Kora. "Next to your uniform. I
borrowed one for you. Had to guess your size."

Kora stepped into the black dress, not at all surprised it was a
little too big. Behind her back, she tightened the strings of the white
ruffled apron she'd avoided most of her life, reminding herself what
was at stake. Everything about the plant was under inspection,

including Commander Martin and the city of Charlotte itself. Kora's cooking skills would go a long way to impress the inspectors before they even stepped foot on the sparkling clean campus, thanks to Maggie's hard work. Maggie had arranged all the details for this evening too, but drew the line at attending herself. Kora thought this odd, but didn't press it.

Catching her reflection in the window, Kora smoothed down the uniform. Time to get to work.

"Welcome gentleman! Please come in out of this awful rain," Grace gushed as she pulled the front door open. "Lucy will get your coats and umbrellas."

From the kitchen, Kora heard their feet stomp on the mat, echoing through the large, two-story foyer on their way to the living room. Several executives from US Rubber Company and their wives were already waiting there.

Kora entered with a silver tray of appetizers, just in time to catch a familiar-looking man in Naval uniform pump George's hand. Kora recognized him from pictures at the plant. Maggie had said the commanding officer would be here tonight. As she circulated with her tray, some of the wives politely thanked her. Most ignored her. Grace clinked a small butter knife against her glass, announcing to everyone that dinner would soon be served.

"Please, everyone, join me in the dining room."

Back in the kitchen, Lucy threw a set of mitts in Kora's direction. "Pull the roast out the oven in two minutes and put it on this platter. I'll start pouring the wine on the table."

"Yes, ma'am," Kora whispered. Listening to the storm outside, Kora thought about James. He wouldn't be happy to know she was here serving white folk. He'd never wanted that for his bride.

A couple of times today, she'd tried to strike up a conversation with Lucy, but got one-word replies. What did Kora ever do to offend, besides cook better than Lucy? Guess that was enough of a crime.

When Lucy returned, they got busy carving the roast and adding steaming sides to fifteen plates, then delivered them to the dining room. When the last plate was lowered onto the table, Kora thought she might get a break. She felt her own hunger start to grow, but Lucy had other ideas.

"Here," she said, shoving full bottles of white and red wines into Kora's hands. "Stand quiet in the corner, but pay attention. Fill the empty fat goblets with red, and skinny ones with white."

This was more than Kora had bargained for, and she suspected Lucy knew that. "Of course," Kora said with a smile before heading for the dining room once again.

Kora tried to fade into the fancy wallpaper, watching for empty glasses among the sixteen formal place settings, though only fifteen sat at the table. Kora still felt the pinches on her fingers from having inserted all three table leaf extensions earlier. The antique wood gleamed, and the dining set now took up the whole room.

Local businessmen with bow ties and trophy wives were staggered between the visiting military guests. The term "corporate-military partnership" popped into Kora's mind, left over from her training classes. These had been hastily formed all over the country to supply the war effort. In Charlotte, the US Rubber Company had joined together with the US Navy, pooling their vast material and labor resources to defeat the enemy. The local men attempted to talk war strategy, until Grace shushed them.

"There'll be plenty of time for that after you gentlemen retire to the study," she said, before redirecting to a conversation more appropriate for mixed company.

Grace and George sat at opposite ends of the long, impressive table, easily controlling the conversation on both fronts. Commander Martin sat to Grace's right. On his other side was an empty seat that Grace had twice apologized for, assuming the commander was married or *at least* bringing a date.

"I guess you could say I'm married to my job," he said with a knowing nod to the other crisply uniformed officers.

Grace smiled, then winked at the other wives. "I'm sure we could change that right quick, Commander Martin. You just say the word and we'll have you introduced to half the eligible ladies in town."

"That's kind of you," he said.

Kora squinted her eyes through the dim lighting to confirm he really was blushing.

"I'll certainly keep that in mind."

"May I ask you a personal question?" Grace said.

"Another one? Why certainly," he answered.

"Have you ever lived in Boston?" The question timed perfectly with a large clap of thunder. Kora didn't know this man from Adam, but he did look nervous for a split second. Then it was gone.

"I spent my first twenty years living there, as a matter of fact."

"I thought so. You pronounce your words exactly like my daughter-in-law. She's from that area."

"Is that so? Well, it was a great place to grow up. Perhaps she would agree."

"Yes, she seems to think so too. Indeed, she hardly passes up an opportunity to compare."

He took another bite, maybe to keep from saying more. Grace appeared to study him.

"In fact, she works down at your plant. You don't know a Maggie Slone, do you?"

The next clap of thunder shook every fancy little teardrop crystal hanging from the chandelier. The chimes faded as he swallowed behind his white cloth napkin. "We just hired our ten thousandth employee. I'm afraid I don't."

"Ten thousand employees!" George exclaimed from the other end. "That makes you Charlotte's largest employer by a landslide."

Grace beamed at her husband. "It does, indeed. Many of those left the employment of my dear friends. Such a large number and I do worry about their safety. I pray daily for our soldiers and now this plant. Commander Martin, perhaps you could ease my burden. I'd love to understand how you keep them all safe."

The storm settled back into rain, offering a pleasant thrumming sound overhead.

"I'd like nothing more than to ease that burden. I've implemented a multi-layered checks and balances protocol here, similar to what I've experienced at other military facilities, only here I added a new tier. All teams—well, almost all—rotate through independent inspection assignments. Shift workers, whose lives are on the line as much as management, are empowered to perform safety inspections in areas where they do not work."

"That's smart," said one of the businessmen, just as Kora refilled his wine. "Removing any biases that might arise from a manager or peer relationship."

"Exactly right, sir. Their impartiality is key to reporting the truth."

Kora passed behind Commander Martin's chair, noticing he hadn't touched a drop of wine.

He paused, maybe for effect, focusing his attention on Grace. "Of course, safety is the shared goal of every soul working down there. Turns out fear of fire is the great equalizer."

George spoke up, ending his wife's interrogation. "It sounds like you have full control of the situation, Commander."

Others nodded.

Finishing the final course, George invited the men to follow him to the study while the women moved to the living room. With aching feet, Kora hauled the last stack of dirty dishes to the kitchen. She was ready for that break, but, once again, Lucy had other plans.

"Go fill drinks in Mr. George's study. I'll take the ladies in the living room."

Kora sighed and slipped into the large wood-paneled room, where everything was some shade of brown. She found the men settled into tanned leather chairs and puffing on cigars. Kora admired the full wall of shelving made of gleaming cherry wood. Maybe James could build those for her someday. She felt bone tired, so kept her focus on the extra money she would collect tonight and add to her house fund.

One uniformed man raised his empty crystal glass. Carrying the heavy decanter, Kora slowly crossed the room to fill it. A young Maggie in a wedding dress smiled from the shelf as she passed. Kora sized up the man standing next to her in Class A uniform. Charlie clearly favored his father, whose glass she filled next.

"Commander Martin, when did you decide on the Navy as your career? Assuming I'm not being too forward."

"Not at all, sir. That's an easy answer, because it was all I ever wanted."

Several nodded, like they shared an understanding of a man's calling. Someone droned on about the importance of having a vision and fulfilling it at any cost.

Kora blended back into the walls. When she scanned the room for empty glasses, she noticed she wasn't the only one interested in Maggie's wedding photograph. Between conversations, Commander Martin seemed struck by it as well, returning his gaze there several times.

The last dish put away, Kora finally got her break. Lucy unwrapped a plate of food and set it down in front of Kora.

"You're a hard worker, when your mind's not up in the clouds," Lucy said.

Though Kora suspected a trap, she was too hungry and tired to second-guess Lucy's intentions. "Thank you," Kora said.

"And you make a decent pie. You come back, now, ya hear?"

Kora didn't know what to say, knowing any wrong words would be shared throughout their neighborhood. "That's kind of you, Lucy. I won't forget it."

Chapter 19

APRIL, 1944
KORA

Riding the bus to work, Kora pulled a hand from her pocket, full of confetti, and laughed. They had gotten her again. The pranks were plenty today, a tradition with her husband's family. How could it be April already? She counted in her head: her third spring without James.

Stepping off the bus and into the rain, Kora protected her head and almost collided with two reporters outside the admin building. She avoided their blinding camera flash just in time. They were gone before she had time to wonder why they'd come.

Inside the change house, she dressed to the sounds of hot gossip buzzing around her. Some big announcement was happening later, with lots of guesses for what it might include.

"Maybe good news about the war?"

"Or *bad* news about the war." Hushed voices followed that unpleasant notion. Kora worried for James.

The belt lines started at seven on the dot. Lulled by routine, the morning sped by until Harry made them all stop, pointing to the speaker high in the corner of the room. They all kept quiet, watching expectantly until a high-pitched male voice came through the black box.

"Good morning, may I have your attention? Please pause production for a brief announcement from Commander Leland Martin." Every Navy man in the room saluted the box hanging on the wall. The sight looked odd to Kora.

"At ease," came the commander's official voice.

Kora watched them obey, wondering if James saluted voice boxes now too.

"Thank you for your attention," the commander continued. "It is with honest pleasure that I relay a letter from Washington yesterday." He cleared his throat. "The US Rubber Company Naval Ammunition Plant has been awarded the E Award for Excellence in Production. It is the highest honor a facility like ours can receive. It's a rare accolade that puts us on even footing with cities like Atlanta and even Detroit.

"I want to thank everyone for your hard work and dedication to safety. Our boys are steps closer to coming home because of you. I hope you feel our government's pride in our work. Your efforts will be formally recognized during the pennant raising ceremony in two weeks. All are invited to attend on the front grounds."

Whistles and applause faded to general accolades, then a conversational hum. What did this mean? More money? More work? Or just another flag on the pole?

Kora leaned toward Maggie to ask, but stopped when she noticed the extra lines on her forehead, like she was thinking hard. Better to ask later, on the drive down to Wateree. Kora looked forward to the drive with Maggie and Harry. She'd heard so much about these famous testing grounds.

The belt started moving again, along with the idle chatter.

"Ruby, how was your date last night?" Kora asked.

"Wonderful! We saw a movie. Say, they showed a preview of the new 'Rosie the Riveter' movie. We should all go see it together next week at the Carolina!"

Kora knew these plans wouldn't include her. She wasn't allowed to see a picture show at the Carolina Theatre. Kora caught Maggie's wrinkled brow, an indication that her friend understood the same.

Maggie began slowly. "I bet our show's also playing at The Grand too. The Carolina's nice, but I've been wanting to try a new theater. We could get a big group of us there. What do you say?"

Kora searched the others' expressions for signs they understood what Maggie was asking. She tried signaling to Maggie that this wasn't necessary; she would gladly see the show with her own friends, but too late. It was official. Nothing left to do but smile.

Plans were made to watch their movie together, in two weeks, at the Grand Theater in Biddleville, near the university Kora hoped James could attend after he came home. Kora wiped her palms on her thighs. She'd never wanted a collision between her two worlds, but it was coming.

❋ ❋ ❋

For some time, Kora had suspected Maggie could be sneaky. Today finally settled it. The woman was downright manipulative.

Alone in the back seat of Harry's automobile, Kora cataloged her suspicions like piecing together a puzzle. She was supposed to be riding with Maggie and Harry to the testing grounds at Wateree Pond, but about an hour ago Maggie had made a big production that something had come up with her girls and she needed Billie to take her spot today.

Of course any problem with Daisy or Demi alarmed her, so Kora pressed Maggie for the cause. After suffering through several vague answers that made no sense, Kora was equally relieved to understand nothing was truly wrong with the girls and annoyed to be played a fool.

Clearly bothered that her two best friends weren't friends with each other, Maggie had engineered a shared experience for Kora and Billie along with Harry to referee if needed. Billie still never smiled or seemed comfortable around her. Kora certainly wasn't holding out for a happy ending between them this evening.

Kora passed the travel time reading Harry's engineering manuals piled in the back seat. Asking for his permission to do so had brought a strange look from Billie. "You and Maggie and your books," she said in a tone that didn't imply a compliment.

Kora kept reading, looking up every once in a while to watch the landscape become more rural as they crossed into South Carolina. She wondered who, if anyone, lived way out here. Approaching a corner, Harry cranked down the window and sent his left arm out. Kora watched his bent elbow and open palm, wondering who he was signaling. The roads were empty except for them.

Fascinated by what she was learning, Kora half-listened to their comments about a majestic old oak on the horizon. The thick trunk and full leaves dazzled Billie and Harry.

Kora looked up, expecting to behold its beauty too, but as they got closer Kora could see nothing but a single, thick rope hanging from the tallest branch. It could've been a swing, one with the seat long separated from the huge knot at the end. But in her heart, Kora knew exactly what that rope meant.

No signs of children, Kora's bones screamed the truth. *That* rope was tied to *that* tree because of its proximity to the road. It sent a clear message—one she'd seen before.

Memories of a similar tree came flooding back—the one she and her cousin Rose used to pass on the way to school. One day, her uncle had borrowed a truck to drive them to school instead. They preferred to walk, but he insisted. He tried to make a game of it, telling them he'd pay them each a penny to keep their eyes covered tight on the tree's stretch of road. Kora's curiosity, as it often did, got the best of her.

The slices of light between her fingers revealed the large man's listless body. The rope looked too taught, like the heavy weight could snap it—or even the branch on the other end—in two. He faced away, thank goodness. She caught sight of one torn overall pocket on his backside, then squeezed her eyes tight, understanding the real reason behind her uncle's game. It was too late. A piece of her innocence was lost and the message hanging from that tree branded into her soul.

The articles she had read this last year in *The Charlotte Post* about the violence in Beaumont and Detroit scared her to death. Kora was certain this tree, growing out in the country all these years, had been a silent witness to violence.

Kora pulled her gaze from the tree, dialing back in on Harry and Billie's discussion. They clearly knew each other from a long time ago. Their reaction to the old tree and its scary rope was different as night and day from hers. This fascinated Kora. Where she saw a threat, they saw love and shared happy memories.

"Do you remember the rope swing you built for me and Katy?"

Harry laughed and detailed the daunting task of hanging the swing. Katy had had her heart set on swinging from the most difficult tree for him to climb, but he couldn't say "no" to the little girl he loved. That same love now brought pain to every part of his face. Kora could read his loss, even from the back seat. She assumed they forgot she was there, because both were quiet for a full minute.

"I'm afraid of what I'd do if I ever saw that snake," Billie said.

"Me too," Harry said. "Gittin' away from ghosts wasn't the only reason I left Gaston County. Running into his smiling face, knowing he got away with murder ... it was too much."

Murder? Kora was horrified. Poor Katy.

"Being kin with half the sheriff's office didn't hurt him none," Billie said. "It never crossed their minds to investigate her so-called accident."

"His parents made sure nobody investigated it. They built a whole new wing on the courthouse in her honor. And the baby's. They even invited me to the dedication. Ain't that something?" Harry's grip on the steering wheel tightened. "I fantasized about what I'd do if I went. Saw myself locked up after. That's when I knew I needed to go."

"Katy came to see me once in Charlotte, after I married Nick. No idea how she found me."

"I never knew that," Harry said.

"She wanted to apologize for ending our friendship. Said she was blinded by love, but she wasn't blind anymore. Told me she was scared sometimes."

"She tried to tell me that too," Harry admitted. "My heart wasn't open to her words. I gave her some speech about a wife submitting to her husband like it reads in the Bible."

Kora jumped when Harry banged his fist several times against the steering wheel.

"Why didn't I listen to her, Billie? I could have stopped it!"

"She was stubborn. We both know that." Billie looked away and wiped her cheek. "It wakes me up at night sometimes."

"Me and Mable was so happy about the baby. I patted myself on the back, congratulating myself for my wonderful, fatherly advice saving her marriage." Harry's voice cracked. "I should have known to save her life and my grandbaby's." He stopped talking.

Billie said, "I should've made her explain what she meant by being scared. I just assumed she had it all figured out, like she always did. I never saw her again. Before she left, I asked if she had any marriage advice for me and Nick as newlyweds. She gave the strangest answer. I feel like I'll say it wrong, but it was something like 'When a man truly loves a woman she becomes his weakness, and when a woman truly loves a man he becomes her strength.' It breaks my heart she didn't believe in her own strength."

More silence followed.

Kora couldn't help herself. She guessed she startled them with her voice. "I think it was Abigail Adams who said, 'Do not put such unlimited power into the hands of husbands. Remember all men would be tyrants if they could.'"

Harry's eyes flashed in the rear-view mirror just as Billie turned around.

"Kora, you've been so quiet back there. I thought you'd gone to sleep."

Feeling like something should be acknowledged, she softly said, "Mr. Stillman, I mean Harry, I'm so sorry for your loss."

Harry nodded, like maybe that was all he could do.

"The wrong side of power can be terrifying," Kora said to the window.

Billie looked at Kora like she was seeing her for the first time. Studying her. Then she turned back to Harry and asked, "Are we almost there?"

"That's the field up ahead."

Soldiers stopped the vehicle and checked all three of their badges. Harry was allowed in and drove over a bridge. After they cleared the water, a huge crater came into view. Kora shielded her eyes, trying to make out the opposite edge of the bowl in the horizon.

"Is this really man-made?"

"It ain't from a meteorite. Dug by America's finest."

Harry parked and led them to what looked like a shack with a single large window on one side. The air smelled fertile. Kora could almost taste the earthiness in the back of her throat. The shack was perched high on the rim of the huge crater, so she could see most of it from the window. Near the center of the hole were several menacing Bofors guns, their swiveling bases firmly grounded and their long barrels pointed at the sky.

Harry made them wear protective gear for their ears and eyes. They would observe every Quality Control test that evening, recording all successful target metrics reached. If this ammunition batch passed, it would be loaded on a train by midnight, on its way to war within twenty-four hours after assembly.

Harry passed them both a clipboard and pencil, showing them where to write in each number they counted. If they disagreed on a number, his count would act as the tiebreaker. The huge headphones and goggles made Kora's head feel heavy, but the rest of her felt exhilarated. James would be busting his buttons to see her now.

Harry asked for two thumbs up. They obliged, then he turned to face the large window, raising his own thumbs high in the air. Kora noticed a second group of military men much farther away, operating several target launchers. The first clay disk was launched high in the sky and the first of the Bofors guns aimed in the disk's direction. Four shells left the barrel and chased each other through the air on their way to destroy the target. Shell number four traced a path of light and smoke through the dusky sky. Kora swelled with pride, witnessing her tracers perform so well.

The explosions rang through Kora's body. Billie must have felt it too, because their wide eyes met. It was surprisingly intense, despite the sound protection they wore—she couldn't imagine how loud these must be for a young soldier hiding inside a ground hole, or teetering near the edge of a huge ship. The smell of acrid smoke reached them in the shack. Almost forgetting to record her number, she refocused on her task.

The rest of the evening flew by. Comparing three sets of numbers, Billie and Kora matched up most of the time, surprising them both to have something in common besides Maggie.

Harry left the shack to turn in their results. Alone with Billie, Kora searched for something to say. Should she acknowledge Katy's sad story?

"Where'd you hear that Abigail Adams quote?" asked Billie.

Kora exhaled, relieved to hear words break through the silence. "My mama had a book on famous first ladies."

"That's funny," she chuckled. "My mama had a soft spot for Mary Todd Lincoln. She had a saying that went something like, 'I would rather marry a good man, a man of mind, with hope and bright prospects ...'" Billie seemed to grapple with the rest.

"... than to marry all the houses, gold, and bones in the world." Kora finished the quote.

Billie smiled, almost like they'd turned a corner.

Harry burst back into the room, holding the door open to signal their exit. "That's that, ladies. This batch will go to war. Let's go home."

They followed him, walking shoulder-to-shoulder to the car. Kora wondered if Billie would give her a turn in the front seat on the way home. Kora was closest to the front car door and Billie to the back, but Kora hesitated a second too long. Billie opened the back door and stepped aside, clearly expecting Kora to resume her spot. Kora swallowed the pain down and slid clear across the wide vinyl seat, as far as she could from Billie's front seat perch. She resigned herself, again, to the way things were. The way they'd always been. When would she learn?

As headlights traced their way back to Charlotte, Harry and Billie picked up their path down memory lane, forgetting her presence again. It was dark, and this morning's drizzle had returned.

As they were about to pass the same oak, this time Kora kept her eyes tightly shut. Knowledge is not always power. You can't fear or miss something that you never knew was there.

Chapter 20

APRIL, 1944
MAGGIE

Maggie had to admit that things were getting better. Her girls were adjusting well to her being at work. The other day she'd overheard them bragging to a friend about their mom's job. Maggie had good friends and a community again. She looked forward to seeing the "Rosie" picture show, with all of them together, including Kora's friends from Brooklyn. She expected a few heads to turn at the theater, but they could handle it.

She was also proud of her part in the E Award, though she hadn't heard a peep from Leland since the inspection. Until now. She was on her way to his office, after being called in. Maybe he wanted to thank her for her a job well done.

Mrs. Sexton looked up when she entered, then toward his closed door. "Please take a seat. He'll be out shortly."

Maggie tried to decipher the muffled tones on the other side of the door. She heard at least one other voice besides his.

The door opened and he ushered her inside. "Maggie Slone, meet Lieutenant Owens."

Accepting the woman's extended hand, her almost aggressive grip took Maggie by surprise. The Lieutenant was older, standing tall and proud in a crisp naval uniform. Though the lieutenant was military fit and makeup free, Maggie noticed deep lines between her brows and not a few gray hairs flash under her too-starched hat. She was one of those WAVES. Maggie couldn't remember what the acronym stood for, but it was something about women volunteers for the Navy.

They all sat. Maggie was still waiting for an explanation.

"I haven't seen you since the inspection, Maggie. I trust you were pleased with the outcome?" Leland asked.

"Yes. It was wonderful news," Maggie replied.

"It was. But now that we've got it, this distinction is ours to lose. If we remain accident-free, they'll add a star to our banner every six months." Leland stopped for effect, she assumed, knitting his hands together. "I want that star, Maggie. And the next one. I know you do too."

He motioned a hand toward their new table guest. "That's why I brought Renata here. Sorry ... Lieutenant Owens. We've worked together before. I'll let her explain her own impressive history with the Navy, but you should know that she started during the Great War."

Maggie looked at Owens, expecting her to chime in, but she kept her gaze on Leland, all business.

Leland continued. "Two hundred more men are leaving here for overseas assignments, many of them supervisors. No choice but to replace them with women. Lieutenant Owens understands how to train women as supervisors. She's done it for years."

Maggie nodded, wondering when anyone else might get a turn to speak.

"What about it, Maggie? You seem to have a good rapport with your line and the other supervisors. The title comes with money and responsibility. Supervisors get more of both."

Supervisor? They were promoting *her* to supervisor. She'd never considered the possibility. Though flattered, she feared taking any more time away from the girls.

They were waiting for an answer. "I appreciate the consideration. I really do, but I'd like time to think about it."

Her words produced an almost imperceptible response from Owens. Was that a *humph*?

"What is there to think about?" Leland asked blankly.

Says the man with no children—not even a dog to care for outside of himself. Instead of saying *that* out loud, she said, "I'm simply asking for one day to discuss it with my family. They keep my girls before and after school. I don't want to assume they can do more without asking."

"If you say so. Take your day." He closed a few file folders and set them aside. "In the meantime, I'd like you to ride with Lieutenant Owens to Wateree Pond today. Show her the testing grounds."

Owens faced Maggie after abruptly standing in her smart, one-inch heels. "I'll pick you up at fifteen hundred hours in front of the Change House." After exchanging salutes with Leland, she left the room.

Maggie excused herself too, then pivoted before reaching the door. "Which line would I supervise?"

"Not the one you work on now."

"Why?"

"Because it's hard enough to make the switch from line worker to supervisor. It's too messy to manage former peers."

Losing her line community was unacceptable. She couldn't bear it, so she came up with another play.

"I know I can make it work, Leland. I've never shied away from messy situations." That was a direct hit, and she knew it. Messy was the word he'd used several times before he broke up with her, in trying to defend his decision. Maggie normally wouldn't go so low, but this was important.

His gaze traveled from her head to her shoes and back again, making her a bit uncomfortable. Was that the point or did he think she couldn't track his roaming eyes? He finally spoke. "Will you accept the promotion today if I assign you to the same line?"

She held his gaze. Always the negotiator—her weakness was his angle. "Yes," she agreed, knowing she could use the new daycare center occasionally if she needed. She heard it was not bad.

"Then I'll allow it. But don't say I didn't warn you," he said.

"I'd never say that."

And she meant it.

The Change House was appropriately named. Women changed from baby-stained dresses into factory coveralls and back again after their shift was over. Their minds switched gears too, from bread bakers to breadwinners. Round-the-clock shifts—at seven, three, and eleven—brought high tides of chattering crowds of women, followed by low tides of emptiness and quiet.

During one of those quieter periods, Maggie changed alone, out of her coveralls and back into her dress, like she always did. She hurried to get ready to ride down to Wateree Pond with Lieutenant Owens, her new boss.

A sound at the door caught Maggie's attention. Firm, confident steps approached her section of lockers. She tried jerking the dress over her head in time, but it got stuck. Her head was barely out when Owens rounded the corner.

"What are you doing?"

"Changing clothes after my shift." She'd grown used to changing in front of strangers over the last year, but this woman made her feel exposed all over again.

"Put your uniform back on. We don't go to testing grounds in dresses. And pin your hair back before we leave." She turned to reveal the tight bun at the nape of her long neck. "Like this. I'll be waiting outside."

Maggie sighed. This was not off to the best start. She put her dirty uniform back on and wrestled her hair into place. She couldn't see the bun, but crossed her fingers it was up to this woman's standards. She wished she had a friend to ask, but they were all on the bus heading home.

Missing her girls, Maggie had called Grace earlier to let her know she wouldn't be home to take them to their second cotillion class. They'd broken her heart last week looking so grown up during their first class. How could they be nine? Halfway to college!

Thoughts of Charlie crept in. Ending this war would bring him home, so she promised her reflection to be a quick study with Lieutenant Owens. She pushed on the exit door, letting in the afternoon sun. Shielding her eyes, she found the Jeep idling near a curb. This was a long trip to take in a loud, windy military vehicle.

She took her seat quickly, with a smile to the driver, then changed her mind about the Jeep. With that stern face looking back at her, she was grateful for any noisy distraction.

They bumped along on gravel until finally hitting pavement and picked up speed. Without doors to hold onto, Maggie grabbed the roll bar and the side of her seat. Like hummingbird wings, the canvas roof cover beat against the steel frame, but as strong as the wind was, it could not touch her hair pinned so tightly back. Perhaps she'd solved the mystery of why WAVES often wore these practical buns.

Maggie knew the most direct route was York Road. She watched Owens choose a different way. "I think you just missed the turn," she offered as loudly as she dared.

"I what?"

"That was the turn back there." Maggie pointed.

"Not our turn," she said, eyes forward. "I've mapped a faster course for us. We're taking the back roads."

Wonderful, thought Maggie. Now she could add dust to the list of elements to endure on this ride. Not to mention awkward conversation, she chuckled.

"What's funny?" Owens asked, surprisingly perceptive.

"Nothing," Maggie said with a quick shake of her bun.

They followed a maze of dirt roads. Maggie was so turned around, they could be headed to Georgia for all she knew. She looked over to see surprisingly long fingernails flank the steering wheel, thumbs tapping to a silent but consistent rhythm hinting at a tune running through the lieutenant's head.

Lost in thought or musical notes, the driver initiated no dialogue, so Maggie took the opportunity to figure out what was expected of her this evening. Should Maggie explain what she knew so far about the testing grounds, or was she expected to learn from this woman and stay quiet?

The silence was driving her insane. "What other plants have you worked in?" Maggie asked with loud, slow words.

Owens leaned in to answer. "Mostly Pennsylvania and several throughout the Midwest. I worked with Commander Martin at a steel shipyard in California on my last assignment."

"*Commander Martin*" echoed in Maggie's head. She'd be sure to always call him that around this woman. She tried to place her accent or lack thereof. "That's a lot of places. Where are you originally from?"

"Everywhere," she shouted. "Preacher's kid. Never stayed one place very long."

More miles passed in silence until the guard house mercifully appeared in the distance. She pointed out where to turn and park, but Owens ignored her. Instead, she stopped the Jeep way too close to the rim of the huge ground hole where testing took place. "How do I get down there?" she asked.

"I have no idea." Maggie pointed out the shack with the big window. "Normally we go in there to watch the testing and make our reports."

Owens craned her neck over the steering wheel. "No," she said, almost to herself as she stomped on the clutch. "I'm going down there with the men."

Owens seized the gear shift column, throwing them into reverse and completing a tight, three-point turn. They wound around the top of the steep rim. Maggie worried about getting in trouble, or worse, driving off the rim, but she stayed quiet. This woman was on some sort of personal mission. Maggie's knuckles were white as they rocked down the steep incline. Eventually, a path emerged, and they followed it down until more parked Jeeps came into view.

Maggie got out of the vehicle to walk a few paces behind Owens as she approached the group of military personnel, breaking up their circle.

"At ease," Owens ordered.

Maggie was confused because not one of them had saluted, but then she watched the men squint at the emblems on this woman lieutenant's sleeve compared to their own. Only then did a few salute—begrudgingly—if Maggie had to guess. Maggie's nervousness turned to fascination. *How will this all play out?*

Owens continued, "We're here to record the results of your testing tonight, but we need to understand your process first. Who would like to show us that?"

"This area doesn't allow women," one man protested.

"It does now," Owens replied.

The men, boys really, glanced at each other. Four of them melted away, leaving two men standing like islands.

"Let's get started," she said.

Owens, Maggie, and the two reluctant volunteers migrated over to the disk launchers.

The men showed them how one person fired the disk launcher at random angles within a certain range, while another soldier about fifty yards away watched to see if the disk was hit. The watcher then looked for the all-clear signal to know the next gunner was ready to fire. Using multiple launchers and guns allowed them to test more rounds in less time. The watchers had the especially important task of making sure one gunner at a time knew when he was "on deck" to fire his respective Bofors gun.

"This minimizes the risk of shooting each other or another person in the hole."

Owens challenged them. "Has that ever happened?"

The men looked at each other and shrugged, silently agreeing to reveal more. "Let's just say it's a rule born out of necessity," one said with a smirk.

"Some might even say experience," the other said.

"I see. So where is your second disk-launcher location?"

"This is the only spot for launching the disks."

Her eyebrows knit together. "You are aware that an enemy plane can come from any direction, correct? They don't always fly in from the right. Your setup neutralizes the element of surprise."

Maggie no longer knew where to look, so she chose the ground. This woman spoke with such conviction her ear had to adjust to it. She imagined the same for the others. When she looked back up, their whole demeanor had changed. Owens pointed to the other side of the hole where a second spot would be ideal for another set of launchers. The men—it appeared, at least—were actually listening.

Owens explained, "The test gunner on deck should not know from what direction these disks will fly. I like the idea of multiple launchers and gunners to minimize loading time, but they need to come from at least two unknown directions. Maybe three. Where are your handie-talkies?"

"We tried using those," one answered. "They aren't reliable at this distance. We use hand signals instead." As if on cue, the other soldier made a signal with his hand. This gained the attention of another man who began walking over.

"I'll have Commander Martin order longer-range talkies," Owens said. "All watchers need to be able to communicate freely while keeping the test gunner's target direction unknown. Any other way puts our boys at risk."

"I guess that makes sense," the soldier replied.

The third man finally appeared in response to the signal. He looked taller, broader, and meaner than the other two. "Can I help you, ladies?"

Oh boy, thought Maggie.

Chin lifted, Owens locked eyes and addressed this new military personnel. "There's room for improvement in your testing process. I'll be communicating my observations to Commander Martin in the morning. I was just giving these men a heads-up on my reasoning."

"And who are you, again?"

"Lieutenant Owens. This is my first visit here, but I couldn't begin to count the number of war production test sites I have observed across our nation."

"I don't care how many sites you've seen, I do not take orders from women." He pointed up toward the small observation building. "You ladies belong safely up there. Not down here."

Maggie jumped at the chance to escape. "We were just on our way there," she blurted out.

"Maggie, please wait for me in the Jeep," a stoic Lieutenant Owens ordered.

Maggie started to leave, then turned back. "Thank you ..." her voice trailed off as her mind ran through the possibilities to end her last sentence: sirs? officers? gentlemen? She gave up and headed for the Jeep.

Silently willing her new boss to follow, she hoped they weren't in trouble. Looking back, she found Owens striding not far behind. What a crazy beginning to Maggie's first day as supervisor. Owens intimidated her, but she was impressed—close to envious—with her steely resolve.

Settled into the passenger seat, Maggie watched the approaching Lieutenant's confident steps, the very ground yielding to her determined heels.

※ ※ ※

Lieutenant Owens had promised a tough first week and didn't disappoint. Maggie's training included critiques on everything from poor posture to the sound of her voice, from clothing to hairdo choices.

"You will work twice as hard to get half the credit," Owens explained more than once. "If men catch a scent of the weakness they constantly assume, you will lose."

Maggie had much to learn, according to Owens. Every answer she gave was used as an example for the others—what not to think, say, or do. Her favorite pearl from Owens so far had to be this:

"Your new role will often place you as the only woman in the room. Your job is to make them forget you are different. Ignore crude comments. Let them bounce off you. Laugh at any and all jokes, but, more importantly, laugh at yourself. This puts them at ease, gives them permission to treat you like one of their own."

Maggie's instincts were turned inside out. Owens saw exactly two colors—black and white—where Maggie saw all shades of gray. Still, she respected the success Owens claimed, and did exactly as told.

The lessons accelerated as the flag ceremony for the E Award approached. Community and military leaders would parade through the grounds that day, hoisting the proud plant's "E" banner atop a flagpole.

Their next visit to the testing grounds was full of respectful salutes for Owens and anyone with her. Maggie wondered if part of those attitude adjustments had come from Leland. She hadn't seen him long enough to ask, but now headed to his office. Aware this was becoming a bad habit, she would make this visit quick.

"Knock, knock."

Looking weary, he still smiled to see her. "Now this is a nice surprise."

"Are you all right? You look tired."

"I'll be much better after tomorrow," he said. "I'd never let a little thing like sleep get in the way." He squeezed a thumb and forefinger across each eye, then blinked back the tiredness. "These are important people coming. They want to use our plant as a model across the country."

"That's a good thing."

"A blessing and a curse."

"Now for another important question," she said, lowering her voice. "I think I've reached my dumb question limit with Owens, but I haven't a clue what a civilian supervisor should wear to this big event. My coveralls, a dress, a suit?"

"You'd look ridiculous in a suit." He shook his head. "I can't see it."

"I don't exactly look distinguished in coveralls either."

"Why don't you ask Owens?"

"I just told you why. She's not the easiest person to talk to."

"But that's why I brought her here. She's very experienced navigating these waters. As a woman, I mean."

Maggie's curiosity got the best of her. "Did you make the changes she suggested to the testing site?"

"Yes, after wading through some tough-guy talk about insubordination. But we all knew she was right. This is not her first rodeo. You'd do well to follow her lead."

"We're … different."

Leland stifled a small yawn. "The Navy's not too keen on different, in case you hadn't noticed."

"Touché," Maggie answered, then paused. "I think I'll compromise with a navy-blue dress."

"Sounds like a good plan."

"And I'll try and melt into the background like she taught me."

Leland leaned over, looking at her feet. "Your sarcasm is dripping all over my nice clean floor."

She laughed at his joke. Owens would be proud.

Leland continued. "In all seriousness, as a woman—much less a supervisor—you shouldn't be so quick to stand out. Or perhaps, you want to give this speech instead of me?"

"I'd rather be boiled in oil."

"I remember that."

"I'll leave you to your speech writing, then. Better you than me. Plus, you always pull it off." She got up to leave but turned back. "You really should get some rest."

"Are you worried about me?"

"Maybe," she said with an almost imperceptible nod, and left.

✳ ✳ ✳

"You're late," Owens barked the next morning. Maggie hustled to join the procession of female supervisors.

"I'm sorry. My daughter had a slight fever," Maggie said to Owens' back, imagining her eyes lifting toward the open sky.

"Children are a distraction. One I wouldn't encourage any of you to pursue, but I guess it's too late for Slone here."

Like rows of ducks, about twenty of them followed their trainer to the front grounds. A few offered a sympathetic glance, careful not to let Owens catch it. The younger girls were sweet but made Maggie feel old. The older ones had grown children and tough skin, less sympathetic to any of Maggie's childcare woes.

Assigned to different buildings, this group was only together under the lieutenant's watchful eye. No time for socializing. Maggie knew their last names, but only because she had heard Owens grumble them so often.

As they reached their destination, hundreds of folding chairs, set in a wide circle of rows, came into view. A naked flagpole stood at the center of the circle. The chairs would seat the VIPs, while several thousand employees would stand behind them, forming an outer circle.

It had rained for days, but today the sun shone against a brilliant Carolina blue sky. Maggie was annoyed at her heels digging into the soft ground. This was never an issue with her steel-toed boots.

Owens clipped off reminders. "Don't speak unless spoken to. Stand up when I do, clap when I clap." Bouncing hair buns relayed their understanding.

Owens led them down the center aisle of the chairs, choosing a middle row for them to sit. Maggie scanned the sizable crowd, relieved to find her friends standing together not far away.

Ruby clapped her hands together silently when she caught Maggie's attention, making a show of her finger running up the back of her leg. Maggie flashed a quick smile, shaking her head to answer no, she had not painted her seams today. The embarrassment of leg paint rubbing off on her blue dress or seat was motivation to risk a run in her last pair of nylons. Ruby's gift was genius, but Maggie felt more genuine in the real thing—and less exposed.

A warm breeze hinted at spring while the crowds filled in quickly. Leland stood and marched up four small steps to the platform, joining several seated men with stern, gray profiles. *Not Leland*, she corrected herself, *Commander Martin* was taking the stage.

What seemed like a million years ago, Charlie had had to give a speech at work. Maggie had helped him prepare and enjoyed critiquing him safely from their couch. Charlie was a good man, but not a great speaker. He was who they all turned to for answers, but inspiring a huge audience was different. It was impossible not to compare them both now.

"Commander" was an appropriate title for Leland. His presence commanded attention, but he also appeared relaxed, like he had just stopped to tell you a funny story in the hallway. He was incredibly good on stage. It wasn't just his words, but his voice—the deep tone balanced between gratefulness for their hard work and inspiring challenge for the phases ahead. A continued flawless safety record for the next six months would add a star to the flag they were about to raise. That was their next carrot to chase.

It felt like he was talking directly to her, but when she looked around, she thought others probably felt the same. When his speech ended, she applauded like everyone else and heard several shouts of "Hear! Hear!" to accept the commander's challenge.

It was time for the flag raising. As Maggie finally laid eyes on the famous "E" banner, she almost laughed out loud. So much pomp and circumstance around a bit of cloth. Responding to Leland's order, a long chain of uniformed men paraded down the aisle until reaching the pole base. Three flags were added to the metal chain, then the crew ceremoniously synchronized their pulls, sending them high.

In silent reverence, every eye followed Old Glory up first, followed by another banner Maggie didn't recognize. Loud cheers erupted. The unassuming pennant was divided in two, the red half on the left held bold white capital letters spelling ARMY, the blue half boasted its own white letters for NAVY. Dead center of the banner was a prominent letter "E" nestled inside a peace wreath.

The blank spaces on either side of the banner held the potential to earn a new star in six short months.

Maggie caught the flash of a newspaper camera. On stage, Leland and the other men posed—humble pride displayed on stoic faces. Thousands of people shared the field, happy to be celebrating any victory.

A receiving line of sorts formed as the VIPs gathered at the base of the stage. Owens grabbed Maggie's elbow, steering her right for them. Leland made formal introductions. He used Maggie and Owens as rare examples of talent left to run the plant. He also highlighted his own success despite the wartime labor challenges. His audience seemed impressed.

"I hear that story all over, Commander Martin." The tallest one adjusted his hat. "These are desperate times finding skilled workers."

Another one, a portly fellow, focused in on Maggie. "Where is your husband?"

"Fighting overseas, sir."

"Does he know you have been promoted to supervisor?" he asked, like he was speaking to a child.

"I mentioned it in my last letter, but there's a lot more to share about our two children."

"So, you're a mother too," he said, even more interested. "Where do you put your children while you work?"

Maggie ignored his strange choice of words. She rattled off the details of her situation, careful to add the benefits of on-site daycare for other women who weren't as lucky to have nearby family.

Owens interrupted her. "We should get back to work." She turned to the distinguished group adding, "We appreciate your time, helping us celebrate this achievement."

"I say, this should be old hat to you by now, Owens. What's this? Your fourth pennant?" The portly one motioned toward Leland. "Not sure how Commander Martin lured you from sunny California," he finished with an elbow poke in Leland's side.

"Leaves a mind to wildly speculate," another one added.

His lewd smirk turned Maggie's stomach.

She searched the circle of faces for any hint of disapproval in the tackiness these men displayed. Owens and Leland offered only wide smiles. *How could they stand it?* Seeking a quick subject change, she blurted out, "I'm curious. What does the second banner signify?" pointing to the three flags above their heads. She remembered learning something about it in training, but honestly couldn't recall.

A deep round of chuckles rippled through the group, leaving Maggie to wonder what was so funny. A man whose sleeve cuff displayed four gold stripes—one more than Leland's—spoke. "Ah, there's the weaker female mind. Don't see these issues in DC. Maybe someday you can join us there, Martin."

Owens took a half-step toward Maggie. "That flag means we're an official wartime production facility. Just like you learned in training." She turned back to the group. "We have already taken up too much of your valuable time. Thank you, gentleman."

Reclaiming Maggie's elbow, harder than before, Owens steered them safely away. Or maybe she had been safer back there, since Owens did not look pleased. Signaling for the others to round up, Owens walked a few paces slower holding Maggie back from the rest.

"I've been doing this a long time, you know," she said in a lower, more strained voice than normal. Unsure if she was being asked a question or even allowed to speak, Maggie kept quiet. "13,000 women, including me, joined the armed forces during the Great War. We were barely tolerated, allowed only jobs men didn't want. As soon as that war ended, I was out on my ear. I won't let that happen again."

Owens paused, perhaps to let it sink in. "This time, over 300,000 women have been allowed to serve. That doesn't even include civilians like *you*." Her mouth formed the last word like it tasted bad.

She continued, "Men make the rules. They decide who stays and who goes. There's an art to playing within their range of expectations. Do a good job, but not one that threatens their position or skill. The single focus of the military is to blend the masses into one efficient machine. Success is achieved only when the individual disappears—into the same uniform, same language, same haircut, daily routine, you name it. As women, we already throw a wrench into their military machine, so we can't draw more attention to ourselves, to our differences. And always, *always* be aware of the chain of command. That's the rule you broke over there."

"I asked an innocent question," Maggie said, her mouth dry.

"To the wrong audience. Drawing too much attention to yourself and to me. You made them question *my* skills to train you to know the answers. Get it?"

Maggie spoke slowly. "So, by asking that question, I made you and Commander Martin look bad in front of the VIPs."

"Yes. In fact, any time you ask a question in front of a man, you are vulnerable, but the situation back there was extreme."

"I understand now," Maggie said. "It won't happen again."

"And, when any joke is made, no matter how bad or wrong it is, you laugh. Even better if you're the butt of the joke, because your laughter proves you aren't different."

Owens stopped, facing Maggie to emphasize her last point. "It proves you belong as one of the boys." Then she spun on her heel, leaving Maggie behind.

One of the *boys*? The last word echoed. She glanced down at her carefully chosen navy dress, smoothed out a wrinkle, checked her stockings for runs, then it bubbled up. Her giggle grew to a laugh. She clamped a hand over her mouth as the next group passed, giving her strange looks.

Maggie wanted to be a good supervisor. She felt that now, surprising even herself. The path to success, according to her new boss, was to mirror a man. That felt like an impossible goal. Wearing a pretty smile, she started walking again to join the others. There had to be another way.

She made up her mind to find her own path.

Chapter 21

APRIL, 1944
MAGGIE

The doorbell rang once, freezing the girls in place. This was the time of day Mr. Fredricks usually made his mail rounds. It rang a second time and the girls raced to the door.

"Well, that might be a world record," Mr. Fredricks said, laughing as he closed the flap over his massive mail bag.

"Is there a letter from Daddy?" Demi asked.

"Of course, there is! You know what that double ring means." Mr. Fredricks descended the porch steps as Daisy and Demi stood on tiptoes to fish the mail out of the brass box. "You ladies enjoy the letter from your soldier." He tipped his navy-colored hat to Maggie.

"Thank you, Mr. Fredricks," Maggie said.

The three of them carried the mail stack back to the kitchen table.

"Hurry, Mama," Daisy said.

"It's just one this time," Demi said, and Maggie could tell she was still excited but a little disappointed. Lately, mail from Charlie came in bunches. Maggie opened the letter fast and sat down next to the girls to read it.

Dearest Maggie, Daisy, and Demi,

I'm coming off a long day of setting up, so if my words aren't quite right, I'll lay the blame there. Tonight, I closed out our meeting with the clever joke from your last letter. Keep 'em coming, because they really lift our spirits! I would return the favor, but the ones my men tell are not for little ears.

Our company has moved twice since my last letter, but I couldn't let another day pass without writing. This new spot plays tricks on the mind. Or maybe it's the heat. If not for the hundreds of loud, snoring men, I might think this the most romantic spot ever. In a different time, you would love it, Maggie. We landed on a sunny, yellow beach covered in wildflowers like I've never seen. Fighting in the middle of such beauty feels surreal. No, it feels unnatural.

Maggie, congratulations on your promotion at the plant! I still wish you didn't have to work, but I'd take bets you'll be running the place before long. Mom writes me about the enormous help she has become for the three of you. It's clear how much she loves her time with the girls. I think she secretly envied the busyness of a big family and she finally has that with the twins.

Did I mention the heat here? Too hot in my tent, so I (and my trusty flashlight) write you this letter under a canopy of more stars than I thought possible. Tomorrow, I'll be one day closer to being home with my family under a Carolina blue sky. Tonight, I will pick out the brightest star and watch it for as long as I can, knowing it will be shining on my girls a few hours later. I will send with it a thousand good wishes.

Be sweet as sugar to Mama, girls, with lots of extra hugs and kisses, like we said. See you in the stars ...

Love,
Daddy

The girls started bouncing in their kitchen chairs. "Can we watch the stars tonight, Mama? Then we can send him a letter right back with a list of our own wishes for Daddy. Like an interstellar game!"

"Wow, that's a five-dollar word, Dem," Maggie said. "Who taught you that?"

"Miss Smithwell … I mean, *Mizz* Smithwell."

"Of course. Your teacher." Maggie pictured the middle-aged woman—quirky was the kindest term that came to mind—and her insistence on the unique pronunciation of her salutation.

"Let's watch the stars tomorrow night. Tonight, Mama is going to see a movie about Rosie the Riveter." The girls start rolling their tongues to mimic the song, making her giggle. "Yes, that Rosie."

"We want to see another movie. Can we come?"

"We'll go another night. The ladies I work with are watching Rosie together. Sally is coming to sit with you two. Remember? You like Sally."

"But we miss you."

Their sad faces made her heart sink. She hated disappointing them. She considered canceling her plans and staying home, but she had made a commitment to Kora and the others. "I promise to make it up to you on Sunday if the weather cooperates. We can set up under the stars, just like Daddy."

The girls cheered, right as the telephone sounded. Maggie made it to the hallway by the third ring, and Billie was on the other end.

Later that evening, after cutting her headlights, Maggie sat behind the wheel a few minutes longer, under the cover of twilight. Patrons, dressed to the nines, strolled in and out of the Grand, hardly noticing her. Laughter radiated from two ladies crossing the theater's parking lot, just in front of Maggie's car. Their gentleman companion offered an arm to each, looking like he had swallowed the canary.

She tried to push down the guilt she'd felt the whole ride over. Leaving the girls with a sitter—their favorite—was not the issue this time. The girls had been excited when the sitter arrived, but on her way out the door, Maggie had overheard Daisy ask her, "Will you check my homework? Sometimes Mama gets too busy to be a mama."

Maggie sighed, longing for the days when her only job was motherhood. She'd been good at that job, before getting pulled in so many different directions. She vowed to make it up to the girls tomorrow. Tonight was for Kora.

Sadly, Maggie's level of commitment seemed to allude Billie, Ruby and Deborah, because their plan to watch their wartime roles play out on the silver screen—all together—had quickly fallen apart. Maggie ran through their flimsy, last-minute excuses. She had felt their anxiety through the telephone. Maybe they were right.

Gripping the wheel, Maggie silently debated. Her strength in numbers plan had boiled down to a solo act. Did she have other things to do? Yes. Was she crazy for coming to the Grand by herself? Yes again, but turning back now felt like letting Kora down.

She walked around the side of the brick, two-story building, sturdy but modest except for one eye-catching feature. Reaching the front entrance, Maggie guessed the builder might have blown his entire budget right here. A beautiful, brick arch framed an elaborate metal door, polished to the point it appeared fictional, like the gateway to Oz.

She started to tug on the twisted black iron handle, but it opened for her, by a man who froze when he saw her standing on the other side. She wasn't sure what to say. Wanting to relax his shocked expression, she offered her most reassuring smile like she did this every day. Excusing herself to pass through, she felt his confused stare linger on her back.

Inside, she caught more curious stares every way she turned. Maggie tried to keep a relaxed smile plastered to her face, one that said she went to colored film houses all the time. She searched the crowd for Kora, relieved to find her waiting near the ticket table.

"Your hair looks good," Kora said once they were in the ticket line. "Nice to see it down."

Maggie gave a shy smile and smoothed her bun-free hair, loose around her neck.

"The others on their way?" Kora asked.

"They aren't coming." Maggie said, relaying their excuses.

"Things do come up." Kora didn't sound convinced either.

As the line shortened, Maggie felt a little panicky, but kept it to herself. Surely they would they sell her a ticket. When she imagined the opposite, she felt her face get red with embarrassment, but there was no turning back now.

It was a packed house tonight. The woman at the counter was head down, focused on trading tickets for coins. As the couple in front of them cleared out, Kora smiled and said, "One please."

Lifting her attention from the money drawer, the counter lady stopped on Maggie's face. As if taking inventory, she looked behind and around where Maggie stood holding her coin. Finally, she looked at Kora, who returned her gaze with the calmest expression, though her eyebrows raised slightly. "She'd like one too," Kora said, plucking Maggie's coin and handing it over to the woman.

Tickets in hand, Kora turned back to speak to Maggie while leading her through the crowd. "I saved seats for us inside. Called in a favor with a friend that works here."

"Sounds perfect." Maggie wished she felt her feigned enthusiasm, but if she was being honest, this was surreal at best. She should be used to feeling like a stranger, but here she was—circus-lady strange.

Reaching their seats, Kora said, "Ladies, you've seen Maggie from the plant. Maggie, these are my neighbors, my friends." Kora rattled off names Maggie tried to memorize. "Maggie works with tracers," Kora said to her left, then turned to Maggie. "They all work the new finishing and fuze lines. You know, the ones they just added."

Maggie knew what that meant. These ladies worked on one of the two, new, all-colored lines. Jaw aching from her permanent smile, Maggie kept eye contact through the rest of their small talk. How beautiful they were in bright head scarves and flowered dresses. She smoothed down her own plain skirt, wishing she'd chosen a brighter color.

"These are great seats." Maggie told a half-truth. The seats were front and center, but they were made of hard wood, not at all as comfortable as the Carolina Theatre.

"I brought a treat to share, y'all." From her satchel, Kora pulled a brown bag full of applesauce cookies. She handed one to Maggie on her right, then passed the bag to her left and watched it travel down the rest of the row. Kora's cooking was well-received as usual. Maggie took a bite and closed her eyes. The cookie was still a little warm and just sweet enough. How could Kora magically create the best-tasting food with half the normal ingredients?

The overhead lights dimmed, and the crowd started cheering for the start of the show. Maggie leaned through the dark and added, "I would love to learn how to make these."

Kora barely acknowledged her comment, focused instead on the dark-skinned, well-dressed gentleman passing them on his way down the aisle. He stopped and turned toward the full house. He raised his arms and looked up. As if on cue, a spotlight illuminated his presence and parts of the screen behind him.

"How's ever'body tonight? You ready to watch Hollywood's version of our wartime working women?"

"Yes!" answered the crowd, getting fired up for the show.

Maggie got a kick out of the audience enthusiasm, but she kept quiet.

"Before we start the show, we'd like to bring up our evening sponsor, Mr. Lester Givens, of Givens Automotive. *Please* show him your *respect* for bringing this first run movie to The Grand!"

While the audience applauded and cheered for Mr. Givens, Maggie leaned over and asked in Kora's ear, "Don't the tickets cover the cost?"

"Not all of it," Kora whispered back. "You don't have sponsors?"

Maggie shook her head.

"These sponsor businesses keep the price low for everyone," Kora explained.

Finishing his live car commercial, including an overacted "testimonial" from a "random" audience volunteer, Givens shook a few hands on the way to his seat. The extinguished spotlight signaled the film's start and the crowd buzzed through the dark.

The camera reel began to clack, barely lighting the faces around her. Maggie stole some quick left/right glances, confirming her face as the only pale one. Was this how Kora felt? For the first time, she questioned if she helped or hurt her friend by convincing Leland to place Kora, the only Black woman on their line.

The screen came alive in true movie magic. Trumpet sounds filled the room, announcing something special was about to start, and distracting Maggie from her musings.

Hollywood seemed to have few roles for women. Actresses had a choice of wife and mother, old servant, innocent girl, or maybe a temptress, if they were lucky. Maggie hoped this movie might be different. She laughed out loud as the plot unfolded. Cheers rose every time protective welding gear was removed to reveal long, flowing hair, expanding the definition of women's work.

Maggie searched, but didn't find, one brown or black face on screen, not like her experience passing through walkways at the plant. Hollywood had chosen to ignore the diversity born of wartime scarcity. She wondered how Kora and the others felt to be removed from this piece of history, when it likely wasn't the first or last time. She glanced left at Kora's perfect, stoic profile following the action on the massive screen, supposing she should remember to ask later.

Blinking from the lights that came from the intermission, the audience adjusted to the brightness. "I need to find a ladies' room," Maggie said.

Kora didn't, so she pointed in the direction of the powder room.

"Is that the one I'm allowed to use?" Maggie asked, not thinking her question through.

Kora froze.

Maggie's embarrassment burned, hot on her cheeks.

Kora slowly revealed the obvious, "There is only one ladies' room here."

Maggie could kick herself. Winding her way through the smoky, crowded lobby, she pushed open the powder room door and took a spot in line. The very charge of the air changed in this intimate space and she felt it physically. Her circus-lady status had returned.

Maggie studied a crack in the wall tile, like its lightning bolt shape was the most interesting thing she'd yet encountered. She breathed a little easier when the lively conversation slowly resumed around her. It was in such contrast to the polite quietness of a white ladies' room.

Finally protected by stall doors, Maggie relaxed, listening to the kindness and community circulating through a powder room, of all places. She giggled along with some of the funny comments.

She stopped short of releasing the lock when she heard a new group of women analyzing what strong wind or circumstances had blown a white woman through the doors tonight.

"Kora brung her," answered one.

"Now why don't that surprise me?" asked another, slapping the sink counter. "That girl's always building a bridge over something."

Maggie sat back down to listen.

"You know her white friends pay her more, that's why she got to keep 'em happy."

"Mmmmm hmmmm."

"Good for her if she gettin' more money. We should all go out and get ourselves a white friend." Hearty laughs exposed the impossible absurdity of this last comment, like they were on sale down at Ivey's.

"And we oughta do it before this war be over. Before everything go back the same."

"Yes, Lord. You know it will."

With the laughter and voices finally fading, Maggie slid the lock slowly to avoid making a sound. She kept her head turned down at the sink, avoiding others who might have overheard the same conversation she had. Her pocketbook was still sitting next to Kora in the theater. Otherwise, she might have gotten in her car right then. Maggie returned to her seat, her posture stick straight.

"Something wrong?" Kora asked immediately.

"Not at all," she clipped, with too much conviction in her voice.

Kora wasn't buying it, though she did hand over another cookie.

The second half of the movie started, sparing her from further explanation of her current mood. Maggie allowed the story splayed across the screen to distract her from sorting through her feelings. She followed the rest of the plot, disappointed to see the riveter plant scenes were just a backdrop for the same tired Hollywood formula.

She should have known.

❊ ❊ ❊

Kora accepted a ride home from Maggie, who wanted a private place to talk. It was dark and Maggie kept her eyes on the road, waiting for a good time to interject, as Kora chatted on about the show.

"Can I ask you a question?"

"Suit yourself," Kora said.

"Do you have to make excuses for being my friend?"

"To whom?"

"To anyone."

"Well, it's not a common sight. I do get questions about how my job came about, but mostly from folks who don't matter. I don't pay them any mind."

Maggie nodded.

"Do you get questions?" Kora asked.

"If I did, I would set them straight," Maggie said, wishing she'd kept her mouth shut. "But no. I don't get questions."

Kora crossed her arms. "That sounds about right. An assumed act of charity."

Maggie stayed quiet, knowing Kora was right, but this seemed to anger her more.

"I am *no* one's charity," Kora said.

Maggie pointed to her own chest. "*I* understand that."

Kora looked out the window a minute, then turned back. "I am not your pet-project and I don't need your help. I got by for thirty years without it."

Maggie was hurt. "I have *never* thought of you as a 'project.' Why are you saying these awful things to your friends? The ones I overheard in the ladies' room tonight." Maggie shared the whole story.

Kora listened, arms folding tighter, but her voice was steady when she finally spoke. "You can trust me when I say this: I do not talk about you to anyone, especially my neighbors. That fool in the bathroom made that story up. They're just trying to explain the unexplainable. Can you blame 'em?"

Maggie felt stung. "I thought you knew why we're friends."

"I thought I did too," Kora said, a little louder than before. "But you've changed. And it's not just me who's noticed. The other girls also." Kora's tone breached on accusatory. "You been acting different ever since your big promotion. As stark as your new hairdo."

"What? The hair bun? Kora, I don't *choose* how to wear my hair anymore. Owens tells me."

"It's not just the hair. We miss the old Maggie."

"I'm still her ... buried under all this pressure. Owens is unrelenting with us—the supervisors, I mean. Most days it's like I've up and joined the military." Maggie's frustration bubbled over. She was disappointing everyone. Tears started to spill down her cheeks.

"Maybe you should pull over," Kora said.

Maggie obliged, resting her forehead on the steering wheel in the now silent car. Before long, she felt Kora's hand cover hers. Maggie stared at their hands together. In the moonlight, she couldn't tell where one set of fingers ended and the other began.

Kora continued, but softer, "It's not easy for us to be friends, but that doesn't mean I'd choose any different."

Maggie sniffed, then smiled. "I thought about not coming tonight after the other girls canceled. I had these grand expectations of all our friends meeting and laughing together at that silly show. I thought it would give us something in common. Like a bridge to build on. I mean, we've all worked at the same place for almost a year. It shouldn't be so hard."

"You're right. It shouldn't."

"I'm glad I came tonight. I know better now." Maggie squeezed her hand. "How you might feel."

"So you and I've got something new in common now," Kora said squeezing back, before letting go. She chuckled. "I almost followed you to that bathroom, you know. I would have too, except for that last comment about which one was yours."

"That was not a proud moment," Maggie admitted. "Can you forgive me?" A car passed them on the driver's side. Maggie watched the lights play across Kora's profile.

After a moment, Kora nodded. "Yes. I can."

"Do you wish you worked one of the finishing lines with your friends?"

"Sometimes," Kora admitted. "But they created those lines after I had just gotten used to you and Ruby and Deborah. Even Billie." She swatted the air, adding, "So I'm staying put."

"Even if you have to suffer my hair bun?"

Kora shook her head and laughed. "That unfortunate bun." Maggie could tell she was teasing, but then Kora got more serious. "It's getting late. Unless there's anything else you need to talk about?"

For the first time, Maggie considered telling Kora about her complicated feelings around Leland and Charlie, none of which belonged inside a happily married woman. Her mouth opened to speak, but nothing fell out. How do you start a conversation like that? She smiled instead and turned the engine over. "No. Nothing else. Let's get you home."

Chapter 22

MAY, 1944
KORA

Nervous about her first safety-check duty, Kora ran through the steps again. Safety was top of mind for everyone who worked here, mostly borne from the basic instinct of self-preservation. It was almost a rubber stamp—several of the girls had called it a piece of cake—but these checks offered a safety net for the one bad apple who didn't care enough about his own life to follow the rules to the letter.

Someone had written "main cafeteria" next to Kora's name on the inspection schedule. She'd certainly spent enough time in that building, at least as a customer. Approaching now as an inspector, the building looked different to Kora. While nothing at the plant was built to last, the cinder blocks in the foundation looked sloppy, like they were stacked in a hurry on soft, tilled soil—too much cement squeezed between cracks—drips frozen in time. Not two years ago, this area was covered in fields of growing crops. Now, the same land was used for destruction in the form of 40 mm shells.

A clipboard hung in every building and held a checklist specific to the building purpose and layout. Kora found it hanging on the wall near the door, just like Maggie and the others had said. For every shift, the workers added their initials to the clipboard, then someone who did not work in that area came by daily to triple check the safety protocol.

Kora inspected the first item on her list, as the linoleum floor gleamed back at her. No wonder—it was constantly cleared for any gunpowder residue that might be clinging to thousands of insulated safety shoes. Kora bent for a closer look. Even the tiny cracks between the floor tiles looked clean. She checked it off the list.

With the clipboard resting on her hip, Kora went outside and walked around the building, glancing through the list to see what she might be looking for back there. Pulling the fence gate closed behind her, she stopped and stared at the "Service Entrance" sign. This would have been *her* door, had she accepted that first job offer at the plant. She looked down and sidestepped a canvas bag like it was a body.

A path was cleared between the fence gate and the back door. This area stored the waste from thousands of daily meals. The clipboard said food waste was stored in the pile of dark blue bags to the right of the aisle. Anything swept from the floors, potentially picking up explosive residue, was collected in the tan bags to the left. The two colors must stay apart, keeping at least ten feet between their combustible contents. Two duct tape lines on the ground marked the aisle.

Kora looked at the lines, then at her pen suspended over the check box, then back at the tape. Stepping back, she measured the distance between the two lines in her head. She crossed to the other side to make sure her eyes weren't playing tricks. The lines still looked too close together.

Appearing in the doorway, a man lifted a blue and tan bag in each hand. Spotting Kora, he appeared confused. His filthy shirt and apron made a valiant effort to cover a large belly, but lost their battle. Kora looked away, not wanting to stare. Heaving his bags onto the correct piles, he missed. Half of one bag fell outside the safety line altogether, but he made no move to fix it.

"Excuse me, do you have a tape measure?" she asked in a tone she hoped was both friendly and authoritative. He looked her up and down.

"What's it to you?"

Warning signals fired through her brain. "I'll just come back with one later if it's a problem."

He reached a greasy arm inside the door, his eyes never leaving her. It must have been hanging nearby, because the tape measure appeared in his hand. He passed it over reluctantly, with the tips of his fat fingers gripping the edge, avoiding any contact.

"These lines appear to be closer than ten feet," Kora explained as she unleashed the metal tail, hooked it to the ground, and walked backwards.

"That's a cause the piles are gettin' high." He drew up both hands to draw invisible quotation marks around the daily special. "It's 'meatloaf' day today and that always brings a crowd. And more of them bags."

Finishing her measurement and confirming her suspicion, Kora recorded the results. Looking down at his carelessly thrown bag straddling the tape, she kicked a tan bag over with her foot and saw the remnants of an older tape line that would have met the distance requirement. Someone had moved that tape. Glancing over at her monitor, now with his hands on hips, she finished up the rest of her tasks quickly.

She wondered if this man understood how these two piles of materials, if allowed to grow together, could ignite a fire. What was eaten and discarded into the trash containers by workers was virtually unknown. The chemical contents had to be kept separate just in case.

As she handed the tape measure back with an outstretched arm, he said, "I ain't never seen a Negro doing no safety checks. You sure you're supposed to be here?"

"That's what they tell me," she said. Inside her head, a warning echoed, *Leave now!*

"Well, I'll be checking up on that, Miss...," he leaned in to read her name badge then pronounced, "Kora." It was impossible not to lean away from his smell, despite her wanting to stand firm.

"It's Mrs.," she corrected him, pointing to her badge. She hated when whites assumed first name familiarity. "Mrs. Bell," she finished, then turned quickly toward the gate.

"I better not be seeing no bad report from you," she heard him say. Forcing herself to turn around, she found he was already facing the doorway and disappeared inside.

✻ ✻ ✻

After what felt like a thousand years, Kora finally saw Maggie come down the long hallway at her usual clip. Signaling her, they ducked into an empty office. Kora closed the door, took a deep breath, faced Maggie, and lifted the lid off her bottled-up questions.

"Okay supervisor, you told me how to run these safety checks, but what do I do when I find a violation? An intentional one. Who do I tell? What if they don't believe me?"

Maggie lightly held Kora's elbows. "Slow down. Tell me exactly what happened."

Starting from the beginning, she finished by showing Maggie her report. The top half contained the safety checklist, the bottom half was dedicated to the details surrounding any observed violations. Kora read that bottom section to Maggie, spelling out the blatant misconduct.

"That's so dangerous." Maggie shook her head. "And he didn't seem to care?"

"If he cared, he wouldn't have moved that tape line. He violated code 4328."

"Honestly, I've never seen the violation section filled out before. Where'd you find the code number?"

"I read all kinds of things around here," Kora said with a waved hand. "Never mind that. The question is will anyone believe *me*? That fool kept going on about how I'm the first Black woman he ever saw do a safety check. I got curious and asked the ladies working the colored lines. Turns out none of them ever been asked to do one of these inspections." She finished her sentence, holding her paper higher in the air between them. "They think maybe it's only for the white lines. Or mostly white, like ours."

Maggie thought a second, then admitted, "They might be right." She tapped an index finger to her lips, then let the hand fall. "What should we do?"

"Why are you asking me? *You're* the supervisor. You should turn in the report and see it through."

"Good. For a second there I thought you might want to rip up the report."

Kora offered her sternest look before saying, "That man is dangerous, and I want to survive this place."

Maggie studied the form. "There's a place for both of us to sign, as a team, so let me find a pen." She rifled around the desk drawer, pulling one out. Kora watched Maggie whisper every word on the page once more, all the way through. They signed it together.

"That's my very last safety check, okay? My nerves can't stand it," Kora said.

"Okay, no more checks for you." Maggie paused and wondered aloud, "Should I take this to Owens?" She shook her head, answering her own question. "No, I'll take it to Harry, as our foreman."

"Let me know how it goes."

The report tucked under her arm, Maggie opened the door wide to let Kora out too. They entered the hallway, heading in opposite directions. Kora turned around when Maggie called her name.

"You did the right thing," she said.

Kora tried to smile and did appreciate the sentiment, but wasn't feeling too righteous at the moment. "For all the good that does me," she replied and continued on.

Chapter 23

JUNE 18, 1944
MAGGIE

L ifting her foot off the gas, Maggie wiggled her throbbing toe, hoping it was only a bruise. She had stubbed it trying to find the ringing telephone, feeling her way through her dark hallway. The official-sounding voice on the other end—thank God it wasn't about Charlie—had told her that management only was to report to the plant as soon as possible.

It had taken her a while to wake the girls and get them to Grace's. She pictured their groggy waves as she backed down the driveway in the dark. Grace had stood next to them, wearing a look of "I told you so." Grace's words at that long-ago Sunday dinner repeated through her mind. *That plant is dangerous.*

Maggie slowed, as did the car ahead, when thick trails of black smoke came into view and dominated the dawning sky. Fire trucks were everywhere, some bearing names of towns she'd never heard of. Sawhorses blocked the main entrance and the now-threatened "E" banner waved as she drove past. For another mile, she followed the parade of red taillights to the south entrance, like she had been told, and found building 79. The manager meeting would take place as far as possible from the main cafeteria.

Maggie grabbed a spot next to some other female supervisors. The room was full and its line equipment was eerily silent. She spotted Leland, standing next to the fire chief, on the other side of the room. The fire chief looked up to say something to Leland, then surveyed the crowd, one hand absently running over his buzz cut. Deep lines carved across the chief's handsome forehead betrayed his nervousness. Maggie wondered if this might have been his first press conference.

A few reporters sat front and center, hands raised high. Leland and the chief took turns answering their questions.

The chief spoke with conviction. "The injured are receiving care at Memorial Hospital and Good Samaritan. Two workers and three firefighters. They are expected to recover."

"None reported missing, but we're still working through rosters at this time," Leland answered.

The chief added, "The plant's largest cafeteria was the only affected building. My causal investigation will begin when we have full daylight."

Adjusting the rim of his hat, a reporter stood to ask his next question. "Commander Martin, how will this affect your safety rating? It feels like we were just out here covering the big flag ceremony."

Leland took his time answering. "That's information we do not have. We need time to isolate the cause. And a formal Naval investigation will likely follow."

The reporter dug in for more dirt. "So, you're saying you could lose it?"

"I appreciate your concern, sir. Next question."

Feeling a little sorry for Leland in his current hot seat, Maggie thought of all the worse outcomes. Thousands of people could have been killed. Yes, something went wrong in that building, but still, they were lucky.

✳ ✳ ✳

Maggie hung up the phone, flipping to the next page of her roster. She'd spoken to most on the list, crossing each worker's name off as safe. When the officer tapped her shoulder and motioned her toward the door, this time she half expected it. Before long, she sat across from Leland Martin. Again.

"I just pulled all cafeteria safety reports submitted in the last thirty days," Leland said, looking more tired than she'd ever seen. "You can imagine my surprise seeing your name on one that matches the potential cause of the fire." He handed her the report just as Harry and Owens showed up, filling two empty seats in Leland's office.

Maggie recognized her signature and Kora's handwriting. That report had crossed her mind but was crowded out by shock and the morning commotion.

"Tell me the story behind this form," he said. "It was filled out three weeks ago. Who is Mrs. James Bell?"

"That's Kora," Maggie said.

"Your Kora?" he asked. She nodded.

Sitting straight and tall, Owens tried to interject. "Commander Martin, as this is now a military matter, I hesitate to involve civilians. You and I can handle this from here."

"I'll decide protocol," he said, eyes never leaving Maggie. "Mrs. Slone, please explain what you know about this report."

Trying to keep the nerves out of her voice, Maggie handed the report back and filled in pieces of the puzzle for Leland, leaving out a few obvious details that Harry and Owens didn't need to know. Kora had taken a turn as an inspector, because she was assigned to Maggie's area. Maggie and Kora's line had rotated through their first safety check assignment last month. Colored-only lines did not rotate through inspection duty, but Leland had agreed to place Kora with Maggie. Now as Kora's supervisor, Maggie had followed instructions and signed the form next to Kora's signature.

After she finished, a stone-faced Leland said, "Thank you, Mrs. Slone. Harry, what happened after this report was brought to your attention?"

Again, Owens butted in. "Sir, if you're through with Mrs. Slone, we have work to—"

"I am not through with her," he said with a slow, measured tone. "Mr. Stillman?"

Harry inhaled deeply before launching his explanation. "These here women did the right thing coming to me. The violation was committed by a person I'm familiar with, but he does not report to me. I went straight to his supervisor, but didn't make much headway. Believe me, I shepherded it as far as I could. There should be something written in his manager's response section." Harry studied the form in front of Leland, like he was trying to read upside down.

Lifting the paper at arm's length, Leland blinked hard, maybe trying to clear the words into focus.

He looks exhausted, Maggie thought.

Leland sighed before he began. "Here's where the matter gets interesting. The manager, a Mr. Miller, did perform an investigation. He summarizes his findings with the following statement: 'As a woman and a Negro, this violation witness is not credible. Upon a valid reinspection, no wrongdoing was found to report, nullifying the original report and closing the matter to further escalation.'"

"There had to be more violations since then," Harry said.

"None that were caught," Leland said, rubbing his eyes with a thumb and forefinger. "I'm waiting on the final cause report, but— off the record—the chief is convinced the fire happened for the very reason these two women reported weeks earlier."

Maggie deadpanned her next two questions. "Does the fire prove Kora's observation was right?" She paused. "Or does it pit her word against these men?"

"I can't answer those questions yet. One thing I can predict is a full DC investigation. I've seen it at other facilities."

"As have I," Owens piped in. "I'm fully prepared to testify on their behalf."

"Testify?" Maggie echoed, an octave higher.

"A formal safety hearing is now inevitable," Owens said.

Leland turned his attention to the lieutenant. "You can't testify." He turned to Harry next. "Nor can you. Only witnesses can testify." He lifted the form in the air, pointing to the bottom. "These two signatures severely limit our witness options."

"But I don't want to testify," Maggie said, picturing herself under a spotlight, in front of a microphone where every "um" and "uhh" stammering from her mouth would be amplified through the room. "I imagine Kora doesn't either."

"Where is she today?"

"Probably at home. The bus routes were canceled."

"Do you know where she lives?"

"I do," Maggie said.

Leland punched a well-worn button on his phone. "Mrs. Sexton, please get me ... ." He stopped, realizing she'd already entered the room.

"What can I get you, sir?"

"Please call a Jeep for Lieutenant Owens and Mrs. Slone." He turned his attention back to Maggie. "I want the two of you to go and get Kora. Meet me back here."

Harry and Leland stood as the ladies exited the room. Maggie caught their exchange before she was out of earshot.

"As their foreman, how can I help?"

"In hindsight, Harry, they should've never signed this form, but here we are. A woman and a Negro as the only cause witness."

"I see."

"As sure as I'm sitting here, Harry. I'll be *damned* if I let this cost *my* plant its reputation."

Chapter 24

JUNE, 1944
KORA

"**K**ora, they's back," came a shout from the living room. Kora didn't need to ask who. Ever since Maggie had driven her big car down the streets of Brooklyn, there was only one *they*.

It hadn't taken long for the rumor to reach her ears. Kora had started cooking the second she learned of the cafeteria fire—anything to distract her mind from poor, sweet Cela. Kora was making her neighbor's favorite skillet corn bread to deliver to the hospital as soon as she could find a ride. What was Cela thinking trying to save those kittens? She never liked cats and complained when they chose to multiply under the kitchen desk rather than kill one solitary mouse.

Slippery from steam and oil, her skillet nearly clattered to the floor when her guests were announced. She wiped her hands and hurried to wind her hair with a scarf just in time to open the door to Maggie and Lieutenant Owens.

Maggie's smile seemed pasted on, where the lieutenant's face held no smile at all.

Kora took a step back. "Maggie, Lieutenant, please come in." Once in the living room, she introduced the few remaining family members who hadn't made a hasty exit. Pulling tighter on her housecoat, Kora offered a seat on her worn but comfy sofa, then fluffed a pillow before taking an opposite chair.

Owens went right to the point. "We require your input at the plant today. We've come to drive you down there."

"What sort of input do you require?" asked Kora, mirroring such formality.

"Why does that matter?" Owens shot back, looking confused.

Maggie interjected. "It's about our safety report."

She knew it. Kora could kick herself for filling that thing out, much less signing her very own name to it, against every instinct. After she had told them about it, her family and friends warned her: keep well below the radar. She'd followed that advice since, but couldn't undo her signature on that blasted form.

Kora looked back and forth between the two white women sitting in her living room; there was a first time for everything. She fantasized about showing them the door, because they didn't belong here. This was her house. She'd played their game, followed their rules—to the letter—and still nobody listened enough to prevent that fire.

Maggie continued, "You and I just have to answer some questions about the report. I'll be right there with you."

Before Kora could fully explore if Maggie's last sentence made her feel better or not, Owens stood abruptly, announcing she would wait exactly five minutes in the Jeep. Enough time for Kora to get ready.

Once alone, Kora started in on Maggie. "How could you let this happen? I took a risk signing that form, and for what? It still caught fire, putting my friend Cela and every soul there at risk. Now there's trouble anyway."

"The whole thing makes me nervous too, but I can't see how we're the ones in trouble. We did the right thing. The safe thing."

"*I* did the right thing," Kora corrected. "You helped." Her statement reflected her raw feelings, a mix of fear and pride. Her instincts about that man from the cafeteria were right.

"Yes, you did the right thing and Harry and I took it as far as we could. Now go get dressed before Owens leaves without us. Keep the scarf," Maggie said, retying her own. "You'll need it in that Jeep."

✳ ✳ ✳

After a rocky ride, Owens parked the Jeep in the dead center of an empty lot. Kora shook her head. Nothing was easy with that woman. She probably enjoyed the exercise. Maggie pulled up her seat, and Kora climbed down from the scariest drive she'd ever taken. If she ever had to ride in this bumpy, wind tunnel on wheels again it would be too soon. Maggie closed the windowless Jeep door, and Kora jumped at the hollow sound.

Once they caught up, Owens spoke her orders. "You two wait for Commander Martin in his office. I'll join you in a bit." She spun to leave, but turned back around. "If he asks you to testify, you should respond that you are uncomfortable doing so. I'm more than capable of speaking on your behalf—I have traveled with him before on several military matters."

They watched her walk away, then headed for the admin building. "What'd she mean by that?" Kora asked.

"Who knows? Can't say I trust her."

"Lord above, I'd rather be just about anywhere but here."

✳ ✳ ✳

Kora hated waiting. She was about to come out of her skin, wishing whatever this was to be over. She shared a bench with Maggie in Commander Martin's waiting room. *Hmph.* Doctors and kings had waiting rooms. Did this man really consider himself that important? She counted the credentials and certificates displayed on the walls, answering her own question.

A deep voice came from the other side of the office door, prompting his graceful secretary to rise, open it, and usher them in. Sitting on the other side of his desk, Kora wondered how he'd speak to her. Perhaps she held the title of the first Black woman invited to sit in this office. Wasn't *that* something?

Commander Martin leaned forward with knitted hands and soft words. "Mrs. Bell, I appreciate you coming on such short notice."

He used her proper name. He must want something. She decided to be nice too. "Well, of course, I'd already planned to be here today. Always sorry to lose a day of work."

"Yes, we all certainly join you in that sentiment." He opened the folder lying before him.

She recognized her report.

Two of his fingers pushed it across the length of the desk, stopping in front of Kora. "Can you confirm your signature, please?"

Kora leaned her neck forward, then sat back up straight. "Yes, that's it."

Harry and Lieutenant Owens came into the room next. The office, filled now with six people, still didn't feel crowded. Kora heard the secretary click the door shut, and felt all eyes fall on her. Only then did the walls contract and she started to feel confined.

She couldn't tell if Commander Martin's tie was half done or half undone, but either case proved he'd been up all night, too tired to fix it or care. He spoke fast, like Maggie. Kora listened as he and Harry traded fancy terms about the fire chief's unofficial cause, matching the violation on Kora's report.

"Sir, I believe these women to be uncomfortable with your request." Owens said, sitting ramrod straight.

"Is that true, Mrs. Bell?"

"Well, I don't know. I'm not sure what you're asking yet."

He leaned forward again, speaking slower. "Any time federal property is damaged to this extent, a safety hearing will occur. Maybe here, but most likely in Washington."

"*The* Washington?" Kora asked.

"The one and only," he answered, a smile finally appearing on his face.

It was a friendly smile, Kora decided. "You want *me* to go to Washington?"

"If it comes to that, yes, we'd take the train to DC."

"What would I have to say?"

"Honestly, you would just answer their questions."

"There's no other way than that—honestly."

"I couldn't agree more. Mrs. Bell, now can I be honest with you?"

"I just said there's no other way." Kora smiled, half enjoying the banter. *Shush*, she told herself. *You're getting over that line.*

"Touché," he chuckled. "I've seen a couple of these play out, and there's two things the government is looking to find. One is workers who put their own agendas ahead of safety and the lives of others. The other is managers who do the same. While they may fault the plant for not reviewing this report in time, it was scheduled to be audited at its appropriate monthly cycle. That the fire occurred before then could just be called bad luck. We could be cited for that, but I've already shortened the audit cycle to weekly going forward."

Kora nodded, and he continued. "Officially speaking, as civilian women you're both 'unreliable' witnesses, but you're also the only eyewitnesses. Your direct testimony could deflect attention away from the plant, and land squarely on the shoulders of these two men." Leland glanced back down at the report for their names. "Mr. Graham and his supervisor, named Miller."

Kora nodded. "I understand all that, but what if they say I had no business as a *Black* civilian woman filling out that report in the first place?"

"I'm not going to sugarcoat it, Mrs. Bell. There's not a grand amount of precedent for that. Your position here at the plant is unique, so it's hard to say how Washington will react."

Kora's heart began to race. What if she just stood up and left? She pictured it, then conceded to stay and listen to the rest of this man's explanation.

He raised one finger and continued, "But… there is a but … no one can deny that you and Mrs. Slone paid attention to the letter of the law. No one can deny that you did your jobs and put the safety of this plant first when you filled out that report. I applaud you both."

Commander Martin looked over his shoulder at the E Award plaque hanging on the wall behind his big old desk. "If we focus on just that, we might keep our 'E' flag too." He turned back, adding quickly, "Not that it matters, but it would be nice."

The commander's stone face seemed to be waiting for her to respond. She glanced at the faces around her, starting with sour Lieutenant Owens. Kora bet her face would always reflect the commander's. Owens hadn't gotten to where she was without playing the game. Maggie's thin smile was impossible to read as her attention bounced between Kora and whoever spoke. Harry's face was appropriately pensive and serious. He certainly didn't speak up for Kora either, but seeing his face did bring to mind her next question.

"Will that man lose his job? The one I named in the report?"

"Pending investigation, both he and his supervisor have been placed on temporary leave," he said.

Kora opened her mouth to ask why it was temporary, then shut it tight, unsure where her line was drawn. She had made up her mind. She wasn't sure she trusted everything Commander Martin said, but enough of it. She put her trust in Maggie too, who seemed comfortable around him. "I'll do whatever's necessary."

Leland rose to his full height, signaling the end of the meeting. He thanked everyone for their time, and asked Harry to stay behind. Kora heard him bark another request to his secretary as she, Maggie, and Owens left the waiting room.

The three women entered the long hallway in silence. Kora was distracted by her own strange mixture of fear and excitement. She was going to Washington. In her head, she started forming her next letter to James. Rumors of fairness and diversity in Washington were legendary in Alabama. When she and James had made the decision to migrate from the deep South, they considered relocating to DC, but with no family there, they settled on Charlotte instead.

Wouldn't it be something when she told James she might see and judge Washington for herself?

Chapter 25

JULY 4, 1944
MAGGIE

The pride of the Seaboard Air Line Railroad stretched before them.

Kora narrowed her eyes and did little to hide a skeptical tone. "Is that thing safe?"

"It looks like it should be on a runway, not tracks," Maggie said, leaning back to find the end.

"The engineering is so sleek. Magnificent," Leland added. "I can't find one ninety-degree angle. Not even a square window."

Maggie raised a hand to shield her eyes. "The glare off that shiny bullet is like staring at the sun."

Large, rounded windows lined both sides of the diesel-powered marvel. On the other side of the windows, curious faces of all ages stared out at them, checking out the latest stop.

Leland looked down at his two travel companions and bent to lift their bags, making his limp more conspicuous. Maggie tried not to stare as he led them to the nearest car.

The steward stopped them before they could climb the first step. "Excuse me, sir, her ticket is for the rear carriage," he said, pointing to Kora.

Maggie wilted, and not from the heat. Despite planning for this, she still wished Kora could ride in the same railcar. Leland handed Kora's bag to the porter. "Carry the satchel and show her the way."

"Yes, sir."

Making sure the porter kept his word, Maggie stayed to watch Kora as long as she could, before rejoining Leland, who watched her from the top stair.

Finding their seats for the seven-hour trip, they removed their hats and stuffed their bags overhead. Maggie ran both hands up and down the armrests of her window seat, enjoying the softness of the deep burgundy fabric.

The train pulled out of the station. Maggie slid her pocketbook under her seat, but it wouldn't go all the way back. Her hand reached down, pulling out the culprit: a *Life* magazine.

"Well, that saved you a dime," Leland said. He pointed to the date in the corner. "Someone left you this week's copy."

Normally Maggie would have thought this was her lucky day. She loved reading *Life,* thinking of the copy she'd saved from the week the twins were born. She stared at the newest cover. The sad faces of two wounded soldiers stared back. They reminded her of Charlie, whose letters were coming less often now.

Charlie had prepared them for mail interruptions. The fighting had intensified, and advancing front lines were complicating mail routes, among other things. She'd received a month's worth of letters all at once, then nothing for weeks now. She and the girls often reread old letters, just to stay connected to him.

"Normandy rages on," Leland said, almost startling her. "But we do gain ground every day."

Puzzled, she asked, "Do you read those details in the paper like everybody else?" She tucked the magazine into the pocket of the seat in front of her. "I don't know why I thought you'd have access to more recent war updates with your job."

He leaned back in his seat. "If I did, I couldn't say, but I did hear one interesting bit of news I can share: our millionth soldier landed in Normandy. The Allies are throwing everything they've got behind that front. The Germans too."

"That's a good thing?"

"Of course. The more men on the ground, the faster we win."

"You're right," she said, thinking, *that's a million families too.*

"Plus, the Navy reached the Marianas. Within air bomb range. They'll clear a path for Army boys like your Charlie."

She looked away from him then, seeing a tobacco farm outside her window. The wide, flat piedmont took a beating from the evening sun. Bent-over field hands stuffed canvas bags that hung from their sunburned shoulders.

"Now that looks like hard work," Leland said. Leaning an elbow onto her armrest, he pointed to more field workers in the next farm. His face was so close to hers, she almost reached out to move a stray hair. There was a time she would have done exactly that.

Maggie lay one hand over her growling belly, flashing a sheepish grin.

"Did that cavernous echo come from you?" he teased.

Her cheeks got warm. "I haven't eaten today. Too much to do."

"Come with me," he said, offering his hand to help her rise. He led her through the maze of interconnected coach cars. He pulled each door open and shut until they finally landed in a dining car booth. Opening two menus between them, he asked, "What are you in the mood for?"

Reviewing the limited options, she was too hungry to be picky. "Can't decide if I want the hot dog with fries, or the club sandwich and pickle."

Maggie made her choice, and he left to go put in their order at the counter.

She watched him walk away. When she turned back, the woman in the next booth caught her eye with a knowing smirk. Maggie looked away, but the heat in her cheeks returned. What was that woman implying? She tried shaking the feeling of judgment, twisting her wedding ring a few times.

Leland returned with heaping plates and full beers. He balanced and lowered them to the table, somehow, without spilling.

The food smelled wonderful. She took a bite and closed her eyes to enjoy it. She opened them to discover Leland's beer raised and waiting for her own.

"To old friends," he offered.

"Old friends," she repeated over the clunk of their green bottles.

While enjoying the food and the quiet, her right foot started to go to sleep. She moved it back to the floor, and felt it graze his shin. When she tried to move it back, her whole leg brushed past his.

He looked up, wide-eyed.

"Sorry," she said, embarrassed. "My foot's asleep."

She scooted left so they were sitting catty-corner across the table, offering more leg room. *Better*, she thought, trying to think of something to distract. "No firecrackers tonight, I suppose."

"I forgot. Today's the fourth of July." He looked out the now darkening window before answering her question. "No, those are banned again this year."

"George found two Roman candles for the girls to light in the backyard. Don't tell anyone. It was their reward for not going to the pool." In case the childless Leland didn't understand, she added, "It's polio season."

"Mum's the word. How are George and Grace?" he asked, like he'd met them more than once.

"Grace is … well, Grace. She had a fit after the fire, insisting I quit my job, even making George back her up. You could cut the guilt with a knife."

"The girls could lose one parent already."

"Whose side are you on? Grace insists it was a miracle no one died in the fire."

She placed an elbow in front of her on the table, nestling her chin in her hand. "Grace did mention you at dinner the other night. Something about 'a top eligible bachelor' in town. She's considering an introduction to a widow from the church parish."

In the middle of wiping his mouth, Leland's sky-high eyebrows appeared over his napkin. "And you talked her right out of it, right?"

Laughter chased down her beer. She covered her mouth and glanced around to see if she'd disturbed the other diners, then leaned over with a loud whisper, "I can't talk her out of *anything*." Maggie wagged a finger. "Consider yourself forewarned."

"Thanks for nothing," he joked, then his smile faded. His expression grew serious. "I hate taking you away from your daughters for this trip."

"They'll be all right," she said, trying to sound convincing. "Grace will keep them too busy to miss me much."

"Any nerves about the hearing?"

"Of course. They won't make me talk at a podium, will they?"

Leland lifted his beer, suspending it in the air between them. "I doubt it," he said, before making his last sip disappear. "If you're expecting the drama you see in movies, you'll be sorely disappointed. Promise."

"Well, that's good. I hope you're right."

"I'm always right," he teased.

Her side vision caught a distant light in the darkening sky. "Was that a firework?"

She got chills, despite the warm air, thinking of people who were dodging real flashes in the sky, from real bombs. She rubbed her arms. It worked for her goosebumps, but not her guilt, safely traveling with Leland.

He changed the subject. "Do you remember that place we used to hang out in Quincy? I'm drawing a blank on the name. Great food." He cocked his head. "Was it Arthur's?"

"Give me a second." Maggie looked down at the table, snapping her fingers in an effort to remember. "Arturo's," she finally said with a final snap, proud of herself for retrieving the name.

"Yes! Wonder if it's still there? Those swell jazz bands would play. Remember?"

"Do I ever." A tune began running through her head.

"And how good their pizza was?"

"Perfect," she said with hands thrown in the air. "Now I'm hungry for pizza!"

"Do you want another hot dog?" His eyes flashed to her empty plate. "For your hollow leg?"

"No," she extended the vowel, giving the plate a push. "I just can't remember the last time I had good pizza."

"Let's make real pizza part of our DC mission," he said with a mischievous grin.

✳ ✳ ✳

Maggie's head slowly dipped forward, then snapped back up with a sharp inhale. She must have slept a little. The whole car was quiet, except for the rhythm of the train wheels. She turned to see what view her window might offer, but the darkness outside only reflected her sleeping seatmate.

She watched him sleep. The train's gentle sway rocked his head just slightly. This complicated man had brought her both happiness and heartache. He was still quite handsome, so how was it possible he'd never married? Knowing she would never ask, she wondered if he still believed women were a career distraction.

She remembered when Leland had returned to Boston every other month to see her after joining the Navy as an officer. He couldn't have been much more than twenty, but had already carved out a very narrow course for his life—while still making it clear she was a part of the picture then. As he had fulfilled his military dreams, his excitement was infectious and easy for her to get caught up in. She dressed to the nines for each of his visits, not knowing exactly during which one, according to his specific plan, he would choose to get down on one knee.

She pictured her oblivious and indignant self, waiting for him to show up to their favorite Italian restaurant. She could still taste the bitter, cold spaghetti sauce over stiffening noodles. As his mother would later reveal, the car that hit him that evening had interrupted Leland's proposal plans. Laid up in a hospital bed for weeks with nothing to do but think, Leland would come to interpret the accident's timing as a sign—or an omen—that would change their path to the altar.

When it became clear his injuries had altered his ability to fulfill his naval ambitions, he blamed himself for being distracted by their relationship. After he shared this with her, it was like talking to a wall. It took more weeks of one-sided conversations at his bedside before Maggie realized what he really meant: *she* was the distraction and *she* bore the blame. They day after his leg recovered, he walked out of her life.

It struck her that this was the first time she'd ever watched him sleep, at least as an adult. Once their parents realized their feelings had matured from childhood buddies to courters, they were never alone, always supervised.

He wasn't snoring but looked like he might start at any moment. His features were beautiful in their sleep-relaxed state. Watching his soft, just-parted lips, she smiled, thinking about their first awkward kiss on her front porch. It had to be quick, because her father was famous for blazing the porch spotlights in time to ruin any mood.

Now Maggie imagined her hand turning his face toward her. Her fingers might graze his temple, leading the way for them to follow along the almost perfect square of his jaw. She imagined her kiss landing on the same temple, idling around one ear, whispering before it followed the trail her finger had just blazed.

He sighed a little in his sleep, drawing her attention to his long, dark lashes. She imagined kissing those too, but only if they stayed closed. After taking the time to visit each feature of his beautiful face with a kiss, she would finally find his mouth. Her hands would raise his face slightly. One finger would trace the outline of his full bottom lip, then continue the thinner trail on top, lingering, not knowing exactly where to go next. Her lips would finally follow her finger's lead, barely grazing one lip, then the other, and melt into both.

She felt the train begin to slow. Worried he might wake up and read her private thoughts, her eyes left his face with regret, traveling down his shirt sleeve, arriving at the hands of his wristwatch. It was after midnight. Turning away for good, she let him sleep the last few minutes of the ride.

Maggie missed capturing the attention of a man. Being with Leland felt easy, normal, because it had once been normal, but it also felt scandalous and forbidden. That added an excitement, a feeling long exiled in her life. She was still a married woman, but husbandless all the same.

She missed every curve and imperfection of Charlie's handsome face. Though marriage wasn't always easy, there was a time she had thought their connection could never fade.

Chapter 26

JULY, 1944
KORA

The moonlight washed over the metal structure—their barracks for the night—looking to Kora like a giant, half-buried can of beans. That made her smile, but she didn't share the joke with Maggie or the commander. Inside it was empty, except for the three of them standing near the door. Kora did a quick survey. Twenty-five bunk beds in four rows, enough to sleep two hundred men.

The commander set their bags down. "Looks like you get your pick of the room," he said, then pointed behind him. "I'll be staying in the officer's quarters just down the sidewalk. If you need anything, turn right. You can't miss it."

They said goodnight as he left. Kora thanked him again. Three hotels had refused to welcome her, but pivoting their plans, Commander Martin deftly found a solution. Uncle Sam had plenty of empty beds at the moment, and would never turn them down.

Kora settled into the top bunk with Maggie right below. Staring at the ceiling, Kora voiced her troubling thought. "Seems like these beds should be full."

"They must be overseas," Maggie replied. "Fighting."

"We should say a prayer for them." Kora prayed for all the soldiers who'd ever watched this same curved ceiling, trying to quiet their minds and fears about their own fate. She asked God to watch over their souls and send them a peace that only He could deliver.

At the end of her prayer, she stifled a yawn. It had been a long trip, but she'd enjoyed her first train ride. Her seat was comfortable and right next to the most interesting man. A businessman, he explained his route to her, rattling off cities she'd never even heard of, up and down the east coast on that Silver Meteor train. He'd also spent time working in Alabama, near her people, and in Charlotte, so they swapped stories.

By now she'd forgotten his name, but she could still see his dark suit, perfectly pressed. He lived somewhere up North. She couldn't imagine all that travel. If she counted that long bus ride through Georgia and South Carolina, Virginia was now the fifth state she'd seen with her own eyes.

Another yawn muscled its way out. Time for sleep. "Goodnight, Maggie."

"Goodnight? That's not how being at 'camp' works, Kora. We have to ask questions and share secrets."

"What questions? For how long? I was looking forward to sleep."

"Until we can't keep our eyes open another minute. I'll go first. Tell me about one of your boyfriends before James."

"This is gonna be a very short conversation, since I didn't have any before James. He's my one and only, unless you count the little white boy I used to chase through the fields when we were nine."

"Kora!" Maggie's laughter floated up from the bottom bunk.

Kora laughed too. "His name was Cephas and he ran like the wind. I never did catch him, but I heard later they done paid him to run track at Auburn."

"Sounds like he should have thanked you for that."

"Indeed, he should have. Is it my turn to ask a question? Give me a second." She paused, then asked, "Which monuments do you want to see while we're here?"

"As many as we can. We don't have too much time. Le—"
Maggie stopped before finishing her word. "Commander Martin
said we might have some time to drive around tomorrow before the
Pentagon. Which ones do you want to see?"

"Definitely Lincoln. Seeing him is a big reason I agreed to come."

"Okay, we'll get you in front of Abe. My turn. Let's see ... okay,
so I've told you how public speaking terrifies me, but what about
you? What's your greatest fear?"

Kora thought it over. There were many, but Maggie had asked
for the biggest. "It's important to me to stay safe. That's why I like
rules and follow them. Shifting rules make me nervous."

"I think Leland would have kept us home if this wasn't safe for
you to do."

Kora raised up on one elbow. "Who's Leland?"

"Sorry. Commander Martin." Her voice was muffled, like it was
coming through her fingers.

Kora's bed squeaked as she leaned over the side. "Now we got
something to talk about, Mizzus Slone. When did you start using
his first name?"

Kora took in the shadow of Maggie slowly lowering her hands.
"When we were five ... maybe six?"

Kora sat straight up, wide awake now, and half-shouted to the
empty room, "You've known him for *thirty years*?" Descending the
bed, Kora found a clear spot at the foot of Maggie's bunk. "Now
we're talking some secrets. Out with it."

The story came out fast and steady, like air escaping a stretched
balloon. After she finished, she seemed to hold her breath, waiting
for Kora to finally respond.

"You're the only person I've told. It feels good to let it out."
Maggie paused. "You probably think the worst of me now."

"Did I say that? No." Kora answered her own question to dismiss
Maggie's insecurities. "I would tell you the truth too. What I *am*
thinking is this is an awful big coincidence."

"What do you mean?"

"This would be like old Cephas coming to work at our plant. The odds are too small, near impossible." Kora crossed her arms. "I think Commander Martin did his homework."

"What do you mean?" Maggie asked. "Like *I* was his homework?"

"Exactly. Aren't there hundreds of naval plants all over this country? After this *random* assignment, he just happens across your name on a roster of thousands. You tell me which is more likely."

Maggie considered her point. "I guess it's possible. My sister Helen still runs into his parents from time to time. I'll have to ask her. But why would he lie about that?"

"I don't know this man at all, so I'm not saying he came to prey on the most vulnerable time in your life. I just think you should think about it some more ... maybe tomorrow." Kora stood up. "Now I'm past the point of tired, Maggie Slone. This camper is going to sleep. Nighty night."

"Of course. Goodnight, Kora," Maggie said as Kora climbed up.

✳ ✳ ✳

All seats were taken around the heavy table, waxed to a shine like everything else in the five-sided building. Sitting on the opposite side, she could see Maggie's reflection on the gleaming surface. It looked like the long reflecting pool between the Washington and Lincoln monuments. The one Commander Martin had pointed out as they drove this morning.

She stole another quick glance at the commander, then at Maggie, still adjusting to knowing they had grown up together. She thought of Maggie as an open book, not the type to have secrets. Not one like that, anyway.

Kora drew a deep breath to calm her nerves. Every uniform here was crisp and wrinkle-free. To reach this room, they'd somehow navigated a maze of odd-angled hallways that seemed to go on for miles. It felt like each person they passed was on his or her way to complete some critical, life-saving task.

The room they filled now was small and on the warm side. It caused her mind to slip, but her attention snapped back like a bent tree when she heard her name.

"Mrs. Bell?"

"Yes?"

"Are these your words written here?"

"Yes, those are my words on the page. I recorded Mr. Graham's violations, as I witnessed them."

"How did you measure the distance?"

"Mr. Graham let me borrow a tape measure. I wanted to be exact."

The man asking the questions was young, with blue-black hair, like he'd just stepped out of a military recruitment poster. "How many of these reports had you filled out before?"

Kora paused, then answered honestly. "This was my very first report."

"So, you were filling out this report at your supervisor's request?"

"Yes."

"And it was your first one?"

"Yes again."

"Is your supervisor in the room?"

Kora pointed across the table at Maggie. "She is."

The officer asked Maggie a few brief questions, then closed the massive file folder. His hand slapped the top, making Kora jump. He stood quickly, leaving everyone else to follow in a rush. Maggie and Kora were the last to rise after they watched the half-dozen officers complete their orderly exit. Commander Martin held their door.

"What just happened?" Maggie asked, crossing into the hallway.

"Exactly what we expected. This meeting was another rubber stamp. You'll both testify tomorrow, separately, like we planned." Not waiting for further questions, he began leading them back through the maze of halls.

They struggled to keep up with his long-legged pace, until all hallway traffic slowed to a stop at the next intersection. They reached the softly murmuring crowd as it watched something approach from the right.

Commander Martin used his height to peek around the corner then signaled back to them. He cleared a spot for Kora and Maggie to see who or what was coming. Trying to see past several men in uniform, Kora caught glimpses of red plaid and a pair of large, spoked wheels. One wheel squeaked with every rotation.

Kora shrugged at Maggie, turning back just in time to get a clear view of the wheelchair. The red blanket lay across the legs of its seated passenger, whose voice finally reached Kora's ears. It sounded familiar, but she couldn't place it.

His full entourage passed right in front of them. Maggie grabbed Kora's hand. She mouthed the word *president,* and Kora clamped her free hand over her mouth, finally grasping the moment's significance. They watched him roll by, as they continued to hold hands.

Kora's heart almost stopped when Franklin Delano Roosevelt looked right at them and smiled as he passed. Kora smiled back, dropping Maggie's hand so she could wave. His blue eyes were intense, but kind, like he was seeing her soul. Commander Martin had to tap her shoulder twice to reclaim their attention and usher them out the nearest doorway. Kora's smile would not fade.

Once back in the car, Maggie burst out, "I cannot believe we just saw the President of America!"

Despite the heat, Kora rubbed gooseflesh from her arms, talking fast. "I just knew it was somebody important, but that wheelchair threw me right off the trail!"

"Exactly. I recognized his voice before his face. Franklin Roosevelt. FDR. I should've shouted that I voted for him three times." Maggie held up three fingers to prove her point. "What about you two? Will you vote for him again this year?"

Kora sat back, shocked into silence, and left Leland to fill the void. "I can't say I voted for him every time, but war requires consistent leadership, so, yes, I'll vote for him this year."

Kora looked back and forth between the front seat occupants. *Did they really assume a red carpet welcome at the voting booth of Kora's choosing?*

Maggie twisted her head, in search of Kora's answer. Instead, she surely read Kora's frustration and anger born of years of humiliating voter disqualification. Maggie's mouth formed a silent "oh" before she faced forward again.

Kora let it sink in for them.

Maggie turned to Leland in the driver's seat and—just like that—changed the subject. "How long has he been like that? In a wheelchair, I mean."

"Since he survived polio," Commander Martin said.

"I had no idea. It never shows in pictures."

"That's by design. It's a sign of weakness. Not the image he wants to display."

Kora broke her silence. "That's sad. He can't be his true self."

Leland's eyes found hers in the rearview mirror. She held them as he spoke. "He's just a man, in the end. Like any other."

Hand-to-heart, Maggie's voice rose an octave. "Well, *I've* never seen a man who also happened to be the president before. Wait 'til I tell the girls. I won't ever forget this day."

Kora leaned against the back seat, trying to catch more of the capitol from her window. "I'll never forget any part of this trip," she echoed, her own heart in hand.

Chapter 27

JULY, 1944
MAGGIE

eal pizza is a work of art, one that can't be hurried, she
reminded her demanding stomach. Still, it was taking too
long. She hated leaving Kora alone back in the Quonset hut.
Insisting to Leland and Maggie that she would be fine, she showed
them her bookmarked page—halfway through a novel Kora was
dying to finish. Maggie told herself to stop worrying and let the
smell of fresh, simmering tomatoes and bubbling cheese—*cheese!*—
distract her.

Leland and Maggie drank their beers in awkward silence. The
place was crowded with couples. Maggie noted all the uniformed
soldiers. "Can I ask you a question?"

"Ask me anything," he said.

"What do you think of Lieutenant Owens?"

Leland shrugged. "Renata's good at her job, but she tries
too hard."

"Renata?"

"That's her name."

"She always calls you Commander Martin."

"Not surprising. She's more military than me at times. Makes me wonder what she does between wars."

"Maybe she hopes it'll be different after this war," she said, just as their number was shouted from behind the counter.

As he returned with their prize, Leland's face was clearly affected by the delicious smell.

"I missed this so much," Maggie gushed between bites of the massive triangle.

"Me too. It's as good as Arturo's."

"Honestly, I miss all Italian food. Grace refused to serve spaghetti until they switched back to our side."

They feasted on more slices while a jukebox, somewhere across the room, spun current hits. It was tucked in a corner in front of a lonely parquet dance floor she barely noticed, until a young couple seized their opportunity. She twisted her chair to get a better view of their dance moves on display and squinted.

"Are they trying to shag?"

"I beg your pardon?" He smiled and cupped one ear to correct whatever he misheard.

She waved off his joke. "It's a dance. Called *The Shag*. Charlie taught all of us in Boston." Her mind went right back to those nights before the war, before motherhood, when they would push back the few pieces of furniture they owned and dance. This music called loudly to that forgotten part of Maggie.

Laying her napkin on the table, she stood up to demand, "Come with me."

"Oh," he said, shaking his head. "No. No, I try to limit my opportunities for humiliation, thank you."

"It's so easy. Nothing to it. I can teach you."

"Meaning what? You'll lead?" He looked right and left before adding, "Like a man?"

"Exactly." Her hand was still suspended, waiting on his.

Her demands and his hesitancy drew the attention of the neighboring table. Lines formed between his brows, but he stayed seated. "I do not enjoy doing things I'm not good at."

"Who does? Just follow me until you get the hang of it. Like I do at work. We all start somewhere, Leland Martin. Up you go."

He shed his jacket, draping it on his empty chair.

She pulled him onto the small dance floor, grinning the entire way. The song ended just as they arrived. Still holding hands, they faced each other, listening to the next record's soft clicks and scratches. The new beat stayed light and quick.

Noticing the younger couple watching her instruction, too, she parroted Charlie's long-ago directions as best she could remember. Leland followed the slower first steps, but grew frustrated when the beat moved quicker than his leg would. Maggie could feel his annoyance, but refused to quit. No one was watching them anyway. Thanks to Maggie's little lesson, the other dancing couple attracted most of the attention.

"Just let me lead," he said, the strain coming through his voice.

"Okay, you lead." She tried to smile and waited for him to start, but instead he pulled her closer to make room for a third couple joining the crowded square.

His face said it all, pleading with her to sit down. She resigned herself, knowing that bumping into the backsides of strangers was not his scene. She felt disappointment flood her face, so she turned quickly and ran right into the chest of a man, new to the tiny dance floor.

"Whoa there!" the stranger said. "I was just coming over to see if your fella'd mind if I cut in?"

Mortified that he thought them a couple, she sputtered, "Oh, he's not ... we were just ..." Her mind processed his question and he looked harmless enough. She started over, "Do you know how to shag?"

"Give a man a chance and I'll show you how well," he said with a confident drawl. The man's shock of red hair was distinctive, the kind of feature you either spend a life hating or use to your advantage. This man, closer to a boy really, was in the latter camp. He looked at Leland, who displayed a thin smile as he handed over Maggie's hand. The moment was truly awkward, but Maggie's head and heart were set on dancing. She was unwilling to let her old self fade so quickly.

The stranger didn't lie. He spun her around the floor like a top, requiring all her focus to keep up and crowding out any thoughts of Leland's bruised ego. A fourth couple joined the floor and it only added to the hilarious abandon she'd rediscovered. Each move had to be precise and tight to fit into the space they'd carved out.

Never seeing one nickel fed to the machine, she thanked the juke box gods who continued to play a perfect shag beat. Surrendering herself to the music, she felt impossibly drunk after one bottle of beer. Daring to try a tight double twirl under the stranger's long arm, raised high in command, she almost clapped for herself when she hit the mark. Their moves were now attracting all the attention.

She was too hot for her cardigan and too embarrassed to remove it. Her breath was coming fast as she almost tripped over a young boy crossing the floor to throw his nickel in the slot furiously pressing buttons. She laughed out loud as this song faded and the music gods orchestrated the next act of this play.

She smiled at the stranger, still holding his hands and trying to catch her breath. Glenn Miller's low croon floated from the juke box, altering the scene. Leland reappeared with the slower rhythm, dispatching the stranger quickly. Leland reversed their roles again, lifting his brows and extending his right hand in silent request to reclaim his proper lead.

She accepted the outstretched hand and let him twine her fingers together with his, bringing her closer. Her other hand had no choice but to rest on his shoulder. His found the small of her back. The years since she had slow-danced collapsed into an unseen void, shocking her with how deeply she missed it. She hadn't danced since her husband left.

Dance was a loose thread connecting different parts of her. Many times, her father had come home from work and spun her around the kitchen as soon as he set down his hat and coat. The strong smell of cigar smoke clung to his uniform. One whiff could send her mind straight back into her daddy's arms and one of the most protected times in her life.

Head resting lightly now on Leland's shoulder, she tried to enjoy the song and quiet her mind's comparison of her three favorite dance partners.

They danced through two more slow ballads. Maggie swayed through the music and the moment. Any hint of his limp disappeared as Leland assumed full command of their steps. She relaxed into his lead.

Her curiosity got the better of her. She looked up and asked, "Can you imagine such a young boy choosing to spend his hard-earned nickel on all these slow songs?" His deep brown eyes darted away from her accusation as she continued, "Unless it wasn't his nickel."

She watched his face play through shock, then fake disbelief and finally surrender with his single word response. "Guilty."

"A lot of that going around." She replayed Kora's words. What *were* the odds of a random assignment landing Leland back in her life? "What else are you guilty of?"

Their swaying stopped. He started to answer, then appeared to change his mind, sliding both hands to frame her face. His lips met hers softly, like he was afraid to move too fast and cause her to bolt. Memories layered in Maggie's mind: their first innocent kiss, their sad last, and every single one in between.

The kiss intensified with the longing of each year that had passed. Her body recognized and responded to him like second nature, like she was coming *Home*.

Home was Boston, before the war, before her life had turned inside out.

No—she argued—home was Charlie, no matter where they lived.

Charlie! She pushed Leland away. They faced one another, stone still, yet rattled as the next record flipped. The other dancers began moving to the faster beat—speeding up her understanding of how far from home she'd strayed.

A too-calm Leland stuffed one hand in his pocket, not hiding an attempt to check his watch on the other, then led her silently off the floor. As they threaded between the rows of tables, Maggie practiced exactly what she would accuse him of when they sat down.

He pointed to the unfinished half of their pizza tray, avoiding her stare. "You must be starved after all that dancing. It might be cold."

"Not hungry, thank you." She crossed her arms. "I want to take the rest back for Kora."

"Of course, I'll get a box," he escaped before she could protest. Returning with the box, he stayed fascinated with his watch, erasing a smudge.

She lifted the remaining slices and closed the lid, finally ready to address the elephant. "You still haven't answered my question. What was that back there?"

He opened his mouth to speak and then closed it as the bells on the door rang loudly, announcing a new patron. She followed his eyes, shocked to recognize the face.

Why was Lieutenant Owens making her way to their table?

Owens pulled a chair out and removed her stiff uniform hat, laying it gently on the table. "No incidents to report from the train," she said, pointing to her own watch. "Right on time."

Leland nodded, as if he had been expecting Owens to arrive. Maggie looked to him for an explanation, still calculating in her head. If Owens had been five minutes early, she would have witnessed their kiss. *Was that part of his plan? To humiliate her and threaten her marriage?* She saved these questions for later, focusing instead on his explanation.

"Renata is here for the testimonies tomorrow. I've been asked to stay behind a few extra days. She'll escort you and Kora back on the train."

She felt Owens watching her closely, ready to judge her first reaction. Maggie refused to let her nerves show. "The more the merrier," she said, smiling, before drawing a water glass to her lips so she wouldn't be expected to speak further.

Owens refused the pizza but agreed to a round of beers. As they watched Leland head off to place the order, Maggie grasped for anything to fill the silence, but the only question occupying her mind was *Why are you really here in Washington?*

The Lieutenant's long fingernails, drumming the tabletop one at a time, distracted Maggie. Bright red this time, they were perfectly done—the one feminine sign Owens offered the world. Maggie absently picked gun powder stains from her own nubs, then tucked them away.

Owens began a slow, sophisticated cigarette ritual Maggie couldn't help but watch. With the pack she made three crisp taps on the table, revealing the brand: Marlboro. The long, skinny tip fit perfectly between two ruby red nails as her lighter softly illuminated her bare face. The women who smoked Marlboro's in the magazine ads came to mind. Had Owens worn lipstick, it would never have clung to a Marlboro tip.

Maggie caught Leland making his way from the bar to the men's room. Jumping on the same excuse, Maggie fled their awkward table. Her return trip revealed Leland and Owens heads down, deep in conversation. What could be coming next, she wondered, seeing them straighten so obviously at her approach. Maggie nursed her beer, waiting, but Owens wasted little time getting to the point.

"Maggie, let's talk about your testimony."

"What about it?"

Her gesture toward Leland cemented their partnership in whatever this was. "We've settled the best way to handle this incident, in favor of the plant." The lieutenant finished and set her glass down roughly, causing a small spill, which she ignored.

Leland sipped, watching her.

"I'm listening." Maggie softened, willing to do anything for the workers back at the plant.

Owens spoke again. "Your incident report appears to match the cause of the fire, but the safety board can judge that two ways.

The report was correct and wrongfully ignored, *or* the report was unreliable and justifiably ignored. The latter signals a rank and file issue. The former points to a more serious systemic issue around management, plus a general disregard for safety." Owens drained her beer. "We need you to say you don't trust the source of the report. Kora should never have been in a position to fill it out and you shouldn't have signed it."

Maggie felt sick. She stared at Leland, forcing him to say something.

"Kora never belonged on your line," he said. "I warned you how messy things could get without segregated lines. She should've been reassigned to one of the colored lines. Those don't rotate through inspection duty."

Maggie glanced quick at Owens, wondering how much she knew about why he had agreed to place Kora with her, as a favor to a friend.

"I'm confused how this would help the plant," she said. "Kora's report could have kept the fire from happening at all. We wouldn't be sitting here if Miller had done his job! Should I lie about that?"

Owens spoke quickly. "We'll never know for sure if the violation directly caused the fire, but we know one hundred percent the only way to save the plant's reputation now. That's for you to do as we say."

"Ah," she nodded. "Of course, save the E Award." Maggie had to look away from Leland, who was now intent on adjusting the napkin in his lap. *All of which benefits your precious military career*, she thought.

Leland looked up and removed any doubt as to what Owens knew. "Just think about it, Mags. You asked me to assign Kora to that line. As a favor. Now we're asking for a favor."

Maggie's stomach lurched. "I was so naïve to think Graham or Miller was the one on trial here."

"It's hard to fault Miller for burying the report, after he learned who wrote it. Plus, these men have families to support." Leland's eyes pleaded with her. "Have a heart, Mags."

Maggie let his words hang in the air, turning them over in her mind. "I get it now." Maggie pushed her glass away, shooting them her best accusatory glare. "Kora has so much less to lose."

Maggie stood quickly and grabbed the pizza box for Kora.

Leland rose too, his face imploring her to reconsider. "Promise you'll trust me and think about it. I'm right about this."

Owens rose slowly, after snuffing out her cigarette. "You don't have to decide tonight, but I know you'll make the right call—the only call—for your employer." Hat in hand, she pointed to the door. "Let's go."

Leland handed the keys to Owens.

Maggie didn't follow right away, she was locked and loaded on Leland's eyes as he spoke. "I'll make sure the big guys at US Rubber know all about you and your cooperation after the fire. They'd be stupid not to hire you on after the war, especially on my recommendation."

Before Maggie could form a response, Owens tugged on her elbow and steered her toward the door. Leland stayed behind, away from further interrogation, as was clearly their plan.

Sleep hardly came to Maggie that night. Partly from sorting through all kinds of confusing thoughts, but mostly because Kora and Owens were in a spontaneous snore off. Her head sandwiched tight between her own pillow and one stolen from the next cot over, she tried to block the noise in exchange for whatever sleep she could grab.

She had answers to some questions, but not others. The man at the Pentagon who had asked Kora and Maggie those odd questions. It felt like *they* were the ones on trial, because now she knew they were. Especially Kora. Owens had been called to DC to do Leland's dirty work.

Maggie ran through tonight's dinner conversation with Leland again. "Shouldn't it be different for Lieutenant Owens?" she'd asked. "This time, I mean. Haven't women, especially WAVES like her, proved themselves enough since this war began?"

"I doubt it," he said behind his napkin, finishing another big bite. "Of course, women have made a difference this time around. You're an example. Nobody denies that, but women can't expect to steal a job that belongs to a man, especially one who just returned from battle. Any more than a man would try to raise babies or run a home." He picked up another slice and added, "You of all people should know this."

Then she replayed Owens' strange lecture as they had ridden back to the barracks tonight. Certain words stuck in Maggie's head—loyalty and trust for what a postwar world could look like for women—carrots Leland must have told Owens to dangle. Everyone wanted the war to end, but worried about it too. Maggie's uncertain future was her weak spot.

Her mind edged toward scarier waters. Charlie's family would take care of her and the girls, but at what cost? She hated relying on them now, but it would be worse if he never came home.

Maggie had learned so much from her job. Most importantly, she learned she was good at it. If she did what they now asked her in DC, would that make a difference later? If Charlie didn't come home, a guaranteed postwar job meant she could support the girls on her own.

And what about Leland and his suspicious timing of that kiss? Had she forgotten what a master manipulator he could be? He wanted to change her testimony. Even his kiss was a setup to soften her to his side.

Her eyes shut tighter, remembering how she'd responded in that moment on the dance floor and recalling her own private fantasy of kissing him on the train. Was this her fault? Maggie sat up, feeling sick from her own answer.

It was quiet. Freed from her pillows, she realized the snoring had stopped, replaced with soft, even breaths coming from Kora above. As she laid back down, she stared at the top bunk.

She remembered Kora pulling her into that empty office back at the Shell Plant, so scared to turn in the report. Maggie had been so imprudent. Now she understood exactly what it meant for Kora to accept responsibility for what she had witnessed. Fear of explosion was the great equalizer at the plant. Black or white, they would suffer the same fate. Kora had put all their safety above her own instinct, and for what?

Somewhere to the left, Owens started up the chainsaw again. Maggie rolled away from the noise and punched up her too-flat pillows as much as she could. She sighed into the muffled racket, giving her tired mind and body over to sleep.

✳ ✳ ✳

"There's simply no time," Owens repeated, tucking her blanket tighter, until her bunk resembled a wooden board.

"But we're getting such an early start. If we leave right now, we can make it to the monument, testify, and still make the train."

Owens looked at Maggie and straightened. "I see the problem now."

Maggie fastened her second shoe and wrinkled up her face, knowing what would likely come next.

"This is exactly why you are always late, Maggie Slone. You push the limit, trying to fit too much into too little time. It gets you in trouble, you know."

Maggie and Kora stayed quiet. Maggie held her breath, hoping Owens would give in.

"Okay. Fine. But I'm starting the car now." Owens marched from the room. "Be out in five—no, make that four!" she ordered, over one padded shoulder.

Soon they were taking quick steps to the top of the Lincoln Memorial. Maggie and Kora approached the stone giant. His expression was serious and pensive, his focus far away.

Kora finally spoke. "I imagined him different."

"What do you mean?"

"My granddaddy could draw right good. He hung his own picture of Lincoln in our Alabama living room and I remember studying that stern face on the wall. Grandmomma caught me once and told me to get on with my chores. I asked her what earned that face his prominent place in our house."

"What did she say?"

"She explained how this man made us free and I remember feeling happy about that. Then she said, 'And they kilt him for it.' Then I felt awful. He's a complicated man, but those were the only two things I knew about Lincoln for so long. No good deed goes unpunished."

Maggie listened, wishing there was something she could say. Kora pulled a notebook and pen out of her bag. "I'm going to take some notes over here."

"Is that a diary?"

"Sort of. I promised the folk back home that I would report back every detail. Like they're here next to me."

Kora stepped through each wing, soaking up the engraved words all around her, then writing furiously in her notebook.

Maggie read the walls too. "Actions and consequences," she said to no one but herself.

Lincoln's bold words continued to inspire visitors almost a hundred years later. Still, his strong arguments hadn't changed enough. Would Maggie's testimony matter in the end? She imagined the bold words she might choose to support Kora's credibility. They would land like a feather on an ocean of inequality, barely causing a ripple.

Kora pulled her elbow, breaking her trance, and they walked back into the sunlight. At the top of the monument stairs, they turned for one last look, heads tilted toward Abe's massive stone features. Almost to herself, Kora said, "He looks like he's remembering something important he forgot to say. Something that would make all the difference."

Their eyes met and Maggie knew what she had to do, even if her words only made a difference for two people.

❋ ❋ ❋

Maggie let go of the suitcase to save her ears from the piercing whistle. She watched an unfazed Owens glide past, completing the distance between Kora's train car and theirs in no time. Drained from the day's events, Maggie followed, hoisting her bag up the stairs. It was going to be a long ride home.

The only two seats left faced each other, with a table in between. With the train in motion, Owens got busy with a stack of files. Maggie tried to feel for another free magazine under her seat, but no such luck. Instead, she watched the twilight settle outside. The landscape blurred as the train picked up speed.

Maggie and Kora had testified separately. That much they had expected. The stenographer, blending into the wall, was the only other woman in the room. Looking back, Maggie could now see that every male mind in that room was already set. Her words, what little stock they had held, were given even less weight.

It was clear, as she sat in that hard, wooden chair and answered their obligatory questions, the only thing Maggie could affect or control was her relationship with Kora. That was the only slate she needed to keep clean and she did, testifying the truth as it happened. The men in that room would believe what they wanted.

Owens knew none of this yet, and Maggie would be damned if she would reveal any more than she had to. She found the upper hand quite enjoyable and let Owens dance all around the subject to no avail.

"You're deep in thought," Owens said.

"It's been a long trip. About to get longer. When I get home, the girls will just be waking up, ready to be entertained like any other Saturday."

"That's right. You have a kid."

She forgot? Should she carry a large "twin mother" sign to help Owens recall the two full-time jobs she juggled? *Deep breath and smile*, she told herself before responding. "Two kids actually, getting ready to turn ten." She tried to read her boss's blank face. "No rest for the weary, unless I can somehow sleep on this train."

"That reminds me. I'm hungry. We should eat before trying to get some rest."

"Wine might help too."

"Sounds like a mission. Let's go."

Maggie led the way to the dining car. It felt like a million years had passed since she and Leland had followed the same path.

Orders placed and glasses poured, they waited on a table to free up. Maggie stood, swaying with the motion of the car, and searched for the right conversation starter for her too-stiff dinner companion.

Maggie noticed others staring at her companion's uniform. Women in the military were still a novelty. "You know, I've never asked you when you realized you wanted to serve in the Navy?"

"My father tried four times for a boy, so he had to get creative with me, the only one of his children who expressed any interest in where he went every morning."

"I thought you said you were a preacher's kid."

"I was, but for a time he was a military chaplain and got pretty high up. He took me to work any time I asked, let me sit in the corner of his office and in meeting rooms." She chuckled. "They really got a kick out of me, like I was their naval mascot. Turns out no one cared what a little girl in a frilly dress overheard, but I paid attention, even after they forgot I was there." Owens drank her wine, "Anyway, I was hooked, and at the front of the line to sign up in '14. Again in '41."

A table came open just as the food was ready. They ate in silence until Maggie could no longer stand it. "Your daddy must be plenty proud of you now."

"At first maybe, during the Great War. Now he's older, more convinced women should know their place." Owens fired up her after-dinner smoke. "He still thinks I could land a man someday, like it's the only respectable option."

"How did you support yourself in between wars?"

Owens took her time to respond, flicking an ash into the cigarette box, then arching one brow. "Now we're getting personal, huh?"

Horrified, Maggie's fingers flew to her chest. "You're right, I'm so sorry. Forget I asked."

"Relax. I'm joking." Owens shook her head laughing. "You're almost too easy."

"And you're too hard," she shot back, shocked by the speed it left her mouth. Only she didn't like being called easy. She braced for a backlash.

Head cocked, Owens looked at her like she had a new haircut. "Maybe I am," she said before pausing. "It's not a pretty story though, what I did in peace time."

Maggie now wished she could take the question back, her mind ticking off wild possibilities. Was Owens a spy between wars, did she gamble, or work in a brothel? She pasted on a smile, preparing for the worst.

"For two long decades, I ran the kitchen at a military base in Kansas. Cooked, cleaned, washed mountains of dishes, served meals, you name it." She pointed at Maggie with a stern face. "Never cleaned a latrine, though. I was firm about that."

Maggie stayed silent as Owens took on a faraway look, then glanced at her pretty nails. "I paint these up nice to remind me of how far I've come since my dishpan hands."

Maggie saw her boss's long, red nails in a new light, but still anticipated another joke coming at her expense. Or was Owens finally showing a humble side?

"What will happen after the war?" Maggie asked. "To your military career, I mean."

With a heavy shrug she said, "That's anybody's guess."

Maggie got curious. "How many plants have you worked for?"

"I never counted. At least ten."

"And how many of those received E ratings?"

"I know that number." She wiggled four of her fingers in the air.

"*Four?*" Maggie asked, genuinely impressed. "And that streak of victories doesn't buy you any leverage? Your record seems to have jumped right off a recruitment poster."

"Who knows? Men are full of hollow promises while they still need you." She stopped and looked Maggie up and down. "You probably have a different experience."

"Maybe, but I've not pushed many envelopes either."

"Well, I've done nothing but."

Maggie's next sentence escaped before she had time to consider its effect. "That's why I couldn't lie about Kora today." Her words hung between them.

Maggie emptied her glass and set it down for emphasis. "Kora Bell is the most reliable *person* I know, much less witness. I can't stop the world from defining her limits, but I knew I couldn't make it worse with my testimony. It's not right."

Owens looked like she was seeing her for the first time. Pointing to her own chest and then to her boss, Maggie continued, "Nor are limits placed on us, regardless how much we might need or want our jobs after the war." Her voice cracked. She felt as drained as her glass.

Owens threw down her napkin, clearly done.

Maggie thought she might be done too, or at least fired on the spot, but Owens surprised her again.

"Didn't think you had it in you, Slone. What's that saying about judging books by covers?" Owens said, rising from her seat, proving they both understood more than the credit they were given.

Chapter 28

After a long night on the train, Kora and Maggie still had a two-hour drive between the Hamlet Depot and Charlotte. Despite their fragile truce on the train, Maggie was glad Owens would drive separately. This had been a long journey and the longest she'd been away from the girls since Charlie left.

"You don't look good," Kora said from the passenger seat. "Don't you fall asleep at that wheel."

"I hardly slept on the train." Maggie yawned through her last word. "You?"

"You know, I thought I'd be anxious after giving my testimony, but I slept like a baby. I've done all I can. The rest is up to God." She raised a hand to the heavens for her last sentence.

Maggie felt like a bad friend, knowing things that Kora didn't—like the intentions to discount her testimony. The Navy would hear what it wanted.

Swapping testimony stories, they confirmed similar questions, and made light of being surrounded by such serious faces. They stopped just short of revealing their own answers.

"Can't wait to tell the girls about the President."

"Ooooh, that still puts butterflies in my stomach. I'm gonna write James about it, first thing." Kora held out both arms, spreading them across her imagined headline. "In all capitals, I'll start the letter ... Mrs. Bell goes to Washington!"

Maggie laughed at Kora's movie reference, but then grew quiet. "You haven't asked me any more about Leland."

"I knew you'd talk when ready."

"I hardly know what to say. You might be right about his intentions for coming, but it doesn't change the fact that he's here."

"No, it doesn't."

The thought of Kora thinking the worst of Maggie kept her quiet about the kiss. She was on her own for unwinding that complication. By the time she pulled down Kora's street, Maggie felt a second wind. She drove straight to get the girls. Grace stood in the front window as Maggie pulled up. Before she could even knock, Grace made a rare venture outside in her housecoat, shuffling the girls out the door. She must have had their little suitcases packed and waiting.

"They're all yours," she sang, already kissing them goodbye. "See you Sunday."

Still in matching nightgowns, her sleepy children forgot their manners. Maggie stopped them, "Ladies, what do you say?"

Daisy and Demi turned back to Grace. "Thank you, Gigi," they said, perfectly synchronized.

Maggie tried to echo their sentiment, but Grace was already pulling on the front door.

Like just-watered plants, the girls began to perk up on the short ride home, dashing her hopes of any daytime shut-eye. The interrogation into her trip launched as soon as they arrived home and didn't stop. Normally proud of their inquisitive nature, today it felt like endless firing rounds of questions meant to break her.

"When can we visit Washington? Why not now? How far is the train? Is Daddy that far away? Did you see the train engineer? Did he blow his whistle? Did Dinah blow her horn?" Their questions rolled through breakfast, lunch, and supper. She replayed her

Roosevelt story at least twice and pinky swore the four of them would return to Washington together. Someday.

When the shadows finally lengthened, she insisted they go outside to play. Maggie craved some quiet time. The last plate put away, she filled a hard-earned glass of wine, one she'd been patient for all day. She considered inviting Grace to join her, but talked herself out of it. Surely she and George had other plans.

Escaping to her patio, she shushed the squeaky back door and sank into the sole surviving lounge chair, once a proud set of four. When did they buy these? It felt like yesterday and like a hundred years ago. When three of them had broken last season, two were donated to a scrap metal drive, but she superstitiously stuffed one chair up in the attic, waiting on Charlie to come home and fix it.

Thankfully, the summer heat had broken too. She pulled in a chest-full of the still night air. Eyes closed, she pictured Charlie playing with the girls in their tiny backyard in Boston and trimming the grass while she tended her flowers. Planting her own flowers was a luxury, one the landlords had never allowed where Maggie grew up.

It was easy to feel Charlie beside her on a night like this, grabbing her hand to bridge the short distance between their two perches. He would playfully notice the back porch needed sweeping and she would ignore his comments until they'd both start to giggle.

When her eyes reopened, she found a much bigger yard sprawled before her, triple the size of their quaint Boston lot. Charlie had left before too many memories could form in this house, but there was one she could never forget.

"Close your eyes," he'd said.

"They're closed!" she said, with fake exasperation. "Plus, your hands are in the way."

"I knew you'd peek. Don't ruin the surprise. I've gone to some trouble here," Charlie said, positioning her body just so. "Ok, now open them."

Compared to other places she'd lived, the house that stood before her was big, but somehow it still looked petite—perhaps even cozy—compared to those on either side. She recognized the signature Myers Park tree canopy above her head.

"Queens Road West is right over there." He pointed. "My parents are five houses up and six houses over. Perfect for borrowing an egg or whatever you might need when I'm gone."

"It looks nice—" she began, but her husband interrupted, like he was bursting with excitement.

"I knew you'd love it." He pulled two metal keys from his pocket, tied with twine. "Let's go see your new house!"

Charlie took two giant steps forward, but Maggie stayed rooted. She couldn't believe her ears. This house looked way out of their budget, especially on his new Army salary. They were supposed to have found a house together that week. A small one. Still tired from the train, she hadn't the energy for a fight, especially when he was leaving in a matter of weeks, not months. She did manage to get out, "That can't be our house."

"Oh, but there's where you're wrong, my Irish Rose. Mom scouted this place out last month and I bought it yesterday, before you arrived. The girls are going to love it. This was a great neighborhood to grow up in. Lots of kids." He pulled back, inspecting her face. "Don't worry, sweetheart. I've got it all worked out." He managed to land a kiss on her cheek. "Now, let's go inside. Wait 'til you see that tub."

Charlie had a money problem. He liked to overspend it. Or maybe she had the problem, because she wanted to save it all. Or *hoard* it, as he liked to throw out during an argument, usually about money. His parents had had to rescue them a few times, and it always bothered her the most.

Something caught her attention now. A twinkle appeared at the edge of the yard—the first firefly emerging for the evening insect social. She smiled, remembering the first time she had heard Charlie call them lightning bugs.

The magic of fireflies—seeing them, chasing them, collecting them in a jar to create a new, stronger light—brought her childhood summers back in a rush. Maggie squinted so the tiny beacons became stars carelessly sprinkled over the lawn, before remembering that was just what she and Leland used to do.

Leland. Her mind replayed Kora's words from the barracks. "I'm not saying he came to prey on one of the most vulnerable times in your life, but what are the odds?"

Should she go to confession tomorrow? She hated confession, afraid to add up how long it had been since her last.

Earlier that morning, she and the girls had written letters to Charlie. Her words dripped onto the page, too syrupy sweet. She threw it away and started over.

"What's wrong with you, Mags?" she whispered into the summer air. A sole firefly landed on the end of her chair. It blinked on and off, as if waiting for an answer.

From the next yard, she heard Demi and Daisy playing with the neighborhood children, most of them boys whose cracked voices announced their in-between years.

"You can't decide what game we play. You're a girl," one wobbly voice called out.

Was he talking to one of her girls? She got her answer when Daisy's voice responded, "Who says boys get to decide?"

"That's the way it is. Boys make the rules. Girls follow."

A second male voice chimed in. "Yeah, if we let you play at all."

"Well, *we* want to catch fireflies, so if you want to play with us, then that's our game." Daisy's voice started out strong. *Attagirl.* There was strength in numbers, but Maggie knew the neighborhood ratio wasn't in the girls' favor.

"We're playing Kick the Can. Don't care if you play or not." Maggie could tell by the boy's tone the matter was settled. She wanted to throttle them. She whispered, "Come on, girls. Don't bend that easy."

The girls tried to engage them in more debate, but the boys were done, their game decided. She craned her neck, trying to catch the action over the fence, but couldn't. She remembered the knothole in the fence.

Matching eye to hole, she could make out a few girl-shaped shadows chasing fireflies with their giggles. Her heart sang, watching the girls stick to their game, but the boys' laughter carried across the lawn, making their affair sound infinitely more fun. One by one, the girls peeled off to join the boys' game. Maggie wilted as her daughters abandoned their own desire for the direction of the masses.

✳ ✳ ✳

Afraid to count the number of hours she'd been awake, Maggie lay across the twins' bedroom floor. On their way to locate nightgowns and toothbrushes, the girls stepped gingerly over her useless body. She should have stolen that nap this morning.

Finally rising from the floor, she pulled covers around their chins and kissed each forehead. "Goodnight, sweet girls. Mama loves you." Her hand hovered over their light switch, so close to the finish line of this marathon day.

"Mama? ..."

Reluctantly returning to Demi's side, the bed sagged with her weight and soft question, "What is it, honey?"

"Why is Daisy smarter than me?"

Her brain buzzed, aware of the importance of this question. "Who told you that?"

"Everybody says it, 'cept maybe you and Daddy. Mizz Smithwell told the whole class Daisy's the smart one."

"When did Miss Smithwell say that?"

"Mommy, it's Mizzzz Smithwell, not Miss." Daisy, propped on one elbow, lectured from the other twin bed.

Maggie ignored Daisy's comment and kept her focus on Demi, whose small, bony shoulders shrugged an answer for when this awful statement was declared aloud in their classroom. "I told Gigi while you were gone."

She dreaded her next question, but she persisted. "And what did Gigi have to say?"

"She said it's okay. It doesn't matter who's smarter, because we both look the same and are more than pretty enough to marry smart husbands."

Maggie breathed in slow and breathed out slower, putting together her next careful sentence. "Listen to my words: you are both equally and exceptionally smart, just maybe in different ways." She paused, praying to get it right or at least minimize the damage. "There's all kinds of smart in this world. There's book smart and street smart. There's art smart and people smart. When I see you two, and *I will always* see you, I see shades of all those smarts rolled up into two perfect people."

The girls looked at one another and giggled as she continued. "And you'll grow up to be confident and yes, very smart women. Whatever Gigi says, that fact has nothing to do with who you marry. Look at Aunt Helen. If she were here right now, she'd tell you she is happily unmarried. She gets to teach women who are already in college. That means she has to be smarter than they are. In fact, you both remind me so much of Aunt Helen—future college women."

Demi smiled wider, hopefully seeing a different version of her future. "I miss Aunt Helen," she softly said.

"And Daddy ..." Daisy's voice trailed off.

"Oh and let's not get started on what Daddy would say to old Mizzzz Smithwell!" Maggie attempted her best man voice. "He'd say, 'You are the most clever girls the world has ever known and if she can't see that then she is woefully mizzzzinformed and probably more than a bit mizzzzerable herself!'"

The girls giggled again. She loved the sound.

"Daddy'd say something funny, just like that," said Daisy. "I can't wait to see him when we turn ten."

Maggie froze. "Why do you think that, honey?"

"I read it in one of his old letters. He promised he would be home to see us blow out the candles this year." Maggie could kick herself. She had always skipped over that detail while rereading Charlie's early letters to them, assuming they'd never catch on because they couldn't read cursive yet. They were getting too smart for her to keep up.

There was no easy way to say the next sentence. "Sweetie, we don't know when Daddy will be home, but it won't be in time for your tenth birthday."

"Oh. Okay." Daisy turned to the side, hiding her expression.

Maggie let her alone, knowing this time there was nothing she could say to make it better. She started to leave again when Demi stopped her.

"Mama, the curtains. You forgot to check for gaps."

When first hung throughout the house, these much-needed, ominous blackout curtains had scared the girls. She explained that the light needed to be held inside the house so planes couldn't see them. After that, the thick fabric had morphed into a sort of bedtime security blanket, keeping them safe from bombers. Ensuring no gaps in their curtains had become part of their nightly routine.

"So I did," she said, getting up to pull them tighter across each window, then she shut the door, slow and quiet. Hearing the soft click of the handle engage, she rested her forehead against their closed door.

Desperate to hang on to their fading innocence, she wished those curtains had the power to keep out other awful truths. Like how boys and grandmothers—not to mention teachers—say all the wrong things. And daddies don't come home, even when you need them the most.

Chapter 29

AUGUST, 1944
KORA

Nell caught the sheet inches before its clean whiteness mixed with the yard's fiery red clay. "Gotchew," she trumpeted, as her arms began to stretch and fold it into more manageable squares. They moved fast against the wind and skies that threatened rain.

"You just about bought yourself another round of laundry," Kora said, yanking some of hers off the line.

"Shoot, laundry for one ain't nothin'."

Nell and Kora shared a rare bond with enlisted husbands and no children to occupy their time.

Kora inhaled the fresh laundry smell, one that usually lifted her mood, but not today. She had shared with her community many stories about her Washington trip, but had not shared one word about what she'd read last week in the official safety hearing report. That was still stewing inside her.

After they'd swapped stories on the latest news from James and Sam, their husbands, Nell asked, "You gone tell me what's eatin' you?"

Kora was impressed with Nell's intuition. She assumed she was hiding it well. "I was thinking about it."

"I'm listenin'."

"They finally let me read that safety hearing report. It came down to my word against theirs."

"Mmmhmm, I told you they wouldn't see your side. Men see 'emselves in the behavior of other men, and facing they own flaws is too big a swalla."

"You were right, Nell."

It's not that Kora was surprised when DC had thrown out her report and testimony, nor when Commander Martin and Lieutenant Owens had celebrated this as good news. She didn't have to think hard to uncover their motivation. Before she had knocked on the door to his office, she knew where they stood—right underneath the "E" safety banner still waving on the pole.

After asking twice, Commander Martin had finally granted Kora's request to read the official report. He must have invited the lieutenant to join them. The two of them sat in his office, watching her read. The term "innocent mistake" jumped out at Kora, who knew in her heart those two words had no business inside a safety report. The term "Negro" taunted her too. It was everywhere and cemented how much she hated it. She scanned through Maggie's section, confirming they both told the truth.

Not waiting for her to finish, he spoke. "Kora?"

Her mind shot back to the last time she had sat in his office, when she'd been *Mrs. Bell*. He'd kept his prize and no longer needed to convince her to play the game.

"I hope you agree this is very good news for our workplace," he continued.

"She does understand that, Commander Martin," Owens interjected.

Kora's vision went red as Southern clay. Lieutenant Owens did not have a right to speak for her. The pinched face of her last boss—the librarian—came to mind. The one she'd kept quiet for, and still lost her job.

"I can speak for myself, thank you." The words marched off her tongue. It felt good to release them.

The other two straightened, glancing at each other. She let them wonder a second longer what was coming next.

"I stand by what I saw, what I measured—twice—and reported. All to keep this place safe." Squaring off with Owens, she punctuated her last words, "Safe for *every*body."

Finishing the story for Nell, Kora was angry for believing it would have turned out any differently, but Nell was too good a friend to repeat her famous words. *I done told you so.*

❋ ❋ ❋

On Monday, Kora was back on the line, deep in thought. She half-listened to Ruby drag out the latest episode of her entertaining love life. Kora calculated the best time to tell Maggie about the report.

She barely felt Harry's tap on her shoulder.

"Miss Kora, could we talk in the hallway?"

Maggie twisted away from the conversation with Ruby. "Is something wrong?"

"Well now, that depends how you see it," Harry answered. He motioned for Kora to follow, with Maggie hot on their heels.

He found a private spot and didn't mince words. "Kora, you've been reassigned to a finishing line."

Kora took this in, unsure what to say.

Maggie looked ready to bubble over with enough questions for both of them. "I'm her supervisor. Why wasn't I informed?"

"Because I'm her foreman. And yours."

Kora watched Maggie fall a half-step back from Harry, from shock or anger. It didn't matter which.

He continued, "This is my call—we need Kora's talent on the finishing lines."

"How neat and tidy." Maggie crossed her arms. "That report came out, didn't it?"

"Yes," Kora said, flatly. She understood the purpose of any investigation report—to recommend changes to prevent future danger. The safety board members felt Kora was assigned an inspection role she had no business taking. Line integration apparently was the root cause to be rectified.

Like some sort of karmic cue, Kora caught sight of Graham and Miller. They were back from paid leave. Maggie's eyes followed them as they passed, her look of disgust clear as day.

Like they knew what conversation Harry was having with Kora and Maggie, Miller slapped Graham's shoulder and said, loud enough for half the hallway to hear, "Time to clear this house, boy!" Kora understood she was the one being cleared from *their* house. Graham's low rumble of a laugh trailed the men out the door. A silent understanding passed from Kora to Maggie, as Maggie's veil lifted.

Maggie looked livid as she turned to face Harry. "I'm going to see Commander Martin about this—"

Harry cut her off, like he anticipated this next move. "No, you won't. He's away on business all week."

"Leaving the dirty work for you." She paused. "How many of these conversations will you have today, Harry?"

He gave his answer by lowering his steel blue eyes to the floor.

Kora pictured the faces of other Black workers assigned to mostly white lines. Her sweet friends.

"What about the executive order?" Maggie argued.

"What about it? This is all coming from DC." Harry shrugged. "No one's losing their job, Maggie. It's a reassignment. Plain and simple."

When Maggie didn't look convinced, he added, "You know I'll put in a strong word. Who knows? Kora'd make a good supervisor on a colored line."

Kora let this sink in, picturing all of her friends already working those lines. "Will my pay be different?"

Hand to heart, Harry answered, "No. That *would* violate the order." Hand raised high, he added, "You can trust me, Kora."

There was that word again. Trust. *No, thank you,* Kora thought. She had been watching over her shoulder for Miller and Graham ever since she filled out that report. That was another reason this new assignment, on the far side of campus, appealed to her. Kora nodded. "I'll go."

Maggie's mouth fell open, then closed, jaw clenched. As Maggie turned toward Harry, Kora sensed that she was about to let him have it.

She took Maggie's hands instead. "It's okay."

"No. No, it's not. This shouldn't happen."

Kora kept her grip on Maggie's hands and met her watery eyes. "I haven't asked too many things of you, Maggie Slone. I'm asking now. I want the power to say 'okay.'"

Maggie's forehead found Kora's. The tears spilled over.

✻ ✻ ✻

The next week, Kora rode a new bus to the plant, through a whole different entrance. She now reported to the other side of the compound, far away from Miller or Graham. She had no interest in witnessing any more of their triumphant return.

Kora and others who had worked on white lines accepted their reassignments quietly, but Kora had one small request and it was granted by Commander Martin after he returned.

As the morning sun peaked over the horizon, she took another gander at her seat mate on the bus. Nell smiled back at Kora, accepting her reassignment from third cafeteria shift to Kora's new first shift line as a gift from God, but Kora knew better. Nell's infectious grin spread to Kora's cheeks. They would make the most of this new experience—together.

Kora kept the reassignment out of her letters to James, not from shame, but because he had enough to say grace over. Opening the door to her new change house, Kora chuckled. James would have seen all this coming a mile away.

When would she learn?

Chapter 30

Maggie pulled into Billie's driveway. She'd already dropped off the others. Before Billie could jump out, she turned off the engine—the signal to talk.

"Something on your mind?" Billie asked.

Maggie stopped. What *wasn't* on her mind might be an easier answer. Her guilt felt thick, layered by Leland's kiss and Kora's reassignment. Since then, Maggie and Billie had grown even closer, but she still held back. "There is something. How did Nick come to enlist?"

"There's not much story to tell. His number came up fast. He was gone within a month."

"So, it was conscription."

"None other than. The notice came in the mail. We knew what it was and left it sitting unopened on the table, quietly staring at it from across the room for a long time like it had landed from outer space. He finally looked at me and said out loud, 'Let's get bombed.'" Billie shrugged. "And then we did. We drained an ancient bottle of whiskey—a wedding present we were saving for a special occasion. The irony of his first words as a draftee hit us later. We could not stop laughing."

"You really laughed about being bombed?"

"Odd as it sounds, it was the only thing left to do. Back then, before Uncle Sam made it indefinite, he was only supposed to serve eighteen months. To cheer ourselves up, we tried to find one thing that took longer than eighteen months to happen. It wasn't easy, but we finally came up with one."

"What?"

"An elephant."

"An elephant?"

"Yeah. Twenty-two months makes a baby elephant. So he would be home way before the next baby elephant was born."

"I think I would really like Nick."

Billie nodded. "Nick's an ass." Her eyes got wide then, and she clamped a hand over her mouth as muffled words continued through her fingers. "I meant to say, *gas*." Billie removed her hand, swatting the air. "Aw heck, he's both. Who'm I kiddin'?"

Laughter filled the car, then Maggie steeled herself to finally say what she'd been thinking. "Maybe Charlie would've been conscripted too. Hard to say, because he enlisted without telling me."

Billie smirked. "So, you've got a husband who doesn't think. What's new?"

"I'm trying to talk about this and you're making wisecracks."

"You're right, I'm sorry." Billie put an imaginary key to her lips, locking them shut.

Maggie sighed, then thought, *Here goes.* "The other night I realized something. I'm not like other women." She stopped for effect.

Billie pointed to her own chest. "Is it okay to talk now?"

"Yes! I said no wisecracks, not no talking."

"Okay, good. How are you 'not normal,' exactly?" asked Billie.

"He left us down here in a house we can't afford and I'm scared our lives won't ever go back to normal. It's been too long. What if he never comes home?"

"They may not talk about it in polite company, but I'm sure there's no shortage of women who are angry about the war. At least behind closed doors."

"I'm not talking about being mad at Hitler or Mussolini."

"Then who?"

"Charlie."

Silence came from the passenger seat, then, "Oh."

"What does 'oh' mean?"

"It just means oh. Give me a chance to think." Billie took over a minute to respond, leaving Maggie to speed through several reasons why she never should have brought this up in the first place. Finally, Billie spoke again, "Nick and I used to fight about having kids all the time. He wanted them bad and thought it'd be easy. I guess I did too, but it turned out to be a lot more complicated. A couple of times I thought I was pregnant, then I wasn't—"

Maggie interrupted. "I'm so sorry."

"Don't be. Anyway, who wants to bring kids into this world? I'd be stuck raising them by myself. No offense."

"None taken."

"See, my relationship was not always tops before Nick got his letter from Uncle Sam. I'm still sore at some of the things he said or did, but I can't say that to him now or even write it in a letter. With my luck, I would write something hurtful and it would be the last thing he ever reads. I don't want that guilt and neither do you."

"You're right, I have enough guilt," Maggie said, thinking of Leland's kiss.

"I wish there was a better answer," Billie said, brushing a scuff mark from her shoe, then her head sprang up and she looked across the street. "Say, I know!"

"What?" she asked, not hiding her skepticism.

"No, this is a good idea. Let's go ask my neighbor what you should do!"

"Which neighbor? Not that strange one?"

"Her name is *Madame* which, okay, does sound strange, but she knows the *future*. My other neighbor swears by her. Come on, it's worth a try."

"I'm not sure, Billie." She looked across the street. "It doesn't even look like she's home."

"She's always home. Her kitchen light's on. See?"

Maggie eyed the little bungalow. It looked harmless enough. The tiny front yard was beautifully trimmed. Maybe it would be okay.

She got out to follow Billie, who was still talking. "Madame told me to stop by anytime I need a reading," she said, before grabbing the door knocker's brass ring, pierced through the nose of a creepy boar's head.

Billie released three hollow beats against the faded wooden door. Not knowing what to expect, Maggie held her breath until the door opened. The woman seemed normal, definitely older, but it was impossible to guess her exact age. A long braid was fastened like a wreath around her head, and her figure was hidden behind an old sweater and skirt.

"Billie! What a pleazzzure." The woman beamed at Billie. "Come inside zee door." Her thick accent was certainly formed thousands of miles from where they now stood, but Maggie couldn't guess where. The folds of her long skirt rustled as she pushed the door closed behind them.

Despite the wide front window, the heavy fabrics chosen for the small living room made it seem darker than it was outside. Not one pattern or color matched, either, unless you counted the fringe to pull it all together.

"Madame, we need your help. My friend Maggie here has a very specific question about her husband who's fighting overseas."

She led them to the front sitting room. "Come. Seet. I get very many questions like zis." She gestured toward three stools and a round table skirted to the floor. Maggie ran her hands over the exotic tablecloth, a paisley tapestry thick with metallic threads.

Madame reached under the table and pulled out a pinewood box. It looked like a tiny coffin and gave Maggie the willies, but it was opened and closed and back under the table so fast there wasn't time to dwell on its meaning. In its place sat a large deck of cards, waiting to tell her future. "Give me both your hands, dahling."

Maggie looked to Billie who nodded. *Here goes nothing*, she thought, placing her hands, palms up, into Madame's. Her fingers were bony, but soft, as Madame examined each line on Maggie's palms. "I like to know a little beet about who seeks answers from zee cards."

Maggie was holding her breath again. She didn't have all day. Grace would be wondering where she was. Still Madame took her time tracing over the surface of one palm. "You have a very long life line. Zis is good. And you have *two* of zee love lines. See right here? Where one ends, zee other begins. Here zis one stops and zee first resumes. You have two lover, no?"

Maggie's face flamed. What was she insinuating? Feeling exposed, she wondered what Billie must think. "No. There's no one else. I love my husband. His name is Charlie Slone. That's who I'm trying to ask you about." Maggie tapped her fingertip to the top of the deck. "With zee cards." Hiding neither tension nor sarcasm, Maggie reclaimed her hands and buried one under each thigh. "Maybe this wasn't a good idea."

"No, no worry. Just asking." Madame's bony hands clapped three staccato beats, startling Maggie. "Now we ask zee cards!" Shuffling the deck and spreading them out, face down in a random pattern, she finally asked, "What is zee question?"

Maggie started to articulate her thoughts, but paused too long and Billie jumped in. "Ask the cards if she should write her husband a letter with her true and honest feelings, even while he's away."

"Yes. I will do zis." Madame closed her eyes while both hands grabbed the end of the table. She whispered words in a language Maggie couldn't begin to translate. Latin maybe? The old woman released the table and her hands flew over the randomly laid mystery cards. One by one, she lifted a card and placed it back in the original pile. She stopped when four cards remained, flipping each one over.

"Ahhh," she said with a certainty Maggie did not share, pointing to the first card, then the second, third, and fourth. "Good, bad, bad, good."

"What does that one mean?" Maggie pointed the card with an ominous-looking horned creature.

"It means," she paused, then exhaled. "If paired to anozer card it would mean somezing, but today ... it mean nozing." She shrugged, elbows on the table, forming a capital Y with her arms and hands. "Zee cards not deciding today. I sorry."

"Is that a bad sign?" Maggie rested her head in hands, then looked up. "I just needed some advice."

Madame jumped up. "Advice? You want advice? Why you not say so? Maman has plenty of advice. *Maman!*" Madame screamed the last word down the hallway before returning to her stool.

From a back room emerged an even older woman, who walked with slow, careful steps, hunched over her shiny cane with a handle polished by years of use.

Madame strung together several foreign sentences. Maman replied in the same clipped cadence. Madame laughed and nodded her head, then gave her mother a clear look of warning.

Madame turned to Maggie to translate. "Maman says you can't talk to your husband, zis Charlie. You could write him, but you can't control zee timing of zee letter. It could be right before he heads into battle or other danger. You don't want zee guilt."

Maggie shook her head in agreement. *You have no idea,* she thought.

"Maman say to write Charlie one long letter. Put everyzing in the letter. No hold back. Then you rip up zee letter. Never send!"

Maggie thought about it for a second. She was a good writer. She pictured the words transcribed from her busy mind to a blissfully blank page. All her pent-up emotions laid out in black and white, then the words torn in pieces with no one the wiser. No harm to

Charlie on the other end of those damning words. "That's a good idea," Maggie said.

"That's a great idea," Billie echoed.

Madame beamed at her mother's stooped frame. "Maman, she has many good advice."

Maman spoke another cryptic sentence and Madame translated again. "She says not that *I*, her daughter, ever took any of her good advice."

They all laughed.

"Please thank her for me." Maggie stood for the door. "I'm sorry, but I have to get my girls."

The three women waved Maggie down the street.

Alone for the drive home, Maggie couldn't believe she hadn't thought of this on her own. It was so simple. *Write it and burn it,* she told herself.

✽ ✽ ✽

She could've chosen any stationery since it would never be mailed, but she selected a single sheet of V-mail paper, banking on its scarcity of space to force her to be direct with her words and emotions. One typed V-mail page served as both letter and envelope, then it was imaged and reprinted overseas. She often wondered where the paper pages went after they were scanned onto film but understood that microfilm was lighter and easier to fly overseas.

It was late. Hating her own messy handwriting, she lugged her typewriter under a desk lamp on the dining room table, then rolled a sheet through the wheel as quietly as she could.

The blankness of the page stared back.

Then it hit her, and she began pressing keys like a woman possessed. Words formed through quick, crisp sounds of each punched letter, and she stopped only to untangle the tiny hammers.

Dear Charlie,

This letter will be different from the others. Things
have changed. No, not things—me. I've changed. That
said, some things will never change. We miss you. We love
you and you remain a topic of conversation throughout
our days.

The girls are learning about Revolutionary history in
school and have grown quite curious on the topic of war.
They pepper me with questions. "When will this war end?
Why did it start? Was it over the price of tea?"

I struggle through the answers as best I can, knowing
you would do a far better job.

I have questions too, Charlie. I was afraid to ask them
before you left, afraid of wasting precious time. I should
have asked though, because they've festered inside my
head ever since. Forgive my stream of consciousness below. It helps to know you will never read these words.

You never once talked to me about re-enlisting. You just
announced it, like I didn't matter. Did you think so little
of me?

When Pearl Harbor shook us to our core, you quietly
poured over newspapers for weeks, looking for answers.
When you finally arrived home that evening, after being
gone half the day, you sailed into the room. It was the
most animated I'd seen you since Pearl. At first, I was so
happy to see the old Charlie back, I didn't care what you
were talking about. Then it sank in.

Why, Charlie? You'd served your country. What about
duty to us? They say a wife should support her husband
regardless, but I'm tired. Your plan was wrong. What
should I tell the girls? You should have included me in the
biggest decision of our lives. Do you regret that now?

I might understand regrets, especially after I found
myself in Leland Martin's arms again. It won't happen a
second time, but it did happen on a work trip to Washington. The guilt is suffocating. If you were here, this never

would have happened. But you're not here and somehow
Leland is.

Where was this in your plan?

I love youu,

Maggie

Except for the annoyance at her one typo, the feeling of relief coursed through her. She felt lighter as she reread her words, pleased with her choices, direct and to the point, like any man would understand. And the best part was no one would ever read them. Yanking the sheet out with one hand, she suppressed a yawn with the other.

From habit, her fingers gripped a pen and wrote her name and his at the top. It had been a long day. She pictured her words catching fire or ripped into shreds, just like Maman had instructed, but her fatigue won out. Lacking the energy to safely light a candle—much less make a fire—she put it off until tomorrow. She looked for a place to hide her letter, where her clever girls wouldn't stumble across it. After trying a few spots, she settled on the safest place in the house. Tucking the letter inside an envelope, she buried it safely under the kitchen counter's endless pile of mail and school forms.

Satisfied, she crawled into bed for a dreamless sleep.

✳ ✳ ✳

"Mommy ... Mama, wake up!" Maggie felt tiny taps on her shoulders and heard Daisy's voice imploring her to action. "It's almost time to take us to Gigi's."

Her sleepy eyes brought into focus two identical faces, studying her like a rare zoo animal. Placing one foot on the floor, she let it pull the rest of her body upright. "Yes. Yes, I'm up."

She dressed quickly, and her car practically drove itself to Grace's, then the plant. Her daily routine had been repeated so many times, it offered deep grooves to ride out the day. She fantasized all the ways she could destroy the letter that evening. She felt lighter all day. Who knew writing a fake letter could be so freeing?

Unable to wait at the end of her day, she pulled into her driveway alone, planning to pick up the girls after. Before turning the front knob, she settled on a good fireplace burning as the letter's dramatic fate.

But her house felt different. Chattering voices filled her ears. It took her a moment to recognize them, because those sounds should still be over at their grandmother's house. Grace and the girls must have walked over early.

Her house looked different too. This morning the entryway had been full of shoes, toys, and stacks of library books waiting to be returned. Now she could see the floor. She found the kitchen in a similar state of spotlessness. She turned to the space on the counter that had held the perennial stack of papers. Gone. A feeling of dread pooled into her feet.

"Hello?" she managed to say.

Finally noticing her presence, the girls ran in for a hug. "Mama, we wanted to surprise you!" Daisy said.

"We've been here cleaning with Gigi since we got out of school," Demi added.

"Where—" she began, but stopped. Her mind felt both light-headed and burdened with the fast-approaching truth all at once. She began again. "Where is that stack of papers?"

"We cleaned it up," she heard them say. "We cleaned out our closet and the cupboards too! What's wrong, Mama?"

Maggie's vision tunneled. "Grace, can I speak to you in the other room?"

Out of earshot, she tried to keep a steady voice. "There was a letter to Charlie inside a plain envelope ..."

"Yes, dear, I know the one. I took care of everything. You don't need to thank me. I pulled it out and mailed it with the rest." Grace flashed her most reassuring smile. "And don't worry, I didn't read one word. We put all of them in the mailbox ... ."

Rushing back to her front porch, Maggie approached the black iron box hanging from the side of the house. She made all sorts of deals with God before lifting the lid. If allowed to beat the postman today, she would never do anything wrong again. Ever. *Please please please*, she silently begged.

The box was empty, except for a few bills. She closed her eyes. The bold typeface of her words flashed in her mind. Harsh words he was never supposed to read were now on their way halfway around the world.

❋ ❋ ❋

With the sun and the girls down for the night, she'd summoned Billie, who now leaned over Maggie's kitchen table to refill their empty glasses. Her attempted consolations weren't helping. "We could always go back and ask Madame," Billie said.

"No more cards," Maggie said rubbing her temples. "There's no magic solution or easy answer to this one."

"Well then, maybe I shouldn't tell you what she said after you left yesterday."

"What? What did she say?"

"Madame was very frustrated at the cards. She swore that rarely happened to her. She wanted to try 'zee stars' instead."

"*Stars?* You mean astrology? Billie, this is bonkers." Maggie paused. "Well, did you let her do it?"

"Of course I did. I was intrigued. She asked me all kinds of stuff about you and Charlie and the girls. Lucky I remembered your birthday is the day after Pearl. Did you know that makes you a Sagittarius?"

"Swell," Maggie said resting her head on her forearm, not sure if she wanted to hear the rest of the story or not.

"And the girls turn ten next week. That makes them Libras, I think, but because they're twins it puts a weird moon in their house of Gemini or something."

"Is there a point coming soon?"

Billie ignored her. "I remembered Charlie was born in June, so we guessed he was a Gemini. Anyway, it was enough for Madame to go on. Astrology's not like a crystal or nothing. She explained that the stars can only offer guidance or ... how'd she say? It can frame the future, but it doesn't fill in the details of the actual picture."

Maggie pushed her empty glass away, making more room for her head to lay on the table.

Billie kept talking to the back of Maggie's hair. "You know Madame charges big bucks for these kinda sessions. She was doing me a favor. Plus, I'm sure she wanted to save some face after the cards crapped out."

Maggie stood. "I'm going to start the dishes."

"Sit your carcass back down, this won't take long. Madame wrote all the signs down, then pulled out a big heavy book. She went back and forth between all these pages, finally landing on one saying, 'Ah-ha.'"

"Did she say what Ah-ha meant?"

"I'm getting there," said Billie, corking the bottle for another day. "Ah-ha meant that she could see the numbers. For a long time there have been three stars in your fifth house or something like that, but eventually a fourth star enters that house making it complete. She thought that might be Charlie coming home. You guys would be a family of four again. It's a good sign."

"Did she say when? The girls are counting down the days before they celebrate double digits." Maggie started stacking dirty plates.

"No, she didn't say when."

"What about the letter, Billie? Does that fourth star mean that Charlie will forgive the terrible things I said in that letter? That he won't read them before a battle and get himself captured or killed?"

"I'm sorry. I wish I could answer those questions for you."

"Me too," said Maggie, on her way to the sink. "It's been the longest day."

Chapter 31

OCTOBER, 1944
KORA

Kora bent over at the waist, gleaning clover from Maggie's backyard, and from the autumn-tinged, weedy mass, picked only those with the fullest leaves in the brightest greens. She surveyed her pretty bouquet, fit for two special birthday girls.

It was her first trip to the house since she and Maggie no longer worked side-by-side. Kora's new supervisor position kept her busy. It had felt like a good enough excuse to cancel their last two book dates.

When the invitation had arrived, Kora checked her emotions and understood enough time had passed. Her skin felt tough enough to try again. She used a neighbor's phone to give her response.

Maggie seemed pleased. "The girls will be over the moon to know you're coming."

"I look forward to seeing them. Seeing all of you."

"Me too. Any chance you could come a little early? The girls would love the extra time with you. We can get ready here and walk over to Grace's."

Kora stopped. "Why would we walk over there?" She double-checked the invitation address, seeing now it was Grace's and not Maggie's street name.

"Grace is hosting, of course. My house isn't big enough to hold all those little girls and their parents. We've all gone a bit overboard. Grace and I saved sugar rations for weeks to make real cupcakes with real sugar. Honey or molasses won't do for this. If we can't get their daddy for them, we can at least bring back a little sweetness of life."

"Those are sweet intentions," Kora began, her mind spinning through possible excuses. "But—"

"What's the matter? You want to come, don't you?"

With both hands on the receiver, Kora came up empty. It was too late to change her mind, and she didn't want to disappoint the girls. "Never mind. I'll see you Saturday," she said before hanging up.

The few times Kora had crossed Grace's threshold, she had come to serve her guests. Today she was an invited guest, and she didn't look forward to defending the difference. But she knew she would have to. Many times. Grace, she could handle. Her housekeeper Lucy was a different story.

Now Kora shook her head, trying to free it from worry and focus on the clovers. The twins were born on the tenth day of the tenth month, and now Kora was here to help make their "lucky birthday" theme come true.

Her mind centered on the sunny skies and gentle breeze, marveling how it could already be October. The cool, dry air whispered over her bare arms and through the turning leaves above. She barely heard the girls come up behind her.

"Find any lucky ones, Miss Kora?"

"I thought they were all lucky. That's why you wanted shamrock green icing for your cupcakes. That indigo and saffron wasn't easy for your mama to come by." Kora plucked four large clovers from her current bouquet, tucking one behind each small ear. Letting her adorn them, the girls stood completely still but for their growing smiles.

"It's lucky that lard fell off the ration list, or there'd be nothing sweet and sticky to fix these on top. Cupcakes don't have ears like you."

Daisy and Demi inspected each other and nodded in approval of their new hairstyles. "Sure, clovers are all lucky, but a four-leaf clover is *extra* lucky," explained Daisy.

"You girls seem pretty lucky to me. I don't recall a fancy party like this for my tenth year."

The girls faced each other, then turned back to Kora, seeming to decide to reveal more. Daisy spoke. "Don't tell Mama, but we gotta wish on a four-leaf clover."

Demi finished her sister's sentence. "To bring Daddy home like he promised, before our real birthday next week."

Kora brought the clover bouquet to her chest, hand over heart, like she could stop it from breaking for these girls. "I see," she said slowly, feeling the weight of response settle on her shoulders.

Maggie's voice boomed through the screen door. "Ladies, the bath is drawn. Gigi expects us at her house to greet your guests in an hour."

Kora was relieved by Maggie's distraction. She couldn't lie to the girls, but she'd given up on luck or magic long ago.

The girls scampered under Maggie's arm as it held the door open wide. Kora followed behind them and listened to their feet thunder up the stairs. She handed half the clovers to Maggie. They were quiet while planting one atop each cupcake and transferring the treats to the waiting silver trays.

"I heard what they asked you," Maggie admitted. "They've pinned all their hopes on a promise he never should have made."

"It's a matter of time before they ask you. What will you say?"

"I've thought a lot about it."

Kora looked up, expecting more, but Maggie slumped.

"And I still can't find the right words. Sometimes I think it'd be worse if they don't ask. Like they've lost all hope."

Maggie lifted a full tray and placed it by the front door. She returned to the kitchen, asking, "Did I ever tell you how much Charlie loved to surprise us?" She snapped her fingers, looking annoyed with herself. "*Loves*. Present tense. Charlie loves surprises."

"How so?"

"If he could, Charlie would love nothing more than to walk through the door right as they blow out the candles."

Not wanting to give false hope, Kora warned, "Be careful with fantasies like that, Maggie. The odds are better to find an extra leaf on one of these." Seeing Maggie's face fall, she thought fast for a brighter topic of conversation. "How did Charlie used to surprise you back in Boston?"

Maggie smiled. "Mostly with parties, and all our friends popping up behind couches and doors. He would create elaborate stories to throw me off the trail." She paused to take another tray to the foyer. "I think my favorite surprise was right before the girls were born. My parents were gone. The doctor had sent me to bed, suspecting I was carrying more than one. Seeing as I felt more pregnant than human, he didn't need to tell me twice."

Elbows on the counter, Maggie continued. "I cried every time Charlie left for work. Friends would stop by, but those were really lonely days and I missed my parents. One day, Charlie came home for lunch. He surprised me with a picnic in bed. He also brought in a stack of books. We spent all afternoon in bed together, taking turns reading books to my enormous belly."

Kora took the sweet story in, trying to imagine James doing the same. "He *is* good at surprises. And he will be again, just not when he thought."

Maggie seemed a million miles away as she asked, "How could that picnic be ten years ago, already?" She shook her head. "We used to joke about our babies turning ten—someday—and how easy our lives would be then."

Kora leaned in for a hug.

Maggie pulled away first. "What am I doing? There's no time. Twelve little girls and their mothers are coming for a party."

"You get the girls ready. I'll finish up down here."

Kora listened to the commotion upstairs as she swept the last crumbs into her hand. Alone with her thoughts, her own insecurities crept in about how this day would go. Lucy worked for Grace and would be there serving. Kora would be there as a guest. Lucy was never warm toward Kora, but she turned downright mean whenever they both found themselves under Grace's roof. It was like the favor of white people was so scarce, it made some Black folks knock each other down to get a handful of these crumbs.

Kora felt that at the plant too. Things had changed since it became fully segregated—some of it for the good. Kora had settled into her new building like it was a cozy set of slippers, realizing how much she had worried before about saying or doing the wrong thing on the old line. She laughed more now.

Kora still double-checked every paystub, half expecting a lesser amount after she left Maggie's line, but Harry had been true to his word. And with Harry's recommendation, Kora was quickly up for a supervisor role. She had lost out to an older Black man, one who convinced the new boss he could keep all the "sisters" in line. When he later bragged about this like it was the natural world order, the women seized every opportunity to prove him wrong.

Kora smiled now at the memory while she checked her just-done hair in Maggie's hallway mirror. That man had never stood a chance—he quit in no time and Kora was promoted. She enjoyed being a supervisor and her ladies seem to like it too.

Balancing the cupcake trays, the four of them walked over and knocked on Grace's door—the *front* door, not the side like Kora had used before. Lucy let them in, warning the girls to keep their outfits clean and telling Maggie and Kora to follow her into the kitchen. There they found Grace in full sergeant mode.

In two sentences, they were divided. Grace pulled Maggie toward the dining room buffet and absently asked Kora to help Lucy, not waiting for an answer. *Here we go*, she thought. Maggie mouthed an apology as the swinging door swallowed her up.

Kora slowly draped her coat over the nearest chairback. She braved a smile, turning to see Lucy assess Kora's outfit—the best one she owned.

"You'll need this." Lucy pulled an apron from a drawer and tossed it in Kora's direction. "Wouldn't want anything to happen to that fancy dress," she said smoothing her own uniform.

Kora gently folded the apron before returning it to the drawer. "I'll take my chances."

Filling a row of crystal pitchers with tea and sugar, Lucy said, "You can't leave that coat in here. It belongs in the entry closet." Her head tilted toward the front entryway. "In fact, that's how you can help, collect the coats of the guests as they arrive."

And there it was. Kora was almost impressed by the swiftness of being put in her place. If she didn't speak up now, the assumptions of every woman and child that came through that door would complete her journey from invited guest to hired help.

"I'm happy to help," she said, holding a steady tone and shaking her head side to side. "But not that way."

Lucy's head snapped up. "Who do you think you are? Miss Maggie's friend?" She huffed, returning to the stove. "Ain't no such thing," she said to the wall.

Before Kora could decide if Lucy was right and form a plan to catch the next bus home, Maggie blew back into the kitchen, freezing in place after clearly reading the room's tension. A hurried Grace followed, almost knocking Maggie down.

Kora and Lucy stood as far apart as possible, stiff-shouldered with their backs to one another. Kora's coat now hung from her crossed arms. Out of the corner of her eye, she could see Grace shrug at Maggie.

"Where in heaven are my manners?" Maggie asked with fake exasperation, finally getting the picture. With one gesture she put the matter to rest. She crossed the large room, peeling off her own coat, then extended a hand toward Kora's.

"Allow me, please."

***

"Cake!" squealed a dozen little girls. The birthday song echoed throughout the dining room soon after. Kora watched Maggie dab away tears as the girls made silent wishes before blowing out twenty candles and stealing glances at a front door that stayed shut.

Balancing the tray full of cupcakes, Lucy did several laps around the dining room. Everyone oohed and aahed over the small, sweet cakes topped with green frosting and perky clovers. Maggie gave credit to Kora's creativity and Grace's hoarded sugar rations.

Kora lifted one off the tray, avoiding Lucy's eyes, then took her first, almost too-sweet bite. Her taste buds weren't as used to the sugar anymore, but by the second she was savoring the treat on her tongue, missing the innocent days before the war, with sugar—the sweetness of life—in abundance.

Charlie did not arrive to help blow out their candles. The girls bounced back from their failed wish, but Kora could tell Maggie didn't share their resilience.

Maggie pulled Kora aside. "I forgot to pull the extra ice cream from my deep freeze. I'll walk over and be back soon."

Kora nodded. "The fresh air'll do you good. Go, I'll be fine."

The noisy room meant Kora could just observe. A photographer was there to capture the moments before and after the sweet and colorful frosting stained the front of each smocked dress. Kora pictured the women who would scrub those stains later. Some of them had arrived with their employers today and found their way to the kitchen.

In a tidal wave of sound, the girls and most of the mothers headed to the backyard. Looking for something to keep her hands busy, Kora stacked some dirty dishes.

"This flash gets so hot. Can I get a glass of tea?"

Kora looked up to find the photographer asking this question of her. She backed toward the kitchen door, holding the stack of sticky green dishes well away from her own dress.

"I'll see what I can scare up," she said, not waiting on a response.

The room went stone silent when she arrived. Three of them, lined up at the sinks, formed an assembly line of dishwashing. Kora recognized one of them from Brooklyn, but couldn't recall a name. She set her dish stack near the others.

Kora considered the right words and, finding none, blurted out, "The photographer is asking for tea."

They stopped their rinsing, washing, drying, and putting away. All eyes fell to Lucy, making Kora feel a bit sick.

Lucy smiled—no she smirked—before nodding toward a full pitcher on the opposite counter. "Clean glasses are right above."

Kora poured the man a glass and left the kitchen as fast as she could. What was taking Maggie so long? Kora found herself in one of the sitting rooms facing the backyard. Two ladies were deep in conversation about the merits of a certain schoolteacher causing all sorts of trouble among the parents.

She found a window with a good view of all the girls playing in the backyard. Daisy and Demi looked so happy. She would bet their happiness was Charlie's wish come true. Wherever he was. They looked like any other group of children, chasing each other in the grass. But these kids had been born lucky, whether they knew it or not.

Not wanting to appear nosy, Kora left the two women to their conversation, and walked toward the entryway. She peeked through front curtains to catch an empty-armed Maggie hurrying up the steps. Maggie blew in and gripped both her hands like a life preserver. After catching her breath, Maggie unfolded a piece of paper from her pocket. Kora caught the Western Union logo at the top, knowing every wife and mother of a soldier feared that Western Union truck showing up in her driveway.

The words "captured" and "prisoner" and "unknown status" floated up from the page. Kora handed it back. Maggie looked shocked, yet desperate to keep it together for her girls.

"I'll never get through this without you," Maggie said, folding the paper and tucking it away before her eyes pleaded with Kora's again. "Please don't leave my side."

Her heart breaking for Maggie, Kora nodded. She would do whatever her friend needed.

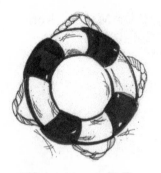

Chapter 32

OCTOBER, 1944
MAGGIE

Behind the podium, Harry stood tall over the room full of supervisors. He read from an official-looking letter and Maggie let his words seep in. "... vicious attack three years ago ... push ourselves to win ... double all production rates on the third anniversary of Pearl Harbor."

Several hands—all from male supervisors—went up as soon as he lowered the letter.

Harry pointed to one and the man stood. "Does this mean our bet on Normandy paid off?"

"Appears so," Harry said and nodded. "Now it sounds like they're gonna double down on that bet."

Another man stood for his question. "Why tie it to Pearl Harbor?"

"Because America loves a challenge. And we'll need every bit of the next two months to prepare for that kind of production jump." Harry gripped both sides of the podium. "Here's the only inspiration I need: if we clear this hurdle on the third anniversary, there likely won't be a fourth while we're at war. Every officer, soldier, and factory needs to double down."

Another hand raised. "But how? We've got the machines, but not the labor. We never stopped recruiting, they just stopped signing up."

"That's right. I didn't say I had all the answers," Harry said. "Next question."

"Is there money for overtime?"

"There's some money for that, but that puts a lot of our workforce in a bind for childcare."

One of the women supervisors finally piped up. "I volunteer my children for extra labor!"

Everyone laughed, including Harry, who responded, "Now in the old days, we coulda put those kids to work and solved both problems." More laughter rose from the seated crowd.

An idea jumped into Maggie's head. Before she could talk herself out of it, she heard Harry say, "Maggie?"

She slowly rose. "I was just thinking. Production is a simple equation: time multiplied by the number of workers, then by the expected daily production rate. Last I checked, there's still only twenty-four hours in a day and if you say there aren't more people to add, then that leaves one number to mess with—the production rate."

Heads turned in Maggie's direction. Too many heads for her taste, but sitting down now would draw even more attention. She pushed on. "What if we had a contest? Teams could compete for who can design the most productive line. The winning design— the one with the fastest time—gets used on December 7 by the whole plant."

Another supervisor added, "We could use the empty full-production line for each team to practice and then run the contest."

"What about QC?" Harry asked the group as Maggie sat back down. "Any shells we make gotta pass those tests or the government won't take 'em."

The same man said, "If a shell from the contest fails testing at the Pond, the whole team's disqualified."

"Huh." Harry thought a moment. "That might could work."

More folks stood with their own questions and comments. Maggie was impressed by the ideas that built upon her own and formed a really good plan for a plant-wide contest. Many of the male supervisors volunteered to lead a design team on the spot.

As the crowd dispersed, Harry caught Maggie's attention and pulled her aside.

"I'm glad you spoke up. I think your idea can work."

"Thank you...."

"You okay?" Harry asked, his brows nearly touching.

"Sure," she said, with as firm a nod as she could muster.

"Well, you look worried. Don't know if it helps or not, but here goes. This war is a numbers game now, Maggie. The one who builds the most airplanes, the most ships, the most bombs and bullets, wins."

Thinking of Charlie and what she now knew about his fate, she felt the world shift beneath her feet. She deadpanned her next words. "The most bodies too."

There was nothing Harry could add to that unfortunate truth. He squeezed her elbow instead. Maggie walked away, deep inside her thoughts, contemplating what might bring an end to the war. She *had to do* something.

❋ ❋ ❋

Elbow deep in paperwork, Leland looked up after Maggie tapped at his office door, cracked about a foot. She pushed it open the rest of the way.

"Come *in*," he said, like she was a welcome sight.

"I couldn't find Mrs. Sexton," Maggie said, pointing behind her.

"Yes, well, contrary to popular opinion, she is human and requires the occasional restroom break." He motioned for her to sit. "To what do I owe the pleasure?"

"I won't keep you long. I know you're busy."

"Never too busy for an old friend." His wide smile faded a bit, replaced with concern. "It's been a while."

Maggie half-smiled. So much had changed since she last sat in this room. She no longer cared what Leland's intentions were in coming to the plant or on their trip to DC. In a way, that devastating telegram had freed her from all worries except uniting her family again. She chuckled at the irony.

"Care to let me in on the joke?" Leland asked.

She shook her head, launching into her request. "I have a question about this new competition."

"It's more of a friendly contest, but go ahead."

"*I* want to lead a team."

"You do?"

"Yes. Let's just say the timing is perfect. I need a distraction." She swallowed hard. "Actually, I need to *win* this contest, not just play the game."

"Uh oh, I just had a flashback to us as kids." Leland laughed. "You used to get so competitive at games."

"None of this is a game," she said, trying to keep the strength in her voice, but her lower lip had a mind of its own.

"What happened? I can tell something's not right."

She took a deep breath. "Western Union came to the house."

"Oh my God. Charlie?"

"Yes," she whispered, eyes closed.

Leland made it to her side of the desk in no time. He leaned back against it. "Come on, Mags, let it out."

She seized another shaky breath. "They believe he's been captured somewhere in the Pacific, but they can't be certain. And they can't tell me everything."

"How long have they known?"

"I'm not sure, but the date on the telegram was a couple of weeks old."

"That is unacceptable. The Army should've telegrammed sooner."

Maggie felt the tears start again, willing them to go away.

"Were your girls there too?"

"No. That was a blessing. We threw a birthday party at Grace's. Little girls were everywhere. I had forgotten to pull something out of the deep freeze and I caught the truck when I walked home to grab it. I don't know how my legs managed to make it the rest of the way."

Leland sat heavily into the chair closest to Maggie. She let him take her hands.

"I don't know if I'm a widow or not. The only communication that's arrived since is a handful of our letters with bold, black *undeliverable* stamps across the top ... that hit me hard." Maggie left out the worst part. The last letter she had sent to Charlie—the one with her confession that never should have been mailed—was not in that batch of returned mail. She told herself letters got lost en route all the time, but in truth, it was killing her not to know if he'd read it before he was captured.

"I'm so sorry, Maggie."

"I'm just thankful I got the news before my family. Grace took to her bed as soon as I told her and George. I haven't had the heart to tell the girls yet. They'll have so many questions and I'm not strong enough to find the right words yet." Maggie took her hands back.

She looked out the window, tucking a runaway curl back in place, before turning back to face him. "I need a distraction, Leland. Can you help me?"

"How?"

"I'm tired of feeling helpless. Turns out the only place I don't feel that way is here. Leading a team for the contest—the national production surge—it's the one thing I can do to bring Charlie home if he's still alive." She shook her head. "If he stays alive. I still have hope."

"You really want to lead one of these design teams? It's going to be a lot of hard work. Are you up for that?"

"I'm not afraid of hard work. I'm drowning, Leland, and this feels like a life preserver."

"Then it's yours, Mags." His hand covered hers. She felt its warmth. "I will always throw you one of those."

Chapter 33

OCTOBER, 1944
MAGGIE

Maggie paid the sitter as soon as she set down her grocery bags. Having no idea how long Grace would be too upset to leave her bed, Maggie was taking it day by day.

As Maggie counted out the money, the sitter wagged a finger and said, "I don't know what those girls up to, but they sneaky today." Pocketing the bills and coins, she added, "They still out there playing, so you might want to fetch 'em home and ask."

Before the woman left, Maggie was relieved to hear her throw over her shoulder, "See you tomorrow."

The food safe in the icebox, she took the sitter's advice to look for the girls. Pushing arms through her coat sleeves, she started down the sidewalk and tried to admire the turning leaves. Despite the vibrant fall colors, everything felt dull to her. She avoided the blue star and gold star flags posted in windows along the way. How long before her own blue star was exchanged for gold?

Father O'Reilly had talked her into meeting with two other women whose husbands were assumed or known prisoners. One woman felt nothing, said she was numb from being in limbo for over a year with no news of his fate. The other one felt everything and wasn't shy in expressing it. Venomous anger at the Germans seemed to ooze from this woman's pores, enough for Maggie to question the same path of hatred for herself. She still wasn't sure if meeting those two had made her feel better or worse. In the days since learning about Charlie's capture, she had yet to shed a real tear.

Her attempt at confession hadn't gone much better. She hated the coffin-like feel of that dark-stained booth. She had planned to tell the priest about Leland, but chickened out, sticking to her more benign feelings of resentment and fear.

Father assigned her four Hail Mary's and seven Lord's Prayers, like they could erase her guilt. They didn't. He did send her off with some advice, similar to the contrite "all's fair in love and war," but more like men aren't themselves to be judged in times of war. It got her to question if Charlie had ever slipped on their marriage vows too, halfway around the world for longer than two years. Strangely, that thought contained layers of jealousy but also comfort. She had yet to sort out why.

Two familiar shapes appeared on the sidewalk, hurrying in her direction. For clues about where they'd been, she scanned their small faces. They had her build, but their faces were all Charlie and never more so than when they were guilty of something. They must have been really guilty today, because it was like seeing a double vision of her husband.

They hugged without meeting her eyes, their hands balled into tight fists. She could almost smell the guilt rising off their down-turned heads. She pressed for answers and her blood went cold. She knew where they had been—playing near the new road, Hampton Avenue, that was under construction—the place Grace had warned them to avoid because captured enemy soldiers were used there as cheap labor.

Seeing their fists balled too tightly, she asked what they held. Finally meeting her eyes, they turned up their palms to reveal a stick of chewing gum in each of their hands. Gum was rationed for them, but the Red Cross was known to provide it for prisoners.

Confiscating the goods, she scolded and sent them to their room to think about their choices. As soon as she saw their guilty postures reach the house, she spun the other way, feeling that new road pull her like a magnet.

What kinds of prisoners are these? she wondered. As her feet quickened on the sidewalk, Deborah's voice echoed through her head. Working the line, Deb had shared many stories of her encounters with German soldiers that frightened the whole team, and her hatred of Germans was understood, given all that Poland had lost.

The rhythm of shovels finally reached her ears. Finding a spot to hide behind a tree, she watched three men in gray coveralls and picked out some German words from their back-and-forth banter.

Maggie thought of the stories she'd heard, like how Hitler had doped his soldiers so they could march for days without sleep. She scrutinized the men for shaky hands or other signs of addiction, but found nothing out of the ordinary. Their movements were sure and heavy chains around their feet were the sole sign that these were prisoners.

A pretty red and gold leaf floated down to land in front of one of them as he worked. She watched him pick it up and roll it between his thumb and forefinger with a smile, then put on the same display for the other two.

Was this how all prisoners of war were treated? She tried to picture Charlie swinging a shovel on the other side of the world. Better than the dark dungeon she'd envisioned before. These men were the enemy, but if she blurred her vision, she could see her own husband in their place, joking, happy for the day's labor and awed by a pretty leaf.

She stepped out from behind the tree. Their shovels ceased, but her heart was hammering so loudly she swore they could all hear it just as well. She placed one foot deliberately before the other, her right palm opened flat, stopping in front of them. Their wide-eyed stares were divided between her face and the four sticks of gum resting in her hand. She pushed her hand and the candy out further until the older, more talkative one finally took the gum back, meeting her eyes.

In the deepest blues she'd ever seen, Maggie saw his recognition of her relation to the twins. He nodded. She did the same.

She turned to walk back up the road, which was still more of a wide dirt path. She'd fully expected to see evil in those eyes, but found the opposite. Somehow she knew. Those eyes were loved—by someone just like Maggie—somewhere far away. A parent, a woman, a child, or all three feared for his safety, just as terrified and tired of their long years of separation.

After a few steps, sadness stole the air from her lungs. She was so tired, exhausted by the unknown, and sad for herself and the world. She stopped and buried her head in her empty hands. She could feel them behind her, watching, but couldn't halt the pent-up tears.

Hearing the slow rattle of chains behind her, she nearly took off in a run. Instead, she felt a tap on her shoulder and gently turned to find the two younger men with the gum back in their own open palms. Wiping away as many tears as possible, she tried to reassure their terrified faces. They must think her insane. Or else maybe they understood all too well. Maybe they'd seen too many half-crazy, near-widows just like her.

"For you," one of them said, offering back the gum.

The sweetness of the words and their gestures reinforced her new knowledge. There was no evil in these men. They only wanted to stop her tears. Her hand shook, taking back the sticks of gum.

"*Danke.*" She croaked one of the few German words she knew, but it was enough. They exchanged smiles, then she started back.

Several times during the rest of her walk home, she checked the contents of her hand. She pictured herself giving the gum back to the girls and thanking them for what they had taught her, though they probably wouldn't understand. She thought of writing this whole experience down, to show Charlie after he came home.

Charlie. Riding the T downtown every day, he'd greet the homeless men living near the street entrance of his stop—men like Abe.

One time Maggie had searched all day for Charlie's dress shoes, certain she'd placed them in the closet the day before. Charlie confessed later at the dinner table. "Abe wears my size. He told me if he could walk in my shoes, he'd be sure to get a job. You should have seen him strut around in those things. Made my day."

Now it was Charlie who relied on the kindness of strangers.

By the time she pulled open her front door, Maggie had resolved two things. First, she would put everything she had behind winning that contest—for Charlie—as the one tiny lever she had the power to flip in this war.

Second, she and the girls would return to that construction site tomorrow, this time with apples or biscuits for the German prisoners, and a prayer that someone, somewhere was doing the same for Charlie.

Chapter 34

OCTOBER, 1944
MAGGIE

Billie strode into Kress's counter, and Maggie waved her over to the large, red vinyl booth she'd already snagged. As the first to arrive, they caught up.

"Do the girls know about Charlie yet?" Billie asked.

"Not yet. I lost my nerve last night." Her daughters' expectant faces, waiting on Maggie's important news, reappeared in her mind. "I'd already sat them down, all serious. I just couldn't." Maggie stopped, feeling those stubborn tears come again. *Not here*, she thought, and forced a smile. "I told them all about the contest instead."

"What'd they say?"

"They were excited. They know we can win."

"Really?" asked Billie, not hiding her surprise.

"Children have a bottomless capacity to believe." Maggie blew on her mug before setting it back down. "Doubts come with age."

The waitress approached and Billie ordered. "Coffee, please."

Maggie made a face. She didn't know how Billie choked down the bitterness of black coffee with no milk or sugar. She'd switched to tea long ago.

Returning to tip her carafe into Billie's mug, the waitress glanced at Maggie and asked, "How many you plan on havin' in this big booth, honey? We got a rush coming."

"I'm hoping to fill it up soon. Maybe five or six more mugs?" The waitress nodded and left.

"So, you're excited about this contest, huh?" asked Billie.

"I am. Scared too."

Billie nodded, wiping a drip from the side of her mug.

Maggie decided to try some of her spiel on Billie. "I'm tired of waiting. For once, I want to influence what happens next."

"You're preachin' to the choir. It's not me you need to convince."

Deborah and Ruby arrived next. As they crossed the checkered tile floor, Maggie whispered to Billie. "Not a word about Charlie. I want to keep this about the contest."

"Hey y'all," crooned Ruby, stripping off her coat and sliding across the vinyl next to Billie. Deborah found a spot next to Maggie.

"Nice sailor top, Rube. Where'd you get it?"

"You like it? Jeffrey bought it. Says it's the closest to a naval uniform he'd want me to get." Ruby adjusted the zipper, showing a hint of cleavage.

More women from their line arrived. More coffee, sandwiches, and gossip were served. The counter filled with hungry patrons and enough white noise to keep their conversation private.

Maggie took one deep breath and began. "I don't have to explain how this war has turned everything in our lives upside down. I used to pray for my old life back, but then I would not know any of you."

"Aw, go on," encouraged one of the ladies.

"No, I'm serious. We've been through a lot together." Maggie took another nervous breath. "You've heard about the design contest, right?"

They nodded.

"Well, I'm forming a team."

Nobody said a word, so she felt the need to fill in. "Let me be clear: I don't know how to double production, but for the first time in my life, I'm not so scared about what I don't know."

A few heads nodded. Finally, some reaction.

"We'll work smart, so as not to be away from our families any more than necessary. What I'm trying to say is: will you join me?" Maggie rushed through her last sentence, despite practicing it differently. She felt raw and exposed as the seconds stretched out.

"I'm in," Billie said before her hand slapped the table. "Who's with me?"

One by one the slaps slowly echoed around the booth.

Maggie was relieved, then panicked, because all eyes fell on her with a look of *Now what?* She hadn't imagined getting this far. These women were willing to follow her, but how would she get them all there? Leaders—good ones at least—knew the right direction. Didn't they?

"Thank you," she said. "I won't let you down." She cleared her throat, trying to keep the strength in her voice. "I heard the main cafeteria reopens tomorrow. Let's meet there at lunch break."

❋ ❋ ❋

The next day, running through her talking points for her new team one more time, Maggie made a quick restroom stop on the way to the main cafeteria.

"Fancy seeing you here," she heard from behind as she washed her hands. Owens emerged from another stall, all smiles. "You came to check out the culinary Phoenix rising from the ashes too?"

Maggie dried her hands. "I'm a sucker for the smell of fresh paint."

Owens was a rare sight these days, busy shaping the newest crop of supervisors. When she did encounter her old boss, it was like their conversation from the train had never happened.

Shaking her hands over the sink, a chatty Owens made up for lost time. "I hear you're recruiting for a design team. The student becomes the rival."

"Pardon?"

"I've formed a team too, mostly military. I half-considered offering you a spot." Pulling the door open, Owens turned back to lock eyes with Maggie. "My experience has what it takes to win. Good luck to your team. You'll need every bit of it."

Maggie stared after her, wondering what had happened to the woman from the train. Entering the rebuilt cafeteria, it looked exactly the same, with one exception: the air was crystal clear. No more wicker baskets filled with lighters, offering weary workers a taste of normalcy. She did notice some spittoons instead and several bottom lips bulging with tobacco wads.

No Smoking signs were on display, matching every other building. Maggie joined the short food line among a sparse lunch crowd, chuckling at the irony of a fire wrecking a good smoke. Kora would have appreciated the irony too, but she now ate on the other side of campus. Maggie hated she was so far away.

Reaching her lunch table and surveying her motley crew, it hit her: what did any of them, herself included, know about winning a production contest? If anyone leaned over to ask, "Say, what's your plan, Maggie?" she would freeze. She needed advice, but from whom? Leland was out. So was Owens, obviously. Harry was her best shot, but it might be against the rules to ask him outright.

Maggie set her tray down, no longer hungry. She grabbed Billie by the wrist. "We'll be right back," she informed the others while pulling Billie away from the table, ignoring her protests.

"Where are you taking me?" Billie asked, her other hand locked around her sandwich. "I'm starving!"

"We're going to find Harry."

❋ ❋ ❋

Her stomach sank with every slow shake of Harry's head. "You know I'd turn the world for you ladies, but rules is rules."

Maggie nodded. "I understand, Harry. I do. It's just ...." She let her sentence trail off with a sideways look at Billie stuffing down her last bite of lunch. Billie nodded too, swallowing hard, then she motioned for Harry to follow her down a side hallway. Maggie stayed put, praying for Billie's history with Harry to tug on his heartstrings. They needed to bend the rules and get his advice, just this once.

When they joined her again, Harry leaned into Maggie for a side hug. "Y'all got what it takes to make a good showing," he said before walking away, then turned to share a wink and a final thought. "I'll be rootin' for you."

As soon as he was out of earshot, Maggie turned to whisper, "Did he give you any clues? What'd he say?"

"All he said was to look through the engineering manuals for the answers. Where do we find those?"

"Do I look like an engineer?"

"Do I?" Billie shot back.

"Let me think." Maggie barely had a chance before Billie erupted.

"Wait, I know! Kora's seen those manuals. She went through 'em cover to cover in Harry's backseat."

"Kora isn't too keen on helping these days," Maggie hesitated. "Not after the way the Navy discounted her testimony."

"You won't even ask?"

"I *asked* her to go to Washington and she agreed. Told her it was the right thing to do. Look how that turned out."

"She's still your friend, though, isn't she?"

Maggie thought back to the girls' birthday party. She wouldn't have made it through the day without Kora. "Yes. A good friend."

"Then ask her as a friend. Besides, the worst she can say is 'no.'"

She considered Billie's words. In the end, it had failed to matter how Maggie chose to testify. Because Maggie was a woman, her words didn't hold enough weight either.

How could Maggie consider asking anything else of Kora?

Billie waited on her answer.

With no other plan coming to mind, Maggie gave in. "All right, I'll drive over to the finishing lines later and ask."

✳ ✳ ✳

Catching Kora in the hallway on the way to her change house, Maggie started with casual small talk, but stopped when she read Kora's suspicious facial expression.

Kora tipped her head left. "You've come too far to be just passing by. What're you up to, Maggie Slone?"

"Nothing," she said, feigning casual disbelief, but soon gave up. "Okay, I need your help."

"Is it Charlie? Did they rescue him?"

"No. Still no word." Maggie shook her head. "The waiting is killing me." Maggie paused. "That's part of the reason I'm here. I can't just sit around and do nothing. I'd do anything to bring him— and James—home. Have you heard about this contest?"

Kora shrugged. "Bits and pieces."

"I might be leading a design team," Maggie stated, then corrected herself. "No, I am leading a design team. And I have to win." Maggie took a big gulp of air. "So, without any right to ask for your help, here I am. Again."

Maggie finished her story, sharing all she knew about the secret of the engineering manuals. Kora was quiet and Maggie let her think it through.

"I saw a couple manuals on my first day in the training room, on a big rolling cart," she finally said. "Might could check if they're still there. The ones about the shells are pointless to read. You can't alter a shell. Bofors guns only accept 'em one way. Find the books that explain the way the actual line process is put together, then find out where you can double or triple up on the steps to save time. You might check Harry's car too. I found some manuals there."

"Thank you, Kora." Maggie leaned in for an awkward hug, but their heads collided.

Kora rubbed her forehead, asking, "Who's your competition?"

Maggie's voice lowered while Kora's eyebrows rose. "Lieutenant Owens for one."

"Well, good luck there." She turned to go.

Maggie watched her back, missing her already. "The girls have been begging for sweet potato pie," Maggie called out, desperate. "I don't know what to tell them, since we never got around to our final lesson."

Kora turned around, shook her head, and seemed mildly entertained by Maggie's paper-thin excuse. "Pick me up next Saturday. We'll make them a pie."

✳ ✳ ✳

The next day, Billie and Maggie passed a message down the line: meet behind the change house after the shift. Before heading out, Maggie caught her reflection in the change house mirror. Thinking of Kora's critique of her bun, she yanked out every pin. Her curls relaxed; if only she could do the same.

Turning the corner, the sight of so many expectant faces caused her stomach to flip. She froze. How had she not seen this coming? Team leaders make big, inspirational speeches. Gathering round, they all stared at Maggie, waiting for something to begin. Who was *she* to have the right words?

Her mind went blank. One man checked his watch and a few women watched the ground, like they were embarrassed for Maggie. Billie's mouth dropped open. Maggie shot her a pleading look, relieved when Billie stepped into the middle.

"We've found out a little more about our competition," Billie began. "It's stiff. They're allowing military to compete, so we need to pull out all the stops. But first, we gotta know what skills we have to work with. We need you to go home and write down every experience that might help. Don't leave anything out, big or small. Did you win a math or spelling bee? Write that down. Shoot your daddy's gun? Put it down. Did you go to college or fly airplanes? Definitely put that down. Bring in your list tomorrow at lunch."

Maggie watched the meaningful nods in response to Billie's confidence. They had a plan, thanks to Billie. Charlie's stoic football captain photograph and his words came to mind. "Eventually you learn more and doubt less, but it takes time." Would she ever be able to experience that?

The crowd broke up and Maggie drove Billie home. Billie wrote down the name of every person on the team. They had no current military, but crossed their fingers that at least one had served in the Great War.

"We need people who can see a multi-step process and find a way to do it better and faster," Maggie mused. "We need more military."

"Who says the military has that market cornered? I'm surprised you—the lady with twins—wouldn't understand that concept just as well."

"Say, you're right." Maggie straightened behind the wheel. "I juggle a hundred things at one time. It's a good point, Billie. Let's frame it that way tomorrow."

"Sure thing," Billie said, adding another column to her list. They ticked off some skills they might be looking for: men who could read blueprints or other drawings, women who plated full meals served hot on the table at a precise hour, travel planners, play directors, and switchboard operators. They got a kick out of how many non-military roles came to mind once they boiled it down. Compared to raising a house full of children, one single repetitive process—like the perfect assembly of a 40 mm shell—was a piece of cake.

Later that night, sleep would not come for Maggie. She saw the faces of Grace and Lieutenant Owens, different as night and day, yet united by one strong opinion: Maggie had no business working as a team leader in this contest. She switched the light back on.

Pulling the tie around her robe, she tiptoed across the room, not wanting to wake the girls. Kora was right about the manuals still being in the back of Harry's car. Taking out the notes Maggie and Billie had furiously copied from those manuals, she studied the words and concepts.

Maggie began to draw out her own understanding of the shell assembly process. The primer, fuze, and tracer lines were the building blocks, then you had to degrease the projectile and consolidate the TNT. The trick in loading was to perfectly insert the smokeless powder propellant into the primer, then add the tracer, projectile flak, and TNT. Finally, the fuze with its booster was added, and the whole shell was snapped together on the finishing line.

Eying her finished drawing of a full assembly line, she smiled. *Not half bad*, she thought, adding stars in places that might be collapsed or shortened. She had arrived early to work last week, wanting to closely observe each of these steps on third shift. She smiled at the irony. Charlie wouldn't recognize his "last-minute Maggie" now.

A deep yawn snuck up on her. Slipping between the covers to give sleep another try, she counted how many days remained to design and test all of their ideas, hoping for enough time.

✳ ✳ ✳

The term "line" was almost overused among the plant workers. There were hundreds of small lines, like the tracer line Maggie supervised. Those smaller lines made up three separate end-to-end production lines, or "full lines," and all three had been constructed in the last half of 1942. Without enough labor to staff, one full line had stood empty with its government-purchased equipment gathering dust. Until now.

Now it was the perfect place for teams to practice and work out bugs in their design, away from the eyes of their competition. Maggie's team settled on an early morning time slot so the women could be home in time to make dinner, and the men in time to eat it.

Billie and Maggie mapped every strength on their list to a part of the line process. They met with each person, explaining why he or she was being assigned to an area, but also allowed for individual vetoes if someone disagreed with their assignment. To Maggie's relief, few vetoes were exercised. The more they confirmed the *why* behind each placement, the faster it was accepted and owned by the person.

"Can I have your attention, please?" Billie asked, rising atop a wooden box. "Raise your hand if you remember learning about the parts of the body in school?" Some hands went up, along with some cracks about the number of years since they'd been in school.

"Okay, let's try again, raise your hand if you *have* a body," Billie said. Every hand raised. "Good, so we're one hundred percent on *that*."

Maggie might have phrased this a little softer, but who was she to criticize Billie from the sidelines?

Billie continued, "When I was in school, we had to memorize all the bones that make up a body. Anybody remember the 'Dry Bones' song?"

Several murmurs rose. "You mean the shin bone connected to the knee bone, that one?"

"Yes, thank you, that one. Now don't laugh, it helped. And it taught me how many little pieces were contained inside one body."

Maggie noticed a few nods.

"Our team is a body," Billie explained. "Together, all our parts make up this very long line. Like the song says, the knee bone's connected to the thigh bone, the thigh bone's connected to the hip bone."

Billie stopped and cleared her throat after attempting to sing her last sentence. "My point is this. You're all experts at your job and we agreed why. But do you understand *how* your work affects the rest of the line, even after your part is done?"

The room was silent, except for the hum of machines. Before she knew it, Maggie heard herself add, "Here's our list. We've put all your names in production order. Find a person who works in the area right above and below you. Ask them the *why* and *how* questions."

Billie stepped down to help Maggie tape the lists to a wall.

The room buzzed with conversation. It was a good exercise, despite the fact that men and women still stood in separate packs whenever they could. *Small steps*, she told herself, feeling a little better about her own leader skills. Afterward, they circled up to share the new things they'd learned.

※ ※ ※

One week later, the planning stage now complete, they all settled in for the team's first timed practice with real shells. The plan looked good on paper, but today would reveal if their design ideas worked, if they had legs or teeth ... or however the saying went.

Walking slowly down the line, she watched everyone get familiar with their stations. On her clipboard, she checked a name off for each face she recognized, which included most.

A sharp tap to her shoulder spun her around. She found Mr. Davis's red, sweaty face much too close to hers. She stepped back as a reflex.

"Maggie, we have a problem," he announced. This was the third time this week he'd raised concerns. She expected his finger to start wagging any second.

"What problem is it now?" she asked, forcing her voice to stay light.

"The fuzes won't implement my changes," he answered.

She tilted her head slightly, like she'd forgotten. "Did we discuss changes for the fuze group?"

"No, but you said to speak up if we see tasks that could be consolidated. I saw one and told those stubborn women to make the dang change."

"Mr. Davis, if you bring your valuable suggestions to me or Billie first, then we can tell the others."

"We're losing time with these extra steps! You and Billie have a labor problem, 'cause these women just won't listen."

"I see," she started, looking over his shoulder to catch Billie's eye. Billie arrived quickly to stand shoulder-to-shoulder with Maggie.

Mr. Davis looked back and forth between them. "No, *I see* what y'all are trying to do," he accused with one swinging finger. "Don't think you can gang up on me." He pointed to his chest. "I've worked production my whole life and I ain't never checked in with no women." He started tugging off his safety gear. "And I ain't startin' now!"

Placing one hand on his arm, Billie calmly said, "These are all unique circumstances, but we need to be a team. One body, remember?"

Davis kept up his rant, unfazed by any words of reason. "The other fellas agree. This is *your* problem, not ours."

Maggie followed his gaze to a large group of men gathered on the other side of the floor. She looked back at Mr. Davis with a sick feeling. Her stomach understood exactly what was coming next.

"We quit! Good luck finding more dames to replace us." He raised one hand high in some kind of signal and, just like that, every man on Maggie's team walked out. Watching them exit, her helpless feeling returned.

Billie signaled the others to pause the line. "Take five, ladies," she said, and the room buzzed in a beehive of gossip over the dramatic walkout. Billie clamped a hand on each of Maggie's shoulders. "Look at me. This is a small, half-expected setback. Those men want to run the show. They, not you, have had a problem from the beginning and can be replaced."

Billie spun her around so Maggie faced the rest of the team. "Now, get it together. For them."

Maggie felt her tight smile widen, confronted by the curious stares of her remaining team.

Billie continued, still behind her. "I'll be back in a bit. I've got to chase those guys down because they just walked out with all our ideas still in their heads. They'd better keep their loose lips shut, or I will personally sink their ships."

Billie left, and Maggie counted the empty spaces along the line where the men had just stood. All eyes stayed on her.

Maggie dug deep for something to say, but all she felt was her nervous laugh pushing to the surface, always at the most inappropriate times. They'd think she was crazy if it showed up now. She swallowed it down as an idea formed.

"I'm bad at spelling," she started slowly, adjusting her voice level. "I wrote a school history paper on Russia once. Proofed it a hundred times—full of pride to include that sneaky silent *p* every time I described the hostile Russian takeover. I remembered that *p* all right, but missed the *u* altogether. I was happy, then mortified, when the teacher held up *my* paper as an example. In front of the whole class, she thanked me for her education on the aggressive Russian chicken coop." Maggie's face flamed from the memory and the silence that followed her story. She was so bad at speaking in front of groups.

One woman finally got the joke and started laughing, then a second and a third, releasing the whole room to laugh at Maggie, whose nervous giggles finally burst through appropriately. "You see, we witnessed another aggressive fowl coup tonight—only this time, it was the roosters."

The stress release of communal laughter wrapped them all tightly together in the moment. It broke the tension as they got back to work, filling in holes left by those proud, stubborn roosters.

"Mistakes will happen, no matter how hard we proof for them. We learn better from our mistakes." Maggie paused, to emphasize her point. "Trust me, I will never forget the correct way to spell the word *coup*."

Maggie walked up and down the line, throwing compliments and encouragements as she passed.

"Ladies, there is no losing in this game. Only winning and learning."

Chapter 35
OCTOBER, 1944
KORA

With all her weight, Maggie forced the knife through the huge sweet potato. The raw, stubborn center yielded suddenly to the blade, smacking the wooden board below. The sound cut through the tension, and both women jumped.

"Watch those fingers," Kora warned, catching the fattest half of the spud before it rolled off the counter. "You'll need them."

"I'll be more careful," replied Maggie. "Did you bring more—"

"Yes, more sugar." Kora nodded, then pointed at Maggie. "You aren't the only one who saves for special occasions."

"Thank you." Maggie got quiet and then whispered, "I told the girls yesterday. About Charlie."

"How'd they take it?"

"As many tears as I predicted, but also more faith than I ever thought. They still believe he'll walk through the door any minute."

"I can't imagine delivering that kind of news," Kora said, shaking her head, "but they're strong girls. Like you."

"If I'm strong, why'd it take me so long to tell them?"

"Because no mother wants to rush into breaking the very hearts she's supposed to protect."

Maggie scraped potato pieces into the pot. They watched them land in the water, a few splashing the stove beneath. Silence settled between them.

They hadn't cooked together or talked books since before the fire. Their new roles made that kind of free time a rarity. By now Kora figured Maggie had read the safety report, but they had yet to talk about it.

The water rolled to a boil. Bright orange potato wedges flipped and tumbled. As if reading Kora's mind, Maggie blurted out, "Can we finally talk about the report? It might help."

"Might hurt too," Kora insisted, curious how Maggie would bridge this particular divide. "You first."

"I understand how you'd feel, like it was all for nothing."

Kora felt the heat of Maggie's hand on her shoulder, for emphasis she supposed. Kora calmly swirled the wooden spoon through the water. "You *understand*. How's that possible when you've never asked how I feel?"

"I wanted to ask, but I was afraid. It's different when I see you now."

"Why do you feel this need to understand?" Kora shook her head. "This world is filled with things I don't understand. Things make no sense to me all the time—things that are just plain wrong, but I got to swallow them down anyway." She tapped the dripping spoon against the side. "Why can't you?"

"Friends are supposed to understand each other," Maggie said softly.

"Friends supposed to listen. Just listen. My mama used to say, 'Understanding without listening is born from an arrogant mind.' It presumes a shared history we don't have."

Kora read the shock on Maggie's face, and continued, "When you say you understand, all I hear is you believe we're the same. We're not." Kora turned off the heat, reaching for a colander to dump the pot. "And we never will be."

Kora felt her anger rise like the steam coming off that colander, impossible to contain. "We're friends—as much as we can be—but you need me more than I need you."

Tears welled in Maggie's eyes, but Kora couldn't stop even if she wanted. "I have a world that I fit into just fine. That first day we met, at the library, it made me sad to know that you didn't. I felt sorry about that and wanted to help."

Kora couldn't decide, after seeing Maggie's crumpled face, if she felt better or worse. *Candora strikes again. But no.* It was true. White women had a long history of relying on Black women to make their lives easier. Enough was enough.

Kora kept the history lesson to herself. Instead, she turned back to the pie. "Pull the flour down. It's time to cut the dough."

Maggie opened the overhead cabinet, silently lifting the flour sack from the shelf. The light changed in the room. Kora peered under the suspended row of cabinets toward the windows, spotting heavy clouds in the distance, as if on cue.

Seeing Maggie flip the kitchen switch on to brighten the one thing she could, Kora felt a sprinkle of guilt. She was a good judge of intent and it wasn't that she doubted Maggie's. Kora supposed she should say that now, but Maggie spoke first.

"You're right, you know. This is all so new to me. There's no excuse for not listening. It should be the easiest thing to do." Maggie stopped to face her friend. "I'm sorry."

Kora nodded, feeling the sincerity in Maggie's words. "You've changed since that day at the library, you know. And not just your hair." Kora cracked a smile, referring to their movie night conversation. "You built your own community at the plant. It wasn't an easy thing to do."

"*We* built it."

"Though we can't work together anymore, I won't forget you getting me the job in the first place." Hands on hips, Kora smiled to lighten the mood. "This pie ain't gone bake itself, ya hear? I used up a month's worth of sugar stamps for this. It's gotta be good. Or my taste buds will be sorely disappointed."

"Right!" Maggie's hands came together. "What's the next step?"

"The crust's the hardest part to get right, so let's try out your improved listening skills."

Kora explained how to measure out the shortening by even teaspoons and drop it in the flour. Maggie followed her lead, while Kora rocked the pastry blender back and forth. Flour and shortening started out so different, but if you mashed them together enough, they formed the beginnings of a beautiful pie.

Kora handed over the blender for Maggie to finish. "Do you remember when we went to see Lincoln's statue?"

"The Lincoln Memorial? I do, yes."

"I was thinking about what he left out of those grand speeches carved into the walls." Kora paused. "Now, that man's kind of like a saint, so forgive my blasphemy, but I'll share with you what I think he could have added at the end."

"I'm all ears."

"His Address said we're all created equal, but we're not. At least, not all the same. And why should we be? The Lord made us different for good reasons. If we're all roaming the earth, equal—the exact same strengths and weaknesses—then one plus one can only equal two. Different people, coming together with different qualities, means one plus one can be greater than two."

Maggie's elbow hung in the air, mid-mash, as she looked up. "That's beautiful. So our different strengths make us more than the sum of our parts. Our differences make the difference."

Kora nodded, repeating the phrase, "Differences make the difference. Yes, like that."

Maggie set the blender down. "Plus, the more we try to prove we are equal, the more they will try and prove us wrong. What if we had a way to prove that our differences make the difference?"

"I'm listening," Kora responded.

"Um. Well." Maggie cringed like she was about to confess. "I didn't want to admit this to you, but every last man on my design team quit on me last week. They walked right over and joined up with Owens instead. Turns out I'm a horrible team leader, and we'll probably need to forfeit on Monday. They knew all our process ideas and we can't find replacements on such short notice."

"Where are you going with this?" Kora asked, suspicious again.

Maggie's nose crinkled through a long pause. "What if we joined our teams together for the contest? I think we've learned how hard it is to be the only difference in the room. What if this team of all women is as Black as it is white?"

Kora let the idea sink in, ready to poke holes. "I don't know. There's not a lot of trust left after the fire."

"I hear that. Maybe together we can build that trust back up? Just think how proud James and Charlie would be. We could win this contest. For them."

Kora's mind started ticking through who she'd pick out of the women on her line—women who could help them win. She started to nod 'okay,' but Maggie's floury bear hug prevented her neck from any further movement.

Kora spoke through one of Maggie's runaway curls. "I'll ask my team, but we still got to convince Commander Martin, don't we?"

"I suppose that'll be our first hurdle," admitted Maggie, finally unwinding from their hug.

"From what I know, it won't be easy to convince that man to give us a chance. I could go with you when you ask him."

"Thanks, but no. This is something I have to do on my own."

It was hard for Kora not to judge Maggie for entertaining thoughts of a man other than her husband. From all the stories she'd shared, Charlie seemed more than enough.

"You want to talk about it?" Kora asked, as their fingers pressed the dough, filling the shape of the pie tin.

Maggie glanced back through the empty hallway. No girls in sight, but she still lowered her voice. "I feel silly. And incredibly guilty. I love my husband." Her soft voice cracked. "Maybe I don't deserve the chance to get to tell him that again."

Kora stopped pressing the dough. She squeezed their floury hands together and locked eyes. "You're human, Maggie. Give yourself grace. This war has drug out longer than anybody knew.

You and I've found strengths we never knew about, but we've tripped over some weaknesses too."

Maggie nodded, but didn't say more.

"Who else knows about you and him? Did Grace's big nose ever sniff it out?"

"No, just your nose."

They both laughed, one giggle feeding off the other, and slowly releasing the tension. Their laughter must have drawn the attention of Daisy and Demi, because twin sets of feet sounded like thunder coming down the stairs. They threw their arms around Kora's middle.

"Kora!" one said.

"You're here! And you're cooking without us," the other added.

Kora kept her floury hands in the air but savored the sweetness of their hug. "Now this ain't fair. I can't tell who's who from the tops of your heads. And it doesn't help when you dress alike." Kora caught Maggie's eye. "So much for differences making a difference here, huh?"

Maggie stopped in her tracks. "You know what? You're right. Girls, you are free to wear whatever outfit suits you." She paused, before adding, "On most days."

The girls turned to their mother. "Really?" they said in unison, like the idea had never entered their mind.

"Really."

One twin looked up at Kora, who immediately recognized Demi's wide smile. "We want to help with the sweet potatoes too."

"You're right on time, my loves. Let's finish this pie."

Chapter 36

OCTOBER, 1944
MAGGIE

Waiting to see Leland, Maggie closed her eyes and pictured her husband's football captain picture. The one that was on proud display in his father's study. Charlie had said that confident stance was just an act—one expected by his team.

Now, keeping up her own act, she held her ground with Leland.

"Let me get this straight," he said from behind his desk, poorly masking his irritation. He had remained quiet while she presented her full case, but now it was his turn. "Half your team quits—the male half—and now you're asking to bend the rules, replacing them with all women? From the colored lines, no less."

"Yes, that covers it," Maggie said.

"Are you aware of how many favors you've asked of me, sitting in that very chair? I do believe Maggie Fraser's taking advantage of our friendship."

"If Maggie *Slone* is taking advantage of anything, I learned it from you," she shot back, thinking of his dance floor kiss. She happily watched him blush.

"You're asking too much. Direct orders coming from that report were crystal clear: fully separate the colored lines. Can't go backward again. And I certainly won't allow an all-woman team."

"Why not? It's probably ninety percent women working here as it is. Of many colors. It's the law of averages that at least one team is all female."

"Because this plant has worked too hard recruiting every man we've got. I won't have them quit in humiliation."

"So you're saying we can win."

"I'm *saying* we aren't the only game in town. Many of these men are skilled and in high demand. Some were already rejected by the military, so yes they come with fragile egos."

That pushed a button. "Why does this matter so much to you? The country's at war and you're putting the male ego above victory." She paused to make her point. "Funny, maybe there's a poster for that?"

He didn't miss a beat. "*When* this country wins the war, men will return to run the factories and the offices." His voice rose slightly. "And women, White and Black, will be relieved and happy to get their pre-war lives back." He looked up, like this was the first time his next thought had crossed his mind. "Besides, you don't have a good track record for returning favors. Not to mention orders."

And there it was. Leland was still sore over Maggie's safety hearing testimony. She hadn't followed orders then, so why should he comply now? A quieter Maggie said, "For all the difference that made. Miller and Graham are back, and Kora's gone."

"She isn't gone," he softened. "She's still here. And so am I. You are going through a lot right now, Mags. I want to help you."

"One chance is all I'm asking. I need to do this, Leland."

He shook his head. "If it were up to me, I'd say yes, but my hands are tied."

Like the team captain she channeled, she wouldn't give up so easily. "That doesn't sound like the Leland Martin I remember. You get what you want." The words flew out of her mouth fast, before she lost her nerve. "Isn't that why you came here? Intentionally, I mean."

He blinked. "Is that what you think?"

"It's what it looks like." She softened her tone but mustered a confident nod. "Yes, it's what I think."

He turned to the wall, avoiding her eyes, before he finally said, "I suppose that would make me the worst kind of person."

She stayed quiet, and felt a little saddened by the pain re-sculpting his handsome profile.

He stood up, signaling an end to their meeting. "Alright, Maggie Slone. You win. You've got your one last favor."

❋ ❋ ❋

When Kora and Maggie had invited their friends to the basement of St. Peter's, everyone filed in, full of chatter at what this was all about. They migrated neatly into Black and white halves of the room. Not a great start for their planned "differences make the difference" speech, which went over like a lead balloon. Maggie and Kora stood at the front of the room, trying to decide the best way to break the ice.

Billie was no help, but at least she had come. Maggie was relieved when she walked in with the others and planted herself in a chair, though anyone in the room could read Billie like a book—arms wrapped tight with one leg crossed and swinging wildly.

Billie's agitation had begun a few days before, when Maggie told her Kora had recruited replacements for the men that quit their team.

"Why them? I was recruiting some replacements myself."

"Well," Maggie said, hands on hips, "who'd you get?"

Pushing out her chin, Billie answered, "I'm still working on it. It's not as easy as it looks, you know. Some are downright suspicious about why we want to band together. Turns out women can be very distrustful of other women."

"I could have told you that." Maggie paused just enough to let Billie know she was proof of the matter.

Billie turned away. "If Kora's so smart, let her help you figure this out. You don't need me."

Maggie dropped it, hoping Billie would come around when she got to know her new team members. Tenacity was Billie's strength and her weakness. Maggie knew one thing for sure. None of this worked without Kora, without Billie, without every woman now sitting in this church basement.

Kora whispered to Maggie that she had an idea. Maggie returned to her seat, curious, and a little nervous. Kora introduced her audience to a game and got not a few grumbles in return.

"Now hear me out. If everyone tries it, we're all in the same boat," Kora reasoned.

Maggie craned her neck right and left, trying to read the audience and finding more than a few skeptical looks. *What was Kora cooking up?* She hoped this same boat wasn't the Titanic.

"Maggie and I done a fair amount of talking this past year. Recently we reached a conclusion. *Everyone* is an outsider somewhere. The names and places may be different, but the feeling is the same, and it sticks with you. There's a sameness to being different. If I were a book, there would be things you could understand about me based on my cover, but if that's all you knew, you'd miss a much larger story inside. Things you can't see." Kora shifted her attention between the Black and white sides of the room. "Things that might show us where we're the same. Not so different."

Kora clapped her hands once, like she was ready for business. Then she invited each woman up to reveal three things found within the pages of her life, not visible on the cover. "Nothing about your kids' ages or where you're from. And nothing that we can see just by looking at you. We want the good parts. Any questions?"

Receiving no response, Kora said, "That's fine. I'll start." She held up one finger. "Let's see. My favorite song is *You Are My Sunshine*, because it makes me cry and smile at the same time. In my book, there's nothing better than the warmth of sunshine." Kora tucked her chin and peered at the audience through perfectly arched brows. "But no offense to the sun, you will never catch me wearing the color yellow." A few chuckles floated over half the crowd.

"I love my neighborhood," she continued. "It's filled with the kindest people a girl could hope to know. I hope and pray to buy a house there. Someday."

Kora paused before flipping over a final finger. "And I'm a good cook, but I shoulda hid it more, because now everyone expects it outta me and it risks being a chore." More chuckles and head nods followed Kora as she found her seat again.

A woman Maggie recognized as Cela stood up to go next. A neighbor of Kora's, she was a bit of a legend, having survived the cafeteria fire. Shortly after Kora had become a supervisor, she'd arranged Cela's childcare and moved her from third to first shift.

Cela's confidence took command of the room as she pivoted up front to face the crowd.

Maggie envied every ounce of her swagger.

"Let's see," she started, looking at Kora. "Just like Miss Kora, I do not wear yellow, but I do like to wear my favorite color. Folks say purple makes me look happier. Okay, that's two things, hate yellow and love purple. Almost done." She fanned herself with her hand. "Whew, this is harder than it looks. Anybody else feeling the heat in here?"

Somebody sitting on the right side of the aisle yelled, "We fine and just waiting on your number three."

Cela thought a second more, then got a big smile on her face while flipping her third finger over. "Kora says I can't tell you how old my kids are, but I got five, all young and wild, and I *do not* want six. But my husband never seems to understand what made all these kids. It causes quite a stir in our marriage some nights. So my sister made me a little pilla and told me to make my bed with it every morning as his signal for that night.

"You can picture this pilla with a red side and a green side—stop and go—if you see what I mean. I told him straight, I was the only one allowed to turn that pilla. He knew I meant it too."

Several snickers floated through both sides of the audience. Maggie glanced around and noticed more than a few rapt faces. Cela had their attention. Even Billie cracked a smile.

"One of those no-no days, I finished my bed making and went to grab the little pilla from the floor. The green side was up, so I flipped it over, then I flipped it over again. That red side was gone and both sides were now green, though it looked like a one-armed child had sewed it together."

Cela paused for effect, waving her three fingers and resting her other hand on one hip. "That man works hard outside our home, but has never lifted a finger inside and certainly never thread a dang needle." She laughed now, raising one hand in the air as if she were swearing on a Bible. "As sure as I'm standing, he taught himself to sew and made sure he never saw *red* again!"

Doubled over, Maggie laughed with the rest, and heard several wisecracks rise from the audience.

"Necessity *is* the mother of invention."

"Wouldn't put it past *my* husband."

Maggie listened to the laughter die down as Cela got serious.

"I'll add one more thing. His short-lived sewing career happened right before the war started. He left to fight a few months later. I miss that man each and every day and I never did change that pilla." She cleared her throat so she could continue. "It's right there, waiting on him to come back."

Cela returned to her seat as a few clapped in support. Maggie, along with likely half the room, could relate only too well with Cela's emotions. A low hum of conversation started up again as they waited on the next volunteer. Maggie had no desire to follow Cela, but clearly no one else did either. Her palms felt sticky, and she tried to dry them on her skirt as she rose.

When she finally reached the front, you could hear a pin drop. She tried clearing her desert-dry throat, only making it worse. *Better get this over fast.*

"One. I hate speaking to crowds," Maggie finally said. "Mostly because I'm afraid I won't have anything interesting to say."

That got some nods, so she released a second finger.

"Let's see, two. Oh, I stole my daddy's car one night. I would've gotten away with it too if I'd remembered to pull the brake and didn't have to fish it out of the pond."

A few snickers floated from the crowd.

She looked down at her two fingers, desperate for a third story to magically appear. It only reminded her why she hated this.

The room was quiet enough to hear distant church bells, giving her an idea. "When I was a kid, when dinner was ready, my mother would ring a cowbell to call us home quickly. She would ring it again if we weren't back fast enough. We were so embarrassed to be treated like cows, we never made her ring it twice. To this day, I have to stop myself from breaking into a full Pavlov's dog sprint whenever I hear a bell, even at work."

Waves of laughter broke the ice clean through. Relief coursed through Maggie's veins as she found her seat. Three more hands popped up to go next. Kora's brilliant idea was working. The game was on to share stories of joy and pain—hidden details uniting them in new ways.

Chapter 37

NOVEMBER, 1944
MAGGIE

At the altar of her steering wheel, she prayed to anyone listening—God, her parents, Charlie, wherever he was. This was it. With all their practice and planning the last few weeks, she expected to feel strong and confident. Inside she felt anything but.

Walking through the lot, she could see the top of the admin building. Leland. She'd likely see him today. The thought made familiar butterflies take flight, but for dread rather than anticipation. The contest had mercifully distracted her from several unresolved problems, including their last uncomfortable conversation.

Walking at a tight clip, deep in thought, she almost ran into Owens coming around the corner of a neighboring building.

"Whoa! Who died?"

"Excuse me?"

"You look upset."

"I'm in a hurry. A lot's on my mind."

Owens offered a haughty smile. "Ah, I see. You must be next up for the contest. We finished this morning." Owens chuckled. "Torpedoed our best time, of course."

Why was Owens being so mean? Their sentimental moment on the train seemed all but forgotten. "Good for you, Lieutenant. Now if you'll excuse me—"

"Honestly, I didn't think they had it in them, but the men you sent over—"

"I did not *send* them over and you know it."

Owens shrugged her shoulders, as if that was enough to clear herself of any malicious intentions. "Well, I was trying to be polite, but I gotta say, they really responded to my style of leadership."

Because you lead like a man, she thought, watching Owens walk away. Maggie turned and continued in the opposite direction, clearing her mind of the distraction.

As she entered the building and squinted down the massive aisle, Maggie caught outlines of Billie and Kora talking over a clipboard. The seats along the line were starting to fill in with her team as she made her way to the end of the line. She greeted them by name as she passed. In return, she got several "Hiya, Rosie" and "Hey, Rosie" comments, followed by a few giggles.

Maggie kept her smile, remembering the unexpected reveal of her real name the week before, when it had finally appeared on Billie's official team roster. A confused Billie had yelled it—loudly, from her call sheet—in front of the whole team.

"Marós Fraser Slone," Billie had said, her voice jumping an octave higher on the *Slone*.

Maggie had felt a stress headache coming on. She rested her head in hand, because this was the last thing she needed in that moment.

"Is that … you?" Billie articulated each word slowly and not softly. "I thought Maggie was short for Margaret or something." Curious eyes followed Billie's gaze, leaving nowhere to hide.

"Can I see the list?" Maggie asked, hoping it was an error. Seeing no reference to Maggie Slone anywhere, she handed it back. Time to confess. "Yes, Marós is my real name. After my grandmother."

Someone else piped up. "Isn't that Irish for Rosemary? I had a grandmother named Marós, but we called her Granny Rosie."

Billie, Ruby, and Deborah looked at each other, mouths open in disbelief. Billie started in first. "Let me get this straight …"

Maggie braced herself for what she knew was coming.

"Your *real* name is Rosie?"

"And you *never* told us in carpool when we were singing that song at the top of our lungs?" Ruby added.

"Well, I …" Maggie hesitated. "You're right. I hid it. But we also made fun of the Rosie cliché and, frankly, I wasn't sure I wanted to be that girl." She checked herself. "Until now," she finished, adding her own laughter to theirs and wondering why she'd kept Marós a secret so long.

Billie was doubled over in laughter. When she came up for air she said, "As long as we're in confession, I was born Wilhelmina Fina." She almost squeaked the last two words, starting a whole new round of laughs. "What were my parents thinking? I couldn't get married fast enough!"

Maggie smiled now at the memory, but sobered quickly when she finally reached Kora and Billie's serious huddle. Billie spoke fast, tapping on the number at the top of the sheet. "That's her time—Owens and her team. Gotta beat *that* time."

"How do you know that's the number?" Maggie asked, suspecting Harry's help.

Billie avoided the question. Instead, she pointed to the handwritten figures in the corner. "Kora says we need to trim five more minutes off our best run to beat Owens. That's a lot of time. So far our biggest shave has been four-and-a-half."

"And quality cannot suffer for speed," Kora added.

Billie nodded too.

For a split second, Maggie basked in the sight—Billie and Kora united on the same side.

"We've got two big hurdles: speed and quality," Maggie said before glancing at the clock. "It's almost time to start. Go find your seats."

Maggie surveyed the line one last time. All were seated except her. Hands of every color were poised and ready for the clock to start. She was so struck by the beautiful scene, she didn't hear Harry approach.

"Ready for the countdown?"

"I hope so," she said, releasing a big breath.

"Ah, you'll do good. Wouldn't be surprised at all if you gals brought the best time." He looked down and smiled. "Just remember why you're doing this."

"Yes, exactly." She bent her elbow and made a fist, swinging her arm in a mock undercut punch. "To win the war and bring the boys home."

"That's a fine reason, but remember it ain't the only one," he finished cryptically, before migrating to the front of the line.

Maggie finally sat and pulled a curled photograph from her coveralls pocket, safely tucking it under the lip of the table, where she could still see it. Her face and Charlie's smiled up at her. Sandwiched between them were the seven-year-old, innocent, toothy grins of their daughters. It was their last picture as a family.

She straightened her stack of tracer discs again. Despite mastering every other assembly track, today Maggie had landed right back where she started, inserting tracer paper. Leaning forward, she scanned left and right. All was ready and in place.

She spotted more photographs too. Brothers and fathers, boyfriends and husbands, looking serious in their uniforms or else hamming it up for the camera. This was Maggie's last-minute idea. No one brought pictures to work, but if they kept them out of the way, why not? During each timed trial, she had told every woman to imagine his next picture, smiling through his thanks for their efforts that day.

Harry reached his perch, officially repeating final instructions, ones they'd memorized. His men placed five hundred empty shells at one end, synchronizing the start of the belt and the timer with the word they'd all been waiting for.

"Go!"

Maggie sat alert, near the center of the line, hands itching to start. The anticipation filtered out everything but this moment.

They were like suspended relay runners, in position, awaiting the baton.

After the shells left their station, the women from the first legs sent quiet words of encouragement down the line. Maggie had delivered similar words up and down the line these past weeks, and they felt good coming back to her now.

"You can do it."

"Keep focus."

"This is your best work."

"We are winning."

The shells finally made it to Maggie's group. Hands flying over the metal and paper, she inserted the discs perfectly, thanks to Billie's invention. A simple kitchen whisk exactly matched the inside of the cone, pushing each disc into place without ripping the paper.

Slamming her last shell back on the belt, Maggie watched them all move down the line, out of her control. So vulnerable to mistakes.

A growing crowd of supporters followed the shell batch as it moved farther down the line. The pull to join them was strong, but she didn't trust her shaky knees. She stayed put, head in her hands. Harry's words played through her mind. *Remember why you're doing this.*

The voices around her grew louder. Must be close to the end. She raised her head just as Billie placed both hands on her shoulders, gently rocking them. "We're doing it! We're really doing it! Kora's been tracking the time and just gave me a thumbs up and a big fat grin. Come *on!*" She pulled Maggie off her stool, giving her just enough time to stuff her picture back in her pocket.

Her knees held out as she followed behind Billie. The crowd reflected a mix of excitement and shock with the last group furiously and meticulously caught up in the energy of shared purpose.

The belt stopped and everybody cheered.

Maggie clapped too, but ducked out on the hugs. Hovering near the men packing their finished batch of shells away, she signed her name across each seal before they were loaded for transport to the test site.

Harry appeared beside Maggie again, speaking louder this time. "This is certainly the liveliest group so far. You'd think somebody won the bottle-top sweepstakes."

"That's a lot of pressure coming off those women, but it's not over yet," Maggie said. She made room for Billie and Kora to join the conversation, asking Harry, "When do they post the times?"

"Six o'clock by the front flagpole, then you can come watch the testing at Wateree," Harry answered.

"We'll be there," Billie said.

"Sounds good, now y'all gotta clear out. We've got two more teams after you."

Maggie half-listened, distracted by the clock on the wall. Two more hours and they would know the winner. And the losers.

✳ ✳ ✳

Hundreds of curious employees huddled under the flagpole. The production "E" banner was freshly minted with a new white star. Leland had saved that flag and his own spotless reputation, earning another quality star six months later.

All the players were here. In front of the crowd, Maggie joined the messy row of team leaders, where she and Owens were the only women. Leland stood by an easel that held a cloth-covered poster board and the results hidden underneath.

Owens goaded her. "Nervous?"

"Are you?" Maggie shot back.

Owens was the picture of confidence. "Not a bit."

Maggie hesitated a second too long. "Me neither," she lied, wishing for a snappier retort.

One of Leland's officers placed a speaker platform box at his feet. He sidestepped it, choosing instead to walk among the crowd and rely on his natural height and strong voice. He thanked everyone for their hard work and good ideas, declaring them all winners in the name of safety and speed to victory. He confirmed rumors of allied battle lines holding firm and advancing every day, forcing the enemy to retreat. Maggie felt sad to learn this was only true for the Atlantic theater.

"One month from today, December 7, 1944, our nation's military factories will come together as a one team to smash our twenty-four-hour production records." After making his way back to the front, he stopped in front of the easel. "Assuming they pass all quality tests, the team at the top of this list will spend the next month executing their design throughout our award-winning plant.

"One more star and that 'E' up there will also stand for exceptional, because ours will be the most decorated plant in the entire Southeast." Cheers rose as Leland pointed to the "E" banner.

Maggie joined the applause, but not as enthusiastically, knowing what had been sacrificed for that star. Leland reached back for the sheet, dramatically uncovering the easel's results.

Getting squeezed out by two taller men, Maggie pushed herself between them, matching their rudeness and not caring one bit. She had planned to slowly scan the list from the bottom up, but instead her eyes went right to the top.

"This brings new meaning to the term 'Ladies First,'" Leland joked. The top spot read "Lieutenant Renata Owens and Team," but Maggie's name was just beneath it. She squinted at the numbers on the far right and did some quick math. Less than thirteen seconds separated her team from a win. She looked at the times just below hers and calculated more than a minute. It didn't matter how close they had come, though. This wasn't a tie.

Maggie backed up to let others see. She ran right into Leland. "Looks like the underdogs almost pulled it off," he said.

"Almost," she said. Her all-female team had come up short, proving his original doubts. Unable to hide her disappointment, she wished to be anywhere but standing there in front of Leland Martin.

Harry sauntered by, in the direction of the parking lot. He tipped an imaginary hat as he passed.

Maggie reached for his arm. "Mind if I tag along with you? The rest of my group is catching a bus down to the Pond."

"Why sure, I'd love the company."

At the car, Maggie pulled the passenger door shut, making a louder sound than intended, but it felt good too.

"You all right?" Harry asked, settling behind the wheel.

"No, but I really don't want to talk about the contest," she said, arms crossed tight. "That's why I couldn't ride with the others. Let's talk about something else. Anything."

"Like what?"

"I don't know, let me think." Maggie remembered his living situation. "How's the widow you rent from?"

"Doing as well as she can, but you never get over losing a child."

Instantly softening, Maggie said, "Her son died in battle?"

"Yeah. Uncle Sam sent her a telegram a few months back. She and I got matching holes in our hearts, not that we ever wanted that in common."

"How is she holding up?"

"Better. She's a strong one." Harry started chuckling. "Can you keep a secret?"

"Yes, I'm very good at secrets."

"I took her out to dinner last week. Drove around the block just to pick her up, all official, in front of the house. We had a real nice time."

"You went on a date with your landlady? How sweet. And scandalous—tell me more!"

Harry's warm, hearty laughter filled the car. "We're far too old for scandals, but it is nice to have someone who understands your pain. It gets real lonely when life don't turn out like your plan."

Maggie considered his words, "someone who understands your pain," feeling a little more ready to talk about work. "Do you ever think about what we do at the plant?"

"All the time. I'm paid to think about it."

"Exactly. We get paid to assemble things that could take a life. And we just had a contest to make more of those things faster. A contest I'm crushed to fall a hair short of winning."

"Well, I got two things to say about that."

"I hoped you might."

"First, this is war. War is ugly. As simple as kill or be killed. We ain't making missiles, but if I had to, I would. I feel good about what we make. Our shells shoot down planes before they can take out our ships."

Harry's two fingers made a V-shape in the air as he continued. "Second, you ladies got razor close. And I probably should keep my mouth shut, but you all scared the pants off Owens and her team."

"We did not. Did we?"

"I wish you could've heard the good Lieutenant yapping out orders, playing on these poor men's fears of being beaten by an all-woman team. Made me forget she even was one."

"Everyone called us the underdog. Do you think it was a fair fight?"

Harry sighed. "Maggie, I'm just a poor boy from Gastonia. I used to think I had it all figured out, until the day I discovered I had nothing figured out. That changed me, but so did the last two years, working so close with folks like you." Harry pointed to his chest. "*I* think differently now."

Maggie nodded, listening.

"To me, if this contest wasn't a fair match, it was your team that had the advantage."

"I don't catch your meaning."

"It's hard to inspire people, Maggie, but I saw you and Kora and Billie do it. Do you know how many times I thought I was motivating my guys at the mill, only to have them quit the next day out of the clear blue? Your team came together better than I've seen in my career. I wish my Katy had been there to see it. What she could've learned from you ...." Harry's voice trailed off.

Maggie couldn't help herself. "Tell me about Katy." He took a long time to respond. She was about to change the subject, when he spoke.

"You woulda loved her. She could light up any room. Always saw the best in folks. Even saw the best in *him* for most of their marriage." Maggie watched the muscles tighten around his jaw. "A good Daddy's supposed to protect his little girl, but I was too blind to save her. Too busy being *right*." His voice caught as they turned into the testing grounds. Turning off the car, he stayed in his seat, eyes forward. "I wish I'd known you back then. I could've told her what strong really is."

It was her turn to point at her chest and shake her head. "Harry, I'm scared every minute. I don't know what I'm doing half the time."

"That don't make you different. It makes you the same as everybody else. They're better at hiding it is all."

Opening his door, he placed one foot in the dirt, then turned back. "That team you built has spirit and focus. You're as good as I've seen build it. That there sounds like a winner to me. No matter what happens tonight."

Beneath a starlit winter sky, the ten fastest teams gathered together again—this time to await the quality test results. Too many bodies sought warmth inside the one-room shack, including Maggie and Billie trying to tune out the lieutenant's painfully loud, boastful words. Kora had reached her limits earlier, blaming claustrophobia and an upset stomach. She joined the rest of their team to pace the aisles and wait in the bus.

Each batch of five hundred shells had to pass inspection and testing, starting with the slowest team. They watched shells explode in the sky before a hazy, three-quarter moon climbing slowly above the horizon.

"Does she have to talk so loud?" Billie whispered.

Maggie knew she meant Owens. "Maybe she's nervous. This could still go our way."

"Let's hope."

"I'd love to wipe that smirk off."

"You and me both."

"She's acting too confident," Maggie said, stealing peeks in the lieutenant's direction. "Like she knows something we don't." She looked around Billie again. "Say, where's she going?"

Billie turned in time to see Owens leave. "Who knows?"

"I'm going to find out," Maggie said fast. "Wait here." As her eyes adjusted to the dark, she caught Owens heading behind the shack. Maggie rounded the opposite corner and found a spot to watch from the shadows. The dull moonlight was enough to reflect off a shell casing. Owens passed the shiny shell over to another woman in a WAVES uniform, who placed it inside a dark bag. Maggie didn't understand what she was seeing, but there was only one way to find out.

"What's going on here?" she demanded, crossing the distance quickly.

"Who's there?" Owens ordered right back. Another exploding shell lit the night and all three faces. "Maggie. Were you spying on me?"

"Where's she going with that shell?" They looked like they were about to deny everything, so she added, "The one inside her bag."

"You don't know what you're talking about. This is official plant business."

"Officially taking place behind a shack? At night?"

"Yes."

"Please, I wasn't born yesterday. Now tell me what's inside that shell."

"Nothing."

"You're lying."

"I don't have to lie, Maggie. There's not one thing inside the shell. It's empty." Her last sentence was softer. "Meant to fail inspection."

Maggie processed this. "I knew it! You're trying to sabotage our test batch. So you'll win."

"You're half-right."

"What do you mean?"

"Your batch will be fine."

"Then where is she taking it?"

"This shell's going to sabotage my team's batch, not yours."

"That makes no sense."

"War doesn't have to make sense, Maggie. I thought I'd taught you that lesson."

"But you'll lose."

"Haven't you heard of losing a battle to win a war?"

Maggie thought she caught Owens looking skyward, but it was too dark to be sure.

Owens continued, "I've given it a lot of thought. There's only one prize I care about. I told you as much on the train."

"You told me a lot of things on the train."

"Including how many awards I've already won. I left out the part where the men always took the credit. My contributions were ruled a fluke."

"That part I can relate to," Maggie said, crossing her arms against the cold.

"Exactly. So, winning another contest means nothing compared to keeping my stripes."

"And staying in the Navy after the war's over," Maggie finished.

"See? I knew you were smart." The lieutenant turned palms up. "It's the ultimate irony. If your team wins, it proves my case. Women can lead and win, without men."

"You're throwing the contest?"

"Let's just say I'm strategically coming in second. I thought for sure you all would beat my time. I'm going to do what I can here, but naturally I can't guarantee your team won't blow your quality check anyway," she said in a voice thick with sarcasm, pulling a mean chuckle from her otherwise silent partner in crime. "Why do you think I've been setting us up as fierce competitors in this contest? To cover my trail. No one will know."

Confident her team's shells would pass QC, Maggie let herself picture Kora and Billie and the joyous faces of those she'd come to love, elated that all their hard work and focus on quality had actually paid off. It was a happy fantasy and almost enough to let the lieutenant's crazy plan play out. Then she imagined having to lie to the same faces and that was too much to bear.

Harry's words played back, "Remember why you're doing this." It almost felt like her next words didn't come from her mouth. "I can't let you throw the contest."

"Why not?" Owens looked genuinely puzzled. "You ladies will be guaranteed a win and no one's the wiser. You're all going back to your kitchen aprons anyway. This would give you a fond memory to tell your 8,000 kids about." The lieutenant's voice dripped with sarcasm, cementing Maggie's decision.

"No." Maggie shook her head. "Besides, we've already won. We're a team." Maggie let that sink in for herself, as much as for them, then she held out one hand. "A team that doesn't need your twisted help. Hand me that shell. Now."

"Suit yourself," Owens said, nodding to the other WAVE. "Let the loser have it."

Maggie pulled it apart, confirming the air inside. She stuffed the metal capsule up the bottom of her coat, inhaling through her teeth as her body absorbed the cold. Before walking away, she couldn't resist getting the last word.

"See you at the finish line."

Maggie stomped her numb feet against the hard ground to feel if they were still down there. Bodies huddled for warmth, not caring if they knew each other or not. Only three per team were allowed to gather for the QC results. The rest of Kora and Maggie's team had to wait on the bus. Maggie had stopped in to say a quick "hello" to them right after she tossed the empty shell into the surrounding field.

Now she recognized the large outline of a man walking toward the crowd. Harry. "Here he comes," she said to Billie and Kora through frosted breath.

She looked at them both, nodding. "Whatever happens is just gravy, because we've already accomplished what we set out to do. We formed the best team."

As the announcement neared, she questioned her own judgment. Maybe she should have let Owens carry out her plan. But for Maggie, that way would have been as hollow as that shell.

Plus, Owens couldn't be trusted. There was a decent chance she was lying through her teeth about her altruistic intentions and that the empty shell sabotage was meant for Maggie's team instead.

Everyone gathered around Harry and got extra quiet. He was all business as he took his time reading from a sheet of paper that rustled with the wind. "Thanks everybody for your patience. Four teams did not pass quality inspection. Those team are led by ..."

Maggie held her breath, praying not to hear her name.

"Walter Fisher."

Maggie exhaled a tiny bit.

"Bob Loman."

Kora grabbed her hand and Billie's.

"Fred Connelly."

Kora was squeezing all feeling out of Maggie's hand.

"And Renata Owens."

Maggie couldn't believe her ears. Maybe they were too numbed by the cold, along with the rest of her. Had they really pulled it off?

She felt Billie and Kora, to her right and left, jump up and down, then hug her tight. "We *won*!" Billie said, elated.

Kora echoed the same, leading Maggie to finally trust her senses.

"We have a new winner," Harry said. "Maggie Slone and team will report to the admin building before first shift tomorrow. Great job everyone. Tomorrow the real work starts, implementing the winning design throughout the entire plant. Now all of you without a job to complete here, please clear out."

Though still stunned, Maggie let Kora and Billie pull her toward the bus. She looked around for Owens, but she had disappeared.

Before ascending the bus stairs to deliver the good news to the rest of their team, Maggie nudged Kora out in front. "*You* tell them."

Kora planted her feet next to the driver. Even he was intrigued by the suspense. Her face started out somber, then morphed into the widest, most beautiful smile Maggie had ever seen.

"We did it!" Kora announced. Still on the ground, Maggie felt it move as the bus erupted with whoops and hollers from inside. The mobile celebration had begun for the ride back. In no time, Kora's neighbor, Nell, pulled out her harmonica to offer a song. The noise receded after Kora shushed the crowd, and Nell stretched the first notes out of her instrument. In no time at all, the crowd recognized *God Bless America*. The stronger voices started singing, until even weaker ones felt safe to join.

Somebody hammed up the high notes on *Foam* and *Home*. They made fun of their own terrible pitch and were rewarded with laughter. Maggie took the time to memorize every detail: the excitement, shared relief, and joy. She never wanted to forget the sound of these voices, all in beautiful harmony.

It was just like raising children: by the time you recognize a moment as *a moment*, it has already slipped through your fingers. Already gone.

Chapter 38

NOVEMBER, 1944
MAGGIE

Winning the contest felt like finally cresting that mile-high peak—only to find a higher, hidden peak waiting to be scaled. The day after the contest, Maggie, Kora, and the rest accepted the daunting tasks of changing the setup for every single line at the plant, and changing the resistant minds of their former competition, still smarting from their losses. *But we have already climbed so far,* Maggie reasoned with herself and the others. *No place to go but up.*

The foremen assigned a group of male engineers to help implement their winning design. Many cracked jokes at their expense.

"Let 'em do it themselves if these broads are so smart."

"Never thought I'd be takin' orders from women," one said, rubbing the dome of his colleague. "Hell, I'd take your bald noodle over their big heads any day."

When Nell and others reported the overheard comments, a hornet-mad Billie started in first. "How are these sore losers allowed to act like this?" She turned to Maggie. "You should say something to Commander Martin."

Maggie shook her head, but not because she hadn't had the same thought. Her mind had changed after she overheard two men placing bets on how long it would take her to run off and do just that. She didn't like what was implied by their undertones. She considered talking to Harry next, but knew that would be perceived the same way.

Between shifts, Maggie pulled the whole team into an empty training room. "We're on our own this time," she said, scanning the faces of her community. "Which is okay, right?"

"Uh huh."

"Guess so."

Underwhelmed by the response, she kept going. "Right now, those engineers think we are a one-act play. Our win was a fluke. Do we agree with them?"

Arms crossed over massive bosom, Nell's voice boomed, "Not me."

Maggie shot her a grateful nod. "Look, what do we know about those engineers?"

"They pigheaded," Nell dead-panned.

"Exactly. So, how do we change minds that don't want to change?"

Kora spoke up. "We let them say 'no.'"

This confused Maggie. "What do you mean? We want them to say 'yes.'"

"I've learned a thing or two about men, especially these engineer types. They need to be right. It feels safer to say no, like they're still in control. So we reword the question."

"How?" asked Maggie.

"Every time we start with a question like 'Is it a bad idea if we ...?' They get a chance to say 'no,' but really they're saying 'yes' to *our* ideas."

"I like it. We could say, 'Would you hate the idea of shaving ten minutes off production by combining these steps ...?' They say 'no' and *also* 'yes' to the modified task."

From the back of the room they heard, "It's a good idea." All heads turned and Owens emerged from behind the cracked door. "You'll need help. Just so happens I've got plenty of experience hearing the word 'no.'"

Maggie knew not to make a big scene over this show of solidarity. Owens wouldn't appreciate the fuss. Instead, she pulled Owens into their circle, then looked around at every face. "Everybody clear? Okay, let's try it!"

"Can I talk to you?"

Maggie did a double take on Kora's long face. They supervised lines in different buildings but met every afternoon, between shifts, to compare progress. After a week, their plan was working, slow but steady.

Alarmed, Maggie pulled her away from loud belts and machines. "Kora, what's wrong?"

"It's Nell."

Maggie's heart sank. Just this week, Nell had shared her fears with Maggie—her husband Sam's letters had stopped coming, just like Charlie's had before he was captured.

"Western Union showed up yesterday." Kora described the scene at Nell's house. Sam's life ended on German soil. His body wouldn't be recovered anytime soon. Not even in a casket for a proper funeral. Maggie considered that an extra cruelty.

"Nell wants—no, she *needs* a proper church service," Kora explained. Sam's life would be remembered on Saturday afternoon at Little Rock Church.

Maggie promised to spread the word. But each time Maggie told Nell's story and heard her team members promise to show up for the funeral on Saturday, her stomach knots tightened.

Hearing music on the other side, Maggie hesitated at Grace's front door, forgetting about the egg she'd wanted to borrow. A familiar set of vibrato and staccato notes were hammering out of the "Christmas" piano, so named for the only time it was played. Most holidays, Grace played lively carols she'd long since memorized, thanking the loud circle of singing voices for drowning out her missed keys.

Maggie quietly entered the living room, with Grace unaware. Her mother-in-law's thick, silver hair was twisted into an effortless chignon and her shoulders were properly held back, except when she missed a note and started over. Then she would curve her spine for just a second, like trying to absorb her error.

When she finally noticed her audience, Maggie could have sworn she saw Grace Virginia Slone blush. A first.

"I'm afraid you caught me."

"Don't stop on my account," Maggie said. "I can't place the tune though."

"Chopin. At least, an attempt at Chopin."

"I've never heard you practice."

"I do practice, dear. On my own time."

"It sounded nice."

"It did not. Don't patronize me, please." Grace wagged a bony finger in the air. "That's worse than any lack of skill."

Maggie crossed the room, and Grace made room for her on the bench.

"Something's wrong," Grace said.

"I'm fine."

"No, I can tell. What's wrong?"

Maggie wilted, tired of holding it in. "Everything." Tears stung her eyes, but she continued. "A friend from work. Her star changed from blue to gold this week. Her husband Sam ... won't be coming home. They won't even recover his ... his body ... behind German lines."

Rubbing her back lightly, like a mother would, Grace offered an occasional, "There, there." Only Grace was clearly affected too. Her own worry for her son chopped up her words as she said, "It'll be alright."

Trying to lengthen her breaths, Maggie explained, "They're having a service for Sam this Saturday. I felt so helpless after Kora told me." Grace pulled out a handkerchief and shared it with Maggie, who continued. "Not to mention these engineers at the plant. They're hell-bent on sabotaging our success. Because they can. Honestly, none of this feels like winning. I don't know why I even tried."

Maggie willed her tears to stop. "Anyway, I was desperate to do something for Nell. I started making plans for our whole team to attend the service. You know, to support her."

Grace's posture went ramrod straight. "Let me guess. You want us to watch the girls this Saturday. Maggie, dear, I don't like to see you so upset, but can I be frank for a moment?"

Maggie nodded yes, while dread pooled into her feet.

"All these extra hours you've spent at your job while our family—especially the two youngest members—is swimming in its own hour of need? There's so much more at stake now with Charlie ...." It was Grace's turn to be overcome.

Maggie swallowed more tears at the thought of hurting her children. "You're right. I keep thinking I'll make it up to them in a few weeks, when this is all over."

"I've always said mothers belong with their children."

"Yes." Maggie hung her head, defeated. "Besides, I don't think I can bear to go Saturday."

Grace seemed to soften, then sighed. "Where will the service be held?"

Maggie sniffed. "Little Rock."

Grace arched a brow. "It would be very awkward for you inside that church."

"That's not why. I can't be strong for Nell when all I can think of is Charlie's fate. Sam's letters stopped coming, just like Charlie's. When will it be my turn to plan a funeral—next week? Next month? I can't shake the thought of switching places with her." Maggie pushed down on a few white keys, proving how little she knew about the instrument. "I might fall apart sitting in that pew."

She banged out what she intended to be a chord, but yielded another rather ugly noise, a perfect fit for her mood. Only three short weeks remained until Pearl Harbor Day. In trying to make it all work, she had failed—failed her team, her family, and her husband by writing that letter. Quitting now would save them all from three more weeks of childcare juggling.

"I'm a mother with two wonderful girls. That should be enough." Maggie finished, waiting for Grace to raise her hands and shout hallelujah that she'd finally seen the light.

No response came. Her silence grew awkward. Unnerved, Maggie was about to ask for her egg and run, when Grace started playing the piano again. The notes came softly at first, then attempted a shaky crescendo climax before trailing off again.

Maggie listened. The music might be called pleasant, but it was such a difficult piece and far from perfect. Grace grimaced through her mistakes, but eventually got through.

"That was lovely," Maggie offered.

"It was not. Don't lie."

"Okay," Maggie confessed, then hurried through her next sentence. "But I enjoyed it. Really."

Grace seemed to settle her mind and accept the second, more honest compliment.

"You should practice more," Maggie said.

"That was the point in my little concert, dear. I do practice, but it's a long road. What has just struck me now is the fact that I allow no one to hear me practice." She paused. "*Because,*" Grace said, dragging out the word like it pained her to continue. "Because, I'm not ... perfect."

"*You're not?*" Maggie feigned a dramatic jaw drop, then got more serious. "Who expects you to be perfect?"

Grace looked like Maggie was the crazy one. "I do."

"That sounds exhausting," Maggie said.

"That's why I chose to play for you just now. You've shown me another side of the coin. If we show only our perfections, how will our children learn to try?"

Maggie felt a bit annoyed. Grace had turned this conversation to be all about her. Again. "I'm confused."

"I'm putting my foot down." Grace patted Maggie's thigh. "You cannot quit and let those engineers have their way."

Maggie was speechless. Grace had gone from critic to champion.

Grace held her fingers an inch above the keys. "You may stumble. You may fall. But that has never been a reason to stop. You must win them over." She started playing again, then stopped abruptly.

"*But,*" Grace said, holding a finger in the air, "I don't think you should go to the funeral on Saturday. The one for poor Nelly."

"Nell."

"I said Nell." Grace nodded, like the case was closed. "It would be too … awkward. You don't need that right now. Stay home with the girls. They need your more." She resumed her inspection of the propped-up sheet music.

After she got the egg, Maggie waved goodbye. She could still hear Grace's notes after the door was softly closed behind her. Walking up the driveway, she heard George call out, "Maggie?"

She turned as he came around the corner of the house. "Yes, George?"

"If I tell you something, will you swear it stays between us?"

Maggie considered this might be the strangest day, and lately that was saying something. "Of course. Mum's the word."

"I overheard you and Grace. Couldn't help it." He pulled her around the corner, making sure they were alone. "Now, I didn't know your father well, only met him a few times. He seemed like a man with good advice, but I *know* my son. If he were here, he'd want you to attend that service Saturday. I've been promising the girls a lunch date at the club anyway."

"You don't have to do that, George. Plus, I'm not sure I have the strength to sit through a soldier's funeral right now."

"I disagree. I've seen you change, Maggie. Your daddy would be proud. Charlie would be proud. I may not always show it, but most of all, *I'm* proud."

Knowing George was a man that said what he meant, she repeated his words. "You think I've changed."

"I played football back in college. You knew that, right?"

Maggie nodded.

"No matter how bad we were down, Coach insisted we play every minute of the game like we had a chance. 'Never give up!' he'd say. But his favorite saying was, 'Courage doesn't always roar. Sometimes it's just the quiet whisper at the end of the day saying, *'I will try again tomorrow.'"*

She smiled.

"I shared that with Charlie once," George said, before looking pained. "I pray he remembers it now."

Grace pushed the front door open. "George?" she yelled, making George and Maggie take a wide step toward the shadowy side of the house so she might look elsewhere.

Giving her father-in-law a huge bear hug, Maggie whispered, "You don't say many words, George Slone, but when you do ..." Maggie gave his broad shoulders one last squeeze. "They're exactly the ones we need to hear."

George smiled like he was pleased, then he winked. "I was taught that makes me the smartest man around."

❋ ❋ ❋

Flanked by two of Sam's sisters, Nell followed the preacher back up the aisle of Little Rock Church, ending the long, beautiful service.

From one of the back pews, Maggie caught Kora rise at the front to speak. "Everyone is invited to my house for food and to pay your respects."

The aisle filled up with smartly dressed adults and children tugging at starched collars. Maggie smiled at the familiar squirming while scanning the pews to see if Billie had ever come.

Maggie shuffled behind her team as they made their way out. They had taken up two pews, which she considered a wonderful showing. In the sunny church parking lot, many chatted about other commitments they had for the day. No time to make it to

Kora's. Maggie was thinking the same, until her eye caught a familiar figure standing next to her car: Billie.

"So nice of you to finally show," Maggie whispered.

"Nell hardly knew any of us were there, poor dear. She won't ever know the difference."

"Oh, yes she will. Get in the car."

"Why?"

"We're going to Kora's house."

"In *Brooklyn*? Maggie, this is too much."

"Too much what? Support for a friend?"

"Keep your voice down."

Maggie turned to find most of their teammates gone. Two white women arguing in a Black church parking lot was attracting some curiosity. They got in the car.

"What's the big deal?" Billie said. "It's not like we're going to get a medal for any of this."

Maggie kept mum on her own hesitancy in coming today. Though her reasons were different, she didn't want to add to Billie's argument. "Why are you so cranky?"

"I'm not cranky!" Billie folded her arms and sat up straighter. "That smarts, Maggie."

"Sorry," Maggie sighed. "But why didn't you come early and sit with us through the service?"

"I changed my mind about a hundred times. I came late and had to stand in the back." Billie slumped, more ready to talk. "I kept hearing my daddy." She wagged a finger, mimicking her father's voice. "'You stick to your own kind, ya hear?'"

"I see."

"He'd have a fit seeing us march over that church threshold. Sometimes I get hung up on … never mind. You'll just call me cranky again. Or shallow."

"Come on. I might have the same thoughts."

"So, you remember Katy?"

"Yes. Harry's daughter. Your best friend."

Billie nodded. "Former best friend. She dumped me, remember? For the richest boy in town and his snooty, rich friends. The last time I saw her alive, we were both married. I asked her what I did wrong. I was hurt all over again when she started laughing, but then she started crying. Turns out she didn't trust anyone who genuinely wanted to be her friend."

Maggie put a hand on Billie's shoulder. "If Katy didn't like herself, that had nothing to do with you."

"Yeah."

"But what's that got to do with Nell?"

"Not just Nell. Why would Nell or Kora or any member of that church want us at that service? I wouldn't."

"Let me be sure I'm getting this straight. You don't think we should've been there, because if you were in their shoes, *you* wouldn't want us there."

"Yes, see? Shallow."

"Oh, it's shallow alright, but I can't say it never crossed my mind either. You think the problem is us?"

Billie shrugged.

"Some of the preacher's words really hit me," Maggie said.

"Like what? I might have missed some of it. Okay, most of it."

"When he talked of victory abroad and victory at home. He praised Sam for his bravery, exchanging his life for our freedom. He said there are victories so big, the whole world can share in them. But just as important, maybe more so, are the small victories that each of us can bring about. Then a handful of men and women sitting in the pews raised both hands high in the air and their fingers formed twin vees. What do you think that meant?"

"Beat's me."

"He also said the world's greatest democracy is fighting the world's greatest racist ... with a segregated army. I never thought about it that way before, did you?"

"No," Billie said. "What do you think it means? Big victories and small ones?"

Maggie started the car and pointed it toward Brooklyn. "Only one way to find out."

Steering through the hard-packed streets, they pulled in behind a line of parallel-parked cars. They watched people carrying food in and out of Kora's place. If the number of mourners meant a thing in this life, Sam had lived a good one.

"We better get out before we change our minds," Maggie said.

"Are we sure about this?"

Maggie gave Billie a look of warning she usually saved for her children. "Get out and smile."

As they walked up to the porch, it was like a sea parted their way. The front room and kitchen were crammed full. Mismatched chairs lined the walls. It was November, but several ladies fanned themselves near an open window. At least Maggie and Billie's black dresses blended in.

No sign of Kora, but Maggie recognized and waved to one of her sisters-in-law who waved back, found them a seat, then disappeared into the kitchen.

Maggie spotted Nell in a comfy chair at the opposite corner. A makeshift line of people had formed, waiting to speak to her. Nell normally filled a whole room with her loud voice and laughter. Not today. She looked like a turtle longing for its shell. Maggie could relate all too well. She glanced at Billie.

Billie met her eyes with a *this-is-not-going-great* look. Recognizing the freedom that comes when things can't get more awkward, Maggie rose and led Billie along with her, adding them to the back of the line to wait for Nell. The stares got worse, making Maggie wish for some punch to occupy her hands. They were here for Nell, she reminded herself, if she would have them.

"We can leave soon," Maggie whispered into Billie's ear.

Billie nodded.

Nell seemed aware only of the folks standing right in front of her. The line cleared out quickly to reveal Maggie and Billie standing before the grieving widow. The room quieted down. Maggie caught

Kora's head pop out of the kitchen, probably curious about how Nell was holding up.

Looking up and recognizing Maggie and Billie, Nell laughed. Not a shallow laugh either. It was her deep, hearty laugh, sorely missing from the room. Billie looked like she might bolt, so Maggie held her arm. Everyone watched for what would come next.

Finally collecting herself, Nell perched on the edge of her chair.

"We're very sorry about Sam," Maggie said taking her hands.

Billie nodded.

"I thank you. And I wasn't laughing at y'all. You two just surprised me is all."

Nell started to rise. Maggie helped her stand. Maybe Nell would show them the door.

"Feels good to be surprised today. Come here." Nell embraced Billie, while a relieved Maggie waited her turn.

Maggie found Kora watching, and returned a smile, before wrapping Nell in her own bear hug. When they separated, it was Maggie's turn to be surprised. Kora and Billie were hugging too. Maggie helped Nell back into her comfy chair to continue the ritual of respect being paid to her husband.

Kora steered Maggie and Billie toward the food, and they helped themselves to steaming plates before some familiar faces from the plant pulled them into the small backyard covered in more chairs and tables. The comfort food lived up to its name. Maggie enjoyed her mashed potatoes and greens, but even better were the smiles and animated stories shared about Sam.

Driving back home, Billie broke their silence. "Well, we got our answer."

"I was just thinking that too."

"I can't believe you were nervous about going. I'm glad we went."

Maggie held her tongue about Billie's forgotten nerves. "Maybe *that's* what the preacher meant today. Small victories."

Chapter 39

DECEMBER 8, 1944
MAGGIE

What a week.

It had started with the girls returning from cotillion, both in full tornado mode. A classmate had overheard and, loud enough for the girls to hear, replayed his parents' recent conversation: prisoners in the Pacific were starved and tortured. Death was preferred over a Japanese camp.

After another mother dropped them off and they banged through the front door, they begged Maggie to tell them it wasn't true—that this boy and his parents had lied. She hugged them, and searched for the right words to calm their fears while wading through her own.

Grace arrived and had to step in. Maggie braced for another lecture. Sitting all four of them at the kitchen table for tea, Grace filled their cups and detailed their long lineage of women who were brave, helpful, and patient any time the world was at war. This story was new to Maggie. Was it true? It was one thing to hide the truth and another to make up a lie.

She couldn't help breaking in. "Who are you talking about?"

"About me and my mother." Grace leveled the teapot over Maggie's cup, stopping the flow midstream. "We were volunteer nurses during The Great War."

"I never knew this," Maggie said, doing the math. "But Charlie was young."

Grace continued to pour. "The soldiers had infected all of Charlotte with the Spanish Lady. We went to Camp Greene every Saturday and George took care of Charlie."

"The Spanish *Lady?*" Maggie asked, as the girls' attention bounced between them. "You mean the flu?"

Grace waved it off with a slender hand. "Yes, a terrible flu sent from Spain, that's just what we all called it."

"Why would they call that devastating virus a *lady?*"

Grace cocked her head in Maggie's direction. "May I finish *my* story now?"

"Sorry," Maggie muttered, feeling like a misbehaved child.

"As I started to say, ladies, my mother and I volunteered every Saturday. It was a very dark time. That virus didn't care if you were rich or poor, man or woman, parent or child."

"A lot like war." Maggie couldn't help herself, but Grace was ignoring her.

"Every person in our city was either sick or taking care of the sick. Mother and I were blessed to be well enough to help care for the poor soldiers." Grace threw a sideways glance at Maggie and added, "Many of them Yankees."

A wide-eyed Daisy asked, "Were you scared of getting sick?"

"Very scared. I witnessed some who didn't make it, but I also cheered when several went home. It showed me the difference between what we can control and what we can't. And it taught me that being brave can feel a lot like fear." She softly pressed each button nose. "But it's fear that's said its prayers."

"We say our prayers about Daddy every night," Daisy confirmed.

"And that's the best way to help your Daddy right now. That, and not listening to any more school friends." Grace stood, pretending to cover her own ears. "I don't want to know their names, because I probably play bridge with their grandmothers."

Maggie rose too, surprising Grace, and herself, with a firm hug. "Oh my!" Grace said.

Before Maggie knew it, the girls wrapped them both in a second layer of arms, then scattered off to play. Maggie pulled away first. "Thank you, Grace. You're a good grandmother."

"Better grandmother than mother-in-law, sometimes."

"You're getting good at both actually," Maggie admitted.

Maggie pulled over, yanking the fallen paper off the floor. How was she going to drive to this armory place if she kept dropping the directions? She leaned back against the headrest.

Thinking about Grace now before restarting the car, she smiled. Charlie might find their new and improved relationship hard to believe if he came home. *When* he came home, she corrected herself.

Directions now firmly in her grip, she continued to find her route to the armory building on the proud east side of town. The parking attendant stood and signaled her to follow the car ahead. Today's big announcement was drawing quite a crowd.

Coming off twenty-four straight hours on the assembly line floor, Maggie had grabbed a few hours of dreamless sleep. For the production blitz, Maggie, Kora, and Billie had once again taped pictures of Charlie, James, and Nick over their employee passes after they tied them like necklaces. Before they knew it, others did the same. The pictures answered the question of *why* they had worked so hard to adjust each line. Despite the unifying spirit, doubling the average daily production was a lofty goal and many expected to fall short. Maggie hadn't wrung her hands like other women, nor covered up with jokes like the men.

You did your best, she told herself for the thousandth time as she crossed the threshold of the massive auditorium that still smelled like fresh paint. But was their best enough to produce over two hundred thousand rounds? Today, they would find out—all together—whether they had succeeded or failed, after Leland would officially announce the total shells assembled by all three Pearl Harbor Day shifts.

✳ ✳ ✳

Maggie was directed to a small room below the armory stage, where Leland was likely practicing his speech for the employees and press. Muffled words came through the door. She knocked.

They hadn't talked alone in months. Wrestling with her own guilt, Maggie had admitted this much to herself: attention from Leland made her feel less lonely. There was a time she had dressed for him at work, wore her hair and makeup for him, and had whole clever conversations with him in her mind. In truth, she craved the distraction—it brought to life a part of herself buried by marriage, by motherhood, and by war.

Today was their mutual birthday, and she wanted to extend an olive branch to Leland. Hearing his voice grant permission from the other side, she pushed her way in. He was on the phone, so her lips formed a silent, "Happy Birthday."

He shifted the receiver to the other ear. "Yes, sir. We couldn't be happier with the results. Appreciate your call ... next month as a matter of fact. Yes, sir, I'll have my girl call yours to set it up. I'd love to come to Washington."

The room's bare, white cinder block walls made a stark setting. Waiting for him to finish, she counted feet shuffling by the small basement window on their way to secure an auditorium seat above. A reporter lugging heavy camera equipment walked by.

"I look forward to seeing you then, sir." He hung up and turned to her with a smile. "Happy birthday to you too. It'll be a good day to celebrate."

"That sounded like good news on the phone."

"We'll see. Yesterday's numbers might just bring some good opportunities."

"Don't tell me the final number." She held up a hand. "I want to hear it when everyone else does."

"I wouldn't dream of it." He paused. "Even if you begged me," he said with a smile.

"I heard you on the phone. Washington, wow, it sounds like they really want you there. It's the military career that you always dreamed of, Leland. Congratulations."

"Maybe," Leland said, looking down at his notes.

"Is something wrong?" Maggie asked. It wasn't like him to shy away from praise.

"It's just, well, can I be honest?"

Maggie nodded as his dark brown eyes locked with hers.

"I hope I never meet Charlie," he said.

She pulled back physically, wondering how he could be so cruel.

He spoke quickly. "Sorry, I'm bad at this ... I'm not saying I hope he never comes home. I know that's what you want. I have a feeling he'll make it back. When he does, I'm certain your life will go back to exactly as it was before the war."

"I'm not sure I'm following you."

"I simply have no interest meeting the guy who gets the war stories *and* the girl I was stupid enough to let go."

"I'm not sure what to say."

"Don't say anything. I just wanted you to know." He checked his watch and stood, shattering the spell. "Almost time to hit the stage," he said.

Maggie rose too. With a mind of its own, her hand sliced through the air for a formal but awkward handshake. He looked surprised, but took her hand, like he did for that first meeting in his office, only this one felt like a last goodbye.

❋ ❋ ❋

Maggie found an open spot near the aisle, between Kora and Billie. On stage, Leland stood in front of a seated panel of VIPs. He began his speech with the latest war news. He rattled off strides achieved by the allied front with more in store for the axis powers, thanks to yesterday's production records broken all over the nation.

All the women on Kora and Maggie's team locked their hands in a chain as Leland, with great fanfare, finally announced the plant's twenty-four-hour production round total on the nation's third Pearl Harbor Day.

"Two hundred ..." Maggie left her seat as soon as she heard his first word, not needing to hear the rest: "*213,143!*"

Everyone jumped to their feet applauding, cheering, and waving to cameras. Arms of friends and strangers came together for handshakes, often ending in hugs. The intoxication of reaching their goal overwhelmed them all. Winning as one team, one nation, and with one objective.

Flash bulbs exploded around them, capturing a stage full of practiced, stoic looks of satisfaction and pride from naval officers and executives at US Rubber, like they had expected these results all along. The cameras also captured the joy radiating from hundreds in the audience, including faces of pure shock and surprise for meeting the goal.

Owens stood awkwardly against the wall of the outer aisle like the happy noise and close contact were too much for her. Giddy from the celebration, Maggie marched right over and hugged her tight. Knowing Owens would hate this attention was sort of the point.

Maggie pulled back. "We did it, Lieutenant. All of us."

"I knew we would."

"That makes one of us." Maggie patted her arm and started to walk away, then turned back and wrapped their hands together. Locking in on her wide eyes, Maggie added, "I really hope that number makes a difference. For you."

A clearly shocked Owens replied, "It'll help us win the war."

"That's not the only difference I hope it makes." Maggie gave a light squeeze and let go of her hands, not needing to explain further. She returned to her seat as Leland's words coming through the microphone finally beat out the cheering.

"Ladies and gentlemen, please, there's more."

Gradually the audience took their seats and got quiet again. Some of the press started to pack up. She wondered what more was left for Leland to say. One by one, he thanked all of the big wigs up on stage. Maggie watched each man puff up with pride in acknowledgment of his minor contribution.

"And now I'd like to invite Maggie Slone to the stage for a few words."

Maggie spun toward Billie, knowing she had misunderstood the words, but Billie just smiled and clapped expectantly along with Kora and the others. The world narrowed, dreamlike.

Leland's surreal sentences continued, "Maggie's team was instrumental to this effort by winning our recent production design contest."

Her ice-cold feet wouldn't budge. Why was he doing this to her? He knew better than anyone how much she hated to speak in public. She had gotten better at it lately, but this was an audience of *hundreds*—a much different ballgame. Was he punishing her? For what she said earlier, beneath the same stage he now called her to?

Her stomach rolled. She turned to Billie. "Please go in my place. You're the speech giver, not me."

"That's true," she nodded. "I am the better speaker, but he's calling for you." She pointed out all the people clapping around them. "They want to hear what *you* have to say this time."

Billie was no help at all. Maggie twisted in the opposite direction toward Kora. "I can't do this. You've got to help me."

Kora nodded slowly. "You *can* do this."

"No, you don't understand. This is too many people. I'll be the fool."

"You can do it," she said, head motioning toward the back of the auditorium. "For them." Following her gaze, Maggie was shocked to find her own children sitting on either side of Grace.

She confronted Kora again. "Why are they here?"

"I asked Grace to bring them."

Maggie looked back at her family. "But why would you do that?"

"I could say the same to you. Why did you ask my family to come today?" Kora asked.

"Because I wanted them to see and hear your accomplishment …" Her words trailed off.

"Sounds about right," Kora finished, looking rather smug.

Maggie filled her lungs as far as they would go and pushed on her knees until she was upright. She found her way to the stage, feeling separated from her body, watching her own self ascend the steps.

As she reached the last stair—as surprised as anyone that her legs held out—Harry rewarded her with a smile and a nod of confidence from the front row. Leland took the seat next to Harry. She glared down at the top of Leland's head as he pretended to be absorbed in his notes. He knew she hated public speaking. He was proving a point, and now she would fail spectacularly in front of her daughters. Her new height revealed a thinning patch of his thick, dark mane. She smiled.

Gingerly, she inched the microphone down to her height. So many people were staring back. Some looked embarrassed for her. The silence was punctured by some clearing throats. Desperate to speak, she felt frozen in place.

Then the beautiful faces of her teammates floated up from the crowd. Their tribe felt primal, and the community they formed came into clear focus. She would do anything for these faces. Even tackle her biggest fear.

And in that moment, she finally understood why Charlie had gone down to the recruitment office that day. Charlie didn't leave her and the girls, *he answered the call to protect his tribe*. Unlike Leland, he knew Maggie was strong, even if she didn't. Charlie knew his community—his army—would need him even more than his family. The need to save his fellow soldiers was separate from his deep love for her and the girls. She was stronger because of his choice to serve. The girls were stronger because of her choice to work.

Maggie's community now took up whole rows of this auditorium. Billie, Kora, Nell, Ruby, Deborah, and the rest met her gaze with patience, like they knew she could do this. Only then did the words trickle out. She leaned in.

"Why ..." Her first word shot through the mic, picking up an echo and a violent screech. She pulled back farther, cleared her throat, and tried again. "Why, at times like these, when I can't think of a single thing to say, do I hear my mother's voice?" She was genuinely asking but got no response. "Does that ever happen to you?"

A small ripple of noise rose up. She scanned the crowd trying to find its origin. Were they laughing at her? With her?

She kept going. "My mother would say ... and to be clear, this comes through my head with the thickest Northern accent you can imagine ... 'Do something today your future self will thank you for.'"

She looked back at her girls. "Of course, most of the time she was just trying to get me to eat broccoli, or do my lessons, but it stayed with me. She lives only in my head now, but my mother was definitely with me the day I signed up to work at our plant. And she was right, because I will always be thankful for the first day I came to work with each of you."

A flash bulb went off, but thankfully didn't blind her. She kept focus, the words coming easier now. "We wear uniforms to show our similarities and our differences." She pointed to her shoulder, where military men divided rank. "But there is no uniform for kindness, for cleverness, for loyalty ...." Maggie found Owens still standing against the wall, apart from the rest. "Nor for self-sacrifice in the face of uncertainty."

Owens cracked a smile for one second, then resumed her mask.

"For those things, you have to open the book cover and read the pages to know what's inside."

Maggie caught some impatient faces and hurried toward her final point.

"We've all lost so much. It's understandable to avoid risk." She shifted her weight between her feet, then stopped, self-conscious of swaying. "I'm glad I took a risk, because I gained the most wonderful community of souls—right there." Maggie pointed at her team, who all cheered in response.

"I'm blessed to know these women and to be known—flaws and all—by them." She beamed in their direction before another revelation hit her hard. "*And* they should be up here with me. We wouldn't be celebrating here today if it weren't for every single one of them. Please come up, ladies." She assessed the space behind her. "There's plenty of room."

She glanced back at the balding panel and asked, "You gentleman don't mind, do you?" Aside from looking a bit shocked, they were already moving their chairs out of the way. Leland didn't look happy about her invitation either, but as he tried to rise, Harry laid a calm hand over his forearm, keeping the commander to his seat.

Some ladies jumped right into the aisle on their way to the stage. Others held back.

"Yes, *you*," she said into the microphone. "Come! This is your time. Your success. None of this happened without each of you." She motioned them down. Maggie called out each name as they reached the top step and filled in around her. After the last name was called, Maggie started clapping. The audience followed suit, filling the room with sound. A reporter quickly unpacked his equipment for this unexpected photo opportunity, asking them to bunch together for a group shot.

Smiling for the cameras, surrounded by her community, her friends, Maggie was overwhelmed. With arms around Billie and Kora, she was too happy to care about going blind from the flash— she would do anything to freeze this rare, perfect moment in time.

The room got quiet again, looking for someone to close this show out. She saw Leland stewing in his chair, arms folded. He shrugged, meaning she was on her own.

She approached the microphone again, thanked everyone for coming and congratulated them again on exceeding their production goal.

"So much has changed. We've changed. We've accomplished goals we never thought possible. That's especially true for me." Catching sight of Grace sitting tall, poised, and beautiful as ever, she found the right words to close it out. "A very wise woman—also a great mother—once told me that courage and fear might look very different from the outside, but inside they feel just the same. Maybe I'm more courageous than I thought.

"Maybe we all are."

Chapter 40

APRIL 12, 1945
KORA

Kora cranked Maggie's car window for a little breeze, being careful not to mess up her hair. Friends had invited her over for dinner tonight, and she wanted to look nice. She admired the afternoon sun, hanging low in the sky.

Maggie hummed softly to the radio.

"What'd you think of the supervisor meeting?" Kora asked.

"Funny, I was about to ask you the same question. It seems like a pivot, all right. Production is going down. On purpose."

Change was coming. Kora could feel it. "I suppose that means the war is winding down."

"I can't see how those two aren't related."

Kora chuckled. "I got one of my feelings, though. Good news is coming soon." Maggie nodded, looking a little sad. "Maybe it'll be good news about Charlie this time," Kora added.

"Or James," Maggie said.

"Yes, my sweet James."

"Your intuition has been right more than a few times. You were right about Leland."

"How so?"

"I talked to my sister last week. Helen finally came clean about how Leland knew exactly where I worked. They bumped into each other at a dinner party. It came up, innocently on her part, but she had forgotten about all that until I told her about his big promotion and move to Washington last month."

Kora felt a little more validated, not surprised to be right about Leland. She watched for signs of emotion written on her friend's profile, but Maggie stayed stoic.

"I can't stay mad at my sister though. She reminded me if Leland hadn't left, I never would have met Charlie."

Kora wished she'd brought up the same good point. "Ain't she a professor? Hmm. That's a smart lady right there." Kora paused before addressing a more serious matter. "The real question is: are you still mad at yourself?"

"Yes, but I've given it some thought, and I think I understand it better. Leland went to great lengths to enter my life again. Deep down, *that* is what drew me to him, because it was the one thing I didn't feel from Charlie."

Kora tried to sort through all that, feeling more and more grateful for her uncomplicated relationship with James.

"I wanted Charlie's regret for leaving us to burn as strong. Maybe it did, and I just didn't feel it at the time. Regardless, I realized that any feelings I had for Leland were twisted inside my love for Charlie. It always comes back to Charlie."

"Back to Charlie," Kora repeated, patting Maggie's shoulder. "And soon Charlie will come back to you."

Cruising the dusty roads back to Charlotte, Maggie kept her speedometer under thirty-five before slowing even more to wind through the sleepy residential streets on the way to Brooklyn. Kora began to point out which trees were starting to bud, when the music on the radio abruptly stopped, replaced with the somber voice of Bob Trout.

"We interrupt this program ..." Static muffled the rest of his sentence. Maggie hurried to a stop, adjusting the knobs on either end to make the broadcast louder and clearer.

"...from CBS World News, the Press Association has just announced that President Roosevelt is dead. The president died of a cerebral hemorrhage. All we know so far is that the President died at Warm Springs in Georgia ...."

Shocked, Maggie and Kora clung to Trout's words and the few known details. A tear rolling down one cheek, Kora finally spoke. "Guess my intuition was wrong. This isn't good news at all ..." *One more loss*, thought Kora. *How much more can this country take?*

Their trip to Washington had seemed a million years ago, but now the memory flooded back. The time they'd seen Roosevelt in person—together. Now they held hands and cried, partly for the passing of a man who had helped the country survive the Great Depression and a World War, but mostly for the finality and uniformity of death, no matter who you were in life.

Maggie dabbed at her tears and offered Kora a handkerchief from the glove box. "We need to get home," Maggie said, restarting the engine.

✳ ✳ ✳

Kora kept her dinner plans. Those friends had a better radio anyway, and many had gathered round it. Kora told them about the day she saw Roosevelt in person. Once she finished her story, the group of friends passed comments around the small living room.

"He had the polio, but stress of this war, *that's* what killed him."

"It's gon' kill us *all*."

"What's this mean for the war?"

"Beats me."

"Shush, they about to swear in the new president."

Their talking stopped as they listened to more sad commentary. Kora shook her head. *So much for my intuition.* They ate and listened and ate some more. Kora must have listened so hard, she was starting to hear things.

"Kora! Kora Bell? Where you at?"

Others turned toward the window at the same time as Kora, so she must not have been the only one who heard. It sounded far away, but when Kora opened the front door, it got louder.

"Kora! Kora Bell? Where you at?" the voice said again, this time she recognized it as her sister-in-law's.

"I'm here!" Kora leaned over the porch railing as far as she could, waving and wondering who needed her this badly. She could see four or five figures coming down the street, but the sun's light was fading fast. She stepped into the street as the group neared. All but one parted to either edge of the road. Her eyes adjusted to see that one, familiar shape set down a couple of large canvas bags, then stand again with outstretched arms.

She took off running toward that man, knowing he was hers and hers alone.

James caught Kora easily, her momentum spinning them both around and making them laugh. He set her down and she counted up all his limbs before checking his head and face—as handsome as ever. He was *whole*! And he was *home*. His sisters, standing on the edge of the road, surrounded them in a family hug, adding to her own tears of joy.

❄❄❄

Late that night, with a brain too busy for sleep, Kora slipped out of bed, careful not to disturb her exhausted husband. His light snoring made her smile. She'd missed even that part of him.

She quietly made herself some tea, wrapped a shawl around her shoulders, and sighed her way into her front porch rocker. After everyone had finally left, Kora and James talked in bed until he couldn't hold his eyes open a second longer. Turns out his company in the Army hadn't seen much combat. Now that she was alone, their conversation replayed in her head.

"When did you know you were coming home?" Kora asked.

"I got orders a few weeks ago. I wrote a letter. Didn't you get it?"

Kora shook her head. "War mail has gotten unreliable lately. More than just me says so."

She tucked herself into her old spot under his arm, feeling more muscle ripple beneath. "What was it really like over there? In Wales, you said?"

"We went all over the English countryside, but mostly Wales. It was beautiful. The Brits didn't know what to do with us at first, but they were sure enough happy we came. The little kids had this saying, 'Got any gum, chum?'"

Kora giggled, then snuggled in even closer.

"I passed out all the gum the Red Cross would give us, because it made those kids happy."

"So you worked all the time?"

"We had some days off. That was the best part, because we were allowed to go inside any pub, dance hall, or restaurant we wanted. Can you imagine?"

"No," Kora said softly.

He squeezed one arm tighter around her shoulder. "I heard about President Roosevelt's G.I. Bill. That's good news. For us."

"It's President Truman now, baby."

"So it is. President Truman," he repeated, through a yawn. "So when you going to put in notice down at the plant?"

Kora propped herself up on one elbow. "What notice?"

"Where you tell them I'm home and you don't have to work no more. I'll find a job, lickety-split. Then we can put all this money you saved up for a house."

Before bed, Kora had revealed the cash stuffed between the mattresses. James gave a soft whoop and she swelled with pride when he called her a hard worker.

Blowing across the top of her teacup, Kora tried out which words she might use to quit the plant. *My husband is home. It's time to go.* They sounded hollow compared to all she'd seen and learned the last year-and-a-half. Then she remembered how a few colored lines had already been let go. *Last hired, first fired.*

Kora watched the bright half-moon play hide-and-seek with a cloud. Rocking slowly in her chair, she gripped the warm mug and mulled her options. Roosevelt was dead. The protections offered through his Executive Order would be dead soon too. James had been right about one thing. This wasn't England. How soon before they shut down all the colored lines? She made the choice then—to leave her job before that happened. On her own terms.

For Kora, there was no other way.

Epilogue

OCTOBER, 1945
MAGGIE

"It's about time that awful billboard came down. I saw them pulling off chunks of her beefy arms just yesterday. By tomorrow, she'll be gone forever," that mother from the school had said loudly in front of Maggie. The woman shook her head and clutched her heart dramatically as she finished her speech. "And I, for one, couldn't be happier."

Maggie drove straight there, needing to see it for herself. She stopped the car behind an empty service truck and got out. Shielding her eyes from the afternoon sun, she tipped her head back. Rosie's face was already gone. Only two narrow strips remained, one showing her blue coveralls, and the other showing bits of brown hair tucked under the red polka dot scarf.

Her strong features were replaced by those of a pretty housewife, beaming over a mop. Mixing the two posters created a strange, hybrid sight Maggie couldn't wrap her mind around. Two workers held extension rods and rubbed down long, sticky strips of the new sign. They watched her with curiosity. She didn't care.

Soon it would be like Rosie had never been there. How could she go from everyplace to no place? The tree of reality, bent by war, had snapped back so fast, making it hard to tell what was real or imagined. Maggie knew where she had to go next. Climbing back in her car, the familiar route allowed time to think. She tried to focus on something besides Charlie. She thought about Daisy and Demi, and the friends she dearly missed since the war had ended two months ago.

Japan had finally surrendered on a hot day in August, after the bombs—Fat Man and Little Boy—had become awkward national heroes. Maggie had been working the sole remaining production line. Only one was needed to fulfill the shrinking demand. The belt stopped. Maggie looked around for the source of the problem.

"Can I have your attention, please," came a voice on the loudspeaker. Everyone froze. "Your attention, please," the voice repeated.

The seconds stretched out with no sound or movement from anyone.

"President Truman has just announced a Japanese surrender. The war has ended. I repeat. The *war is over!*"

Any further news from the speakers was drowned out by hundreds of cheers mixed with sounds of back slapping, weeping, laughing, and many hallelujahs. As they waited on further instructions, Maggie let out the breath she'd been holding for over three years. Picturing the elated faces of her girls hearing this announcement at school, she wished they'd hurry and restart the line so she could finish and get home to celebrate with her family.

Harry entered the room behind a soldier carrying a large wooden box. Everyone gathered around the box as Harry climbed on top. His deep voice boomed. "We got glorious news today. News we've been waitin' on for a lotta years."

Maggie started another round of clapping, and others followed. Harry smiled and waited patiently. "Y'all played your parts well in ending this war. I know you're proud, but it don't come near as proud as I've been to work beside you."

"Thank *you*, Harry!" someone shouted.

Others echoed, "Let's hear it for Harry!"

"I appreciate the words. I do. But I don't want to keep you from celebrating with your families. I just gotta read this here statement from US Rubber." Harry unfolded an official-looking piece of paper from his back pocket while everyone got quiet again.

"The Executive Board of the US Rubber Company, in partnership with the United States Navy, appreciates your answer to our brave nation's call of duty. Your commitment to our resulting victory has led us to this historic day." Harry paused for another wave of cheers to die down. "Thankfully, your valiant service is no longer necessary, and your employment is hereby terminated, effective immediately."

Harry let the letter fall to his side. "Go home folks. Hug your family. It's over." He probably said some more things after that, but Maggie didn't hear them. It was all over. Including her job. Turning on a dime, everything changed back. Most people couldn't wait to put the war behind them.

That was two months ago. Now, finding her way to Billie's house, she knocked at the door and Billie pulled it wide, looking happy to see her. "Come in! I'll get us a soda."

"Is Nick here?" Maggie asked, trailing her to the kitchen.

"Nah, he's still at work. Lucky stiff. I kinda miss going somewhere every day." Billie pulled two glasses from the cabinet and filled them with cola.

Maggie watched the bubbles cling to the side of her glass, unsure where to start.

Billie, of course, dove right in. "How is he?"

She sighed, picturing her husband's face as he tried to smile through too pale, too thin features. "Charlie's alive. It's enough for now."

"Did Grace cancel the party?"

Maggie nodded. "He insisted, adamant he didn't want a hero's welcome."

"What does that mean?"

Maggie raked fingers through her curls, thinking of his second night home, when they were finally alone.

Maggie had summoned all her courage to ask him about reading her last letter. She had to know. Was this where he'd reveal his hatred of her—or worse—his disappointment? She asked the question.

He hesitated a bit too long and stopped meeting her eyes. Her heart stopped and she wanted to bolt from the room, but she stayed, stooping a bit to force his eyes back up where they belonged—locked with hers.

"Maggie, I ...."

Facing him, she took both his hands as they stood in the middle of the room—the very center of the world as far as she was concerned. Somewhere she'd heard it was harder to stay mad at someone if you were holding hands. She gave him time.

"... There's so much I'm trying to forget over there. I can't say I remember this last letter. What did it say?"

Everything clicked into place. Her world—no, their world—started up again. This was her Charlie. Whether he had read that letter or not, he was making a choice to move forward, not back. She stretched on her tiptoes and hugged his neck. Feeling his stubble against her cheek, she said to the wall behind him, "It was a weak moment. I had lots of those, but what it said isn't important any longer."

He pulled back, and now she felt his focus, intent on her hearing his words. "Maggie, I understand weak moments. Before I left, I thought I had everything figured out. I was wrong. You, me, the kids—us—that's what matters. That is the only thing that has ever mattered."

He found her hands again and attempted to twine their fingers, but his still trembled, making it hard. The shaking—one of the first things she'd noticed after he came home—scared her. That, and how he almost recoiled from his family's half-mad excitement upon his arrival. Charlie always had such strong, steady hands.

Her grip stilled his, and he continued. "Me—standing right here, in the same room again with you—is the only thing I prayed for. Everything else, including any weak moments, will work itself out."

She squeezed him tight as he kissed away her doubts.

"Maggie, did you hear what I said?" Billie now asked.

Realizing Billie was awkwardly waiting for an answer, Maggie found her words. "He won't say exactly what happened over there. I've gotten bits and pieces. Father O'Reilly may be the only one who knows. He's going to confession twice a week."

"It's an adjustment for everyone. Including you."

Maggie shook her head and chuckled. "Grace and Lucy keep trying to feed him, but he swears he's not hungry. In fact, my icebox is overflowing. Maybe I'll bring some over for you and Nick."

"Works for me. I've been eating a lot lately." Billie admitted.

"I even cooked him some new recipes, the ones Kora taught me, but they took more than pounds from that man. The thought of Charlie Slone never being the same ...." Stubborn tears reappeared. "Can we talk about something else?"

"Of course. I didn't mean to pry." Billie paused before asking, "Any luck finding a job? I hear the insurance biz is buzzin'."

Sipping her cola, Maggie half-smiled and said, "I think I've applied for every single job in Charlotte. Outside of the bank, I mean."

"We all know you're going to end up there. Why fight it?"

"You know, a lot *has* changed for me, but I still don't want my father-in-law's handouts. I was pretty good at what I did during the war. Before every soldier returning triumphant got in line ahead of me."

"One of those soldiers was mine," Billie reminded her.

"You're right," a guilty Maggie added quickly, wishing she could take it back. "The bank wouldn't be so bad."

Billie nodded, as their conversation comfortably lagged.

"She came down today, you know," Maggie said. "Replaced by a mop model."

"You came all the way to tell me that? I thought the billboard was already gone."

Maggie felt a little stung. Billie must have sensed it, because she laid a hand on Maggie's arm. "It's not your fault things changed.

Hey, there was a time when you wanted everything to go back the way it was."

"What's that saying?"

They answered together. "Careful what you wish for."

Maggie swallowed the irony then washed her glass in the sink, dried it, and returned it to the cabinet. Billie let her. "I need to get back home. Thanks for the drink and the ear."

On their way to the front door, Maggie caught sight of their newspaper clipping, lovingly framed and hung in Billie's tiny foyer. She ran a finger over each smiling face, as they proudly celebrated their accomplishment from atop the armory stage. So many dear faces she hardly saw anymore.

Despite the picture's black, white, and shades of gray, their happiness jumped off the page like a sunny yellow. Maggie could close her eyes now and feel the powerful group hug she and Kora had dived into after that picture was taken. It was an unforgettable moment.

"How *is* Kora?" asked Billie from behind her.

Kora. Maggie's hand stopped just under Kora's smile beaming in the photo. She hadn't seen that smile since the day she learned Charlie had been rescued.

Kora had been at Maggie's house when the military messengers arrived. Kora's expression turned to stone when they handed their hats to her, but she silently accepted them anyway.

Distracted by their message—their very presence in her home—Maggie was silent too. After the messengers left, Kora held Maggie, who sobbed through waves of relief and anxiety. Maggie had missed the opportunity to correct those officers right away, but it had happened so fast.

When Maggie telephoned later to apologize, Kora agreed it had happened fast, but insisted nothing about the officers' behavior was shocking. Maggie understood James and Kora were trying to rebuild their lives too, but faced their own tree snapping back— their own contributions to the war becoming erased.

Billie patiently waited for Maggie to answer. Again. She must think Maggie insane. "I called Kora last week. No job yet, but James found work. He's running the picture show at The Grand. Says he'll apply for college in the spring. They're hoping to buy a house too." Maggie let her hand fall from the frame, and turned for the door.

"I'd better hurry," Maggie said. "The girls hate when I'm gone now. That's another complication for finding a job. Grace took them for a sundae, and she'll fuss about why I'm late. Just like the old days, huh?"

"Some things never change."

Grabbing her keys from the hall table, she looked at Billie. "It's scariest when he wakes up, not knowing where he is. He feels bad later and does his best to pretend everything's okay."

"At least he's back," Billie offered, with a light hand atop Maggie's shoulder. "He can heal now."

"He is home," Maggie's voice trailed off. "And I would only say this to you, but it feels like Charlie is still trying to find his way back to us."

Billie leaned in for a hug. Pulling back, she asked, "Want to hear my news? I guess it's good. I was going to wait."

"Let's hear it. I could use some good news."

Billie's words came out slow and hesitant, like she was auditioning them for future revealing moments. "Well, it appears … I'm going to have … a baby."

"Billie!" Maggie threw her arms around her neck again. "That's the best news I've heard since Charlie came back!"

Billie let herself be hugged but stayed a little stiff. When they finally separated, her pretty blue eyes found the floor before asking, "Is it?"

Maggie took a hand to each shoulder and held Billie's eyes in all seriousness. "Being a mother is the best job I've ever had. Honest."

"I'm gonna hold you to that." Billie held up a hand to signal *enough* as Maggie went in for a third hug.

Billie held the door open for Maggie, who waved and started down the sidewalk. She breathed in the late afternoon air, finally tinged with signs of fall.

"Maggie?" Billie called out, making her turn around.

"Yeah?"

Billie let the door shut behind her. The crickets were starting to sing. "What if it's a girl?"

"What do you mean?" Maggie began, then stopped herself, realizing exactly what Billie meant. Despite all they'd proved in so little time, the world would soon forget. Everything Maggie, Kora, Billie, and the others had accomplished was already being forgotten—washed away in a national sigh of relief.

Maggie chose her next words carefully. "There you go, Billie, proving what a wonderful mother you'll be. Already wanting the best for your baby."

Maggie thought of her own girls. Would it be different for them someday? She could never blame Billie for wanting her baby to have every opportunity this world had to offer. She understood all too well.

Since the plant had closed, Maggie tried to put a name to her sadness. There was a void that sometimes crept in underneath the joy of Charlie's return. Her community was gone, and she was alone with new goals to tackle. To find a new job. To face fears of Charlie not getting well. She was back where she started, on her own with a unique set of circumstances the world wasn't built to expect.

Maggie pulled the car door shut and rolled down the window.

Billie took a step closer to the car, reading Maggie's mind. "She never just existed on that billboard, you know. It will be different for Daisy and Demi."

"You're right," Maggie said. "They can't paper over everything we did."

This was why she had needed to see Billie today—for something to hold onto. Her hand turned the ignition, and the engine broke the spell.

"Thanks, Billie. I'll see you soon." She started to reverse, then remembered. "My best to Nick."

"Mine to Charlie." Billie nodded. "Call me tomorrow?"

"I will."

Acknowledgments

Years ago, I learned that my father, Tom Fidelle, wrote a book. He showed my mother a few chapters, but grew frustrated and never finished or showed it to anyone else. Had I known how rare it is to finish a book, I might never have started, but I did start it and it's being held in your hands thanks to an amazing community of people to whom I will always be grateful.

I want to thank the amazing folks at Warren Publishing for selecting my manuscript and bringing this book to life. Mindy Kuhn, Amy Ashby, and Lacey Cope, thank you for your expertise and patience. I also had the privilege of working with a lot of editors along the way. Though I may never truly understand the full difference between developmental, line, and proof editors, I do understand that Betsy Thorpe, Kim Wright, and Rachel Logan made my story better.

Creative writing is an art form I had to learn. I am grateful to Paul Reali and Kathie Collins at Charlotte Center for Literary Arts, and the wonderful members of its Authors Lab class of 2019 for the perfect classroom setting. From that class grew my AWE Circle of fellow writers and friends that critiqued some chapters over and over until I got them right. Thank you, Daphne Thompson, Jennifer Halls, Rebecca Jones, Nancy Zupanec, and Rebecca Wallace.

While storytelling is an art, I still stand in awe of the visual artists who enhanced this book. Thank you to the amazing artist, Eva Crawford, and model, Joy Farley, for the perfect cover art. Thank you to my brilliant, talented, and dear friend, Randi Koistinen, for sharing her gift of illustration to perfectly represent all forty chapter headings.

Thank you to my mother, Linda Fidelle, and my mother-in-law, Susie Ritchie, for their combined inspiration for the character Grace. I hope you understand your impact on motherhood for me and how many of your wise words live inside my head. Thank you to my rockstar sister-in-law, Ann Deister, as my beta reader, cheerleader, and "dream catcher" who woke up one day with an idea for the perfect cover art.

This book would not be possible without support from my longtime besties Kelly Masters, Julie Mata, and Carol Lawrence, who took time from their busy lives to read and give feedback on multiple versions of the novel. I will forever be grateful for your consistent encouragement to cross the finish line. Carol, that Rosie bobblehead got me through more days of writing than you'll ever know. We can do it!

I relied on many experts and eyewitnesses to research this story. I am thankful for the wonderful resources at the Charlotte Mecklenburg Library, including the Robinson-Spangler Carolina Room for the few pictures left of the Shell Plant, and for the Fiction Writing Group led by Surabhi Kaushik. I have a special gratitude for Sally Robinson, Ruth Helms, and Marilyn Price, whose childhood memories growing up in Charlotte were written into this story. I am also grateful to the historians who met with me or wrote wonderful books to reference on Charlotte's history, including Tom Hanchett, David Erdman, Willie Griffin, Mark Wilson, and Brandon Lunsford. Thank you also to my friend and fire-protection engineer, Michael Masters, for his first-hand knowledge on how fire spreads and how it might have been extinguished in the 1940s.

I cannot understate how critical beta readers are to the writing process. Thank you to my power betas, April Whitlock and Marla

Mahon, for being early adopters and story influencers. I am also incredibly thankful to Kim Moran, Cissy Carlson, Ann Linde, Anne Perper, Barb Pearson, Ingrid Cochard, Julie McGraw, and Anne Schmitt for their time and honest critique of the story as readers.

Every author begins their journey with a love of books and learning. I am so grateful for the commitment, community, and support of my ASK Bible study and the Babes Book Club. Half of any success is just showing up, and I'm grateful to fellow "bankers" and bibliophiles Lee Rhodes, Christy Livoti, Pamela May, Barbara Morrow, Anne Carter Craddock, and Lisa Sicard for their monthly accountability and friendship spanning over two decades.

The support of my family is the most important. Since the day they came into the world at 3:37, 3:38, and 3:39 p.m., my children have taught me more than they will ever know. Thank you, Meg, Ben, and Will, for making me a mom. I'm so proud of the adults you've become and look forward to even more shared experiences and memories to be made. You can do anything, and I'll always be cheering you on.

Finally, to my husband David, I am grateful for your partnership in life, your support in every crazy idea I've tried, and your patience as I wrote this book. I guess I should also thank the ever-expanding Charlotte music and brewery scene for keeping you occupied during all the Saturdays I spent in front of my computer. Thank you for reading my story, encouraging my latest project or "hobby," and being my best friend.